SEASONS OF LIFE

SEASONS OF LIFE

STORIES OF THE HUMAN CYCLE

EVA TAUBE

Copyright © 1985 by Eva Taube

Reprinted 1994

Canadian Cataloguing in Publication Data

Main entry under title:

Seasons of life

ISBN 0-7710-8440-4

1. Short stories – 20th century. 2. Short stories, Canadian – 20th century. I. Taube, Eva, 1932-

PN6120.2.S4 1985   808.83'1   C84-099710-8

Printed and bound in Canada by Webcom Ltd.

McClelland & Stewart Inc.
The Canadian Publishers
481 University Avenue
Toronto, Ontario
M5G 2E9

Preface

Seasons of Life explores the human cycle through the art of the short story. It traces the human journey from childhood to old age through a collection of stories arranged in four units following the seasons of nature. Recent studies by such contemporary social scientists as Erik Erikson and Daniel Levinson and works by their distinguished forerunner Carl Jung have noted that we pass through various stages of life in a definite pattern of progression. At each stage we experience a gradual unfolding of biological and intellectual capacities that impose on us different responsibilities and different roles in our relations with others. Nancy Mayer, in her book *The Male Mid-Life Crisis*, writes, "There is no cure for time, but there are different ways to look at the cycle of life. And the view we adopt dramatically reflects how much reverence our culture has for the individual and for its humanity."

Students can benefit from life cycle education. It will evoke in them a reverence for human life and for the mystery of the human personality and will add a dimension of understanding to their own lives. Such a study will help them not only to understand the meaning and importance of their own stage in life and of the problems that affect them as a generation but also to anticipate their personal futures and to deepen their sensitivity to the needs and problems of other generations that they encounter in their daily lives. For such a study, the art of fiction is uniquely qualified. Story-tellers can provide an authentic guide to the drama of the human seasons. Through their skilful use of language and narrative techniques and through their profound insight, they express their individual visions of life and accurately reflect the quality of human experience.

This text attempts to fulfil the need for a study of the life cycle. Each unit in the book represents a season of life that, like the human personality, has unique characteristics. The stories in the first unit, "Spring: Childhood and Adolescence," portray the fresh, imaginative, bewildering world of the child. They present adolescents awakening to new perceptions, capacities, and desires with their undercurrent of conflicting emotions. In the second unit, "Summer: Early Adulthood and Adulthood," young adults are testing beliefs, locating social roles, experiencing their first fragile romance and its dissolution, preparing with apprehension for the voyage into independence. Adults plant roots and confront the complexities inherent in marriage, parenthood, and the challenge of building careers. The stories in "Autumn: Mid-Life," the third unit, dramatize turning points in their protagonists' lives, periods of evaluation: considering possible options, assessing objectives and goals, facing the problem of setting off in new directions. In the final unit, "Winter: Old Age," the aged, having discarded their occupational roles, experience the rewards of old age: the fullness of life. At the same time, they struggle with such problems as maintaining their independence with dignity, sometimes against pressure from their adult children, and must come to terms with aging and the prospect of death.

Each story in this book has been chosen for its literary excellence, its powerful portrayal of the season of life that it explores, and its ability to engage the interest and enthusiasm of students in the classroom. The authors range from classic favourites to contemporary masters to experimental writers. Together they provide a rich blend of stories that contribute freshness and vitality to a reading program.

To provide another lens through which to view the life cycle, brief introductions to each of the four seasons contain excerpts from a variety of sources: sociologists, psychologists, and literary masters, as well as personal accounts of the process of growing up and aging in our society.

If a text is to be an effective educational tool, it should help students to read fiction with sensitivity and understanding. For this purpose, I have included a brief introduction to each story, establishing a context by explaining the author's characteristic style and, where necessary, the literary convention or tradition within which the story was written. The objective is to deepen enjoyment through greater understanding.

Questions following each story will evoke a diversity of responses and guide students to their own discoveries. The questions move from problems of content and theme to consideration of the different strategies available to the story-teller. Another group of questions contains suggestions for writing designed to engage students' imaginative participation in the experience that the story dramatizes and to encourage them to draw from their own experience. Both types of writing exercises should result in self-discovery. Finally, a set of questions examines social issues and stages in the life cycle, drawing attention to the broader implications of the story. The questions on social issues, which should be of particular interest to family study courses, include psycho-sociological quotations that explore questions raised in the stories on human relations, family problems, stages in human development, and a wide range of compelling issues relevant to youth in a dynamic, multicultural society. Although the social questions call for discussion, they too can easily be adapted to written exercises and can generate research projects on human issues.

The four sets of questions, under the headings "Discovering Meaning," "Exploring Method," "Suggestions for Writing," and "Examining Social Issues," are arranged to reflect the way we read: noting details and meaning, examining techniques, considering implications, and discovering insights into ourselves and into our culture. As every teacher well knows, such an echo between life and literary art is part of the appeal and power of fiction.

Contents

Seasons of Life

The imagery of seasons takes many
forms . . . . First, there is the idea of a
PROCESS or JOURNEY from a starting
point . . . to a termination point. . . . To speak
of a general, human life cycle is to propose
that the journey from birth to old age
follows an underlying, universal pattern on
which there are endless cultural and
individual variations. . . . But as long as the
journey continues, it follows the basic
sequence.

Second, there is the idea of SEASONS: a
series of periods or stages within the life
cycle. The process is not a simple,
continuous, unchanging flow. There are
qualitatively different seasons, each having
its own distinctive character. . . . Change
goes on within each, and a transition is
required for the shift from one season to the
next.

Daniel Levinson
The Seasons of a Man's Life

1

SPRING

Childhood and Adolescence

Childhood

Childhood is the world of miracle and
wonder: as if creation rose, bathed in light,
out of the darkness, utterly new and fresh
and astonishing. The end of childhood is
when things cease to astonish us. When the
world seems familiar, when one has got
used to existence, one has become an adult.

Eugene Ionesco
Fragments of a Journal

Have you ever felt like nobody
Just a tiny speck of air,
When everyone's around you,
And you are just not there?

Karen Crawford, age nine

First Day in School

W. O. Mitchell

"First Day in School" is taken from Who Has Seen the Wind *(1947), the acclaimed novel of the western Canadian writer W. O. Mitchell. With a blend of humour and pathos, the novel perceptively charts the transition of the young protagonist, Brian O'Connal, from childhood in a small town on the Saskatchewan prairie to early maturity. As he develops, Brian experiences the tension between the mysterious lure of the prairie and the demands of the town. The primitive, hauntingly beautiful prairie promises him freedom, excites his imagination, but also reveals its frightening power of destructiveness and its threat of chaos; the town demands commitment and social responsibility.*

In the foreword to Who Has Seen the Wind, *Mitchell explains his purpose: "In this story I have tried to present sympathetically the struggle of a boy to understand what still defeats mature and learned men – the ultimate meaning of the cycle." This purpose is dramatized in Brian's relation with the prairie. In the perfection of a dewdrop one morning, Brian intuits the unity between the human and the natural world. In the sweep of the wind on the prairie, he senses "a feeling" of divine presence. In this episode of the novel, the Brian O'Connal we meet is six years old, eager to "find out all about things."*

As a dramatist who has written a radio series, Jake and the Kid *(1961), depicting prairie life in the Forties, and other plays, Mitchell demonstrates a strong sense of the dramatic and an accurate ear for authentic dialogue. As a writer of novels and short fiction, he has a keen eye for detail and fresh, vivid imagery. In an introduction to his anthology of five plays, Mitchell expresses what he regards as the objective of a writer of fiction: "A novelist wants his readers not only to watch and to listen but to enter envelopes of consciousness as well, giving the illusion of inner dimensions belonging to human beings alone."*

In "First Day in School," Mitchell provides his readers with a view of this inner dimension of his characters and the fictional world they inhabit.

On the morning of the first day of September, the bright noise of sparrows woke Brian. The curtains in his room breathed in and out with the fall breeze as he lay still beside his brother; he could see his clothes folded over the foot of the white-enameled iron bed. His mother had put them there the night before. Today was to be his first day in school.

From under the bed came a frantic scrabbling of sound; the red and white fox terrier jumped up. His one red ear gave to his head an archly tilted look; a saddle-shaped patch of red spread over his back. "Down, Jappy." Brian pushed him from the bed; he flung back the covers. Bobbie slept on, his plump fist against his fat face, his tightly curled red hair bright against the rumpled pillow.

The dog jumped against Brian's leg as the boy stood a moment by the side of the bed. Brian O'Connal was short for his six years and slight with the leanness and darkness of an Indian boy; as his grandmother had often said, it was the black Scotch MacMurray in him. He held his head back and upright with a sureness that was also his grandmother's.

With the dog trotting after him, he went to the open window. He would not have to say that next year he was going to school, thought Brian – or next fall, or next week: he was going today. He was going to school just as Artie Sherry did. He was old enough now. He would find out all about things. He would learn. He wouldn't get the strap.

"You up?" Bobbie was sitting, his red hair tousled, the sleep in his blue eyes not quite able to dim their wild twinkle. He was a chunky boy, four now, and solid, in his Uncle Sean's words, as a brick outhouse. "I wish I was going to school."

"You will when you get old enough." Brian turned from the window. He began to dress while Bobbie watched him from the bed.

Downstairs Maggie O'Connal stood at the stove in the kitchen; she prepared the family breakfast with quick, birdlike movements. Brian said good morning to her as though it were any morning, trying his best to hide the excitement that was in him, to act as though he were used to going to school every morning. He was not very successful. There was a strange tightness in his mother's face; a look of concern in her brown eyes with their fine crow's-feet at the corners.

"Off to school, Spalpeen?" Brian felt a rush of emotion, as he always did when his father spoke to him. Gerald O'Connal ruffled his son's hair as he passed Brian; he sat down at the opposite end of the table. His dark red hair with gray beginning to grizzle it had a roan look along the sides of his head. In the last year his complexion had lost the blood-flush that had warmed it. He cleared his throat. "You – uh – do as they tell you, Brian."

"He will," Brian's mother said quickly. "I'm sure he will."

"I'm six now," said Brian as he picked up his spoon.

"I'm four," Bobbie said. "I'm going to school next year. I don't want any porridge."

"Porridge makes ye grow," said the grandmother, who had come in with him. Her hair was thinner now; her skin had taken on a transparency new to it. Lace hung from the velvet band around her throat; it failed to hide completely the gentle swell of a goiter there.

"I still think I should go with him – "

"No, Maggie," Brian's father interrupted her.

"You don't have to go," said Brian. "Forbsie's starting too, and his mother isn't going with him."

The look upon Maggie O'Connal's small face deepened; it was not a happy one.

"I'm not very fussy about porridge," Bobbie announced.

"Well, ye must eat it," said the grandmother; "it makes ye grow."

"I'm not fussy about growing."

"Eat it up, Son," his mother said with the tone in her voice that Bobbie knew meant no further argument. He began to eat his oatmeal, stuffing it in with great, heaping spoonfuls. Actually he was very fond of it.

As he broke up stale bread and poured milk over it for his dog, Brian wished that parents wouldn't act as they were doing. They seemed to think it was awful to go to school. He'd heard Artie talk of getting the strap, and of Mr. Digby's getting after a person for shouting in the halls; still, that was no reason for his mother and father's acting as they were. He straightened up from the dog's dish by the sink.

"It's not time yet," said his mother.

"I know. I'm going upstairs for a minute."

In his room he picked up the pistol that lay on the table by the bed; it was a water pistol with a rubber bulb for a handle, crosshatched with creases, the rest of it cast-lead. He carried it with him always and was not truly dressed without it, or without the gloves that had red stars sewn on the fringed, funnel-shaped parts that covered his sleeves. He went downstairs again.

". . . He's so young," he heard his mother saying.

"She says you're awful young to go alone," said Bobbie.

"No, I'm not. What time is it?"

His father looked at his watch. "Half-past eight."

"I better be going."

His mother went over to him quickly and bent down. He kissed her and felt her arm tighten on his shoulder. When he straightened up and felt that his cheek was damp, he was impatient with her.

He left the kitchen after instructing Bobbie to hold the dog until he'd got away from the house. Dogs did not go to school.

"I thought," Gerald O'Connal said when Brian had gone, "that it was only the Irish who were sentimental."

Maggie O'Connal, with her back to him as she faced the stove, did not answer him.

"There's only one kind of Irishman," said the grandmother, "shanty Irish. They're not sentimental. They're dirty."

"And the Scots are tight," said O'Connal.

"Not tight," returned the grandmother, "canny."

"Another name for it," said Brian's father.

"He's so – so – *damned* independent," said Maggie O'Connal. She turned to Bobbie and spoke with unusual sharpness. "Don't you go any farther than MacTaggart's Corner – understand?"

Bobbie, who frequently strayed far from home, was intent on his porridge.

Forbsie's fat face shone. "Do we have to line up?" he said to Artie.

"Everybody does," Artie answered, his face contorting at the offending glasses. "The girls go in the girls' door an' the boys go in the boys' door. You better not let 'em catch you going in the girls' door."

"Why not?" asked Brian.

"You're not s'posed to. There's two toilets. There's the girls' toilet on the girls' side – an' the boys' on the boys' side – in the basement."

"Is there!" said Forbsie.

"That's where old Tinhead is." Artie referred to Mr. Briggs, the school janitor, said to have a silver plate in his head ever since he had served with the Princess Pats in the war.

Ahead of them and behind them small groups of children made their way to the school on the eastern edge of the town. "There's the China Kids," said Artie.

Brian saw them, the Wongs, Tang and Vooie. It was Vooie's first day at school, and his sister, Tang, with the protectiveness of an older sister, had the collar of his coat clenched tight in her hand. Brian had seen the Wong children often, for they had grown up on that section of gray cement that ran before their father's Bluebird Café. Now that the mother, a small amber woman brought from China by Wong to bear him Tang and Vooie, had died, the father had left Vooie to his sister's care. He cooked meals for the children, and that was all. Brian knew Wong too, a small, stooped Chinese with a white mustache, who wore summer and winter a rooster-comb-red toque. Brian had seen him often behind the café counter with its welter of cigarette and tobacco packets, its jaw breakers, licorice plugs, whips, pipes, and staring fried-egg candies.

Brian's confidence ebbed as they neared the schoolyard on the prairie edge and as Artie regaled the other boys with stories of the terrible Miss MacDonald. She was cranky; she hated kids; it was she, he told Forbsie and Brian, who would be their teacher.

Until the bell rang, Forbsie and Brian stood with their backs to the orange brick of Lord Roberts School, watching other boys play catch, or wrestle in the bare dirt. The swings on the town side were occupied; girls swinging idly with one foot trailing, the boys pumping high and mightily. When the bell rang somewhere in the depths of the school, the children formed reluctantly into two lines at the doors; those left outside the lines were the beginners, forlorn little souls whom Miss MacDonald came out to shepherd in to the school. She assigned them their seats in the lower grades room, at the head of the stairs, told them to sit quietly and play with the colored plasticine Mariel Abercrombie had passed out. Then she turned to hand out the readers to the Grade Threes, of which Artie Sherry was a member.

The first excitement over, Brian began to find school a rather disappointing affair. Forbsie sat across from him, Artie two rows over. He would go over and see Artie for a while, Brian decided; he got up and started down the aisle. Miss MacDonald, at the board, turned and saw him. "Sit down, Brian."

"I'm just going over to see Artie."

"You'll have to sit down." She turned back to the board.

Brian continued on his journey to Artie. She wasn't his mother; he wasn't hurting anything; he wasn't doing anything wrong.

"I said to sit down!"

He stopped at the end of the aisle. "I just want to see Artie for a minute."

"You must put up your hand if you want something. Then I'll give you permission to see Artie."

He stood watching her.

"Sit down in your seat!"

He continued to stand. Miss MacDonald's thin face reddened slightly. She bit her lip. "*Sit down!*"

Brian stood. Utter classroom quiet had descended. Outside the window a meadow lark went up his bright scale with a *one-two-three-and-here-I-go*. Miss MacDonald began to walk down the aisle in which Brian was standing. He reached into his hip pocket and felt the comfort of the water pistol there. Miss MacDonald stopped three seats ahead of him. "Will you sit down!"

Wordlessly he drew the pistol out, being careful not to squeeze the butt. He held it behind his back. Miss MacDonald reached out her hand to guide him back to his seat. It paused in mid-air as Brian brought the water pistol to view. One clear drop of water hung from the end pointing at Miss MacDonald's midriff. Her mouth flew open. She stared at the pistol and at the slight drip of water from the small hand holding it.

"I filled it," Brian assured her, "out of the fountain."

Her face flamed. "Give me that pistol!"

He made no move to hand it to her.

Her hand darted out to the water pistol. Startled, Brian squeezed. The pistol squirted. Miss MacDonald, with her dripping hand, jerked the pistol from his grasp. She propelled him from the room.

As he walked ahead of her to the end of the hall where the Principal's office was, Brian's heart pounded; he was in for it. The front of her dress dripping, Miss MacDonald knocked on the Principal's door. It opened, and Mr. Digby, tall and sandy-haired, a questioning look upon his rough face, stood there.

With emotion poorly concealed, Miss MacDonald told him what had happened, the indignant spray of saliva from her thin lips unheeded, the corners of her mouth quivering. When she had finished, Digby said: –

"You'd better let your classes go. Miss Spencer has, hers. I'll attend to Brian."

The door closed on Miss MacDonald's outraged back.

Mr. Digby walked to the desk, sat down; he leaned forward with his elbows on the top. "Well, Brian?"

The boy stared at him.

"Little trouble?"

With his dark gaze deliberately unflinching, Brian continued to stare.

Mr. Digby's long fingers began to drum the desk top. He leaned back in the chair; the fingers drummed on. He cleared his throat. "Don't – Won't you talk to me?"

Unchanged, Brian's face looked up to the Principal; no expression was there, certainly no inclination to talk was indicated. Mr. Digby rose from his chair, Brian's eyes lifting with him.

"You – Don't you like school, Brian?"

20

No sign betrayed Brian's response one way or the other to the institution of education.

"We're only trying to – to – " What were they trying to do? He'd talked it over enough with Hislop when he'd been here. Each year a new crop. Teach them to line up six times a day, regulate their lives with bells, trim off the uncomfortable habits, the unsocial ones – or was it simply the ones that interfered with . . . ? "We . . . want to help you. You want people to like you, don't you?"

He could see the gentle swell and ebb of the boy's chest under his sweater, that and nothing more.

"You want to get along with people. You want to grow up to be . . ." An individual whose every emotion, wish, action, was the resultant of two forces: what he felt and truly wanted, what he thought he should feel and ought to want. Give him the faiths that belonged to all other men.

His mind shied from his thinking like a horse from too high a jump. The thing was to get the child to talk – without frightening it out of him. "Miss MacDonald is your teacher now. You must do as she says. It's – it's like . . ." He cast about for something to say, any wedge to slip under the barrier between them. "You do what your mother tells you," he pried. "You don't disobey her."

Still no interest or understanding showed in the boy's dark eyes.

What would the boy understand?

"Have you a dog, Brian?"

There was a flicker of the boy's eyes. That was it.

"He does what you tell him. You expect him to do what you want him to. A dog isn't much good if he won't do what he's told." He looked for a moment at the boy with his erect back, his legs slightly apart. "Does he do any tricks?"

"He can jump over – " The words spilled out, then stopped.

"Over your arms if you hold them out?"

"Over a stick," Brian corrected him.

"Oh." The teacher was silent because he knew it was the right moment to say nothing.

"Tricks aren't any good. He's going to catch gophers. That isn't a trick."

The Principal nodded.

"They're *for* catching gophers."

"That's right."

"Fox terriers. He's a fox terrier. I don't like her."

"Don't you?"

"She tried to make me sit down. I didn't feel like sitting down. I wasn't hurting anything."

"What if everyone in the room wanted to stand up? She couldn't teach very well then, could she?"

Brian considered a moment. "She stands up."

"That's because she's the teacher."

"Does she have to stand up to teach people things?"

Digby nodded.

"Maybe I have to stand up to learn things," suggested Brian.

"Do you *have* to?"

"Maybe I do," said Brian. "Does she?"

"Maybe she does," said Digby.

"Well, I don't."

"You could learn anyway," suggested Digby, "couldn't you?"

"Yes, I could. But I don't think I'll learn from her. I better have another teacher."

"I don't think that could be arranged," Digby explained to him. "You see, she's the only one we have for Grade One. You want to go to school, don't you?"

"Oh, yes, I'm going to find out about things."

"Then you'd better try to get along with Miss MacDonald." There was a note of firmness in Digby's voice.

Brian was silent. Digby reached into his desk drawer; he drew out the water pistol and handed it to Brian. "She'd like you to have this back," he said, knowing that it was the farthest thing from Miss MacDonald's desires.

"Thank you. It doesn't work very good anyway."

"All right. No more school today – this afternoon. Think about what I said."

For some time after Brian had left, Digby sat at his desk. On the half-opened window behind him a fly, lulled to languor by the morning sun, bunted crazily up the pane, fell protestingly, and lay half-paralyzed on the sill, the numbness of his sound lost in the emptiness of the office.

Questions for Writing and Discussion

Discovering Meaning

1. How would you describe Brian? Compare Brian with the minor characters Forbsie and Vooie, for whom this is also the first day in school.
2. Compare Brian's relations with his mother and with his father. Is there a difference? Why or why not?
3. Brian's father accuses his wife of sentimentalism: an excessive

emotional response to a situation that does not warrant it. What is your view of the mother's response to her son's leaving home for the first time to go to school?

4. Artie Sherry describes Miss MacDonald for Brian and Forbsie before they meet her. Is his characterization accurate? What is your impression of her?

5. Describe the character of Mr. Digby, the principal.

6. Contrast Mr. Digby's and Miss MacDonald's treatments of Brian. Why is Mr. Digby more successful?

Exploring Method

1. Mitchell uses the third-person omniscient narrator to tell his story; that is, the narrator describes scenes, provides background information, and portrays characters through description and dialogue. He enters the thoughts of only two characters, Brian and Mr. Digby. What does Mitchell gain by presenting the inner world of his central characters and presenting an external view of his minor characters?

2. How does the opening scene prepare the reader for Brian's behaviour in school?

3. Mitchell uses a few carefully selected images to create scenes and characters that are indelibly etched in the reader's mind: he uses words that name colours, sounds, smells, taste, and texture to create vivid scenes and to portray the environment. What is your impression of Brian's home environment? Select the images and dialogue that formed your impression.

4. What is Artie Sherry's function in the story?

5. What is the significance of the image of the fly at the end of the story? How is the image related to Brian's conflict with the school authorities?

Suggestions for Writing

1. In Brian's confrontation with Miss MacDonald, we see the situation from contrasting viewpoints: through Brian's thoughts and through Miss MacDonald's behaviour. Rewrite the scene in the classroom focusing on Miss MacDonald's thoughts and how she views Brian's behaviour.

2. Through Mr. Digby and Miss MacDonald, Mitchell portrays two views of education. Compare these two approaches. Describe your portrait of an ideal teacher.

3. Examine Mr. Digby's thoughts when he confronts Brian. What is his view of the school system and of what education should be? Evaluate his view and present your own.

4. Write a narrative describing your first day in school. Use dialogue and descriptive detail to portray your impression of the setting and characters.

Examining Social Issues

1. Brian's mother and father disagree about whether to accompany Brian to school on the first day. Who is right? Should a parent take a child to school on the first day? Why or why not?
2. Mitchell portrays the children on swings in the schoolyard: the girls are timid, swinging "idly with one foot trailing"; the boys are daring, "pumping high and mightily." Are all boys and girls like this? Do rural children behave differently from city children? The story is set in the 1940s. Do you think children have changed since then? Why or why not?
3. When Brian says to Mr. Digby, "Maybe I have to stand up to learn," he is questioning the validity of discipline in school. Is Brian right? Should schools be more permissive? Defend your view.
4. The psychologist Dr. Clark E. Moustakas, in *The Young Child in School*, describes a child's first encounter with school:

   So the day before the day of kindergarten arrives and images of magic and curious fantasies lie in his heart and in his mind. He comes with wonder and awe, with gladness and rapture. Which of us as parents has not seen this limitless joy suddenly turn to indifference or even violent objection to any idea of school? What happens to destroy the ecstatic joy that exists before the child's entrance? What happens to kill his dream?

   Discuss the causes of students' disillusionment with school.
5. Brian's conflict with school authorities could eventually turn him into a school drop-out. What influences contribute to his decision to return to Miss MacDonald's class? Discuss what causes students to drop out of school.
6. In confronting his first day at school, Brian has reached a transition in his life: he is moving towards greater independence. With it, he must comply with new demands and assume new responsibilities but also lose certain rights and privileges. Identify the responsibilities he must assume and the privileges he has lost.
7. From Brian's behaviour and from your observations of six-year-olds you know, construct a psychological profile of a typical six-year-old.

The Doll's House

Katherine Mansfield

Along with the Russian dramatist and short-story writer Anton Chekhov and the Irish novelist and writer of short fiction James Joyce, Katherine Mansfield played a major role in shaping the contemporary short story.

The action in modern stories is slight; the scenes are highly detailed in description. The focus is on the consciousness of the central characters, whose inner thoughts are revealed through interior monologue. Stories centre on their protagonists' development: their impressions, feelings, thoughts in response to a situation. The modern story builds up to a revelation at the end when the reader's understanding of the significance of the situation is deeper than that of the character who is involved in the action. The modern writer's technique is closer to that of poetry in its use of images, metaphors, and symbols.

Katherine Mansfield is a master of this poetic technique; she creates a tight framework for her simple stories with a network of carefully interwoven images so that the ordinary is transformed into the artistically meaningful. Her aim, as she expressed it, was to make the reader see. Her plots are simplified to intensify the emotional impact. Her stories dramatize a brief moment in her characters' lives, a moment that assumes a universal significance. Mansfield's purpose in her stories is to present a critical psychological crisis when a character recognizes the meaning of the experience. Her themes are the breakdown of social values, emotional isolation, human contact that is never genuine communication, people living wasted lives that are destructive both to themselves and to others, moments of joy that carry an undertone of sadness, love always inadequately realized.

The setting of her stories is generally Europe. But the emotional crisis she experienced at the death of her brother in World War I induced Mansfield to return to memories of her native New Zealand and to devote herself to recreating life as she remembered it as a child. "The Doll's House," "Prelude," "At the Bay," and "The Garden Party," Mansfield's major stories, are set in New Zealand. They are spontaneous, delicate, reflecting her own heightened response to the blend of beauty and pain in human life. "The Doll's

House," which was published several months after her death in 1923, is one of her most perceptive studies of New Zealand middle-class life.

When dear old Mrs. Hay went back to town after staying with the Burnells she sent the children a doll's house. It was so big that the carter and Pat carried it into the courtyard, and there it stayed, propped up on two wooden boxes beside the feed-room door. No harm could come to it; it was summer. And perhaps the smell of paint would have gone off by the time it had to be taken in. For, really, the smell of paint coming from that doll's house ("Sweet of old Mrs. Hay, of course; most sweet and generous!") – but the smell of paint was quite enough to make anyone seriously ill, in Aunt Beryl's opinion. Even before the sacking was taken off. And when it was . . .

There stood the doll's house, a dark, oily, spinach green, picked out with bright yellow. Its two solid little chimneys, glued on to the roof, were painted red and white, and the door, gleaming with yellow varnish, was like a little slab of toffee. Four windows, real windows, were divided into panes by a broad streak of green. There was actually a tiny porch, too, painted yellow, with big lumps of congealed paint hanging along the edge.

But perfect, perfect little house! Who could possibly mind the smell. It was part of the joy, part of the newness.

"Open it quickly, someone!"

The hook at the side was stuck fast. Pat pried it open with his penknife, and the whole house front swung back, and – there you were, gazing at one and the same moment into the drawing-room and dining-room, the kitchen and two bedrooms. That is the way for a house to open! Why don't all houses open like that? How much more exciting than peering through the slit of a door into a mean little hall with a hat-stand and two umbrellas! That is – isn't it? – what you long to know about a house when you put your hand on the knocker. Perhaps it is the way God opens houses at the dead of the night when He is taking a quiet turn with an angel. . . .

"Oh-oh!" The Burnell children sounded as though they were in despair. It was too marvellous; it was too much for them. They had never seen anything like it in their lives. All the rooms were papered. There were pictures on the walls, painted on the paper, with gold frames complete. Red carpet covered all the floors except the kitchen; red plush chairs in the drawing-room, green in the dining-room; tables, beds with real bedclothes, a cradle, a stove, a dresser with tiny plates and one big jug. But what Kezia liked more than anything, what she liked frightfully, was the lamp. It stood in the middle of the dining-room table, an exquisite little amber lamp with a white globe. It was even filled all ready for lighting, though, of course, you couldn't light it. But there was something inside that looked like oil and moved when you shook it.

The father and mother dolls, who sprawled very stiff as though they had fainted in the drawing-room, and their two little children asleep upstairs, were really too big for the doll's house. They didn't look as though they belonged. But the lamp was perfect. It seemed to smile at Kezia, to say, "I live here." The lamp was real.

The Burnell children could hardly walk to school fast enough the next morning. They burned to tell everybody, to describe, to – well – to boast about their doll's house before the school-bell rang.

"I'm to tell," said Isabel, "because I'm the eldest. And you can join in after. But I'm to tell first."

There was nothing to answer. Isabel was bossy, but she was always right, and Lottie and Kezia knew too well the powers that went with being eldest. They brushed through the thick buttercups at the road edge and said nothing.

"And I'm to choose who's to come and see it first. Mother said I might."

For it had been arranged that while the doll's house stood in the courtyard they might ask the girls at school, two at a time, to come and look. Not to stay to tea, of course, or to come traipsing through the house. But just to stand quietly in the courtyard while Isabel pointed out the beauties, and Lottie and Kezia looked pleased. . . .

But hurry as they might, by the time they had reached the tarred palings of the boys' playground the bell had begun to jangle. They only just had time to whip off their hats and fall into line before the roll was called. Never mind. Isabel tried to make up for it by looking very important and mysterious and by whispering behind her hand to the girls near her, "Got something to tell you at playtime."

Playtime came and Isabel was surrounded. The girls of her class nearly fought to put their arms round her, to walk away with her, to beam flatteringly, to be her special friend. She held quite a court under the huge pine trees at the side of the playground. Nudging, giggling together, the little girls pressed up close. And the only two who stayed outside the ring were the two who were always outside, the little Kelveys. They knew better than to come anywhere near the Burnells.

27

For the fact was, the school the Burnell children went to was not at all the kind of place their parents would have chosen if there had been any choice. But there was none. It was the only school for miles. And the consequence was all the children of the neighbourhood, the Judge's little girls, the doctor's daughters, the store-keeper's children, the milkman's, were forced to mix together. Not to speak of there being an equal number of rude, rough little boys as well. But the line had to be drawn somewhere. It was drawn at the Kelveys. Many of the children, including the Burnells, were not allowed even to speak to them. They walked past the Kelveys with their heads in the air, and as they set the fashion in all matters of behaviour, the Kelveys were shunned by everybody. Even the teacher had a special voice for them, and a special smile for the other children when Lil Kelvey came up to her desk with a bunch of dreadfully common-looking flowers.

They were the daughters of a spry, hard-working little washer-woman, who went about from house to house by the day. This was awful enough. But where was Mr. Kelvey? Nobody knew for certain. But everybody said he was in prison. So they were the daughters of a washerwoman and a jailbird. Very nice company for other people's children! And they looked it. Why Mrs. Kelvey made them so conspicuous was hard to understand. The truth was they were dressed in "bits" given to her by the people for whom she worked. Lil, for instance, who was a stout, plain child, with big freckles, came to school in a dress made from a green art-serge tablecloth of the Burnells', with red plush sleeves from the Logans' curtains. Her hat, perched on top of her high fore-head, was a grown-up woman's hat, once the property of Miss Lecky, the postmistress. It was turned up at the back and trimmed with a large scarlet quill. What a little guy she looked! It was impossible not to laugh. And her little sister, our Else, wore a long white dress, rather like a nightgown, and a pair of little boy's boots. But whatever our Else wore she would have looked strange. She was a tiny wishbone of a child, with cropped hair and enormous solemn eyes – a little white owl. Nobody had ever seen her smile; she scarcely ever spoke. She went through life holding on to Lil, with a piece of Lil's skirt screwed up in her hand. Where Lil went, our Else followed. In the playground, on the road going to and from school, there was Lil marching in front and our Else holding on behind. Only when she wanted any-thing, or when she was out of breath, our Else gave Lil a tug, a twitch, and Lil stopped and turned round. The Kelveys never failed to understand each other.

Now they hovered at the edge; you couldn't stop them listening. When the little girls turned round and sneered, Lil, as usual, gave her silly, shamefaced smile, but our Else only looked.

And Isabel's voice, so very proud, went on telling. The carpet made a great sensation, but so did the beds with real bedclothes, and the stove with an oven door.

When she finished Kezia broke in. "You've forgotten the lamp, Isabel."

"Oh yes," said Isabel, "and there's a teeny little lamp, all made of yellow glass, with a white globe that stands on the dining-room table. You couldn't tell it from a real one."

"The lamp's best of all," cried Kezia. She thought Isabel wasn't making half enough of the little lamp. But nobody paid any attention. Isabel was choosing the two who were to come back with them that afternoon and see it. She chose Emmie Cole and Lena Logan. But when the others knew they were all to have a chance, they couldn't be nice enough to Isabel. One by one they put their arms round Isabel's waist and walked her off. They had something to whisper to her, a secret. "Isabel's *my* friend."

Only the little Kelveys moved away forgotten; there was nothing more for them to hear.

Days passed, and as more children saw the doll's house, the fame of it spread. It became the one subject, the rage. The one question was, "Have you seen Burnells' doll's house? Oh, ain't it lovely!" "Haven't you seen it? Oh, I say!"

Even the dinner hour was given up to talking about it. The little girls sat under the pines eating their thick mutton sandwiches and big slabs of johnny cake spread with butter. While always, as near as they could get, sat the Kelveys, our Else holding on to Lil, listening too, while they chewed their jam sandwiches out of a newspaper soaked with large red blobs.

"Mother," said Kezia, "can't I ask the Kelveys just once?"

"Certainly not, Kezia."

"But why not?"

"Run away, Kezia; you know quite well why not."

At last everybody had seen it except them. On that day the subject rather flagged. It was the dinner hour. The children stood together under the pine trees, and suddenly, as they looked at the Kelveys eating out of their paper, always by themselves, always listening, they wanted to be horrid to them. Emmie Cole started the whisper.

"Lil Kelvey's going to be a servant when she grows up."

"O-oh, how awful!" said Isabel Burnell, and she made eyes at Emmie.

Emmie swallowed in a very meaning way and nodded to Isabel as she'd seen her mother do on those occasions. "It's true – it's true – it's true," she said.

Then Lena Logan's little eyes snapped. "Shall I ask her?" she whispered.

"Bet you don't," said Jessie May.

"Pooh, I'm not frightened," said Lena. Suddenly she gave a little squeal and danced in front of the other girls. "Watch! Watch me! Watch me now!" said Lena. And sliding, gliding, dragging one foot, giggling behind her hand, Lena went over to the Kelveys.

Lil looked up from her dinner. She wrapped the rest quickly away. Our Else stopped chewing. What was coming now?

"Is it true you're going to be a servant when you grow up, Lil Kelvey?" shrilled Lena.

Dead silence. But instead of answering, Lil only gave her silly, shamefaced smile. She didn't seem to mind the question at all. What a sell for Lena! The girls began to titter.

Lena couldn't stand that. She put her hands on her hips; she shot forward. "Yah, yer father's in prison!" she hissed spitefully.

This was such a marvellous thing to have said that the little girls rushed away in a body, deeply, deeply excited, wild with joy. Someone found a long rope, and they began skipping. And never did they skip so high, run in and out so fast, or do such daring things as on that morning.

In the afternoon Pat called for the Burnell children with the buggy and they drove home. There were visitors. Isabel and Lottie, who liked visitors, went upstairs to change their pinafores. But Kezia thieved out at the back. Nobody was about; she began to swing on the big white gates of the courtyard. Presently, looking along the road, she saw two little dots. They grew bigger, they were coming towards her. Now she could see that one was in front and one close behind. Now she could see that they were the Kelveys. Kezia stopped swinging. She slipped off the gate as if she was going to run away. Then she hesitated. The Kelveys came nearer, and beside them walked their shadows, very long, stretching right across the road with their heads in the buttercups. Kezia clambered back on the gate; she had made up her mind; she swung out.

"Hullo," she said to the passing Kelveys.

They were so astounded that they stopped. Lil gave her silly smile. Our Else stared.

"You can come and see our doll's house if you want to," said Kezia, and she dragged one toe on the ground. But at that Lil turned red and shook her head quickly.

"Why not?" asked Kezia.

Lil gasped, then she said, "Your ma told our ma you wasn't to speak to us."

"Oh well," said Kezia. She didn't know what to reply. "It doesn't matter. You can come and see our doll's house all the same. Come on. Nobody's looking."

But Lil shook her head still harder.

"Don't you want to?" asked Kezia.

Suddenly there was a twitch, a tug at Lil's skirt. She turned round. Our Else was looking at her with big, imploring eyes; she was frowning; she wanted to go. For a moment Lil looked at our Else very doubtfully. But then our Else twitched her skirt again. She started forward. Kezia led the way. Like two little stray cats they followed across the courtyard to where the doll's house stood.

"There it is," said Kezia.

There was a pause. Lil breathed loudly, almost snorted; our Else was still as stone.

"I'll open it for you," said Kezia kindly. She undid the hook and they looked inside.

"There's the drawing-room and the dining-room, and that's the – "

"Kezia!"

Oh, what a start they gave!

"Kezia!"

It was Aunt Beryl's voice. They turned round. At the back door stood Aunt Beryl, staring as if she couldn't believe what she saw.

"How dare you ask the little Kelveys into the courtyard!" said her cold, furious voice. "You know as well as I do, you're not allowed to talk to them. Run away, children, run away at once. And don't come back again," said Aunt Beryl. And she stepped into the yard and shooed them out as if they were chickens.

"Off you go immediately!" she called, cold and proud.

They did not need telling twice. Burning with shame, shrinking together, Lil huddling along like her mother, our Else dazed, somehow they crossed the big courtyard and squeezed through the white gate.

"Wicked, disobedient little girl!" said Aunt Beryl bitterly to Kezia, and she slammed the doll's house to.

The afternoon had been awful. A letter had come from Willie Brent, a terrifying, threatening letter, saying if she did not meet him that evening in Pulman's Bush, he'd come to the front door and ask the reason why! But now that she had frightened those little rats of Kelveys and given Kezia a good scolding, her heart felt lighter. That ghastly pressure was gone. She went back to the house humming.

When the Kelveys were well out of sight of Burnells', they sat down to rest on a big red drainpipe by the side of the road. Lil's cheeks were still burning; she took off the hat with the quill and held it on her knee. Dreamily they looked over the hay paddocks, past the creek, to the group of wattles where Logan's cows stood waiting to be milked. What were their thoughts?

Presently our Else nudged up close to her sister. But now she had forgotten the cross lady. She put out a finger and stroked her sister's quill; she smiled her rare smile.

"I seen the little lamp," she said softly.

Then both were silent once more.

Questions for Writing and Discussion

Discovering Meaning

1. The viewers' reactions to the doll's house reveal their characters. Discuss the various attitudes and what they reveal about each character.
2. Why is Kezia fascinated by the lamp? What qualities does she appreciate in it? Why does she disregard her parents' prohibition and invite the Kelveys to see the doll's house?
3. Contrast Lil and Else. Why is the younger Kelvey child called "our" Else?
4. Why do the children taunt the Kelveys? Why are they "wild with joy" after their cruel remark about the Kelveys' father?
5. Explain the reasons for Aunt Beryl's sudden rage at the end of the story.
6. In the ending, Mansfield presents an "epiphany"; that is, the crucial moment that reveals the meaning of the story. What meaning do you derive from the ending?

Exploring Method

1. In telling the story, Mansfield shifts from the third-person narrator's voice to idioms that the characters would use. Select these phrases and sentences and identify the character whose thoughts they record.

2. Mansfield describes the doll's house in three different passages. How are the images logically related? Through whose eyes is the doll's house seen in each passage? How does Kezia's response to the doll's house prepare the reader for her behaviour later in the story?
3. Mansfield uses parallel characters and parallel scenes to develop her theme. Discuss the significance of the following parallels.
   a) Two pairs of children outside the social circle in the school yard: the Burnell children, Lottie and Kezia, and the Kelveys, Lil and our Else.
   b) Two scenes using dialogue: the children in the schoolyard, taunting the Kelveys about their father, and Kezia at her gate, inviting the Kelveys to see the doll's house.
   c) The use of the buttercup image: in relation to Lottie and Kezia as Isabel says she will tell their friends about the doll's house, and to the Kelvey children as they approach Kezia on the road, with the heads of their elongated shadows in the buttercups.
4. Discuss the use of the lamp as a symbol in the story.
5. Describe the ways in which Mansfield uses circle images and their significance in the story.

Suggestions for Writing

1. At the end, after the Kelveys have seen the doll's house, the narrator asks, "What are their thoughts?" Rewrite the ending, recording what you imagine the Kelveys' thoughts are.
2. Examine the words describing the doll's house. Note the precise details, words naming colours, textures, smells, and sounds that appeal to the senses. Using Mansfield's technique, describe one of your possessions and make it vivid and immediate to your reader.
3. Narrate an incident you witnessed, experienced, or imagine in which you, like Kezia, discover that a child's sense of good and evil conflicts with the adult reality.
4. Describe a scene that involves prejudice, once from the victim's point of view and a second time from the prejudiced person's point of view.

Examining Social Issues

1. Discuss the influence of the adults in the children's cruelty to the Kelveys. Select examples from the story that illustrate this

influence. Do you see this influence around you? Give examples from your own experience.

2. What insights into the causes of prejudice are revealed through the behaviour of the following characters towards the Kelveys: Isabel and her friends, the teacher, Aunt Beryl, Mrs. Burnell.

3. Imagine Else at Lil's age. Will she be more assertive, or will she accept humiliating treatment as timidly as Lil? How should a victim of prejudice react?

Wing's Chips

Mavis Gallant

Mavis Gallant's childhood in Quebec and her bilingualism have fostered in her an interest in a variety of characters, customs, and sensibilities from diverse origins. Her settings are either Quebec or Europe (where she is currently living), settings that she creates vividly with a few crisp details. She portrays with amusement, affection, and compassion characters who are exiles, expatriates, rootless transients, people transplanted from their native surroundings. In her European settings, Canadians are uneasy residents, unable to accept the life-styles they encounter. In her Quebec settings, French Canadians and Anglo-Saxons are separated by barriers of historical mistrust that limit their perceptions of one another.

The narrator in "Wing's Chips" (1954) explores the past as she reconstructs the lost world of her childhood. By using two points of view simultaneously, the child's and the adult's, the author allows the reader to understand the child's response to her experience through an adult's perspective. The double focus affects the tone of the story, adding a dimension of objectivity, irony, and humour.

Often, since I grew up, I have tried to remember the name of the French-Canadian town where I lived for a summer with my father when I was a little girl of seven or eight. Sometimes, passing through a town, I have thought I recognized it, but some detail is always wrong, or at least fails to fit the picture in my memory. It was a town like many others in the St. Lawrence Valley – old, but with a curious atmosphere of harshness, as if the whole area were still frontier and had not been settled and cultivated for three hundred years. There were rows of temporary-looking frame and stucco houses, a post office in somebody's living room, a Chinese fish-and-chip store, and, on the lawn of the imposing Catholic church, a statue of Jesus, arms extended, crowned with a wreath of electric lights. Running straight through the center of town was a narrow river; a few leaky rowboats were tied up along its banks, and on Sunday afternoons hot, church-dressed young men would go to work on them with rusty bailing tins. The girls who

35

clustered giggling on shore and watched them wore pastel stockings, lacy summer hats, and voile dresses that dipped down in back and were decorated low on one hip with sprays of artificial lilac. For additional Sunday divertissement, there was the cinema, in an old barn near the railway station. The pictures had no sound track; airs from "My Maryland" and "The Student Prince" were played on a piano and there was the occasional toot of the suburban train from Montreal while on the screen ladies with untidy hair and men in riding boots engaged in agitated, soundless conversation, opening and closing their mouths like fish.

Though I have forgotten the name of this town, I do remember with remarkable clarity the house my father took for that summer. It was white clapboard, and surrounded by shade trees and an untended garden, in which only sunflowers and a few perennials survived. It had been rented furnished and bore the imprint of Quebec rural taste, running largely to ball fringes and seashell-encrusted religious art. My father, who was a painter, used one room as a studio – or, rather, storage place, since he worked mostly out-of-doors – slept in another, and ignored the remaining seven, which was probably just as well, though order of a sort was kept by a fierce-looking local girl called Pauline, who had a pronounced mustache and was so ill-tempered that her nickname was *P'tit-Loup* – Little Wolf.

Pauline cooked abominably, cleaned according to her mood, and asked me questions. My father had told her that my mother was in a nursing home in Montreal, but Pauline wanted to know more. How ill was my mother? Very ill? Dying? Was it true that my parents were separated? Was my father *really* my father? "*Drôle de père,*" said Pauline. She was perplexed by his painting, his animals (that summer his menagerie included two German shepherds, a parrot, and a marmoset, which later bit the finger of a man teasing it and had to be given away to Montreal's ratty little zoo, where it moped itself to death), and his total indifference to the way the house was run. Why didn't he work, like other men, said Pauline.

I could understand her bewilderment, for the question of my father's working was beginning to worry me for the first time. All of the French-Canadian fathers in the town worked. They delivered milk, they farmed, they owned rival hardware stores, they drew up one another's wills. Nor were they the only busy ones. Across the river, in a faithful reproduction of a suburb of Glasgow or Manchester, lived a small colony of English-speaking summer residents from Montreal. Their children were called Al, Lily,

Winnie, or Mac, and they were distinguished by their popping blue eyes, their excessive devotion to the Royal Family, and their contempt for anything even vaguely queer or Gallic. Like the French-Canadians, the fathers of Lily and Winnie and the others worked. Every one of them had a job. When they were not taking the train to Montreal to attend to their jobs, they were crouched in their gardens, caps on their heads, tying up tomato plants or painting stones to make gay multicolored borders for the nasturtium beds. Saturday night, they trooped into the town bar-and-grill and drank as much Molson's ale as could be poured into the stomach before closing time. Then, awash with ale and nostalgia, they sang about the maid in the clogs and shawl, and something else that went, "Let's all go down to the Strand, and 'ave a ba-na-ar-na!"

My father, I believed, was wrong in not establishing some immediate liaison with this group. Like them, he was English – a real cabbage, said Pauline when she learned that he had been in Canada only eight or nine years. Indeed, one of his very few topics of conversation with me was the England of his boyhood, before the First World War. It sounded green, sunny, and silent – a sort of vast lawn rising and falling beside the sea; the sun was smaller and higher than the sun in Canada, looking something like a coin; the trees were leafy and round, and looked like cushions. This was probably not at all what he said, but it was the image I retained – a landscape flickering and flooded with light, like the old silents at the cinema. The parents of Lily and Winnie had, presumably, also come out of this landscape, yet it was a bond my father appeared to ignore. It seemed to me that he was unaware of how much we had lost caste, and what grievous social errors we had committed, by being too much identified with the French. He had chosen a house on the wrong side of the river. Instead of avoiding the French language, or noisily making fun of it, he spoke it whenever he was dealing with anyone who could not understand English. He did not attend the English church, and he looked just as sloppy on Sundays as he did the rest of the week.

"You people Carthlic?" one of the fathers from over the river asked me once, as if that would explain a lot.

Mercifully, I was able to say no. I knew we were not Catholic because at the Pensionnat Saint-Louis de Gonzague, in Montreal, which I attended, I had passed the age at which children usually took the First Communion. For a year and more, my classmates had been attending morning chapel in white veils, while I still wore a plain, stiff, pre-Communion black veil that smelled of convent parlors, and marked me as one outside the limits of grace.

"Then why's your dad always around the frogs?" asked the English father.

Drôle de père indeed. I had to agree with Pauline. He was not like any father I had met or read about. He was not Elsie's Mr. Dinsmore, stern but swayed by tears. Nor did he in the least resemble Mr. Bobbsey, of the Bobbsey Twins books, or Mr. Bunker, of the Six Little Bunkers. I was never scolded, or rebuked, or reminded to brush my teeth or say my prayers. My father was perfectly content to live his own summer and let me live mine, which did not please me in the least. If, at meals, I failed to drink my milk, it was I who had to mention this omission. When I came home from swimming with my hair wet, it was I who had to remind him that, because of some ear trouble that was a hangover of scarlet fever, I was supposed to wear a bathing cap. When Lon Chaney in *The Hunchback of Notre Dame* finally arrived at the cinema, he did not say a word about my not going, even though Lily and Winnie and many of the French-Canadian children were not allowed to attend, and boasted about the restriction.

Oddly, he did have one or two notions about the correct upbringing of children, which were, to me, just as exasperating as his omissions. Somewhere in the back of his mind lingered a recollection that all little girls were taught French and music. I don't know where the little girls of the England of his childhood were sent to learn their French – presumably to France – but I was placed, one month after my fourth birthday, in the Pensionnat, where for two years I had the petted privilege of being the youngest boarder in the history of the school. My piano lessons had also begun at four, but lasted only a short time, for, as the nun in charge of music explained, I could not remember or sit still, and my hand was too small to span an octave. Music had then been dropped as one of my accomplishments until that summer, when, persuaded by someone who obviously had my welfare at heart, my father dispatched me twice a week to study piano with a Madame Tessier, the convent-educated wife of a farmer, whose parlor was furnished entirely with wicker and over whose household hung a faint smell of dung, owing to the proximity of the outbuildings and the intense humidity of summer weather in the St. Lawrence Valley. Together, Madame Tessier and I sweated it out, plodding away against my lack of talent, my absence of interest, and my strong but unspoken desire to be somewhere else.

"*Cette enfant ne fera jamais rien,*" I once heard her say in despair.

We had been at it four or five weeks before she discovered at least part of the trouble; it was simply that there was no piano at home, so I never practiced. After every lesson, she had marked with care the scales I was to master, yet, week after week, I produced only those jerky, hesitant sounds that are such agony for music teachers and the people in the next room.

"You might as well tell your father there's no use carrying on unless you have a piano," she said.

I was only too happy, and told him that afternoon, at lunch.

"You mean you want me to get you a *piano?*" he said, looking around the dining room as if I had insisted it be installed, then and there, between the window and the mirrored china cabinet. How unreasonable I was!

"But you make me take the lessons," I said. How unreasonable *he* was!

A friend of my father's said to me, years later, "He never had the faintest idea what to do with you." But it was equally true that I never had the faintest idea what to do with him. We did not, of course, get a piano, and Madame Tessier's view was that because my father had no employment to speak of (she called him a *flâneur*), we simply couldn't afford one – the depth of shame in a town where even the milkman's daughters could play duets.

No one took my father's painting seriously as a daily round of work, least of all I. At one point during that summer, my father agreed to do a pastel portrait of the daughter of a Madame Gravelle, who lived in Montreal. (This was in the late twenties, when pastel drawings of children hung in every other sitting room.) The daughter, Liliane, who was my age or younger, was to be shown in her First Communion dress and veil. Madame Gravelle and Liliane drove out from Montreal, and while Liliane posed with docility, her mother hung about helpfully commenting. Here my father was neglecting to show in detail the pattern of the lace veil; there he had the wrong shade of blue for Liliane's eyes; again, it was the matter of Liliane's diamond cross. The cross, which hung from her neck, contained four diamonds on the horizontal segment and six on the vertical, and this treasure he had reduced to two unimpressive strokes.

My father suggested that Madame Gravelle might be just as happy with a tinted photograph. No, said Madame Gravelle, she would not. Well, then, he suggested, how about a miniature? He knew of a miniaturist who worked from photographs, eliminating sittings, and whose fee was about four times his own. Madame Gravelle bore Liliane, her cross, and her veil back to Montreal, and my father went back to painting around the countryside and going out with his dogs.

His failure weighed heavily on me, particularly after someone, possibly Pauline, told me that he was forever painting people who didn't pay him a cent for doing it. He painted Pauline, mustache and all; he painted some of the French-Canadian children who came to play in our garden, and from whom I was learning a savory French vocabulary not taught at Pensionnat Saint-Louis de Gonzague; he very often sketched the little Wing children, whose family owned the village fish-and-chip store.

The Wing children were solemn little Chinese, close in age and so tangled in lineage that it was impossible to sort them out as sisters, brothers, and cousins. Some of the adult Wings – brothers, and cousins – ran the fish-and-chip shop, and were said to own many similar establishments throughout Quebec and to be (although no one would have guessed it to see them) by far the richest people in the area. The interior of their store smelled wonderfully of frying grease and vinegar, and the walls were a mosaic of brightly painted tin signs advertising Player's Mild, Orange Crush, Sweet Marie chocolate bars, and ginger ale. The smaller Wings, in the winter months, attended Anglican boarding schools in the west, at a discreet distance from the source of income. Their English was excellent and their French-Canadian idiom without flaw. Those nearest my age were Florence, Marjorie, Ronald, and Hugh. The older set of brothers and cousins – those of my father's generation – had abrupt, utilitarian names: Tommy, Jimmy, George. The still older people – most of whom seldom came out from the rooms behind the shop – used their Chinese names. There was even a great-grandmother, who sat, shrunken and silent, by the great iron range where the chips swam in a bath of boiling fat.

As the Wings had no garden, and were not permitted to play by the river, lest they fall in and drown, it was most often at my house that we played. If my father was out, we would stand at the door of his studio and peer in at the fascinating disorder.

"What does he do?" Florence or Marjorie would say. "What does your father do?"

"He paints!" Pauline would cry from the kitchen. She might, herself, consider him loony, but the privilege was hers. She worked there, not a pack of Chinese.

It was late in the summer, in August, when, one afternoon, Florence and Marjorie and Ronald and Hugh came up from the gate escorting, like a convoy, one of the older Wings. They looked anxious and important. "Is your father here?" said the grown-up Wing.

I ran to fetch my father, who had just started out for a walk. When we returned, Pauline and the older Wing, who turned out to be Jimmy, were arguing in French, she at the top of her voice, he almost inaudibly.

"The kids talk about you a lot," said Jimmy Wing to my father. "They said you were a painter. We're enlarging the store, and we want a new sign."

"A sign?"

"I told you!" shrieked Pauline from the dining-room door, to which she had retreated. "*Ce n'est pas un peintre comme ça.*"

"*Un peintre, c'est un peintre,*" said Jimmy Wing, imperturbable.

My father looked at the little Wings, who were all looking up at him, and said, "Exactly. *Un peintre, c'est un peintre.* What sort of sign would you like?"

The Wings didn't know; they all began to talk at once. Something artistic, said Jimmy Wing, with the lettering fat and thin, imitation Chinese. Did my father know what he meant? Oh, yes. My father knew exactly.

"Just 'Wing's Chips'?" my father asked. "Or would you like it in French – *'Les Chips de Wing'*?"

"Oh, *English,*" said all the Wings, almost together. My father said later that the Chinese were terrible snobs.

He painted the sign the next Sunday afternoon, not in the studio but out in the back garden, sitting on the wide kitchen steps. He lacquered it black, and painted – in red-and-gold characters, fat and thin – "Wing's Chips," and under this he put the name of the town and two curly little letters, "P.Q.," for "Province of Quebec."

Tommy and Jimmy Wing and all the little ones came to fetch the sign the next day. The two men looked at it for a long time, while the little ones looked anxiously at them to see if they liked it. Finally, Jimmy Wing said, "It's the most beautiful thing I ever saw."

The two men bore it away, the little Wings trailing behind, and hung it on a horizontal pole over the street in front of their shop, where it rocked in the hot, damp breeze from the river. I was hysterically proud of the sign and, for quite the first time, of my father. Everyone stopped before the shop and examined it. The French-Canadians admitted that it was *pas mal, pas mal du tout,* while the English adults said approvingly that he must have been paid a fine penny for it. I could not bring down our new stature by admitting that he had painted it as a favor, and that it was only after Jimmy and Tommy had insisted that he had said they could, if they liked, pay for the gold paint, since he had had to go to Montreal for it. Nor did I tell anyone how the Wings, burdened with gratitude, kept bringing us chips and ice cream.

"Oh, yes, he was paid an awful lot," I assured them all.

Every day, I went to look at the sign, and I hung around the shop in case anyone wanted to ask me questions about it. There it was, "Wing's Chips," proof that my father was an ordinary workingman just like anybody else, and I pointed it out to as many people as I could, both English and French, until the summer ended and we went away.

Questions for Writing and Discussion

Discovering Meaning

1. Describe the narrator's father. Compare him with the other fathers in the story. Why does he irritate both the French Canadians and the English?
2. Describe the character of the protagonist, the eight-year-old child. Why is she beginning, for the first time, to question her father's behaviour? Why does she join with those who disapprove of her father?
3. Why do the Wings admire the girl's father?
4. Why does the father refuse to complete the portrait of Madame Gravelle's daughter for a fee, yet agree to paint Jimmy Wing's sign without payment?
5. The narrator reports that her father said Jimmy Wing was a snob. What are the reasons for his view? Do you agree with him? Why or why not? Why are the Wing family and the narrator and her father able to establish communication with each other?
6. In the final scene, the author presents various attitudes towards the father's sign. Compare the daughter's attitude with the others.

Exploring Method

1. We hear two voices telling the story, the adult narrator recalling her childhood experience and the voice of the child who is involved in the action. How does the adult narrator's view of her father differ from the child's view? Select passages in the story that express the adult narrator's judgement. What is your impression of the father? Is it closer to the child's or to the adult narrator's? Why?

2. What is the function in the story of each of the following characters: Pauline, Madame Gravelle, Madame Tessier?
3. The narrator describes three settings: the Canadian St. Lawrence valley town as a generalized picture in her memory, the house that she remembers with remarkable clarity, and the English landscape of her imagination, based on her father's stories about his boyhood. Examine the details she uses to describe each and discuss the differences between a generalized memory, a vivid memory, and a memory of an imaginary image.

Suggestions for Writing

1. Gallant examines the different expressions of art in the story: the statue of Jesus with the neon sign, the sea-shell-encrusted religious art in the house, the unfinished portrait of Madame Gravelle's daughter, and Wing's sign. Using the father's viewpoint, write a review in which you examine the merits of each.
2. Expressing the father's thoughts, write a monologue in which he describes his position as an artist in the community.
3. The father in the story is a permissive parent. The Wing children have restrictive parents. Which upbringing seems more successful? Illustrate your opinion by describing two of your friends, one with permissive parents, another with strict parents.
4. The narrator says, "My father was content to live his own summer and let me live mine, which did not please me in the least." Did you have such feelings when you were eight? Describe yourself at that age. Illustrate your description with a personal experience in which you narrate a typical incident that dramatizes your relationship with your parents.

Examining Social Issues

1. What restrictions should parents impose on young children? What changes should occur in parental control during teen-age years?
2. Compare the effects on the Wing children of living in an extended family with the effects on the narrator of living in a single-parent family. Consider the benefits and the problems of each.
3. In describing the Wing family, Gallant portrays only the oldest generation clinging to their Chinese customs and names. Is this

a typical portrait of families outside the mainstream culture? Discuss the tensions resulting from the assimilation of the younger and the middle generations in such families.

4. The story portrays several economic levels: the poor French Canadians, represented by Pauline; the middle class, represented by Madame Tessier and the English summer residents; and the wealthy, represented by Madame Gravelle and the Wing family. Account for the differences between the two wealthy families, the Wings and the Gravelles. Discuss the relative influences of economic differences and racial tension as sources of conflict among the different groups. Support your answer with examples of prejudice in the story.

5. Discuss the effects of having a diversity of racial minorities in a community. Use some examples that you have observed. How can appreciation of such pluralism be cultivated?

6. David Elkind, in his book *A Sympathetic Understanding of the Child*, presents a psychological profile of the eight-year-old. According to Elkind, a psychologist, eight-year-olds are outgoing, curious, extremely social, critical both of themselves and of others, and mature in social relations. They are ambivalent about growing up, combining a critical attitude towards adults with an eagerness to know more about the adult world and to assume some of its privileges. Compare the eight-year-old in this story with Elkind's profile.

The Outlaw

Sinclair Ross

*Sinclair Ross, an author of major importance in Canadian litera-
ture, writes in the tradition of the early realist Frederick Philip
Grove. Ross influenced such writers of prairie fiction as Margaret
Laurence, Robert Kroetsch, and Rudy Wiebe. The best of his writing is based on his own childhood on a prairie farm. As a chron-
icler of the period of the drought and the Depression, he made a
significant contribution to Canadian literary history.*

*Margaret Laurence, in her introduction to the collection of his
stories,* The Lamp at Noon *(1968), describes Ross's typical setting:
"The farm stands far apart, only distantly related to whatever
town is the focal point for buying and selling. The human community is, for most of the time, reduced to the smallest unit, one
family. The isolation is virtually complete."*

*In this setting, Ross creates portraits of frustrated, emotionally
repressed men and women on barren landscapes, an external reflection of their inner lives, where their experiences mirror the
position of human beings in the cosmos. His characters are
farmers who survive with dignity, endurance, and pride against
hard, unyielding nature with its cycles of treacherous winds and
droughts; women disappointed with the bleak conditions of their
lives and concerned for their children; children, impressionable,
imaginative, isolated, for whom the future still holds the promise
of excitement.*

*In his fiction, the recurrent theme is the need for fantasy in a
person's life. For Ross, the dream is a defence against the indifference of the universe. It is an escape from the dreary restriction of a
limited world, a means of heightening and intensifying life, and a
way of cultivating one's best self. In taut, economical, rhythmic
prose that evokes the bleak landscape and mirrors the inner lives
of his protagonists, he portrays the tension between a world
hostile to illusion and the need for illusion in a hostile world.*

She was beautiful but dangerous. She had thrown one man and killed him, thrown another and broken his collar bone, and my parents, as if they knew what the sight of her idle in her stall was doing to me, never let a day go by without giving lurid details, everything from splints and stitches to the undertaker, of the painful and untimely end in store for me should I ever take it into my fool young head to try to ride her.

"I've got troubles enough without having you laid up with broken bones and doctor bills. She's a sly one, mind, and no good's ever come of her."

"Besides, you're only turned thirteen, and a grown man, a regular cowboy at that, would think twice before tackling her. Another year and then we'll see. You'll both be that much older. In the meantime nobody expects it of you."

In the meantime, though, she was a captive, pining her heart away. Week after week she stamped and pawed, nosed the hay out of her manger contemptuously, flung up her head and poured out wild, despairing neighs into the prairie winds and blizzards streaming past. It was mostly, of course, for my benefit. She had sized me up, evidently, as soft-hearted as well as faint-hearted, and decided there was just a chance that I might weaken and go riding. Her neighs, just as she intended they should, tormented and shamed me.

She was a good horse, but a reprobate. That was how we came to own her. At the auction sale where she was put up, her reputation as a killer spread among the crowd, and my father got her cheap. He was such a practical, level-headed man, and she was so obviously a poor investment, that I suspect it was because of me he bought her. As I stood at his side in the front row of the crowd and watched them lead her out, poised, dramatic, radiant, some of the sudden desire that overwhelmed me must have leaped from my face and melted him.

"Anyway, she's a bargain," he defended himself that evening at the supper table. "I can always sell her and at least get back what I paid. But first I want to see what a taste of good hard work will do."

He tried it. His intention was to work her on the land a month or two, just till she was tamed down to make an all-round, serviceable saddle horse, but after a painful week of half-days on the plow he let her keep her stall. She was too hard on his nerves, he said, straining ahead and pulling twice her share. She was too hard on his self-respect, actually, the slender limbs, the imperious head.

For she was a very lovely reprobate. Twenty years of struggle with the land had made him a determined, often hard man, but he couldn't bring himself to break her spirit with the plow.

She was one horse, and she was all horses. Thundering battle chargers, fleet Arabians, untamed mustangs – sitting beside her on her manger I knew and rode them all. There was history in her shapely head and burning eyes. I charged with her at Balaklava, Waterloo, scoured the deserts of Africa and the steppes of the Ukraine. Conquest and carnage, trumpets and glory – she understood, and carried me triumphantly.

To approach her was to be enlarged, transported. She was coalblack, gleaming, queenly. Her mane had a ripple and her neck an arch. And somehow, softly and mysteriously, she was always burning. The reflection on her glossy hide, whether of winter sunshine or yellow lantern light, seemed the glow of some fierce, secret passion. There were moments when I felt the whole stable charged with her, as if she were the priestess of her kind, in communion with her deity.

For all that, though, she was a very dangerous horse, and dutifully my parents kept warning me. Facts didn't lie, they pointed out. A record was a record.

Isabel did her utmost to convince me that the record was a slander. With nuzzling, velvet lips she coaxed and pleaded, whispered that the delights of fantasy and dream were but as shadows beside the exhilarations of reality. Only try reality – slip her bridle on. Only be reasonable – ask myself what she would gain by throwing me. After all, I was turned thirteen. It wasn't as if I were a *small* boy.

And then, temptress, she bore me off to the mountain top of my vanity, and with all the world spread out before my gaze, talked guilefully of prestige and acclaim.

Over there, three miles away, was the school house. What a sensation to come galloping up on her, the notorious outlaw, instead of jogging along as usual on bandy-legged old Pete. What a surprise for Millie Dickson, whose efforts to be loyal to me were always defeated by my lack of verve and daring. For it was true: on the playground I had only a fair rating. I was butterfingers when it came to ball, and once in a fight I had cravenly turned tail and run. How sweet to wipe out all the ignominy of my past, to be deferred to by the older boys, to bask in Millie's smiles of favour.

And over there, seven miles away, the cupolas of its grain elevators just visible on the horizon, was town. Where fairs were sometimes held, and races run. On such a horse I naturally would win, and for all I knew the prize might be a hundred dollars. Well, then – supposing I could treat Millie to ice-cream *and* a movie!

Here Isabel would pause a moment, contemptuous of one so craven, then whinny shrill in challenge to some other rider, with heart and spirit equal to her own. There was no one, of course, to hear the challenge, but still it always troubled me. Johnny Olsen, for instance, the show-off Swede who had punched my nose and made me run – supposing he should come along and say, "I'll ride her for you – I'm not scared!" What kind of figure then would I cut? What would Millie Dickson say?

Isabel's motives, in all this, were two. The first was a natural, purely equine desire to escape from her stall and stretch her legs. The second, equally strong, was a perverse, purely feminine itch to bend me to her will.

For it was a will as imperious as her head. Her pride was at stake; I had to be reduced. With the first coaxing nuzzle of her lips she had committed herself to the struggle, and that as a male I was still at such a rudimentary stage made it doubly imperative that she emerge the victor. Defeat by a man would have been defeat, bitter but endurable. Defeat by a boy, on the other hand, would have been sheer humiliation.

On account of the roads and weather school was closed for two months after Christmas, and as the winter wore on it became increasingly difficult to resist her. A good deal of the time my father was away with wheat to town, and it was three miles to the nearest neighbour where there was another boy. I had chores, books, and the toolshed to keep me busy, but still there were long hours of idleness. Hungry for companionship, it was only natural that I should turn to Isabel. There were always her tail and mane to comb when we wearied of each other conversationally.

My association with her, of course, was virtual disobedience. I knew that she was charging me with desire, that eventually under its pressure I must burst like a blister, but still, despite conscience and good intentions, I lingered. Leaving her was always difficult, like leaving a fair or picnic, and going home to hunt the cows.

And then one clear sharp day, early in February, Millie Dickson and her mother drove over to spend the afternoon, and suddenly the temptation was too much for me.

They came early, country-fashion, so that Mrs. Dickson would have time for a long talk and tea, and be home again before nightfall. My father was away to town, and when they drove up in their bright red cutter I hurried out to take the horse. Mrs. Dickson was generous in her thanks, and even Millie smiled invitingly from beneath her frosted yellow curls. She had always liked me well enough. It was just that my behaviour at school made it difficult to be my champion.

I was shy when I returned to the house, but exceedingly happy. We all sat in the kitchen, not only because it was the largest, warmest room, but also because it gave my mother a chance to entertain her guest and at the same time whip up fresh biscuits and a cake in their honour. Mrs. Dickson asked so many friendly questions that I squirmed with pleasure till the varnish on my chair fairly blistered. What could it mean but that at home Millie did champion me, that she suppressed the discreditable and spoke only of the best?

She and I talked, too. We leafed through old magazines, gossiped about school, speculated on the new teacher, and gradually established a sense of intimacy and good will that made me confident my past was all forgotten, my future rosy and secure. For an hour it was like that – socially the most gratifying hour I had ever spent – and then, as nearly always happened when my mother had visitors, the delinquencies and scandals of the community moved in, and the kitchen became a place unfit for innocent young ears.

There must have been a considerable number of these delinquencies. It was indeed a very upright, fine community, but it must have had its wayward side. Anyway, surveying my entire boyhood, I am sure I could count on the fingers of one hand the time I was *not* sent out to chop wood or look for eggs when my mother and her friends got started on the neighbours. Usually I had a fair idea from the thread of conversation who it was who had been up to what, but this time, absorbed in my relationship with Millie, I heard nothing till my mother tapped my shoulder.

"Come along," she said brightly, affecting concern for our appetites and health. "It's too fine a day for you and Millie to be sitting in the house. Run out and play in the fresh air, so you'll be ready for your tea."

But at thirteen you don't play with a girl. You can neither skin the cat with her up in the loft among the rafters, nor turn somersaults down a strawstack. I did suggest taking the .22 and going after rabbits, but the dear little bunnies were so sweet, she said, she couldn't bear to hurt them. Naturally, therefore, after a chilly and dispiriting turn or two around the barnyard, I took her in to visit Isabel.

Isabel rose to the occasion. She minced and pawed, strained at her halter shank to let us see how badly she wanted to be taken out, then nipped our sleeves to prove her gentle playfulness. And finally, to remind us that despite such intimacies she was by no means an ordinary horse, she lifted her head and trumpeted out one of her wild, dramatic neighs.

Millie was impressed. "The wonderful way she holds her head," she said, "just like a picture. If only you could ride her to school."

"Nobody rides her – anywhere," I replied curtly. "She's an outlaw." And then, as her mouth drooped in disappointment, "At least nobody's *supposed* to ride her."

She jumped for it. "You mean you do ride her? And she doesn't throw you?"

"Of course," I conceded modestly, "she's very easy to ride. Such speed – and smooth as a rocking chair. When you look down the ground's just like water running past. But she could throw me all right if she had a mind to."

Millie sighed. "I'd like so much though to *see* you ride her. Today – isn't it a good chance, with them in there talking and your father away to town?"

I hesitated, overcome by a feeling of fright and commitment, and then Isabel too joined in. She begged and wheedled, looked so innocent, at the same time so hurt and disappointed, that Millie exclaimed she felt like going for a ride herself. And that settled it. "Stand at the door and see no one's coming," I commanded. "I'll put her bridle on."

Isabel practically put it on herself. She gave a shrill, excited whinny as I led her out, pranced like a circus pony, pushed me along still faster with her nose. "No," I answered Millie shortly, "I don't use the saddle. You don't get sore, she rides so easy. And in case she turns mean I won't get tangled in the stirrups."

With a flutter in her voice Millie said, "Do you really think you should?" and in response I steeled myself, nonchalantly turned up the collar of my sheepskin. "At the rate she goes," I explained, "the wind cuts through you like a knife."

To myself I reflected, "There's plenty of snow. At the worst it will only be a spill."

Isabel stood quite still till I was mounted. She even stood still a moment longer, letting me gather myself, take a firm grip of the reins, crouch low in readiness. Then with a plunge, a spasm of muscles, she was off. And it was true: the wind cut sharp and bitter like a knife, the snow slipped past like water. Only in her motion there was a difference. She was like a rocket, not a rocking chair.

It was nearly a mile, though, before I began properly to understand what was happening. Isabel the outlaw – the horse that had killed a man, that people talked about for fifty miles – here was I, just turned thirteen, and riding her. And an immense pride filled me. Cold as I was I pushed my sheepskin collar down and straightened recklessly to feel the rush of wind. I needed it that way, a counteracting sting of cold to steady the exhilaration.

We had gone another mile before I remembered Millie, and at once, as if sensitive to my concern, Isabel drew up short for breath. She didn't drop to a trot or walk as an ordinary horse would have done, but instead, with the clean grace and precision of a bird alighting on a branch, came smoothly to a halt. And for a moment or two, before starting home again, she rested. The prairie spread before us cold and sparkling in the winter sunlight, and poised and motionless, ears pricked forwards, nostrils faintly quivering, she breathed in rapturously its loping miles of freedom.

And I too, responsive to her bidding, was aware as never before of its austere, unrelenting beauty. There were the white fields and the blue, metallic sky; the little splashes here and there of yellow strawstack, luminous and clear as drops of gum on fresh pine lumber; the scattered farmsteads brave and wistful in their isolation; the gleam of sun and snow. I wanted none of it, but she insisted. Thirteen years old and riding an outlaw – naturally I wanted only that. I wanted to indulge shamelessly my vanity, to drink the daring and success of my exploit in full-strength draughts, but Isabel, like a conscientious teacher at a fair, dragging you off to see instructive things, insisted on the landscape.

Look, she said firmly, while it's here before you, so that to the last detail it will remain clear. For you, too, some day there may be stalls and halters, and it will be a good memory.

But only for a moment or two, and then we were off again. She went even faster going home. She disdained and rebelled against her stall, but the way she whipped the wind around my ears you would have thought she had suddenly conceived a great affection for it. It was a strong wind, fiercely cold. There was a sharp sting in my ears a minute, then a sudden warmth and ease. I knew they were frozen, but there wasn't time to worry. I worked my collar up, crouched low again. Her mane blew back and lashed my face. Before the steady blast of wind my forehead felt as if the bone were wearing thin. But I didn't mind. I was riding her and holding on. I felt fearless, proud, mature. All the shame and misgivings of the past were over. I was now both her master and my own.

And then she was fifteen or twenty feet away, demurely watching me, and I was picking myself up and spitting snow.

She had done it with the utmost skill, right head first into a snowdrift, where I wouldn't hurt myself, less than a quarter of a mile from home.

And not even to toss her head and gallop off so that Millie would think she had done it in a fit of fright or meanness. Just to stand there, a picture of puzzled innocence, blandly transferring all the blame on me. What was wrong? Just when we were getting on so splendidly – why on earth had I deserted her?

For in her own way, despite her record, Isabel was something of a moralist. She took a firm stand against pride that wasn't justified. She considered my use of the word "master" insufferably presumptuous. Being able to ride an outlaw was not the same thing at all as being accorded the privilege of riding one, and for the good of my soul, it was high time I appreciated the distinction.

She stood still, sniffing in my direction, until I had almost reached her, then gave a disdainful snort and trotted pertly home. At the stable door she was waiting for me. I approached limping – not because I was hurt, but because with Millie standing back a little distance, goggle-eyed, I felt it looked better, made my tumble less an occasion for laughter – and as if believing me Isabel thrust her nose out, all condolence, and felt me tenderly where I was pretending it was sore. From the bottom of her heart she hoped I wouldn't be so unfortunate another time. So far as she was concerned, however, she could make no promises. There had been one fall, she explained to Millie, and there might easily be another. The future was entirely up to me. She couldn't be responsible for my horsemanship.

"Your ears are frozen," Millie changed the subject. "And your mother knows everything – she's going to let your father handle you."

I looked at her accusingly, but in a smug, self-righteous tone she explained, "She called you twice, and then came out to see why you didn't answer. Just in time to see it happen. I'll rub your ears with snow if you like before we go in for tea."

It was a good tea, but I didn't eat much. My ears were not only swelling badly and turning purple; they were also starting to drip. My mother pinned a wash cloth to each shoulder, then sprinkled on talcum powder. She said nothing, but was ominously white-lipped and calm – saving herself up, I didn't doubt, until we were alone. I was in misery to escape upstairs to a mirror, but she insisted, probably as a kind of punishment, that I stay and finish my tea. Millie, I noticed, didn't eat much either, and kept her eyes turned fastidiously away.

When finally Mrs. Dickson and Millie were gone – and as an additional humiliation, I wasn't allowed out to bring round their horse – my mother replaced the wash cloths with towels. Still silent, still white-lipped, and since there was no need, now that we were alone, for her to keep on saving herself up, it struck me that perhaps the condition of my ears was really serious.

"They're smarting bad – and throbbing," I said hopefully. "It must have been colder than I thought."

"It must have been," she agreed. "Go up to your room now out of my way till suppertime. I'd better talk to your father before he sees you anyway."

I knew then that she was as afraid of what was in store for me as I was. Her expression remained stern, but there was a softness in her voice, a note of anxiety. It was a good sign, but it was also a bad one. It meant that she expected my father's anger to be explosive and extreme.

Upstairs, swollen and tender as they were, I gave my ears a brisk rubbing. They were already dripping and unsightly. A little worse, a darker, a more alarming purple, and they might get me out of a hiding.

While waiting I also rehearsed a number of entrances, a number of defences, but at the last minute abandoned all of them. The heat in my ears as I went downstairs was spreading like a prairie fire, and when I entered the kitchen there was such a blaze of it across my eyes that I could make out my father only as a vague, menacing form. A desperate resolve seized me; should he so much as threaten the razor strap I would ride away on Isabel and be lost to them forever.

But instead of pouncing he looked me over critically a minute, then hitched in his chair to the table and began buttering a piece of bread. "Some bronco buster," he said at last, in a weary, disillusioned voice. "All you need now is a ten-gallon."

"I didn't have the saddle – and she stopped short and shied." My voice climbed defensively. In dramatization of the suddenness of the stop I drove a clenched fist into an open palm. "I had been sticking on all right though – for four miles or more."

"Anyway," he said resignedly, "you've got yourself a pretty pair of ears."

I raised a quick, self-conscious hand to touch them, and my mother assured me, "They're still there all right – don't worry. They made a hit with Millie too, judging by the look on her face. I think she'll be seeing them tonight in her sleep."

"But the mare," my father interrupted in a man-to-man tone of voice, abruptly cold-shouldering my mother, "how did you find her? Mean as she's supposed to be?"

"Not mean at all. Even when I was getting on – she stood and let me."

"Next time, just the same, you'd better play safe and use a snaffle. I'll hunt one up for you. It won't hurt her so long as she behaves."

"The next time!" my mother cried. "Talking about the next time when you ought to be taking down his breeches. She's no fit horse for a boy. If nobody'll buy her you ought to give her away, before she breaks somebody else's neck."

She went on for a long time like that, but I didn't pay much attention. Pride – that was what it amounted to – pride even greater than mine had been before I landed in the snowdrift. It sent me soaring a minute, took my breath away, but it also brought a little shiver of embarrassment and shame. How long, then, had I kept them waiting? How many times in the last few months had they looked at me and despaired?

"One thing," my mother declared with finality, "you're not riding her to school. The things I'd be thinking and seeing all day – I just couldn't stand it."

"You hear," my father agreed. "I'll not have you carrying on with a lot of young fools crazy as yourself – being a good fellow, like as not, and letting them all ride her."

I was about to protest – as if any of them dared or *could* ride Isabel – but instead, remembering in time, went on docilely with my supper. Outwardly impassive, I was sky-high within. Just as Isabel herself had always said, what a sensation to ride foaming up to school at a breakneck, hair-raising gallop. In the past I had indulged the prospect sparingly. Indeed, with so many threats and warnings in my ears, it had never been a prospect at all, but only a fantasy, something to be thought about wishfully, like blacking both Johnny Olsen's eyes at once, or having five dollars to spend. Now, though, everything was going to be different. Now, in their peculiar parental idiom, they had just given their permission, and Isabel and the future were all mine. Isabel *and* Millie Dickson. In accompaniment to a fervent resolve to be worthy of them both, my ears throbbed happily.

Questions for Writing and Discussion

Discovering Meaning

1. From the father's several appearances in the story, Ross creates a vivid portrait of him. What characteristics of the father emerge in the story? Describe the mother's character.

2. The boy's fantasy life is centred on the horse. Describe his fantasy world. What conditions in the boy's life make him peculiarly susceptible to such flights of imagination?
3. The boy imagines the horse whispering to him that "the delights of fantasy and dream were but as shadows beside the exhilaration of reality." Contrast the reality of the ride with the dream.
4. During the ride, the boy compares the horse to a "conscientious teacher." What does the horse teach the boy?
5. At the end of the story the boy is overjoyed when his parents in their "peculiar idiom" grant him permission to ride his horse to school. Examine the language used between the parents and the child that causes the boy to draw such a conclusion. Contrast the surface meaning of the parents' words and their deeper meaning. What conclusions can you draw about the parents' attitudes to their son and to themselves?

Exploring Method

1. What does Ross gain by using a first-person narrator: by presenting events and characters through the eyes of a thirteen-year-old boy?
2. What is Millie Dickson's function in the story?
3. The story is divided into three parts. Examine the opening and closing sentences of each section. How do they control the structure of the story?
4. The beauty and violence of the prairie landscape come alive in Ross's story. Select the details that demonstrate each of these characteristics.
5. Ross's critics admire his style for its precision, economy, rhythm, and effective repetition. Select examples from the story to support this assessment of Ross's style.

Suggestions for Writing

1. The story portrays an initiation of not only exhilaration and adventure but also hardship and pain. Write an account of an experience of your own that brought the exhilaration of measuring up to a challenge but also involved hardship.
2. Most initiation stories portray the experience as disillusioning, one in which reality falls short of expectations. This story portrays an opposite result. Narrate an experience in your life when the reality was more exciting than the fantasy.
3. The boy experiences a sense of freedom while riding his horse.

In what sense is Ross using the word "freedom"? Evaluate his view and give your own definition. Illustrate your definition with a description of an activity or a sport that gives you this sense of freedom. Use descriptive details to help your reader share your experience.

4. Impelled by a strong desire, the boy ignores his parents' wishes and rides the Outlaw. Narrate an incident in which you experienced a similar conflict. Heighten the dramatic power of your narrative with dialogue, monologue, and vivid descriptions of your feelings and thoughts, and build your story up to a climax that suggests how the experience affected you.

Examining Social Issues

1. To what extent does the mother's anxiety about the boy contribute to his timid behaviour at school? Can parents, in their desire to protect their children, make them timid, shy, and unsure of themselves?

2. After the boy rides the horse successfully, the father says to him, "Some bronco buster. All you need now is a ten-gallon." How are the boy's elation and the father's pride in his son related to their society's expectations of men's behaviour? Have such expectations changed today? Support your answer with examples.

3. From the brief glimpse of the parents together in the last scene, what can you conclude about their relationship? How does the relationship between parents influence their children?

4. As the boy experiences the urge to ride the horse, he explains Isabel's motive for tempting him as a "purely feminine itch to bend me to her will." Support or oppose this view of feminine psychology.

5. In an essay, "The Prairie: A State of Mind," the Canadian novelist Henry Kreisel describes two opposing reactions to the prairie: "Man the conqueror and man the insignificant dwarf always threatened by defeat." He attributes the difference to "the state of mind produced by the sheer physical fact of the prairie." Which of these two responses to life on the prairie does Ross portray in this story? Support your answer with references to details in the story.

Growing Up in Victoria

Joan Mason Hurley

As a Canadian playwright, Joan Mason Hurley skilfully uses dramatic techniques to recreate, with vibrant immediacy, the Victoria of her childhood in the Thirties. Through realistic dialogue and visually dramatic scenes, Hurley presents the opulent world of her heroine's mother. Shielded by huge protecting lawns, chromium-plated cars, and servants eager to please, the mother creates a dream world that excludes the existence of unemployment, war, and Hitler, and denies her daughters contact with the realities of life.

But the first-person narrator, the artistic child, Stephanie, sensitive and curious, reaches beyond this world. Obsessed with the quest for experience, she creates a fictional hero, Stephen, and provides him with adventures that she herself is not allowed to experience. Her journey to Cromwell Street is an encounter with reality. Within the drab, shadowy realm of poverty, she discovers a woman who possesses a genuine love for her children. In the end, Stephanie's compassion and understanding have liberated her from her mother's restricted, indifferent existence into the fullness and variety of the real world.

Even on Saturdays we were down to breakfast at eight o'clock, hair combed, buttons fastened, no bedroom slippers. Slovenly habits, declared our mother, were only for the lower classes. Mam'zelle, Sally and I always got there first. I would like to have read the comics, but it was as much as one's life was worth to touch the newspapers, one at each end of the table, most carefully folded and placed by Ellen.

With the entrance of our mother, formal good mornings were exchanged:

"Bonjour, Mam'zelle."

"Bonjour, madame."

"Good morning, Mummy," Sally and I would chirp and mumble.

"How's my pet, today?" my mother would reply to Sally.

In the morning she and our father did not feel like speaking, and, therefore, neither could we. So while we worked our way through porridge, boiled eggs, and toast in silence, I entertained myself by squinting at the outside of their papers.

Of the two, I liked my father's *Times* the best. It was, of course, the *Times* of London. It arrived from England in bunches, several together, tied with coarse brown string, and four weeks old at least. Ellen kept them in chronological order, so my father could read one each day at breakfast, just as if he'd never left home.

This being Saturday, I'd planned to work on my story. Today, I decided, I'd choose my names from the *Times*. So while my father read the inside pages, where the news was, I tried to determine if anyone interesting had been Hatched, Matched or Dispatched.

> *To Rosalind*, I read
> *wife of the Hon. Peregrine Postlethwaite,*
> *a son, Benedict, on March 8, 1933, at . . .*

"Stephanie," my mother's voice was cutting as ice. "Do pay attention. Eleven years old and there's egg all over your jumper. More work for poor Mam'zelle, as usual."

I was prepared for a lecture, but fortunately her attention was diverted by something in the *Daily Colonist*.

"Well, really, listen to this would you, Edward?"

> Colonel and Mrs. F. T. St. John entertained at dinner, Wednesday, at their gracious home, Glenduffe, in the Uplands. Covers were laid for sixteen.

She paused, bursting with indignation, waiting for him to speak. He made a noise, supposed to be sympathetic.

"If I'd known," she said, "I would certainly not have asked them this evening." She twitched the paper shut. Her eye fell on the front page, which she always looked at last, and which was full of unpalatable news:

> Men in Relief Camps Strike
>
> Unemployment Procession Broken up
>
> Mounted Police Charge, Use Whips to Disperse Crowd

"In my opinion," she declared, "far too much attention is paid to the unemployed. Anyone with the will to work can find a job. Look at you, Mam'zelle, you're employed, and you're not even British."

"*Vraiment*," said Mam'zelle, in a low voice.

"That's not true, Mummy," I had to interrupt. "Mr. Robinson

says it's terrible on his street. More than half the men are out of work, and they've all tried and tried to find jobs."

"Stephanie, I've told you before, it is not *Mr.* Robinson when referring to the gardener."

"Oh, Mummy," I exclaimed, exasperated.

"Edward!" said my mother.

"Don't speak to your mother like that," said my father in a tired, automatic way from behind the *Times*. Then immediately changed the subject.

"There's more in here about this Adolf Hitler. Comical-looking chap, but he seems to be making a stir in Germany."

"Fortunately what happens in Germany doesn't affect us," retorted my mother. "Isn't that what Richie and John died for?"

My father said nothing. We three, being finished, Mam'zelle asked if we might be excused. As we were leaving the room, my mother called me back.

"Stephanie, I want you to come downtown with me this morning and carry parcels."

"Me?" I exclaimed, outraged.

"What a selfish child you are. Always thinking of yourself. Now, get ready. And tell Mam'zelle I want you looking presentable."

I stumped upstairs, furious. Mam'zelle was in the bathroom washing our hairbrushes.

"I've got to go downtown with Mummy, dammit," I said.

"Do not zay ze dammit," said Mam'zelle, "or you will get in ze 'ot water."

I scowled.

"I hate going downtown."

"*Alors*, your mother will want you to look *comme il faut*, 'ow about ze blue skirt and ze blue coat with ze fur collar?"

"I tore it last Sunday, remember?"

"*Mon Dieu*, I 'ave forgot. I will 'ave to mend it."

"Sorry, Mam'zelle."

The April sun was warm when I went outside to wait in my brown skirt and beret. Robinson was working in the front rose bed.

"Hullo, Mr. Robinson, how's everything?" He was my friend, and I refused to patronize him.

"The wife's birthday, today," he said, his brown face crinkling into a smile. "We're going to the movies this after."

He looked so happy, I asked him what he was going to give her.

He didn't answer. Looked down at his spade. I understood and was mortified. He could not afford to give her anything, for there were two small children as well, all living off what he made digging our garden.

"It's her birthday treat, y' understand," he said. "Fred Astaire and Ginger Rogers."

Then my mother emerged into the sunshine from the shadows of the porte cochere.

"Good morning, Robinson."

"'Morning, madam."

"Let me look at you, Stephanie."

I turned and faced her.

"Well, I suppose you'll pass. But you might have worn your blue. For Heaven's sake pull up your socks, child, and do try to look more agreeable. You'll never get a husband with a face like that."

"I don't want a husband," I muttered under my breath. But I pulled up my socks.

She, herself, was elegant as always. Today she wore a pale green coat and skirt my grandmother had sent her from Dickins and Jones in London. I must be adopted, I decided, and no one had had the courage to tell me. Then my father came out in his gardening clothes.

"Dear Edward," trilled my mother, "you do look a tramp. Anyone seeing you, would think Robinson owned the property and you were the gardener."

She gave a silvery laugh. But I was watching my father's face. He was holding open the door of the car, and he was not amused.

My mother and I got in, and with a grinding of gears and a jerk, we took off, scattering gravel over the lawn.

"I loathe shopping on a Saturday," she remarked, as we proceeded along the avenue, the McLaughlin Buick jouncing in and out of potholes. Then we were hung up behind a streetcar. Every time we tried to pass it would stop to take on passengers, and we would be obliged to stop too, or risk a ten-dollar fine.

"Now then, Stephanie, you've come to be of use," she said, when we had finally reached Fort Street and angle-parked against the curb. "Pick up the basket."

She started down the street. I followed her, servile and mutinous, a slave attending Queen Cleopatra.

Town was full of the usual Saturday crowds. Automobiles vied for position with horse-drawn milk and ice carts. Paper and rubbish blew about, occasionally flying up into the air and catching some unwary person in the face. Dogs ran at large, and if anybody crossed the road he had to watch where he stepped for horse dung.

Our first stop was Clark's, the fishmonger's. Mr. Clark was large and pink, with little half glasses over which he peered at his customers. He was dressed like the British shopkeeper he once had been, in cloth cap and blue and white striped apron. His store had a nice cold sea smell, with huge blocks of ice on which he kept the fish. Thick sawdust covered the floor. I stood behind my mother tracing my initials with the tip of my toe, S.C.C., then seeing her eye upon me, I hastily scuffed them out. She herself was drumming impatiently on the counter with white-gloved fingers, for someone was ahead of us, a thin woman with two ragged children with runny noses. Did he have any fish heads, she was asking.

"I'll see," said Mr. Clark. Then to my mother. "Just be a moment, madam." He disappeared into the back, returned with a pile of heads, all bulbous eyes and gaping mouths. He put them on the scale.

"Nineteen cents," he said.

The woman had been poking at some coins in a worn change purse.

"I have only sixteen cents," she said, in a humble, apologetic whisper, casting an anxious glance at my mother.

Mr. Clark looked over the top of his spectacles.

"Righty-ho," he said. But from where I stood I could see that while the woman was counting out her nickels and pennies upon the counter, he was actually adding a bit of cod to the white grease-paper parcel.

"Here you are, madam." He handed over the packet. "And thank you very kindly."

The woman gave him a little frightened smile as she walked out. Mr. Clark shook his head.

"Hard times," he said.

"Indeed," said my mother coldly.

"Well, well, Mrs. Croft, sorry to keep you waiting."

I knew she had come for shrimp. And there they were, the most expensive commodity in the shop, all rosy and hairy-looking with tiny black eyes, like Mr. Clark's. She picked one up with her neat white glove, and snapping it in two, held it to her nose.

"Are these fresh?"

"Came in this morning, madam."

"Are you certain?"

Mr. Clark remained as courteous, as imperturbable as a bishop while he explained that he'd bought them, himself, straight off the fish boat at Johnson Street bridge.

"Well, then, three pounds, and charge to my account, please."

The damp and fishy parcel was deposited in my basket.

"Now," said my mother, "the florist's."

She swept along the crowded sidewalk, I dodging behind.

"For goodness' sake, Stephanie," said she, turning round. "Can't you keep up?"

But when we arrived at Kirkwood's, instead of going in, she halted outside.

"Where are your manners, Stephanie? Will you never learn? Open the door for your mother."

I shoved at the heavy door, the basket of shrimp banging against my legs.

"Can't you see it says, pull."

I tried to pull, but at the same moment another lady was coming out. The door flapped into my face, almost breaking my glasses.

"Really, Stephanie," she was beginning again. Then she recognized Mrs. St. John. Would she remark on the party to which she had not been asked? Not her.

"Dear Jane, good morning, good morning. We are so looking forward to seeing you this evening. No, only a small party. Just twelve. Yes, Stephanie is a great help. Say how do you do, Stephanie. Indeed I am lucky to have a daughter to go shopping with."

I wondered how she could do it, as I stood on one leg then the other, staring at the carnations in Kirkwood's window.

Inside the shop, my mother discovered her American friend, Mrs. Plunkett.

"Harriet, darling, what a *lovely* surprise. No, I never come down on a Saturday. Such dreadful crowds," dropping her voice, "of lower class people. But there were one or two things I just had to get fresh. These roses," she pulled one out of its container, "do they look all right to you? If only there were a really *good* florist in this town. Oh, there you are, Mr. Kirkwood, I didn't see you behind that fern. Are these roses fresh, or will they drop dead as soon as I get them home? I see. Well, give me a dozen. White, please, and charge to my account. A cup of coffee, Harriet? There's nothing I'd like better. Shall we go across the street? Stephanie can wait in the car. Oh, you have Bryce over there already? Then Stephanie must come, too. Do fix your beret, child, and for heaven's sake be careful of those roses."

Miserable, resentful, carrying the wretched basket, I trailed behind my effusive mother to the Acorn Tearoom. Bryce, in my class at school, was seated at a table behind a milkshake. He stood up when we approached.

"Such nice manners. A regular young gentleman," bubbled my mother. "How are you, Bryce, dear?"

"Fine thanks, Mrs. Croft."

"Carruthers-Croft," his mother corrected him.

"Oh well, I don't really mind," lied my mother.

With a sucking noise, Bryce finished his milkshake. "Mom," he said. "Okay if I meet you at the car?"

"Oh, sure, honey. Don't be long, though."

So that's what he thought of us. If I'd been as pretty as Diana Cunningham, he wouldn't have left in such a hurry. The idea was vaguely distressing.

"Wouldn't you like to go with Bryce, Stephanie," my mother was saying.

"No, thank you." I was aghast at the idea. How could she be so unperceptive.

"Do pull your beret down, and what's the matter with your spectacles, they're all fogged."

"Poor child, I do believe she's shy," said Mrs. Plunkett.

The waitress brought coffee, and in my mortification, reaching up to wipe my glasses, my elbow caught her hand, one of the cups flew onto the floor, broke and splashed in all directions.

"Really," said my mother. "How can you be so clumsy?"

"Sorry," I said, ready to die of embarrassment. "Has it ruined your skirt, Mrs. Plunkett?"

"No, honey, no harm done. Don't be cross with her, Celia. It was an accident."

"She has too many accidents," retorted my mother. But seeing the expression on Mrs. Plunkett's face, she said no more, until we got back to the car. Then she let me have it. I'd ruined her morning. She had a splitting headache. She's been obliged to tip the girl three times as much to make up for the trouble I'd caused. Now I'd turned eleven she had hoped there might be some improvement. But obviously not. Obviously it was high time I went off to boarding school and learned to behave like a lady.

I was in despair. And yet I knew why she was angry. She was always on edge before one of her dinner parties. Twelve guests were more than Ellen could easily manage, even with the help of the cleaning woman. The two of them had set the table when we got home. The sun was flooding in at the long dining-room windows, shining on the silver, the crystal, and the white damask napkins. My mother straightened a candle in one of the Georgian candlesticks, on which was engraved the family crest.

"The table looks charming, Ellen," she said. She believed in being gracious to servants, one got the best out of them that way. "I'll arrange the flowers after lunch."

"Yes," I said, "when's lunch. I'm starving."

"Always thinking of yourself, Stephanie. Ellen's far too busy to cook a hot lunch today."

Everyone was busy, it seemed. My father and Mr. Robinson were still toiling outside, and when I walked into the kitchen to deposit the basket, I found Mam'zelle and Sally sitting at the table peeling almonds.

"Mam'zelle's a meany," said Sally, pretending to pout. "She'll only let me eat one in ten."

"I am not meany," said Mam'zelle, "ze almonds are for ze guests."

"Quite right," said my mother, who had come in behind me. "And, Mam'zelle, I would be much obliged if you'd be so kind as to shell these shrimps. Ellen has still to stuff the ducks, and I don't know how she'll get everything done in time."

"Shall I help?" I asked, an attempt to atone for my sins.

"No. You'll only break something. You and Sally had better take sandwiches upstairs, and keep out of the way."

"Let's go to Sherwood Forest," suggested Sally.

"*Alors, changez* ze clothes," said Mam'zelle.

"And Sally must wear a jersey," said my mother.

Instructions. Instructions. But Sherwood Forest was populated with attractive characters – Robin Hood, Hiawatha, the Swiss Family Robinson. It was the wild part at the bottom of the garden. Here grew a tree, an ancient and massive oak, among the branches of which Robinson had built us a platform.

What could be pleasanter than lunch at the top of a tree? Birds sang. Sunshine dappled through budding leaves. Today, we decided to be on board ship.

"Stores loaded," I called up to Sally, as I tied the picnic basket to a rope. "Heave away, Bo'sun."

"Aye, aye, sir."

Sally pulled from above. I tucked my cotton play dress into its matching knickers, grabbed the bottom branch and began to climb. The rough bark stung and scratched my bare legs. If only girls could wear trousers, I thought. Once I'd reached the platform I soon forgot the horrors of the morning.

"How are your rations, Captain?" Sally was asking.

"Ship's biscuit's not bad," I said, taking a bite out of my egg sandwich.

Sally giggled. "It's fun up here in the raven's roost."

"Crow's nest, silly Sally."

She was peering through the branches.

"I spy, with my little eye . . ."

"If you don't learn the proper words . . ."

"Mummy!"

"Where?"

"To port," said Sally, surprising me, as she often did. "Talking to Mr. Robinson on the drive."

"Telling him to go home, I should think. Goodness, he'll be late for his movie if he doesn't watch out."

"That's his funeral." It was an expression Sally had just learned and was forbidden to say.

"But it's his wife's birthday."

"Christopher's birthday, too," said Sally. "His nanny's coming for me after lunch."

"Goodness," I said. "Then we'd better go ashore. Will you take the basket back?" I asked as I helped her off the bottom branch. "I'm going to the woodshed."

"Whatever do you do in the woodshed?"

"Oh, nothing much."

The woodshed was dark, private, pleasantly scented of cedar, a much better place to write, less public and distracting than the tree. I took out the exercise book I kept hidden between the logs, and pushing the chopping block against the wall, sat down to compose my new story, Stephen's adventures in Africa. I had just finished reading *King Solomon's Mines*, and my head was full of exotic happenings.

> *Stephen and his friend, Benedict*

I wrote, then scratched out Benedict and substituted Peregrine.

> *Peregrine, were standing at the top of the shaft when . . .*

The door of the shed opened suddenly. I jumped up, trying to conceal my book, but it was only Robinson, who was in on the secret.

"Hullo, hullo," he said gruffly, picking up a rake, "you here."

"You here, yourself," I said, hurt by his attitude. "I thought you were taking your wife to the movies?"

"Was, you mean."

"What's happened?"

"Your ma wants the drive raked. She's got company coming."

"But you're not supposed to work Saturday afternoons."

"I know." Robinson heaved a sigh.

"Well, tell her. It's Saturday, and it's your wife's birthday."

Robinson looked at me, said nothing.

I had no patience with such spinelessness.

"I'll speak to her for you, then." I started to leave.

Robinson gripped my arm like a vice. "Not on your life, you don't."

"Why not?"

"Cos I'm damn lucky to have a job. If I don't do what she wants, ten others'd be glad to take my place."

I was stymied.

"What about your wife?"

Robinson's kind, brown face creased with anxiety.

"She'll be worriet sick. She's got a great imagination, has that girl. Every time I'm late, she thinks I've met with me end."

"Then I'll telephone her for you. I can go upstairs, no one'll hear."

"We don't have no phone." He paused. "Of course if you was to go down to our place on the streetcar . . ." he hesitated, eyeing me. "I hate to disappoint her like, and have her all worked up and worriet as well."

"Well," I considered, "I don't know." It was absolutely unheard of, my going off alone, downtown, to wherever Robinson lived. I tore a page out of my book, handed him my pencil.

"Draw me a map, then."

"You're a brick," said Robinson, showing all his broken and missing teeth, and he wrung my hand with his hard and dirty one.

When I got into the house, Sally was sitting in the hall, tidily dressed, waiting for Christopher's nanny. She opened her mouth to speak, but I put my finger to my lips as I dashed past. Upstairs, in the nursery, I found some streetcar tickets. No point in changing, I thought, as I pulled my dress out of my knickers. I picked up my tam and a jacket. Passing back through the hall, Miss Inquisitive asked in a loud whisper,

"What've you got your tam on for?"

I shook my head at her, and quickly made my escape. In a few minutes, slightly out of breath, I was standing on the avenue amongst a little clutch of people waiting for the streetcar, which could be heard whirring and banging along its tracks, long before it came in sight. At last it drew up in front of us, the folding doors flew open with a jerk.

"Hurry along, there," called the conductor, an elderly, cross-faced man perched on a high black stool. We straggled across the road in front of the traffic, mothers with small children, young people with library books and roller skates, an old woman with a dachshund on a leash.

"Watch that dog. Move back in the car, please. No, no change for five dollars. Whatcha think I am, a bloody bank?"

I was the last to get in. There was one place left, next to a fat woman, sitting legs apart, with a plant on her lap. I squeezed down beside her, the plant tickled my face. I had not been on a streetcar alone before. I saw, as if for the first time, how lumpy and shabby were the yellow straw seats, how dirty the ridged floor stuck with chewing gum and littered with cigarette ends and papers. The barred windows were grimy, one could hardly see out.

But it was exciting, nevertheless, going off alone, an adventure of the kind I had so often imagined for my friend, Stephen. What if this streetcar were the trans-Siberian railway? What if I were daring, handsome Stepanovich, bearer of messages for the revolution.

"Goodness me, if it isn't Stephanie Carruthers-Croft?"

Handsome Stepanovich vanished. Standing in front of me, her green cloak swaying all over the aisle, was friendly Mrs. Stewart.

Realizing that a whole swarm of people had got on, I rose to offer my seat.

"Thank you, dear," she said, quirking an eyebrow at the lady with the plant.

Standing beside her, holding the strap from the ceiling, I was deeply conscious that I had on my old play dress, that my hair was a mess, my legs bare and scratched, and that I looked a sight in front of one of my mother's friends.

"What a surprise, Stephanie, meeting you here of all places."

"I've been sent on an errand," I replied quite truthfully.

"One doesn't often see you out without that nice Mademoiselle."

"No." And I wondered whether she'd tell my mother.

"My car's being repaired," she explained, leaning away from the plant.

Fortunately, she soon got off. I studied the directions Robinson had given me. I must go along Douglas Street to the Hudson's Bay Company, walk three blocks east and two north to Cromwell Street.

It wasn't complicated. But once I'd left the security of the streetcar my confidence began to fade. Was it wise to have come? Was it safe to walk in this part of town? Men stood in doorways, silently staring. Stray dogs followed me, or barked as I passed. I took off my tam and stuffed it in my pocket. Sally and I were never allowed out without hats, but the girls I saw around me now were all bare-headed.

Cromwell Street, when I came to it, was a shock. If ever I'd thought about where Robinson lived, I'd imagined a whitewashed cottage, covered with rambling roses, set in a small but lovely garden with blue lupins and pink hollyhocks. I'd seen a picture like that once, in an English children's annual. It had been entitled 'The Gardener's Cottage.'

My romantic notion could hardly be further from the truth. There were no whitewashed cottages on dusty, unpaved Cromwell Street, only sad, tired houses, ramshackle, tumbledown, set in unkempt patches of grass on either side of rotting wooden sidewalks. Ragged children grubbed in the dirt, or skipped with frayed pieces of rope. A few older girls, about my age, were playing hopscotch. They had no chalk to mark their squares, and were using handfuls of grass with which to stain green lines on the wooden boards. They stared at me. I walked quicker. A few of the houses I passed had porches on which sat men with bitter, careworn faces. One or two had an arm or a leg missing, victims of the Great War, in which my uncles Richie and John had fallen.

I dreaded arriving at Robinson's house. But there it was. I recognized the number on the gate, and the lilac bush he'd told me about. It was a little neater, a little tidier than its neighbours, the garden cultivated into a vegetable plot. But so small. Why you could drop the whole thing, chimney and porch included, into our front hall and still have room to spare.

A young woman stood in the open front door, peering up the street with an anxious expression. She might have been pretty, if she hadn't been so thin. She gazed at me inquiringly as I opened the tiny gate and took the four steps that brought me to the porch.

"Good afternoon," I said, a feeble copy of my mother's manner. "Are you Mrs. Robinson?"

She nodded without speaking.

"I've come with a message from Mr. . . . from your husband."

"Why? What's the matter? Is he all right?" She spoke with a feverish kind of intensity.

"He's awfully sorry. He has to work this afternoon."

She'd been gazing at me with big grey eyes. Now she looked as if she might crumble to the ground with relief and disappointment. I hurried on.

"He said maybe you can go next Saturday." Robinson had explained to me they couldn't afford to go in the evenings. "By the way," I added, "Happy Birthday."

I hadn't meant it unkindly. I had spoken without thought, out of embarrassment and nervousness. To my horror large tears began to roll down her cheeks. Happy birthday, indeed.

"I bet it was her idea, him working," she said bitterly. "He says it's always her."

"I'm sorry," I said, oddly torn between a bizarre loyalty to my mother, and genuine sympathy.

She took out a handkerchief and blew her nose.

"You must be Stephanie. Your hair's much redder than he said."

"Is it?" I was self-conscious, as always, when anyone commented on my appearance.

"Did you come down special?"

I nodded.

"Won't you come in and have some lemonade?"

She led the way. I stepped over the threshold into a room, perfectly clean and tidy, but so pathetically bare of comfort. Linoleum floor, sagging sofa, coal stove, kitchen table with glass jam jar filled with lilac.

She must have read my thoughts.

"We're going to get better stuff when we can. We spent all we got on the kids' room." She opened the door with obvious pride to show me a small bedroom which contained a painted cot and crib, a tiny square of frayed carpet, a dresser with some of the handles missing, and new-looking curtains decorated with nursery figures which were too short for the window.

"I like your curtains."

"Aren't they pretty?" she answered, pleased. "It was a remnant. I was real lucky to find it. My sister's taken the kids for the afternoon." She gave a laugh. "It ain't usually so quiet around here."

She brought me some lemonade. The glass had a chip in it. Surreptitiously, I turned it round to the other side.

"I've made a cake," she said. "It's Robbie's favourite." She lifted up a pudding basin to display a large round cake with currants. "I'd offer you some only . . ."

"Oh, you mustn't cut it till he comes," I said. "Anyway, I'm not hungry. Only thirsty. The lemonade's delicious," I added politely.

"I had to save out of the housekeeping for two months to buy the sugar and currants. It was a surprise, for when we came home from the movie."

She looked as if she might cry again. I felt as if I might cry, too, when I thought of Mrs. St. John, who, according to my mother, sometimes buried in the garden the too-rich cakes her Chinese cook would insist upon making. I stood up.

"Thank you for the lovely lemonade, but I must get back now."

"It was real nice of you to come."

She escorted me down the little path, and as I walked away I could feel her standing by the gate watching me.

It was getting on for five o'clock when I arrived home. I peeked through the gates. The drive did look beautiful, like a piece of grey herringbone tweed. I tiptoed over it carefully. With luck, I could get upstairs before anyone saw me.

In the hall, which was full of the smell of roasting duck, I met Sally.

"You're going to catch it. It's going to be your fun-er-al."

"Did you tell on me?"

"I said I saw you wearing your tam." As she followed me up the staircase, she justified herself. "I had to. They were going on and on at me."

On the landing we encountered Mam'zelle.

"Steph-an-ee, where 'ave you been? We 'ave been searching and searching for you."

Unhappily, like George Washington I could not tell a lie.

"I went out."

"What eez zees out? I weesh to know. Where did you go?"

"Downtown in the streetcar."

"Oooo," said Sally. "All by yourself?"

"And dressed like that?" My mother had come out of her bed-room, attired in a pale blue negligee.

"I felt like going out, so I did," I said defiantly, to forestall fur-ther questions. "I went as far as the Hudson's Bay and then came back again."

"I was just about to telephone the police," said my mother. "As soon as I'd had my bath, that is. I visualized all sorts of terrible accidents, and on the day of my party, too."

How trying that would have been, I couldn't help thinking.

"You're so selfish, Stephanie," she went on. "Never consider anyone but yourself. As a punishment you can go to bed right now, without any supper."

"Poor Steffy," said Sally. "She'll be hungry."

But I wasn't. In spite of the smell of roasting duck, I could not have eaten anything.

Questions for Writing and Discussion

Discovering Meaning

1. Describe the central character, Stephanie. To what extent is

she conditioned by her family? To what extent is she independent of her family's influence?

2. What is your impression of Stephanie's mother? Support your answer with illustrations from the story. Discuss her relationship with her daughters and with her husband.

3. Stephanie makes two journeys, one to Fort Street with her mother and one to Cromwell Street alone to deliver a message to Mrs. Robinson. What does she learn from each journey?

4. Discuss the role of fantasy in Stephanie's life.

5. What is the significance of the story's ending?

Exploring Method

1. The author uses a first-person narrator to tell her story. We see events and characters through the eyes of a sensitive, rebellious child. Is she a reliable narrator? That is, is she an accurate observer or are her impressions exaggerated and coloured by her rebellion? Support your answer.

2. The author presents several settings in the story. Each is a vivid physical setting but also assumes symbolic significance. What do the following symbolize?
   a) The Crofts' garden and the Robinsons' garden.
   b) Sherwood Forest and the woodshed.
   c) Crowded Fort Street and Cromwell Street, where the Robinsons live.

3. How does the author prepare the reader for Stephanie's decision to visit Mrs. Robinson's home?

4. Structurally the story is divided into three parts: the scene at breakfast, the journey downtown, and the journey to the Robinsons' home. What is the function in the story of each part? How does the contrast between the two social classes enter each section of the story?

5. The story achieves a neat symmetry through the author's pairing of contrasting characters. Contrast each pair: Mr. and Mrs. Croft, and Stephanie and her sister Sally.

Suggestions for Writing

1. When Stephanie arrives at Mrs. Robinson's home, it is different from the romantic image her imagination has created. Describe one of your own experiences in which the reality was different from your romantic expectations.

2. The story can be read on several levels:
   a) social comedy: a satire directed against Mrs. Croft and her insistence on class distinctions;

b) an initiation: the journey to the Robinsons' home;

c) social history: a portrait of Victoria during the Thirties.

Analyze the story, using one of these approaches. Select details in the story to support your analysis.

3. Katherine Mansfield's "The Doll's House," set in New Zealand, and this story, set in Victoria, both portray prejudice based on social class. Compare and contrast the treatment of the theme through the following:

a) the central characters Stephanie and Kezia;

b) the portrayal of the upper-class adult;

c) the portrayal of the lower class.

Examining Social Issues

1. Stephanie is the oldest daughter. How has her character been influenced by her position in the family? Discuss how the birth order of children in a family affects their personalities.

2. In this story, Stephanie is a young writer. According to Freud, artists' repressions and frustrations find their outlet in creative expression. Artists' heightened sensitivities allow them to translate their frustrations into complex works of art. To what extent does this theory about the artist apply to Stephanie? Do you agree with Freud about the source of artistic creativity? Why or why not?

3. This is psychologist David Elkind's profile of an eleven-year-old, from *A Sympathetic Understanding of the Child*:

> At age eleven we begin to see changes that will mark adolescence. Self-doubts and insecurity are present. Relations to parents and siblings are conflictual, and the eleven-year-old finds much to criticize in her parents. She believes that she is being discriminated against. Only her relations with her friends remain unruffled. . . . At this stage young people do not have the energy to invest in concentrated learning; they expend it too generously elsewhere.

How does this sketch apply to Stephanie in this story? Use your experience to provide illustrations for an expanded portrait of an eleven-year-old.

Adolescence

Adolescents are excessively egoistic, and yet
at no time in later life are they capable of so
much self-sacrifice and devotion. They form
the most passionate love-relations, only to
break them off as abruptly as they began
them. They oscillate between blind
submission to some self-chosen leader and
defiant rebellion against any authority. They
are selfish and materially minded and at the
same time full of lofty idealism. Their
moods veer between light-hearted optimism
and blackest pessimism.

Anna Freud
The Ego and the Mechanism of Defense

A Teenager's View

Growing up is a time of confusion and
uncertainty. You begin to question
principles that you had always considered
concrete fact. Ideas, all conflicting, pour in
from all directions – parents, teachers,
adults, and teenage friends, movies, radio,
TV, books. You decide you are for one thing,
then someone talks you into the opposite
side. Adults are confused also, but they have
had time to form their opinions and
standards, whereas the teenagers are
floundering in the sea of indecision.

Ruth Strang
The Adolescent Views Himself

Red Dress

Alice Munro

Alice Munro, one of Canada's most talented writers of short stories, has won the Governor General's Literary Award twice, in 1968 and 1978. Based on her childhood in Protestant rural Ontario, her fiction explores the experiences of the adolescent trying to come to terms with the adult world. In her early collection Dance of the Happy Shades *(1968), from which "Red Dress" is taken, and in* Lives of Girls and Women *(1971), she portrays with compassion and humour the sensitive, introspective adolescent's experience in a rigid, limiting society in the Forties.*

Munro's typical themes are isolation and rejection. Her protagonists feel disconnected from their families. They view themselves as outsiders in a strange world, which they describe with the careful attention of alien explorers. They record with fascinating precision the shapes, colours, sounds, and textures that their more prosaic friends and relatives do not perceive.

In an interview Munro said, "I am not a writer who is very concerned with ideas. I'm not an intellectual writer. I'm very excited by what you may call the surface of life." Although her fiction is firmly rooted in the social realities of the rural and small-town world of her own experience, she insistently illuminates what lies beneath the familiar comfortable surface – the less discernible, shadowy area of irrational impulses that make human communication so difficult. Alice Munro's stories are memorable for the understanding and sympathy with which they portray the complexity of human relationships.

M y mother was making me a dress. All through the month of November I would come from school and find her in the kitchen, surrounded by cut-up red velvet and scraps of tissue-paper pattern. She worked at an old treadle machine pushed up against the window to get the light, and also to let her look out, past the stubble fields and bare vegetable garden, to see who went by on the road. There was seldom anybody to see.

The red velvet material was hard to work with, it pulled, and the style my mother had chosen was not easy either. She was not really a good sewer. She liked to make things; that is different. Whenever she could she tried to skip basting and pressing and she took no pride in the fine points of tailoring, the finishing of buttonholes and the overcasting of seams as, for instance, my aunt and my grandmother did. Unlike them she started off with an inspiration, a brave and dazzling idea; from that moment on, her pleasure ran downhill. In the first place she could never find a pattern to suit her. It was no wonder; there were no patterns made to match the ideas that blossomed in her head. She had made me, at various times when I was younger, a flowered organdie dress with a high Victorian neckline edged in scratchy lace, with a poke bonnet to match; a Scottish plaid outfit with a velvet jacket and tam; an embroidered peasant blouse worn with a full red skirt and black laced bodice. I had worn these clothes with docility, even pleasure, in the days when I was unaware of the world's opinion. Now, grown wiser, I wished for dresses like those my friend Lonnie had, bought at Beale's store.

I had to try it on. Sometimes Lonnie came home from school with me and she would sit on the couch watching. I was embarrassed by the way my mother crept around me, her knees creaking, her breath coming heavily. She muttered to herself. Around the house she wore no corset or stockings, she wore wedge-heeled shoes and ankle socks; her legs were marked with lumps of blue-green veins. I thought her squatting position shameless, even obscene; I tried to keep talking to Lonnie so that her attention would be taken away from my mother as much as possible. Lonnie wore the composed, polite, appreciative expression that was her disguise in the presence of grownups. She laughed at them and was a ferocious mimic, and they never knew.

My mother pulled me about, and pricked me with pins. She made me turn around, she made me walk away, she made me stand still. "What do you think of it, Lonnie?" she said around the pins in her mouth.

"It's beautiful," said Lonnie, in her mild, sincere way. Lonnie's own mother was dead. She lived with her father who never noticed her, and this, in my eyes, made her seem both vulnerable and privileged.

"It *will* be, if I can ever manage the fit," my mother said. "Ah, well," she said theatrically, getting to her feet with a woeful creaking and sighing, "I doubt if she appreciates it." She enraged me, talking like this to Lonnie, as if Lonnie were grown up and I were still a child. "Stand still," she said, hauling the pinned and basted dress over my head. My head was muffled in velvet, my body exposed, in an old cotton school slip. I felt like a great raw lump, clumsy and goose-pimpled. I wished I was like Lonnie, light-boned, pale and thin; she had been a Blue Baby.

"Well nobody ever made me a dress when I was going to high school," my mother said, "I made my own, or I did without." I was afraid she was going to start again on the story of her walking seven miles to town and finding a job waiting on tables in a boarding-house, so that she could go to high school. All the stories of my mother's life which had once interested me had begun to seem melodramatic, irrelevant, and tiresome.

"One time I had a dress given to me," she said. "It was a cream-coloured cashmere wool with royal blue piping down the front and lovely mother-of-pearl buttons, I wonder what ever became of it?"

When we got free Lonnie and I went upstairs to my room. It was cold, but we stayed there. We talked about the boys in our class, going up and down the rows and saying, "Do you like him? Well, do you half-like him? Do you *hate* him? Would you go out with him if he asked you?" Nobody had asked us. We were thirteen, and we had been going to high school for two months. We did questionnaires in magazines, to find out whether we had personality and whether we would be popular. We read articles on how to make up our faces to accentuate our good points and how to carry on a conversation on the first date and what to do when a boy tried to go too far. Also we read articles on frigidity of the menopause, abortion and why husbands seek satisfaction away from home. When we were not doing school work, we were occupied most of the time with the garnering, passing on and discussing of sexual information. We had made a pact to tell each other everything. But one thing I did not tell was about this dance, the high school Christmas Dance for which my mother was making me a dress. It was that I did not want to go.

At high school I was never comfortable for a minute. I did not know about Lonnie. Before an exam, she got icy hands and palpitations, but I was close to despair at all times. When I was asked a question in class, any simple little question at all, my voice was apt to come out squeaky, or else hoarse and trembling. When I had to go to the blackboard I was sure – even at a time of the month when this could not be true – that I had blood on my skirt. My hands became slippery with sweat when they were required to work the blackboard compass. I could not hit the ball in volley-ball; being called upon to perform an action in front of others made all my reflexes come undone. I hated Business Practice because you had to rule pages for an account book, using a straight pen, and when the teacher looked over my shoulder all the delicate lines wobbled and ran together. I hated Science; we perched on stools under harsh lights behind tables of unfamiliar, fragile equipment, and were taught by the principal of the school, a man with a cold, self-relishing voice – he read the Scriptures every morning – and a great talent for inflicting humiliation. I hated English because the boys played bingo at the back of the room while the teacher, a stout, gentle girl, slightly cross-eyed, read Wordsworth at the front. She threatened them, she begged them, her face red and her voice as unreliable as mine. They offered burlesqued apologies and when she started to read again they took up rapt postures, made swooning faces, crossed their eyes, flung their hands over their hearts. Sometimes she would burst into tears, there was no help for it, she had to run out into the hall. Then the boys made loud mooing noises; our hungry laughter – oh, mine too – pursued her. There was a carnival atmosphere of brutality in the room at such times, scaring weak and suspect people like me.

But what was really going on in the school was not Business Practice and Science and English, there was something else that gave life its urgency and brightness. That old building, with its rock-walled clammy basements and black cloakrooms and pictures of dead royalties and lost explorers, was full of the tension and excitement of sexual competition, and in this, in spite of daydreams of vast successes, I had premonitions of total defeat. Something had to happen, to keep me from that dance.

With December came snow, and I had an idea. Formerly I had considered falling off my bicycle and spraining my ankle and I had tried to manage this, as I rode home along the hard-frozen, deeply rutted country roads. But it was too difficult. However, my throat and bronchial tubes were supposed to be weak; why not expose them? I started getting out of bed at night and opening my window a little. I knelt down and let the wind, sometimes stinging with snow, rush in around my bared throat. I took off my pajama top. I said to myself the words "blue with cold" and as I knelt there, my eyes shut, I pictured my chest and throat turning blue, the cold, greyed blue of veins under the skin. I stayed until I could not stand it any more, and then I took a handful of snow from the windowsill and smeared it all over my chest, before I buttoned my pajamas. It would melt against the flannelette and I would be sleeping in wet clothes, which was supposed to be the worst thing of all. In the morning, the moment I woke up, I cleared my throat, testing for soreness, coughed experimentally, hopefully, touched my forehead to see if I had fever. It was no good. Every morning, including the day of the dance, I rose defeated, and in perfect health.

The day of the dance I did my hair up in steel curlers. I had never done this before, because my hair was naturally curly, but today I wanted the protection of all possible female rituals. I lay on the couch in the kitchen, reading *The Last Days of Pompeii*, and wishing I was there. My mother, never satisfied, was sewing a white lace collar on the dress; she had decided it was too grown-up looking. I watched the hours. It was one of the shortest days of the year. Above the couch, on the wallpaper, were old games of Xs and Os, old drawings and scribblings my brother and I had done when we were sick with bronchitis. I looked at them and longed to be back safe behind the boundaries of childhood.

When I took out the curlers my hair, both naturally and artificially stimulated, sprang out in an exuberant glossy bush. I wet it, I combed it, beat it with the brush and tugged it down along my cheeks. I applied face powder, which stood out chalkily on my hot face. My mother got out her Ashes of Roses Cologne, which she never used, and let me splash it over my arms. Then she zipped up the dress and turned me around to the mirror. The dress was princess style, very tight in the midriff. I saw how my breasts, in their new stiff brassiere, jutted out surprisingly, with mature authority, under the childish frills of the collar.

"Well I wish I could take a picture," my mother said. "I am really, genuinely proud of that fit. And you might say thank you for it."

"Thank you," I said.

The first thing Lonnie said when I opened the door to her was, "Jesus, what did you do to your hair?"

"I did it up."

"You look like a Zulu. Oh, don't worry. Get me a comb and I'll do the front in a roll. It'll look all right. It'll even make you look older."

I sat in front of the mirror and Lonnie stood behind me, fixing my hair. My mother seemed unable to leave us. I wished she would. She watched the roll take shape and said, "You're a wonder, Lonnie. You should take up hairdressing."

"That's a thought," Lonnie said. She had on a pale blue crepe dress, with a peplum and bow; it was much more grown-up than mine even without the collar. Her hair had come out as sleek as the girl's on the bobby-pin card. I had always thought secretly that Lonnie could not be pretty because she had crooked teeth, but now I saw that crooked teeth or not, her stylish dress and smooth hair made me look a little like a golliwog, stuffed into red velvet, wide-eyed, wild-haired, with a suggestion of delirium.

My mother followed us to the door and called out into the dark, "Au reservoir!" This was a traditional farewell of Lonnie's and mine; it sounded foolish and desolate coming from her, and I was so angry with her for using it that I did not reply. It was only Lonnie who called back cheerfully, encouragingly, "Good night!"

The gymnasium smelled of pine and cedar. Red and green bells of fluted paper hung from the basketball hoops; the high, barred windows were hidden by green boughs. Everybody in the upper grades seemed to have come in couples. Some of the Grade Twelve and Thirteen girls had brought boy friends who had already graduated, who were young businessmen around the town. These young men smoked in the gymnasium, nobody could stop them, they were free. The girls stood beside them, resting their hands casually on male sleeves, their faces bored, aloof and beautiful. I longed to be like that. They behaved as if only they – the older ones – were really at the dance, as if the rest of us, whom they moved among and peered around, were, if not invisible, inanimate; when the first dance was announced – a Paul Jones – they moved out languidly, smiling at each other as if they had been asked to take part in some half-forgotten childish game. Holding hands and shivering, crowding up together, Lonnie and I and the other Grade Nine girls followed.

I didn't dare look at the outer circle as it passed me, for fear I should see some unmannerly hurrying-up. When the music stopped I stayed where I was, and half-raising my eyes I saw a boy named Mason Williams coming reluctantly towards me. Barely touching my waist and my fingers, he began to dance with me. My legs were hollow, my arm trembled from the shoulder, I could not have spoken. This Mason Williams was one of the heroes of the school; he played basketball and hockey and walked the halls with an air of royal sullenness and barbaric contempt. To have to dance with a nonentity like me was as offensive to him as having to memorize Shakespeare. I felt this as keenly as he did, and imagined that he was exchanging looks of dismay with his friends. He steered me, stumbling, to the edge of the floor. He took his hand from my waist and dropped my arm.

"See you," he said. He walked away.

It took me a minute or two to realize what had happened and that he was not coming back. I went and stood by the wall alone. The Physical Education teacher, dancing past energetically in the arms of a Grade Ten boy, gave me an inquisitive look. She was the only teacher in the school who made use of the words social adjustment, and I was afraid that if she had seen, or if she found out, she might make some horribly public attempt to make Mason finish out the dance with me. I myself was not angry or surprised at Mason; I accepted his position, and mine, in the world of school and I saw that what he had done was the realistic thing to do. He was a Natural Hero, not a Student Council type of hero bound for success beyond the school; one of those would have danced with me courteously and patronizingly and left me feeling no better off. Still, I hoped not many people had seen. I hated people seeing. I began to bite the skin on my thumb.

When the music stopped I joined the surge of girls to the end of the gymnasium. Pretend it didn't happen, I said to myself. Pretend this is the beginning, now.

The band began to play again. There was movement in the dense crowd at our end of the floor, it thinned rapidly. Boys came over, girls went out to dance. Lonnie went. The girl on the other side of me went. Nobody asked me. I remembered a magazine article Lonnie and I had read, which said *Be gay! Let the boys see your eyes sparkle, let them hear laughter in your voice! Simple, obvious, but how many girls forget!* It was true, I had forgotten. My eyebrows were drawn together with tension, I must look scared and ugly. I took a deep breath and tried to loosen my face. I smiled. But I felt absurd, smiling at no one. And I observed that girls on the dance floor, popular girls, were not smiling; many of them had sleepy, sulky faces and never smiled at all.

Girls were still going out to the floor. Some, despairing, went with each other. But most went with boys. Fat girls, girls with pimples, a poor girl who didn't own a good dress and had to wear a skirt and sweater to the dance; they were claimed, they danced away. Why take them and not me? Why everybody else and not me? I have a red velvet dress, I did my hair in curlers, I used a deodorant and put on cologne. *Pray*, I thought. I couldn't close my eyes but I said over and over again in my mind, *Please, me, please,* and I locked my fingers behind my back in a sign more potent than crossing, the same secret sign Lonnie and I used not to be sent to the blackboard in Math.

It did not work. What I had been afraid of was true. I was going to be left. There was something mysterious the matter with me, something that could not be put right like bad breath or overlooked like pimples, and everybody knew it, and I knew it; I had known it all along. But I had not known it for sure, I had hoped to be mistaken. Certainty rose inside me like sickness. I hurried past one or two girls who were also left and went into the girls' washroom. I hid myself in a cubicle.

That was where I stayed. Between dances girls came in and went out quickly. There were plenty of cubicles; nobody noticed that I was not a temporary occupant. During the dances, I listened to the music which I liked but had no part of any more. For I was not going to try any more. I only wanted to hide in here, get out without seeing anybody, get home.

One time after the music started somebody stayed behind. She was taking a long time running the water, washing her hands, combing her hair. She was going to think it funny that I stayed in so long. I had better go out and wash my hands, and maybe while I was washing them she would leave.

It was Mary Fortune. I knew her by name, because she was an officer of the Girls' Athletic Society and she was on the Honour Roll and she was always organizing things. She had something to do with organizing this dance; she had been around to all the classrooms asking for volunteers to do the decorations. She was in Grade Eleven or Twelve.

"Nice and cool in here," she said. "I came in to get cooled off. I get so hot."

She was still combing her hair when I finished my hands. "Do you like the band?" she said.

"It's all right." I didn't really know what to say. I was surprised at her, an older girl, taking this time to talk to me.

"I don't. I can't stand it. I hate dancing when I don't like the band. Listen. They're so choppy. I'd just as soon not dance as dance to that."

I combed my hair. She leaned against a basin, watching me.

"I don't want to dance and don't particularly want to stay in here. Let's go and have a cigarette."

"Where?"

"Come on, I'll show you."

At the end of the washroom there was a door. It was unlocked and led into a dark closet full of mops and pails. She had me hold the door open, to get the washroom light, until she found the knob of another door. This door opened into darkness.

"I can't turn on the light or somebody might see," she said. "It's the janitor's room." I reflected that athletes always seemed to know more than the rest of us about the school as a building; they knew where things were kept and they were always coming out of unauthorized doors with a bold, preoccupied air. "Watch out where you're going," she said. "Over at the far end there's some stairs. They go up to a closet on the second floor. The door's locked at the top, but there's like a partition between the stairs and the room. So if we sit on the steps, even if by chance someone did come in here, they wouldn't see us."

"Wouldn't they smell smoke?" I said.

"Oh, well. Live dangerously."

There was a high window over the stairs which gave us a little light. Mary Fortune had cigarettes and matches in her purse. I had not smoked before except the cigarettes Lonnie and I made ourselves, using papers and tobacco stolen from her father; they came apart in the middle. These were much better.

"The only reason I even came to-night," Mary Fortune said, "is because I am responsible for the decorations and I wanted to see, you know, how it looked once people got in there and everything. Otherwise why bother? I'm not boy-crazy."

In the light from the high window I could see her narrow, scornful face, her dark skin pitted with acne, her teeth pushed together at the front, making her look adult and commanding.

"Most girls are. Haven't you noticed that? The greatest collection of boy-crazy girls you could imagine is right here in this school."

I was grateful for her attention, her company and her cigarette. I said I thought so too.

"Like this afternoon. This afternoon I was trying to get them to hang the bells and junk. They just get up on the ladders and fool around with boys. They don't care if it ever gets decorated. It's just an excuse. That's the only aim they have in life, fooling around with boys. As far as I'm concerned, they're idiots."

We talked about teachers, and things at school. She said she wanted to be a physical education teacher and she would have to go to college for that, but her parents did not have enough money. She said she planned to work her own way through, she wanted to be independent anyway, she would work in the cafeteria and in the summer she would do farm work, like picking tobacco. Listening to her, I felt the acute phase of my unhappiness passing. Here was someone who had suffered the same defeat as I had – I saw that – but she was full of energy and self-respect. She had thought of other things to do. She would pick tobacco.

We stayed there talking and smoking during the long pause in the music, when, outside, they were having doughnuts and coffee. When the music started again Mary said, "Look, do we have to hang around here any longer? Let's get our coats and go. We can go down to Lee's and have a hot chocolate and talk in comfort, why not?"

We felt our way across the janitor's room, carrying ashes and cigarette butts in our hands. In the closet, we stopped and listened to make sure there was nobody in the washroom. We came back into the light and threw the ashes into the toilet. We had to go out and cut across the dance floor to the cloakroom, which was beside the outside door.

A dance was just beginning. "Go round the edge of the floor," Mary said. "Nobody'll notice us."

I followed her. I didn't look at anybody. I didn't look for Lonnie. Lonnie was probably not going to be my friend any more, not as much as before anyway. She was what Mary would call boy-crazy.

I found that I was not so frightened, now that I had made up my mind to leave the dance behind. I was not waiting for anybody to choose me. I had my own plans. I did not have to smile or make signs for luck. It did not matter to me. I was on my way to have a hot chocolate, with my friend.

A boy said something to me. He was in my way. I thought he must be telling me that I had dropped something or that I couldn't go that way or that the cloakroom was locked. I didn't understand that he was asking me to dance until he said it over again. It was Raymond Bolting from our class, whom I had never talked to in my life. He thought I meant yes. He put his hand on my waist and almost without meaning to, I began to dance.

We moved to the middle of the floor. I was dancing. My legs had forgotten to tremble and my hands to sweat. I was dancing with a boy who had asked me. Nobody told him to, he didn't have to, he just asked me. Was it possible, could I believe it, was there nothing the matter with me after all?

I thought that I ought to tell him there was a mistake, that I was just leaving, I was going to have a hot chocolate with my girl friend. But I did not say anything. My face was making certain delicate adjustments, achieving with no effort at all the grave absent-minded look of these who were chosen, those who danced. This was the face that Mary Fortune saw, when she looked out of the cloakroom door, her scarf already around her head. I made a weak waving motion with the hand that lay on the boy's shoulder, indicating that I apologized, that I didn't know what had happened and also that it was no use waiting for me. Then I turned my head away, and when I looked again she was gone.

Raymond Bolting took me home and Harold Simons took Lonnie home. We all walked together as far as Lonnie's corner. The boys were having an argument about a hockey game, which Lonnie and I could not follow. Then we separated into couples and Raymond continued with me the conversation he had been having with Harold. He did not seem to notice that he was now talking to me instead. Once or twice I said, "Well I don't know, I didn't see that game," but after a while I decided just to say "H'm hmm," and that seemed to be all that was necessary.

One other thing he said was, "I didn't realize you lived such a long way out." And he sniffled. The cold was making my nose run a little too, and I worked my fingers through the candy wrappers in my coat pocket until I found a shabby Kleenex. I didn't know whether to offer it to him or not, but he sniffled so loudly that I finally said, "I just have this one Kleenex, it probably isn't even clean, it probably has ink on it. But if I was to tear it in half we'd each have something."

"Thanks," he said. "I sure could use it."

It was a good thing, I thought, that I had done that, for at my gate, when I said, "Well, good night," and after he said, "Oh, yeah. Good night," he leaned towards me and kissed me, briefly, with the air of one who knew his job when he saw it, on the corner of my mouth. Then he turned back to town, never knowing he had been my rescuer, that he had brought me from Mary Fortune's territory into the ordinary world.

I went around the house to the back door, thinking, I have been to a dance and a boy has walked me home and kissed me. It was all true. My life was possible. I went past the kitchen window and I saw my mother. She was sitting with her feet on the open oven door, drinking tea out of a cup without a saucer. She was just sitting and waiting for me to come home and tell her everything that had happened. And I would not do it, I never would. But when I saw the waiting kitchen, and my mother in her faded, fuzzy Paisley kimono, with her sleepy but doggedly expectant face, I understood what a mysterious and oppressive obligation I had, to be happy, and how I had almost failed it, and would be likely to fail it, every time, and she would not know.

Questions for Writing and Discussion

Discovering Meaning

1. Describe the narrator.
2. Describe the narrator's mother. What conditions have shaped her life?
3. Examine the relationship between mother and daughter. Is the narrator sympathetic or unsympathetic towards her mother? Why?

4. Compare Raymond Bolting's adjustment to the institution of school dances with the narrator's.
5. Describe the atmosphere in the final episode when the two teenagers, the narrator and her escort, walk home sharing a tissue. Is this episode an appropriate ending to the dance? Why or why not?
6. In the final image of her mother after the dance, what emotions does the daughter experience? How will their relationship develop now?

Exploring Method

1. How reliable is the first-person narrator in her judgements of events and characters? Select instances in the story in which your judgement does not coincide with hers. In which instances do you agree with her?
2. How do these pairs of characters function in the story: Lonnie and Mason Williams; and Mary Fortune and Raymond Bolting?
3. In Munro's stories, settings help define the limits that her characters struggle to overcome. What insights into the central character's conflict are provided by the opening paragraph and by the description of the gymnasium as the narrator enters?
4. In the story, the author alternates pain and comedy. Identify the elements of each.

Suggestions for Writing

1. The author aims her satire at several targets. What social criticism does she direct against teenage magazines, school dances, and double-dating? Describe your own view of these familiar props of teenage life.
2. Write a narrative in which you describe your first dance.
3. The story portrays a high school in the Forties. Compare a modern high school with the one in the story. Illustrate your comparison with an account of your experience at high school.

Examining Social Issues

1. The protagonists in "The Outlaw" and "Red Dress" are both early adolescents, both thirteen-year-olds. At this stage, young people ask two urgent questions: "Who am I?" and "Where am I?" The first question concerns identity: a struggle to develop a

perception of themselves as emerging adults; the second question is concerned with developing an understanding of the world in which they live.

Here is a psychological profile of the early adolescent period from *The Adolescent Views Himself*, by Ruth Strang:

> The early adolescent period ... is usually considered the most difficult time for youngsters and for their elders. The emotions are often intense; their changes in mood are often rapid and violent. They seek excitement. Being treated like children almost always arouses their anger. Yet underneath their rebellion, their sloppy clothes or simulated sophistication, and their valiant efforts to grow up is a pervasive feeling of insecurity and bewilderment. They worry about their appearance and about being normal. They worry a great deal about being liked and being accepted in groups of their own age.

How does Strang's psychological portrait apply to the protagonists in the two stories in their preoccupation with identity and with understanding their world? Compare this portrait with the portrait of teenagers of the protagonists' age in situation comedies and commercials on television. Which is a truer reflection of today's teenagers? Why?

2. The story portrays an oppressive mother-daughter relationship. Suggest ways in which the relationship could be made less frustrating for both mother and daughter.

3. Before the dance, the thirteen-year-old narrator says, "I longed to be back safe behind the boundaries of childhood." Do you think teenagers are pressured into sexual competition before they are emotionally ready for the experience? Support your answer with examples.

4. Discuss the advantages and disadvantages of junior high school as an intermediary step towards senior high school. How would your high school experience have been different if you had or had not attended junior high school first?

5. The narrator confesses, "At high school ... I was close to despair at all times." Reread the account of her classroom experience. What is it about high school that drives students to "despair"?

The Loons

Margaret Laurence

Margaret Laurence, one of Canada's most gifted writers, expresses the objective of her fiction in this way: "One would like to convey a feeling of flesh-and-blood immediacy, a feeling that this is what it was like to be this particular person with all the complexity that implies, all the irrelevancy and paradoxical quality of life itself. Which is not possible to convey, really, as life is not art." Margaret Laurence, in her vital portrayal of individualized characters within vividly realized settings, has come as close to the complexity of life as art can achieve.

Just as William Faulkner, the novelist of the American South, modelled his fictional world of Yoknapatawpha County after his home in the state of Mississippi, with its racial tensions centred on black-white divisions, so Margaret Laurence has created a setting for all her Canadian novels, the fictional Manawaka, a prairie town like her own native Neepawa in Manitoba. Hovering on the fringes of the action in her stories and novels is the presence of the Tonnerres, a family descended from the Metis. In Laurence's Manawaka, the abused Tonnerre family symbolizes the nation's collective guilt because of its unjust treatment of the Metis.

The stories in Laurence's collection A Bird in the House *(1970), from which "The Loons" is taken, are linked by the character of the narrator, Vanessa MacLeod, whose fictional experience is based on Laurence's own life. Laurence, through her narrator, is looking back on her own younger self, tracing her development for a period of ten years beginning from 1935. Like Mavis Gallant in "Wing's Chips," Margaret Laurence in "The Loons" uses a double focus to tell her story. We see events simultaneously through the child's and the adult narrator's eyes: the child's partly uncomprehending awareness, confused by an undercurrent of conflicting emotions, and at the same time the older narrator's memories, which add a dimension of compassion, understanding, and acceptance. The result is that the adult narrator, reflecting on her childhood, gains an unfolding insight into her personal history and into the history of the nation. The Tonnerres, the impoverished family we meet in "The Loons," are a perpetual reproach to Manawaka's conscience, symbolizing the divisions, distrust, and frustrated longings of one of Canada's oldest oppressed minorities.*

Margaret Laurence has said of her writing that she wants to put down on paper what everyone knows but no one has thought of expressing. In our media, we have observed the suffering of people like the Tonnerres. But in this story, Laurence has brought their plight vividly and movingly to life through the character of Piquette.

Just below Manawaka, where the Wachakwa River ran brown and noisy over the pebbles, the scrub oak and grey-green willow and chokecherry bushes grew in a dense thicket. In a clearing at the centre of the thicket stood the Tonnerre family's shack. The basis of this dwelling was a small square cabin made of poplar poles and chinked with mud, which had been built by Jules Tonnerre some fifty years before, when he came back from Batoche with a bullet in his thigh, the year that Riel was hanged and the voices of the Metis entered their long silence. Jules had only intended to stay the winter in the Wachakwa Valley, but the family was still there in the thirties, when I was a child. As the Tonnerres had increased, their settlement had been added to, until the clearing at the foot of the town hill was a chaos of lean-tos, wooden packing cases, warped lumber, discarded car tires, ramshackle chicken coops, tangled strands of barbed wire and rusty tin cans.

The Tonnerres were French halfbreeds, and among themselves they spoke a *patois* that was neither Cree nor French. Their English was broken and full of obscenities. They did not belong among the Cree of the Galloping Mountain reservation, further north, and they did not belong among the Scots-Irish and Ukrainians of Manawaka either. They were, as my Grandmother MacLeod would have put it, neither flesh, fowl, nor good salt herring. When their men were not working at odd jobs or as section hands on the C.P.R., they lived on relief. In the summers, one of the Tonnerre youngsters, with a face that seemed totally unfamiliar with laughter, would knock at the doors of the town's brick houses and offer for sale a lard-pail full of bruised wild strawberries, and if he got as much as a quarter he would grab the coin and run before the customer had time to change her mind. Sometimes old Jules, or his son Lazarus, would get mixed up in a Saturday-night brawl, and would hit out at whoever was nearest, or howl drunkenly among the offended shoppers on Main Street, and then the Mountie would put them for the night in the barred cell underneath the Court House, and the next morning they would be quiet again.

Piquette Tonnerre, the daughter of Lazarus, was in my class at school. She was older than I, but she had failed several grades, perhaps because her attendance had always been sporadic and her interest in schoolwork negligible. Part of the reason she had missed a lot of school was that she had had tuberculosis of the bone, and had once spent many months in hospital. I knew this because my father was the doctor who had looked after her. Her sickness was almost the only thing I knew about her, however. Otherwise, she existed for me only as a vaguely embarrassing presence, with her hoarse voice and her clumsy limping walk and her grimy cotton dresses that were always miles too long. I was neither friendly nor unfriendly towards her. She dwelt and moved somewhere within my scope of vision, but I did not actually notice her very much until that peculiar summer when I was eleven.

"I don't know what to do about that kid," my father said at dinner one evening. "Piquette Tonnerre, I mean. The damn bone's flared up again. I've had her in hospital for quite a while now, and it's under control all right, but I hate like the dickens to send her home again."

"Couldn't you explain to her mother that she has to rest a lot?" my mother said.

"The mother's not there," my father replied. "She took off a few years back. Can't say I blame her. Piquette cooks for them, and she says Lazarus would never do anything for himself as long as she's there. Anyway, I don't think she'd take much care of herself, once she got back. She's only thirteen, after all. Beth, I was thinking – what about taking her up to Diamond Lake with us this summer? A couple of months rest would give that bone a much better chance."

My mother looked stunned.

"But Ewen – what about Roddie and Vanessa?"

"She's not contagious," my father said. "And it would be company for Vanessa."

"Oh dear," my mother said in distress, "I'll bet anything she has nits in her hair."

"For Pete's sake," my father said crossly, "do you think Matron would let her stay in the hospital for all this time like that? Don't be silly, Beth."

Grandmother MacLeod, her delicately featured face as rigid as a cameo, now brought her mauve-veined hands together as though she were about to begin a prayer.

"Ewen, if that half-breed youngster comes along to Diamond Lake, I'm not going," she announced. "I'll go to Morag's for the summer."

I had trouble in stifling my urge to laugh, for my mother brightened visibly and quickly tried to hide it. If it came to a choice between Grandmother MacLeod and Piquette, Piquette would win hands down, nits or not.

"It might be quite nice for you, at that," she mused. "You haven't seen Morag for over a year, and you might enjoy being in the city for a while. Well, Ewen dear, you do what you think best. If you think it would do Piquette some good, then we'll be glad to have her, as long as she behaves herself."

So it happened that several weeks later, when we all piled into my father's old Nash, surrounded by suitcases and boxes of provisions and toys for my ten-month-old brother, Piquette was with us and Grandmother MacLeod, miraculously, was not. My father would only be staying at the cottage for a couple of weeks, for he had to get back to his practice, but the rest of us would stay at Diamond Lake until the end of August.

Our cottage was not named, as many were, "Dew Drop Inn" or "Bide-a-Wee," or "Bonnie Doon." The sign on the roadway bore in austere letters only our name, MacLeod. It was not a large cottage, but it was on the lakefront. You could look out the windows and see, through the filigree of the spruce trees, the water glistening greenly as the sun caught it. All around the cottage were ferns, and sharp-branched raspberry bushes, and moss that had grown over fallen tree trunks. If you looked carefully among the weeds and grass, you could find wild strawberry plants which were in white flower now and in another month would bear fruit, the fragrant globes hanging like miniature scarlet lanterns on the thin hairy stems. The two grey squirrels were still there, gossiping at us from the tall spruce beside the cottage, and by the end of the summer they would again be tame enough to take pieces of crust from my hands. The broad moose antlers that hung above the back door were a little more bleached and fissured after the winter, but otherwise everything was the same. I raced joyfully around my kingdom, greeting all the places I had not seen for a year. My brother, Roderick, who had not been born when we were here last summer, sat on the car rug in the sunshine and examined a brown spruce cone, meticulously turning it round and round in his small and curious hands. My mother and father toted the luggage from car to cottage, exclaiming over how well the place had wintered, no broken windows, thank goodness, no apparent damage from storm-felled branches or snow.

Only after I had finished looking around did I notice Piquette. She was sitting on the swing, her lame leg held stiffly out, and her other foot scuffing the ground as she swung slowly back and forth. Her long hair hung black and straight around her shoulders, and her broad coarse-featured face bore no expression – it was blank, as though she no longer dwelt within her own skull, as though she had gone elsewhere. I approached her very hesitantly.

"Want to come and play?"

Piquette looked at me with a sudden flash of scorn.

"I ain't a kid," she said.

Wounded, I stamped angrily away, swearing I would not speak to her for the rest of the summer. In the days that followed, however, Piquette began to interest me, and I began to want to interest her. My reasons did not appear bizarre to me. Unlikely as it may seem, I had only just realised that the Tonnerre family, whom I had always heard called halfbreeds, were actually Indians, or as near as made no difference. My acquaintance with Indians was not extensive. I did not remember ever having seen a real Indian, and my new awareness that Piquette sprang from the people of Big Bear and Poundmaker, of Tecumseh, of the Iroquois who had eaten Father Brebeuf's heart – all this gave her an instant attraction in my eyes. I was a devoted reader of Pauline Johnson at this age, and sometimes would orate aloud in an exalted voice, *West Wind, blow from your prairie nest; Blow from the mountains, blow from the west* – and so on. It seemed to me that Piquette must be in some way a daughter of the forest, a kind of junior prophetess of the wilds, who might impart to me, if I took the right approach, some of the secrets which she undoubtedly knew – where the whippoorwill made her nest, how the coyote reared her young, or whatever it was that it said in Hiawatha.

I set about gaining Piquette's trust. She was not allowed to go swimming, with her bad leg, but I managed to lure her down to the beach – or rather, she came because there was nothing else to do. The water was always icy, for the lake was fed by springs, but I swam like a dog, thrashing my arms and legs around at such speed and with such an output of energy that I never grew cold. Finally, when I had had enough, I came out and sat beside Piquette on the sand. When she saw me approaching, her hand squashed flat the sand castle she had been building, and she looked at me sullenly, without speaking.

"Do you like this place?" I asked, after a while, intending to lead on from there into the question of forest lore.

Piquette shrugged. "It's okay. Good as anywhere."

"I love it," I said. "We come here every summer."

"So what?" Her voice was distant, and I glanced at her uncertainly, wondering what I could have said wrong.

"Do you want to come for a walk?" I asked her. "We wouldn't

need to go far. If you walk just around the point there, you come to a bay where great big reeds grow in the water, and all kinds of fish hang around there. Want to? Come on."

She shook her head.

"Your dad said I ain't supposed to do no more walking than I got to."

I tried another line.

"I bet you know a lot about the woods and all that, eh?" I began respectfully.

Piquette looked at me from her large dark unsmiling eyes.

"I don't know what in hell you're talkin' about," she replied. "You nuts or somethin'? If you mean where my old man, and me, and all them live, you better shut up, by Jesus, you hear?"

I was startled and my feelings were hurt, but I had a kind of dogged perseverance. I ignored her rebuff.

"You know something Piquette? There's loons here, on this lake. You can see their nests just up the shore there, behind those logs. At night, you can hear them even from the cottage, but it's better to listen from the beach. My dad says we should listen and try to remember how they sound, because in a few years when more cottages are built at Diamond Lake and more people come in, the loons will go away."

Piquette was picking up stones and snail shells and then dropping them again.

"Who gives a good goddamn?" she said.

It became increasingly obvious that, as an Indian, Piquette was a dead loss. That evening I went out by myself, scrambling through the bushes that overhung the steep path, my feet slipping on the fallen spruce needles that covered the ground. When I reached the shore, I walked along the firm damp sand to the small pier that my father had built, and sat down there. I heard some- one else crashing through the undergrowth and the bracken, and for a moment I thought Piquette had changed her mind, but it turned out to be my father. He sat beside me on the pier and we waited, without speaking.

At night the lake was like black glass with a streak of amber which was the path of the moon. All around, the spruce trees grew tall and close-set, branches blackly sharp against the sky, which was lightened by a cold flickering of stars. Then the loons began their calling. They rose like phantom birds from the nests on the shore, and flew out onto the dark still surface of the water.

No one can ever describe the ululating sound, the crying of the loons, and no one who has heard it can ever forget it. Plaintive, and yet with a quality of chilling mockery, those voices belonged to a world separated by aeons from our neat world of summer cottages and the lighted lamps of home.

"They must have sounded just like that," my father remarked, "before any person ever set foot here."

Then he laughed. "You could say the same, of course, about sparrows, or chipmunks, but somehow it only strikes you that way with the loons."

"I know," I said.

Neither of us suspected that this would be the last time we would ever sit here together on the shore, listening. We stayed for perhaps half an hour, and then we went back to the cottage. My mother was reading beside the fireplace. Piquette was looking at the burning birch log, and not doing anything.

"You should have come along," I said, although in fact I was glad she had not.

"Not me," Piquette said. "You wouldn't catch me walkin' way down there jus' for a bunch of squawkin' birds."

Piquette and I remained ill at ease with one another. I felt I had somehow failed my father, but I did not know what was the matter, nor why she would not or could not respond when I suggested exploring the woods or playing house. I thought it was probably her slow and difficult walking that held her back. She stayed most of the time in the cottage with my mother, helping her with the dishes or with Roddie, but hardly ever talking. Then the Duncans arrived at their cottage, and I spent my days with Mavis, who was my best friend. I could not reach Piquette at all, and I soon lost interest in trying. But all that summer she remained as both a reproach and a mystery to me.

That winter my father died of pneumonia, after less than a week's illness. For some time I saw nothing around me, being completely immersed in my own pain and my mother's. When I looked outward once more, I scarcely noticed that Piquette Tonnerre was no longer at school. I do not remember seeing her at all until four years later, one Saturday night when Mavis and I were having Cokes in the Regal Café. The jukebox was booming like tuneful thunder, and beside it, leaning lightly on its chrome and its rainbow glass, was a girl.

Piquette must have been seventeen then, although she looked about twenty. I stared at her, astounded that anyone could have changed so much. Her face, so stolid and expressionless before, was animated now with a gaiety that was almost violent. She laughed and talked very loudly with the boys around her. Her lipstick was bright carmine, and her hair was cut short and frizzily permed. She had not been pretty as a child, and she was not pretty now, for her features were still heavy and blunt. But her dark and slightly slanted eyes were beautiful, and her skin-tight skirt and orange sweater displayed to enviable advantage a soft and slender body.

She saw me, and walked over. She teetered a little, but it was not due to her once-tubercular leg, for her limp was almost gone.

"Hi, Vanessa." Her voice still had the same hoarseness. "Long time no see, eh?"

"Hi," I said. "Where've you been keeping yourself, Piquette?"

"Oh, I been around," she said. "I been away almost two years now. Been all over the place – Winnipeg, Regina, Saskatoon, Jesus, what I could tell you! I come back this summer, but I ain't stayin'. You kids goin' to the dance?"

"No," I said abruptly, for this was a sore point with me. I was fifteen, and thought I was old enough to go to the Saturday-night dances at the Flamingo. My mother, however, thought otherwise.

"Y'oughta come," Piquette said. "I never miss one. It's just about the on'y thing in this jerkwater town that's any fun. Boy, you couldn' catch me stayin' here. I don't give a shit about this place. It stinks."

She sat down beside me, and I caught the harsh over-sweetness of her perfume.

"Listen, you wanna know something, Vanessa?" she confided, her voice only slightly blurred. "Your dad was the only person in Manawaka that ever done anything good to me."

I nodded speechlessly. I was certain she was speaking the truth. I knew a little more than I had that summer at Diamond Lake, but I could not reach her now any more than I had then. I was ashamed, ashamed of my own timidity, the frightened tendency to look the other way. Yet I felt no real warmth towards her – I only felt that I ought to, because of that distant summer and because my father had hoped she would be company for me, or perhaps that I would be for her, but it had not happened that way. At this moment, meeting her again, I had to admit that she repelled and embarrassed me, and I could not help despising the self-pity in her voice. I wished she would go away. I did not want to see her. I did not know what to say to her. It seemed that we had nothing to say to one another.

"I'll tell you something else," Piquette went on. "All the old bitches an' biddies in this town will sure be surprised. I'm gettin' married this fall – my boyfriend, he's an English fella, works in the stockyards in the city there, a very tall guy, got blond wavy hair. Gee, is he ever handsome. Got this real classy name. Alvin Gerald Cummings – some handle, eh? They call him Al."

For the merest instant, then, I saw her. I really did see her, for the first and only time in all the years we had both lived in the same town. Her defiant face, momentarily, became unguarded and unmasked, and in her eyes there was a terrifying hope.

"Gee, Piquette – " I burst out awkwardly, "that's swell. That's really wonderful. Congratulations – good luck – I hope you'll be happy – "

As I mouthed the conventional phrases, I could only guess how great her need must have been, that she had been forced to seek the very things she so bitterly rejected.

When I was eighteen, I left Manawaka and went away to college. At the end of my first year, I came back home for the summer. I spent the next few days in talking non-stop with my mother, as we exchanged all the news that somehow had not found its way into letters – what had happened in my life and what had happened here in Manawaka while I was away. My mother searched her memory for events that concerned people I knew.

"Did I ever write you about Piquette Tonnerre, Vanessa?" she asked one morning.

"No, I don't think so," I replied. "Last I heard of her, she was going to marry some guy in the city. Is she still there?"

My mother looked perturbed, and it was a moment before she spoke, as though she did not know how to express what she had to tell and wished she did not need to try.

"She's dead," she said at last. Then, as I stared at her, "Oh, Vanessa, when it happened, I couldn't help thinking of her as she was that summer – so sullen and gauche and badly dressed. I couldn't help wondering if we could have done something more at that time – but what could we do? She used to be around in the cottage there with me all day, and honestly, it was all I could do to get a word out of her. She didn't even talk to your father very much, although I think she liked him, in her way."

"What happened?" I asked.

"Either her husband left her, or she left him," my mother said. "I don't know which. Anyway, she came back here with two youngsters, both only babies – they must have been born very close together. She kept house, I guess, for Lazarus and her brothers, down in the valley there, in the old Tonnerre place. I used to see her on the street sometimes, but she never spoke to me. She'd put on an awful lot of weight, and she looked a mess, to tell you the truth, a real slattern, dressed any old how. She was up in court a couple of times – drunk and disorderly, of course. One Saturday night last winter, during the coldest weather, Piquette was alone in the shack with the children. The Tonnerres made home brew all the time, so I've heard, and Lazarus said later she'd been drinking most of the day when he and the boys went out that evening. They had an old woodstove there – you know the kind, with exposed pipes. The shack caught fire. Piquette didn't get out, and neither did the children."

I did not say anything. As so often with Piquette, there did not seem to be anything to say. There was a kind of silence around the image in my mind of the fire and the snow, and I wished I could put from my memory the look that I had seen once in Piquette's eyes.

I went up to Diamond Lake for a few days that summer, with Mavis and her family. The MacLeod cottage had been sold after my father's death, and I did not even go to look at it, not wanting to witness my long-ago kingdom possessed now by strangers. But one evening I went down to the shore by myself.

The small pier which my father had built was gone, and in its place there was a large and solid pier built by the government, for Galloping Mountain was now a national park, and Diamond Lake had been re-named Lake Wapakata, for it was felt that an Indian name would have a greater appeal to tourists. The one store had become several dozen, and the settlement had all the attributes of a flourishing resort – hotels, a dance-hall, cafés with neon signs, the penetrating odours of potato chips and hot dogs.

I sat on the government pier and looked out across the water. At night the lake at least was the same as it had always been, darkly shining and bearing within its black glass the streak of amber that was the path of the moon. There was no wind that evening, and everything was quiet all around me. It seemed too quiet, and then I realised that the loons were no longer here. I listened for some time, to make sure, but never once did I hear that long-drawn call, half mocking and half plaintive, spearing through the stillness across the lake.

I did not know what had happened to the birds. Perhaps they had gone away to some far place of belonging. Perhaps they had been unable to find such a place, and had simply died out, having ceased to care any longer whether they lived or not.

I remembered how Piquette had scorned to come along, when my father and I sat there and listened to the lake birds. It seemed to me now that in some unconscious and totally unrecognised way, Piquette might have been the only one, after all, who had heard the crying of the loons.

96

Questions for Writing and Discussion

Discovering Meaning

1. Trace the narrator's developing relationship with Piquette. What is her father's role in this relationship?
2. The author presents three portraits of Piquette: at thirteen, at seventeen, and at twenty. Describe each portrait and explain the social and personal influences that shape each phase in Piquette's life.
3. How does Piquette's concept of herself differ from the narrator's view of her? Why does Piquette angrily reject the narrator's attempt to identify her with an idealized vision of Indians?
4. At the news of Piquette's death, the narrator remembers "the terrifying hope" she saw in her eyes. Explain the meaning of the look in Piquette's eyes.
5. Why does the narrator conclude that "Piquette might have been the only one . . . who had heard the crying of the loons"?

Exploring Method

1. In the story, the first-person narrator is an adult remembering her childhood. What does the author achieve by using an adult's rather than a child's point of view to tell the story?
2. What is the function of the first two paragraphs in the story?
3. Against each portrait of Piquette, the author sets a parallel portrait of the narrator. Contrast the girls in each phase of their lives. What is the author's purpose in developing the contrasts?
4. How does the author foreshadow the failure of Piquette's marriage?
5. What is the function of the parallel scenes on the pier: the scene of the narrator and her father listening to the loons and the final scene of the narrator alone thinking about the loons?
6. Explain the use of the loon as a symbol and its relation to Piquette.

Suggestions for Writing

1. As the narrator listens to the cry of the loons, she thinks, "No one can ever describe that ululating sound . . . plaintive, and yet with a quality of chilling mockery." Describe the sounds and sights of nature that have impressed you. Create a poem by

using a new line for each image. Describe each sight or sound so that it appeals to as many of your reader's senses as possible. Here is an example:

> The steady rhythm of the rain beating on the window,
> The sun setting in a blaze of molten gold,
> Large footsteps on wet sand,
> The howling wind lashing my face,
> The swish of skis skimming over the crunching, crystal snow.

2. While telling her daughter about Piquette's death, the narrator's mother says: "I couldn't help wondering if we could have done something more at that time." Reread the scene in the story between Piquette and the narrator at Diamond Lake, from the narrator's asking "Do you like this place?" to Piquette's reply "Not me. . . . You wouldn' catch me walkin' way down there jus' for a bunch of squawkin' birds." Add another scene of dialogue between the two girls that does not end with Piquette's rejection and in which they reach some degree of understanding and friendship.

3. Of her home in Diamond Lake, the narrator tells Piquette, "I love it." Examine the details that suggest her love for the area. Select a passage as a model and describe a place you appreciate.

Examining Social Issues

1. Piquette's marriage to an Anglo-Saxon Canadian does not survive. Why do you think it failed? Can interracial marriages survive? Why or why not?

2. Who was responsible for the Tonnerre family's condition, the community, the government, or the Tonnerres themselves? Give reasons for your opinion.

3. The Tonnerres, as Metis, are neither Cree nor French. Would their lives have been improved if they had been living on the Galloping Mountain reservation? Why or why not?

Grids and Doglegs

Clark Blaise

Clark Blaise is a French-Canadian novelist and short-story writer born in Quebec. While he was still a child, his family emigrated to the United States and, in their search for economic stability, lived in many cities. His early history, then, enables him to portray what it means to be an alien.

"Grids and Doglegs" appeared in Blaise's collection Tribal Justice *(1974). The characters in these stories, mostly adolescents, must adjust to an America divided into diverse, isolated groups suspicious of one another. When someone from one group penetrates another, the intruder encounters a "strange justice." Blaise identifies these intruders by their vulnerability, their need to be loved. Rejected, they tend to strike out blindly against family, peers, strangers. The stories portray the feeling of being a different kind of teenager – an outsider in a community of peers.*

Blaise's stories are joltingly alive. Like autobiography, they portray pockets of chaotic life that move the story forward. And again like autobiography, they convey the sensation of living at a certain time in a certain place without seeming to enclose the experience in the structure of a story. A narrator in one of Blaise's stories speaks for him when he says, "I used to write miniature novels, vividly imagined, set anywhere my imagination moved me. Then something slipped. I started writing of myself and these vivid moments in a confusing flux."

The narrator in "Grids and Doglegs" experiences such "vivid moments" and records them with striking immediacy.

When I was sixteen I could spend whole evenings with a straight-edge, a pencil, and a few sheets of unlined construction paper, and with those tools I would lay out imaginary cities along twisting rivers or ragged coastlines. Centuries of expansion and division, terrors of fire and renewal, recorded in the primitive fiction of gaps and clusters, grids and doglegs. My cities were tangles; inevitably, like Pittsburgh. And as I built my cities, I'd keep the Pirates game on (in another notebook I kept running accounts of my team's declining fortune – "Well, Tony Bartirome, that knocks you down to .188" – the pre-game averages were never exact enough for me), and during the summers I excavated for the Department of Man, Carnegie Museum. Twice a week during the winter I visited the Casino Burlesque (this a winter pleasure, to counter the loss of baseball). I was a painter too, of sweeping subjects: my paleobotanical murals for the Devonian Fishes Hall are still a model for younger painter-excavators. (Are there others, still, like me, in Pittsburgh? This story is for them.) On Saturdays I lectured to the Junior Amateur Archaeologists and Anthropologists of Western Pennsylvania. I was a high school junior, my parents worked at their new store, and I was, obviously, mostly alone. In the afternoons, winter and summer, I picked up dirty clothes for my father's laundry.

I had – obviously, again – very few friends; there were not many boys like me. Fat, but without real bulk, arrogant but ridiculously shy. Certifiably brilliant but hopelessly unstudious, I felt unallied to even the conventionally bright honor-rollers in my suburban high school. Keith Godwin was my closest friend; I took three meals a week at his house, and usually slept over on Friday night.

Keith's father was a chemist with Alcoa; his mother a pillar of the local United Presbyterian Church, the Women's Club, and the University Women's chapter; and the four children (all but Keith, the oldest) were models of charm, ambition, and beauty. Keith was a moon-faced redhead with freckles and dimples – one would never suspect the depth of his cynicism – with just two real passions: the organ and competitive chess. I have seen him win five simultaneous blindfold games, ten-second moves – against tournament competition. We used to play at the dinner table without the board, calling out our moves while shoveling in the food. Years later, high school atheism behind him, he enrolled in a Presbyterian seminary of Calvinist persuasions and is now a minister somewhere in California. He leads a number of extremist campaigns (crackpot drives, to be exact), against education, books, movies, minorities, pacifists – this, too, was a part of our rebellion, though I've turned the opposite way. But this isn't a story about Keith. He had a sister, Cyndy, one year younger.

She was tall, like her father, about five-eight, an inch taller than I. Hers was the beauty of contrasts: fair skin, dark hair, gray eyes, and the sharpness of features so common in girls who take after their fathers. Progressively I was to desire her as a sister, then wife, and finally as lover; but by then, of course, it was too late. I took a fix on her, and she guided me through high school; no matter how far out I veered, the hope of eventually pleasing Cyndy drove me back.

100

In the summer of my junior year, I put away the spade, my collection of pots and flints, and took up astronomy. There's a romance to astronomy, an almost courtly type of pain and fascination, felt by all who study it. The excitement: that like a character in the childhood comics, I could shrink myself and dismiss the petty frustrations of school, the indifference of Cyndy and my parents; that I could submit to points of light long burned-out and be rewarded with their cosmic tolerance of my obesity, ridicule from the athletes in the lunch line, and the Pirates' latest losing streak. I memorized all I could from the basic texts at Carnegie Library, and shifted my allegiance from Carnegie Museum to Buhl Planetarium. There was a workshop in the basement just getting going, started for teen-age telescope-builders, and I became a charter member.

Each week I ground out my lens; glass over glass through gritty water, one night a week for at least a year. Fine precise work, never my style, but I stuck with it while most of the charter enthusiasts fell away. The abrasive carborundum grew finer, month by month, from sand, to talc, to rouge – a single fleck of a coarser grade in those final months would have plundered my mirror like a meteorite. Considering the winter nights on which I sacrificed movies and TV for that lens, the long streetcar rides, the aching arches, the insults from the German shop foreman, the meticulous scrubbing-down after each Wednesday session, the temptation to sneak upstairs for the "Skyshow" with one of the chubby compliant girls – my alter egos – from the Jewish high school: *considering all that*, plus the all-important exclusiveness and recognition it granted, that superb instrument was a heavy investment to sell, finally, for a mere three hundred dollars. But I did, in the fine-polishing stage, because, I felt, I owed it to Cyndy. Three hundred dollars, for a new investment in myself.

Astronomy is the moral heavyweight of the physical sciences; it is a humiliating science, a destroyer of pride in human achievements, or shame in human failings. Compared to the vacant dimensions of space – of time, distance, and temperature – what could be felt for Eisenhower's heart attack, Grecian urns, six million Jews, my waddle and shiny gabardines? My parents were nearing separation, their store beginning to falter – what could I care for their silence, their fights, the begging for bigger and bigger loans? The diameter of Antares, the Messier system, the swelling of space into uncreated nothingness – these things mattered because they were large, remote and perpetual. The Tammany Ring and follies of Hitler, Shakespeare, and the Constitution were dust; the Andromeda galaxy was *worlds*. I took my meals out or with the Godwins, and I thought of these things as I struggled at chess with Keith and caught glimpses of Cyndy as she dried the dishes – if only I'd had dishes to dry!

The arrogance of astronomy, archaeology, chess, burlesque, baseball, science-fiction, everything I cared for: humility and arrogance are often so close (the men I'm writing this for – who once painted murals and played in high school bands just to feel a part of something – they know); it's all the same feeling, isn't it? Nothing matters, except, perhaps, the proper irony. I had that irony once (I wish, in fact, I had it now), and it was something like this:

In the days of the fifties, each home room of each suburban high school started the day with a Bible reading and the pledge of allegiance to the flag. Thirty mumbling sounds, one fervent old woman, and me. It had taken me one night, five years earlier, to learn the Lord's Prayer backwards. I had looked up, as well, the Russian pledge and gotten it translated into English: this did for my daily morning ablutions. The lone difficulty had to do with Bible Week, which descended without warning on a Monday morning with the demand that we, in turn, quote a snatch from the Bible. This is fine if one's name is Zymurgy and you've had a chance to memorize everyone else's favorite, or the shortest verse. But I am a Dyer, and preceded often by Cohens and Bernsteins (more on that later): Bible Week often caught me unprepared. So it happened in the winter of my senior year that Marvin Bernstein was excused ("We won't ask Marvin, class, for he is of a different faith. Aren't you, Marvin?") and then a ruffian named Callahan rattled off a quick, "For God so loved the world that he gave his only begotten Son . . ." so fast that I couldn't catch it. A Sheila Cohen, whose white bra straps I'd stared at for one hour a day, five days a week, for three years – Sheila Cohen was excused. And Norman Dyer, I, stood. "Remember, Norman," said the teacher, "I won't have the Lord's Prayer and the Twenty-second Psalm." She didn't like Callahan's rendition either, and knew she'd get thirty more. From me she expected originality. I didn't disappoint.

"Om," I said, and quickly sat. I'd learned it from the Vedanta, something an astronomer studies.

Her smile had frozen. It was her habit, after a recitation, to smile and nod and congratulate us with, "Ah, yes, Revelations, a lovely choice, Nancy . . ." But gathering her pluckiness she demanded, "Just what is that supposed to mean, Norman?"

"Everything," I said, with an astronomer's shrug. I was preparing a justification, something to do with more people in the world praying "Om" than anything else, but I had never caused trouble before, and she decided to drop it. She called on my alphabetical shadow (a boy who'd stared for three years at my dandruff and flaring ears?), another Catholic, Dykes was his name, and Dykes this time, instead of following Callahan, twisted the knife a little deeper, and boomed out, "Om . . . amen!" Our teacher shut the Bible, caressed the marker, the white leather binding, and then read us a long passage having to do, as I recall, with nothing we had said.

That was the only victory of my high school years.

I imagined a hundred disasters a day that would wash Cyndy Godwin into my arms, grateful and bedraggled. Keith never suspected. My passion had a single outlet – the telephone. Alone in my parents' duplex, the television on, the Pirates game on, I would phone. No need to check the dial, the fingering was instinctive. Two rings at the Godwins'; if anyone but Cyndy answered, I'd hang up immediately. But with Cyndy I'd hold, through her perplexed "Hellos?" till she queried, "Susie, is that you?" "Brenda?" "Who is it, please?" and I would hold until her voice betrayed fear beyond the irritation. Oh, the pleasure of her slightly hysterical voice, "Daddy, it's that *man* again," and I would sniffle menacingly into the mouthpiece. Then I'd hang up and it was over; like a Pirates loss, nothing to do but wait for tomorrow. Cyndy would answer the phone perhaps twice a week. Added to the three meals a week I took with them, I convinced myself that five sightings or soundings a week would eventually cinch a marriage if I but waited for a sign she'd surely give me. She was of course dating a bright, good-looking boy a year ahead of me (already at Princeton), a conventional sort of doctor-to-be, active in Scouts, Choir, Sports, and Junior Achievement, attending Princeton on the annual Kiwanis Fellowship. A very common type in our school and suburb, easily tolerated and easily dismissed. Clearly, a girl of Cyndy's sensitivity could not long endure his ministerial humor, his mere ignorance disguised as modesty. Everything about him – good looks, activities, athletics, piety, manners – spoke against him. In those years the only competition for Cyndy that I might have feared would have come from someone of my own circle. And that was impossible, for none of us had ever had a date.

And I knew her like a brother! Hours spent with her playing Scrabble, driving her to the doctor's for curious flaws I was never to learn about . . . and, in the summers, accompanying the family to their cabin and at night hearing her breathing beyond a burlap wall . . . Like a brother? Not even that, for as I write I remember Keith grabbing her on the stairs, slamming his open hands against her breasts, and Cyndy responding, while I ached to save her, "Keith! What will Normie think?" And this went on for three years, from the first evening I ate with the Godwins when I was in tenth grade, till the spring semester of my senior year; Cyndy was a junior. There was no drama, no falling action, merely a sweet and painful stasis that I aggrandized with a dozen readings of *Cyrano de Bergerac*, and a customizing of his soliloquies . . . "This butt that follows me by half an hour . . . An ass, you say? Say rather a caboose, a dessert . . ." All of this was bound to end, only when I could break the balance.

We are back to the telescope, the three hundred well-earned dollars. Some kids I knew, Keith not included this time, took over the school printing press and ran off one thousand dramatic broadsheets, condemning a dozen teachers for incompetence and Lesbianism (a word that we knew meant more than "an inhabitant of Lesbos," the definition in our high school dictionary). We were caught, we proudly confessed (astronomy again: I sent a copy to *Mad* magazine and they wrote back, *"funny, but don't get caught. You might end up working for a joint like this"*). The school wrote letters to every college that had so greedily accepted us a few weeks earlier, calling on them to retract their acceptance until we publicly apologized. Most of us did, for what good it did; I didn't – it made very little difference anyway, since my parents no longer could have afforded Yale. It would be Penn State in September.

I awoke one morning in April – a gorgeous morning – and decided to diet. A doctor in Squirrel Hill made his living prescribing amphetamines by the carload to suburban matrons. I lost thirty pounds in a month and a half, which dropped me into the ranks of the flabby underweights (funny, I'd always believed there was a *hard* me, under the fat, waiting to be sculpted out – there wasn't).

Tight new khakis and my first sweaters were now a part of the "New Look" Norman Dyer, which I capped one evening by calling the Arthur Murray Studios. I earned a free dance analysis by answering correctly a condescending question from their television quiz the night before. Then, with the three hundred dollars, I enrolled.

I went to three studio parties, each time with the enormous kid sister of my voluptuous instructress. That gigantic adolescent with a baby face couldn't dance a step (and had been brought along for me, I was certain), and her slimmed-down but still ample sister took on only her fellow teachers and some older, lonelier types, much to my relief. I wanted to dance, but not to be noticed. The poor big-little sister, whose name was Almajean, was dropping out of a mill-town high school in a year to become . . . what? I can't guess, and she didn't know, even then. We drank a lot of punch, shuffled together when we had to, and I told her about delivering clothes, something she could respect me for, never admitting that my father owned the store.

But I knew what I had to do. For my friends there was a single event in our high school careers that *had*, above all, to be missed. We had avoided every athletic contest, every dance, pep rally, party – everything voluntary and everything mildly compulsory; we had our private insurrections against the flag and God, but all that good work, all that conscientious effort, would be wasted if we attended the flurry of dances in our last two weeks. The Senior Prom was no problem – I'd been barred because of the newspaper caper. But a week later came the Women's Club College Prom, for everyone going on to higher study (92 per cent always did). The pressure for a 100 per cent turn-out was stifling. Even the teachers wore WC buttons so we wouldn't forget. Home room teachers managed to find out who was still uninvited (no one to give Sheila Cohen's bra a snap?). The College Prom combined the necessary exclusiveness and sophistication – smoking was permitted on the balcony – to have become the very essence of graduation night. And there was a special feature that we high schoolers had heard about ever since the eighth grade: the sifting of seniors into a few dozen booths, right on the dance floor, to meet local alums of their college-to-be, picking up a few fraternity bids, athletic money, while the band played a medley of privileged alma maters. I recalled the pain I had felt a year before, as I watched Cyndy leave with her then-senior boy friend, and I was still there playing chess, when they returned around 2 A.M., for punch.

It took three weeks of aborted phone calls before I asked Cyndy to the College Prom. She of course accepted. Her steady boy friend was already at Princeton and ineligible. According to Keith, he'd left instructions: nothing serious. What did *he* know of seriousness, I thought, making my move. I bought a dinner jacket, dancing shoes, shirt, links, studs, cummerbund, and got ten dollars spending money from my astonished father. I was seventeen, and this was my first date.

Cyndy was a beautiful *woman* that night; it was the first time I'd seen her consciously glamorous. The year before she'd been a girl, well turned-out, but a trifle thin and shaky. But not tonight!

Despite the glistening car and my flashy clothes, my new near-mesomorphy, I felt like a worm as I slipped the white orchid corsage around her wrist. (I could have had a bosom corsage; when the florist suggested it, I nearly ran from the shop. What if I jabbed her, right *there*?) And I could have cried at the trouble she'd gone to, *for me*: her hair was up, she wore glittering earrings and a pale sophisticated lipstick that made her lips look chapped. And, mercifully, flat heels. The Godwin family turned out for our departure, so happy that I had asked her, so respectful of my sudden self-assurance. Her father told me to stay out as long as we wished. Keith and the rest of my friends were supposedly at the movies, but had long been planning, I knew, for the milkman's matinee at the Casino Burlesque. I appreciated not having to face him – wondering, in fact, how I ever would again. My best-kept secret was out (Oh, the ways they have of getting us kinky people straightened out!); but she was mine tonight, the purest, most beautiful, the *kindest* girl I'd ever met. And for the first time, for the briefest instant, I connected her to those familiar bodies of the strippers I knew so well, and suddenly I felt that I knew what this dating business was all about and why it excited everyone so. I understood how thrilling it must be actually to touch, and kiss, and look at naked, a beautiful woman whom you loved, and who might touch you back.

The ballroom of the Woman's Club was fussily decorated; dozens of volunteers had worked all week. Clusters of spotlights strained through the sagging roof of crepe (the lights blue-filtered, something like the Casino), and the couples in formal gowns and dinner jackets seemed suddenly worthy of college and the professional lives they were destined to enter. A few people stared at Cyndy and smirked at me, and I began to feel a commingling of pride and shame, mostly the latter.

We danced a little – rumbas were my best – but mainly talked, drinking punch and nibbling the rich sugar cookies that her mother, among so many others, had helped to bake. We talked soberly, of my enforced retreat from the Ivy League (not even the car stealers and petty criminals on the fringe of our suburban society had been treated as harshly as I), of Keith's preparation for Princeton. Her gray eyes never left me. I talked of other friends, two who were leaving for a summer in Paris, to polish their French before entering Yale. Cyndy listened to it all, with her cool hand on my wrist. "How I wish Keith had taken someone tonight!" she exclaimed.

Then at last came the finale of the dance: everyone to the center of the floor, everyone once by the reviewing stand, while the orchestra struck up a medley of collegiate tunes. "Hail to Pitt!" cried the president of the Woman's Club, and Pitt's incoming freshmen, after whirling past the bandstand, stopped at an adjoining booth, signed a book, and collected their name tags. The rousing music blared on, the fight songs of Yale and Harvard, Duquesne and Carnegie Tech, Penn State, Wash and Jeff, Denison and Wesleyan . . .

"Come on, Normie, we can go outside," she suggested. We had just passed under the reviewing stand, where the three judges were standing impassively. Something about the King and Queen; nothing I'd been let in on. The dance floor was thinning as the booths filled. I broke the dance-stride and began walking her out, only to be reminded by the WC president, straining above "Going Back to Old Nassau," to keep on dancing, please. The panel of judges – two teachers selected by the students, and Mr. Hartman, husband of the club's president – were already on the dance floor, smiling at the couples and poking their heads into the clogged booths. Cyndy and I were approaching the doors, near the bruisers in my Penn State booth. One of the algebra teachers was racing toward us, a wide grin on his florid face, and Cyndy gave my hand a tug. "Normie," she whispered, "I think something wonderful is about to happen."

The teacher was with us, a man much shorter than Cyndy, who panted, "Congratulations! You're my choice." He held a wreath of roses above her head, and she lowered her head to receive it. "Ah – what is your name?"

"Cyndy Godwin," she said, "Mr. Esposito."

"Keith Godwin's sister?"

"Yes."

"And how are you, Norman – or should I ask?" Mr. Wheeler, my history teacher, shouldered his way over to us; he held out a bouquet of yellow mums. "Two out of three," he grinned, "that should just about do it."

"Do what?" I asked. I wanted to run, but felt too sick. Cyndy squeezed my cold hand; the orchid nuzzled me like a healthy dog. My knees were numb, face burning.

"Cinch it," said Wheeler, "King Dyer."

"If Hartman comes up with someone else, then there'll be a vote," Esposito explained. "If he hasn't been bribed, then he'll choose this girl too and that'll be it."

I have never prayed harder. Wheeler led us around the main

dance floor, by the rows of chairs that were now empty. The musicians suspended the Cornell evening hymn to enable the WC president to announce dramatically, in her most practiced voice, "The Queen approaches."

There was light applause from the far end of the floor. Couples strained from the college booths as we passed, and I could hear the undertone, ". . . he's a brain in my biology class, Norman something-or-other, but I don't know her . . ." I don't *have* to be here, I reminded myself. No one made me bring her. I could have asked one of the girls from the Planetarium who respected me for my wit and memory alone – or I could be home like any other self-respecting intellectual, in a cold sweat over *I Led Three Lives*. The Pirates were playing a twi-nighter and I could have been out there at Forbes Field in my favorite right-field upperdeck, where I'm an expert . . . why didn't I ask her out to a baseball game? Or I could have been where I truly belonged, with my friends down at the Casino Burlesque. . . .

"You'll lead the next dance, of course," Wheeler whispered. Cyndy was ahead of us, with Esposito.

"Couldn't someone else?" I said. "Maybe you – why not you?" Then I said with sudden inspiration, "She's not a senior. I don't think she's eligible, do you?"

"Don't worry, don't worry, Norman." I had been one of his favorite pupils. "Her class hasn't a thing to do with it, just her looks. And Norman" – he smiled confidentially – "she's an extraordinarily beautiful girl."

"Yeah," I agreed, had to. I drifted to the stairs by the bandstand. "I'm going to check anyway," I said. I ran to Mrs. Hartman herself. "Juniors aren't eligible to be Queen, are they? I mean, she'll get her own chance next year when she's going to college, right?"

Her smile melted as she finally looked at me; she had been staring into the lights, planning her speech. "Is her escort a senior?"

"Yes," I admitted, "but *he* wasn't chosen. Anyway, he's one of those guys who were kept from the Prom. By rights I don't think he should even be here."

"I don't think this has ever come up before." She squinted into the footlights, a well-preserved woman showing strain. "I presume you're a class officer."

"No, I'm her escort."

"Her *escort*? I'm afraid I don't understand. Do I know the girl?"

"Cyndy Godwin?"

"You don't mean Betsy Godwin's girl? Surely I'm not to take the prize away from that lovely girl, just because – well, just because *why* for heaven's sake?"

The bandleader leaned over and asked if he should start the "Miss America" theme. Mrs. Hartman fluttered her hand. And then from the other side of the stand, the third judge, Mr. Hartman, hissed to his wife. "Here she is," he beamed.

"Oh, dear me," began Mrs. Hartman.

"A vote?" I suggested. "It has to be democratic."

The second choice, a peppy redhead named Paula, innocently followed Mr. Hartman up the stairs and was already smiling like a winner. She was a popular senior, co-vice-president of nearly everything. Oh, poise! Glorious confidence! Already the front rows were applauding the apparent Queen, though she had only Mr. Hartman's slender cluster of roses to certify her. Now the band started up, the applause grew heavy, and a few enthusiasts even whistled. Her escort, a union leader's son, took his place behind her, and I cheerfully backed off the bandstand, joining Cyndy and the teachers at the foot of the steps. Cyndy had returned her flowers, and Mr. Wheeler was standing dejectedly behind her, holding the bouquet. The wreath dangled from his wrist.

"I feel like a damn fool," he said.

"That was very sweet of you, Normie," Cyndy said, and kissed me hard on the cheek.

"I just can't get over it," Wheeler went on, "if anyone here deserves that damn thing, it's you. At least take the flowers."

I took them for her. "Would you like to go?" I asked. She took my arm and we walked out. I left the flowers on an empty chair.

I felt more at ease as we left the school and headed across the street to the car. It was a cool night, and Cyndy was warm at my side, holding my arm tightly. "Let's have something to eat," I suggested, having practiced the line a hundred times, though it still sounded badly acted. I had planned the dinner as well; *filet mignon* on toast at a classy restaurant out on the highway. I hadn't planned it for quite so early in the night, but even so, I was confident. A girl like Cyndy ate out perhaps once or twice a year, and had probably never ordered *filet*. I was more at home in a fancy restaurant than at a family table.

"I think I'd like that," she said.

"What happened in there was silly – just try to forget all about it," I said. "It's some crazy rule or something."

We walked up a side street, past a dozen cars strewn with crepe.

"It's not winning so much," she said, "It's just an embarrassing thing walking up there like that and then being left holding the flowers."

"There's always next year."

"Oh, I won't get it again. There are lots of prettier girls than me in my class."

An opening, I thought. So easy to tell her that she was a queen, deservedly, any place. But I couldn't even slip my arm around her waist, or take her hand that rested on my sleeve.

"Well, I think you're really pretty." And I winced.

"Thank you, Norman."

"Prettier than anyone I've ever – "

"I understand," she said. Then she took my hand and pointed it above the streetlights. "I'll bet you know all those stars, don't you, Normie?"

"Sure."

"You and Keith – you're going to be really something someday."

We came to the car; I opened Cyndy's door and she got in. "Normie?" she said, as she smoothed her skirt before I closed the door, "could we hurry? I've got to use the bathroom."

I held the door open a second. *How dare she*, I thought, that's not what she's supposed to say. This is a date; you're a queen, my own queen. I looked at the sidewalk, a few feet ahead of us, then said suddenly, bitterly, "There's a hydrant up there. Why don't you use it?"

I slapped the headlights as I walked to my side, hoping they would shatter and I could bleed to death.

"That wasn't a very nice thing to say, Norman," she said as I sat down.

"I know."

"A girl who didn't know you better might have gotten offended."

I drove carefully, afraid now on this night of calamity that I might be especially accident-prone. It was all too clear now, why she had gone with me. Lord, protect me from a too-easy forgiveness. In the restaurant parking lot, I told her how sorry I was for everything, without specifying how broad an everything I was sorry for.

"You were a perfect date," she said. "Come on, let's forget about everything, O.K.?"

Once inside, she went immediately to the powder room. The hostess, who knew me, guided me to a table at the far end of the main dining room. She would bring Cyndy to me. My dinner jacket attracted some attention; people were already turning to look for my date. I sat down; water was poured for two, a salad bowl appeared. When no one was looking, I pounded the table. *Years of this*, I thought: slapping headlights, kicking tables, wanting to scream a memory out of existence, wanting to shrink back into the stars, the quarries, the right-field stands – things that could no longer contain me. A smiling older man from the table across the aisle snapped his fingers and pointed to his cheek, then to mine, and winked. "Lipstick!" he finally whispered, no longer smiling. I had begun to wet the napkin when I saw Cyndy and the hostess approaching – and the excitement that followed in Cyndy's wake. I stood to meet her. She was the Queen, freshly beautiful, and as I walked to her she took a hanky from her purse and pressed it to her lips. Then in front of everyone, she touched the moistened hanky to my cheek, and we turned to take our places.

Questions for Writing and Discussion

Discovering Meaning

1. In the opening paragraph, the narrator is laying out imaginary cities in grids and doglegs. Relate the title and the opening to his hobbies, his interests, and his relationship with Cyndy.
2. The narrator describes himself as "arrogant but ridiculously shy . . . certifiably brilliant but hopelessly unstudious." Where are these traits revealed in the story?
3. Why does the narrator spoil Cyndy's chance of winning the title of Queen at the dance?
4. After they leave the dance, why is the narrator frustrated and angry?

Exploring Method

1. The author uses the first-person reflective point of view to tell his story; that is, the narrator recollects each episode of his earlier life in high school and interprets it before he proceeds to the next one. What is the effect on the reader of this method of telling the story?
2. Examine the passages in parentheses. What insight does each provide into the adult narrator looking back at his adolescent experience? How do these interruptions affect your response to the narrator? Do they draw you closer to him or distance you from him? Why?
3. After the narrator's account of building a telescope and selling it, he refers to a three-hundred-dollar investment that he made

on himself. But before he returns to this episode, he recalls two earlier experiences – his rebellion against "Bible Week" and his anonymous phone calls to Cyndy. How do these intervening episodes prepare the reader for his behaviour at the dance and after it?

Suggestions for Writing

1. Examine the narrator's thoughts while waiting for Cyndy in the restaurant, in the sentence, *"Years of this . . .* things that could no longer contain me." Are such impulses to strike out at victims and the longing to "shrink back into the stars," to escape one's identity and become a part of the impersonal world in moments of crisis, typical of teenage feelings or characteristic only of this narrator? Describe a moment of frustration that you experienced and your response. Include details that will help your reader share your experience.
2. The narrator believes that "astronomy is the moral heavy-weight of the physical sciences"; it is "humiliating." Why does he come to this conclusion? What are the attractions of astronomy for him? Select an interest or hobby and describe its attraction for you.
3. The narrator says, "Humility and arrogance are often so close (the men I'm writing this for – who once painted murals and played in high school bands just to feel a part of something – they know)." Does this description apply to anyone you know? Write a narrative putting yourself or another character in a situation to which your response was arrogance to conceal insecurity.

Examining Social Issues

1. What is your view of Cyndy's behaviour in the story? How do you assess her relationship with the narrator and her concept of herself?
2. The narrator and his friends frequently visit the Casino Burlesque. On his first date, when Cyndy appears dressed for the College Prom, the narrator thinks, "For the first time, for the briefest instant, I connected her to those familiar bodies of strippers I knew so well, and suddenly I felt that I knew what this dating business was all about and why it excited everyone so. I understood how thrilling it must be actually to touch, and kiss, and look at naked, a beautiful woman whom you loved, and who might touch you back." What is your view of the influ-

ence on teenage behaviour of explicit sexual displays in magazines and in movies?

3. In describing his behaviour in class, the narrator observes, "I had that irony once"; that is, as a teenager he was able to expose the absurdity of illogical or harmful customs. Then he adds, "(I wish, in fact, I had it now)." As an adult he has lost the will to attack outdated or harmful customs. Are adults more timid social critics than teenagers? Why or why not?

4. Why does the narrator rebel against "Bible Week"? What is your view of Bible reading and prayer at school?

5. The narrator is a curious, intelligent, imaginative sixteen-year-old, yet he is by his own admission "hopelessly unstudious" and a rebel. What can high schools do to sustain the gifted student's interest in school?

6. The narrator observes that in the suburban high school he attends, 92 per cent of students go on to higher study. He suggests that students are pressured to go to university. Does such pressure still exist in high school? What is your view of schools' and parents' pressures on high school graduates to go on to university? What are the alternatives to enrolling in university directly after high school? Evaluate each option.

The Immortals

Ed Kleiman

Ed Kleiman, the author of "The Immortals" (1976), was born in the North End of Winnipeg, the area he describes in his story. He brings its vitality, its seething energy, to life in his catalogue of its residents and their activities: "labouring classes, small foreign-language newspapers, watch-maker shops, a Jewish theatrical company, a Ukrainian dance troupe, small choirs, tap-dancing schools, orchestral groups, chess clubs, and more radical political thinkers per square block than Soviet Russia had known before the Revolution." Set against these vibrant survivors are the residents of the fashionable South End, respectable, immaculate, powerful. In this context, the central episode in the story, the football game, becomes more than an athletic event. It is a battle of the poor against the affluent members of the establishment. In this setting, Kleiman dramatizes the outrageously comic football game.

Many critics have tried to define comedy through its tendency to evoke laughter. Although laughter is not the sole purpose of comedy, it frequently accompanies it. Comedy is based on the need to merge our lives with the lives of other people rather than to guard our separateness, our individuality, as in tragedy. It implies that we need to adjust our wills and even our characters to the community in which, by choice or by necessity, we live.

The kind of comedy in which laughter is the sole purpose is called farce. In this form of humour, situations contrast sharply with the way life normally runs. The laughter that farce evokes can be refreshing because it gives us a holiday from life as it is. Farce may occur in comedy where scenes are impossibly at odds with ordinary human life.

A further element in comedy is the picaresque – the story about the rogue who makes his way in society. In such stories, our sympathy is engaged because we tend to sympathize with the underdog, the little man. Besides, we derive a flattering awareness, through the hero's adventures, that although we are little and helpless, our spirits are not defeated by those in positions of power. Charlie Chaplin is the classic picaresque hero – he is the little tramp who manages to survive his adventures with his dignity intact. The picaresque hero stirs our feeling of empathy because

we discover in him a little of the scapegoat. Watching him over-
come his anxieties and tensions, we are able to lessen our own feel-
ings of inadequacy just a little. But the picaresque hero appeals to
another habit of mind: the desire to shed the responsibility we owe
to society without paying a severe price.

The charm, then, in Kleiman's football game lies in its comic ele-
ments, which evoke laughter because of the game's incongruities.
We find the North End players so endearing because they contain
aspects of the picaresque hero – they engage our sympathy with the
underdog and appeal to our underground impulses to rebel
against duty.

For days in the early fall of forty-nine, St. John's High had
buzzed with rumours about whether or not Torchy Brownstone
would be allowed to play in the football game on Friday. Torchy
was our first-string quarterback, a two-year veteran with the
school, and if we were to have any chance of beating Kelvin – our
arch-rivals from River Heights – then the team could not afford to
see him sidelined with a knee injury. The injury had been sus-
tained in a practice session last week when a second-string line-
backer had gotten carried away with enthusiasm and tackled
Torchy just as he was coming around the end on a double reverse.
So one of our own players had done what the rest of the league
would've been trying to do all through the fall.

What hurt the most was that Torchy should be sidelined when
we were playing Kelvin. The game itself didn't count for anything. It was an exhibition game, a warm-up before the regular
season began. But what did count was that this was a contest between the North and South ends of the city. And that was no small
matter.

The North End consisted mainly of immigrants from Eastern
Europe, labouring classes, small foreign-language newspapers,
watch-maker shops, a Jewish theatrical company, a Ukrainian
dance troupe, small choirs, tap-dancing schools, orchestral
groups, chess clubs, and more radical political thinkers per
square block than Soviet Russia had known before the Revolution. The South End – or River Heights, as it is more fashionably
called – was basically what that revolution had been against. The
mayor, most of the aldermen, the chairman of the school board,
and many of the civic employees – not the street sweepers, of
course – lived in River Heights.

Actually, when you think about it, they had chosen a curious
name for their end of town. If you've ever passed through Winni-

peg, you'll realize that it rests on one of the flattest stretches of land in the world. In fact, I read in the school library once that the land falls at the rate of no more than two feet per mile as it extends northward toward Lake Winnipeg. So the Heights, you see, can't amount to much more than six or eight feet, at the most. But people there like to think of themselves as living on a plateau overlooking the rest of the city, as in a sense they do. For the heights they've attained are built on political and economical foundations that give them a vantage point of something like six or eight hundred feet.

Another way of distinguishing between the two parts of the city is by looking at the street names. In the North End, you'll find such names as Selkirk Ave., Euclid St., Aberdeen, Dufferin – names steeped in history, names which suggest the realm of human endeavour, anguish, accomplishment. But if you look at the street names in River Heights, what you'll find, with few exceptions, are such names as Ash St., Elm, Oak, Maple. Vast expanses of velvet lawns, well-treed boulevards – the area looks like a garden, a retreat from the toil and anguish everywhere visible in the North End. The two cultures meet downtown, where the South End gentry immediately head for the managerial offices, and the North End rabble file past the company clocks with their time cards. After work countless numbers of expensive cars sweep grandly across the Maryland Bridge back into Eden, while street cars and buses pass northward beneath the CPR subway into a grim bleak underworld of steel fences, concrete walls, locked doors, and savage dogs that seem capable of looking in three directions at once.

But at the Osborne Stadium in the fall, the traditional roles can be reversed for an evening. There, on Friday nights, the North End may once more experience the heady hours of triumph it knew during the 1919 Strike, when it seemed the World Revolution might begin right here in Winnipeg. So, you see, the fact that Torchy Brownstone had injured his knee in football practice was of major concern to us all.

And then to add insult to injury, the English teacher Mr. Rockwood caught our star tackles, Norm Mittlehaus and Sam Markewicz, in Room 41 the day before the game and tried to have them disqualified from playing on Friday. Room 41 is Goldman's Drugstore – just across the street from the high school – and kids are always sneaking across during the day to have a soda, read a magazine, or have a smoke. And Rockwood is always catching them. Rockwood is about five foot two and weighs about a hundred and eighty, so he's a fairly stocky little guy with huge shoulders and a neck like a bull dog. Needless to say, Rockwood lives in River Heights, and he would have still been teaching at Kelvin if he hadn't swatted one of his pupils one day – the son of a school trustee, as it turned out – and since then he's been our affliction. He often tries to have kids expelled, banned from writing exams, or disqualified from playing football – which drives the football coach, Mr. Powalski, wild. It always seemed to us that Mr. Rockwood would have been much happier, would have felt more free to express himself, and would have achieved a greater degree of fulfillment if he'd been a guard at Auschwitz.

Anyway, as soon as Mr. Powalski learned that Rockwood had disqualified our star tackles Mittlehaus and Markewicz from playing the next night, he rushed up to the principal's office and threatened to resign – again, for what must have been the tenth time that year – if they weren't reinstated.

On the Friday night of the game, the stands were packed. Would Torchy play? And what about Mittlehaus and Markewicz? Even I came to the game that night, and I rarely go to football games – or any kind of sports event for that matter. I'm more interested in the finer things in life, in art and poetry, and all my evenings then were taken up by an epic poem in hexameters I was working on. But the whole school was caught up in the game that night, and Joel Greenberg, my partner in Chem. lab who was running for student president, finally persuaded me that I couldn't stay behind.

So there we all were, glaring across the field at the River Heights stands, where, sitting shamelessly among the staunch supporters of the opposing team, we could make out Rockwood; Peg-Leg Dobson – our Physics teacher; Mr. Atkinson – our Chemistry teacher; and Mr. Clearwater – the principal. Still, Kleinberg, Schultz, Rasmussen, and Pollick – all loyal North Enders – had stationed themselves prominently in our end of the stadium.

Rumours abounded. Kelvin was supposed to have all-new football equipment donated by the president of a huge department store. It was also whispered that the team had been practising secret plays to be unveiled that night. They had a new fullback – a huge 200 pounder, who would make mincemeat of our line. And, most ominous of all, there was talk that the chief referee had bet $5.00 on the River Heights team.

But each new rumour of impending doom simply sent our spirits soaring higher. We shouted taunts across the field, blew up Sheiks and let them float skyward, unveiled posters that displayed a hammer and sickle beneath which were the words "Workers, Arise!", bombarded the officials with over-ripe tomatoes and rotten eggs which we'd saved especially for the occasion, and flung rolls of toilet paper into the playing area. Until an exasperated voice in an Oxford accent that had obviously just been acquired that summer asked us all to stand for the National Anthem.

Then the whistle blew, and we kicked off to Kelvin and, to our horror, that 200-pound fullback really did exist because he caught the ball and ran over three of our tacklers for a touchdown. Less than sixty seconds after the game had started, they had six points and we had three injuries. Suddenly our players in their ripped sweaters and torn pads looked like a pretty shabby lot in comparison with that Kelvin team, which moved with such military precision in their new uniforms and shiny helmets.

On the next kick-off, our star runner, Cramer, caught the football, and was promptly tackled by their 200-pound fullback, whose name, we learned, was Bruno Hogg. When Cramer finally managed to get up, he was limping. A mighty groan escaped from the North End stands. Jerusalem had just been taken and we were all being marched off to captivity in Babylon. We could see Torchy, down on the sidelines, pleading with the coach to let him in – knee injury and all – but Powalski sent in Marty Klein instead.

When they first caught sight of Marty, the military discipline of the Kelvin team threatened to disintegrate. Marty's all of five foot two and can't weigh much more than 125, so his appearance caused first titters, then guffaws. Of course they didn't realize that Marty uses his size to advantage. He's the sneakiest player you'll ever see.

Right away, Marty calls a plunge by the fullback. But when they peel the players off our boy, he doesn't have the ball. Then the Kelvin line pounces on the two halfbacks, but they don't have the ball either – and so they throw them away and begin looking around with murder in their eyes for the tailback. By the time they start looking around for Marty, it's too late: he's waving to them with one hand, the ball in the other, from behind their goal line. Marty had jumped right out of harm's way once the ball had been snapped, and then he strolled off down the sidelines while the Kelvin team pounced upon one player after another in their frantic search for the missing football. Somehow we managed to finish the quarter with a six-all tie.

But in the second quarter, disaster struck. We'd managed to hold Kelvin in their own end of the field until they had to kick on third down. Out of their huddle they marched in that military precision of theirs, and we knew right away something tricky was up.

118

Three of their backfielders pranced out to one side behind the kicker, who booted the ball no more than fifteen yards, and those three ballet stars danced away with the ball while we were left looking like jerks, with our coach hastily thumbing through his handbook to see what it was all about. When Kelvin tried the same stunt a few plays later, all three of their ballerinas were immediately flattened. But that was strictly *verboten*, according to the officials, and we were penalized fifteen yards. Then that 200-pound fullback of theirs got the ball again, and we were behind another six points. But at last Powalski found the section in the rule book dealing with on-side kicks and brought an end to that particular gimmick.

When we finally got the ball again, Marty Klein called another plunge by the fullback, but now the whole line piled on top of poor Marty, and so the fullback – who did have the ball this time – was bulldozing across the field all by himself toward the Kelvin goal line when his bootlace came undone, and he tripped over the loose end. Of course Kelvin recovered the fumbled ball, and we were lucky to finish the half only six points down.

During the intermission, more rumours swept through the stands. A doctor had been seen racing down to the stadium from the North End with a special drug and a set of splints that would enable Torchy to play in the second half. This was immediately contradicted by another rumour: the same doctor had warned that Torchy would limp for the rest of his life if he played that night.

Someone else hinted that there was a special reason for those Kelvin players moving about with such stiff, jerky motions and spastic gestures. All that talk about military precision and strict training was a bunch of nonsense. Joel Greenberg had sneaked into the Kelvin dressing room before the game and sprinkled red pepper into every one of their jock straps. A little later somebody spotted Joel sitting beside me, and soon a couple of dozen people were cheering him as the new student president. None of us suspected then that twenty years later, long after he had become a doctor, gotten married, and had two children, he would take an overdose of drugs and walk off the MacIntyre Building smack on top of the five o'clock rush. Joel stood up in the stands that evening, smiled in that sly way of his, and waved his hand to the cheering crowd.

Later still, a few students from the Grade Twelve Industrial Class stormed across the field to pick a fight with some of the River Heights fans, but they got thrown out of the stadium by the police for their efforts. Afterwards, we heard that they had peed in the gas tanks of all the posh cars parked around the stadium – cars which after the game that night were seen to be lurching and stalling through the streets leading back into River Heights.

Then the players came back on the field, and that 200-pound fullback of theirs got the ball, and now we were behind twelve points. It was during the third quarter that they really began to grind our team into the turf. They seemed to be getting stronger by the minute, while our crew looked shabbier than ever. We couldn't understand it. It didn't make sense. Unless perhaps they'd discovered the red pepper. From the way they paraded and strutted across the field, it was clear they'd be prepared for any contingency. We couldn't put anything past them.

When calling plays, they didn't huddle, as we did. Instead their team would line up in two rows, with their backs to us, and their quarterback would stand facing them and bark out the number of the play. They couldn't have cared less if we overheard or not, they were so confident. Then the centre would march out and crouch over the ball, while the rest of the team moved with just as much military precision to their positions. The ball would be snapped and – Quick March! – they had fifteen more yards, while, as likely as not, we had a few more lumps.

Just as we were getting used to the fact that they weren't trying anything fancy now – that this was going to be one of those bruising games where each side tries to pound the other into the earth – their 200-pound fullback started to come round one end, then handed the ball off to the tailback, who scooted round the other end on a double reverse. And we were eighteen points behind.

The mood on our side of the stadium became grim. On the field the game was turning into a rout. Marty Klein, who was playing safety, as well as quarterback, got creamed when he intercepted a Kelvin pass on our one-yard line, and the Ambulance Corps had to carry him off the field. Down on the sidelines, Torchy Brownstone was still pleading with the coach to let him in.

I guess we should have known when Torchy appeared on the bench dressed for the game that the fates had decreed he would play that night. We knew it was crazy, but on to the field he limped with the first-string line: Norm Mittlehaus – a savage tackle who was later to sing with the Metropolitan Opera and eventually become a cantor; Harvey Zimmerman – who'd recently met a bunch of pretty nurses at the General Hospital and was playing with the reckless abandon of someone determined to break a collar-bone at least; Sammy Markewicz – who never quite came up to expectations, and who, when he was sent to Los Angeles to study dentistry, married the daughter of a clothing manufacturer instead; and Sheldon Kunstler – who later moved to New York and got rich by inventing a machine that bent, folded, and stapled computer cards. Across the field they moved, as the voice on the P.A. system announced that Torchy Brownstone was playing against doctor's orders, and we all cheered mindlessly.

St. John's huddled behind their own goal line. A couple of Kelvin linemen – huge Goliaths that seemed to have just wandered in from the battle plains of Judaea – let long thin streams of spit slide from between their teeth to the grass. Their teammates looked no less contemptuous.

Then the St. John's huddle broke, and Izzy Steinberg, who'd played the Lord High Executioner in *The Pirates of Penzance* the year before, marched with an exaggerated goose step to his position as centre. Above him the rest of the team marched with stiff jerky steps to their places also. Dressed in their torn sweaters and oversize pants, held up by bits of string and old suspenders, they turned smartly to salute Torchy, who promptly returned the salute, and then as one man they all whirled about to give a "Sieg Heil" to the members of the Kelvin team. As the full impact of the caricature was taken in by the spectators, laughter began to gather within the North End stands until it washed over the Kelvin fans.

The laughter and noise quietened into an expectant hush as Torchy began to call signals. Everyone in the stadium knew that Torchy had the largest sleight-of-hand repertoire of any high-school quarterback in the city. Consequently, once the play began, anyone who could conceivably get his hands on the ball – backs, ends – all were immediately flattened by those Kelvin behemoths that came roaring through our line. Which meant that nobody laid a hand on Torchy as he limped down the field, paused briefly to fish the ball out of the hole in his sweater, and then crossed over the River Heights goal line. The quarterback sneak had travelled the whole length of the field.

While the Kelvin players were still complaining to the officials, we could see Torchy calling the St. John's team into a huddle. I don't know what he said, but after the kick-off, our players charged down the field as if they'd been transformed. In the fading sunlight, their torn uniforms looked like golden armour, ablaze with precious stones; their helmets shone with emeralds and sapphires; and they moved with a grace and power that was electrifying. That 200-pound River Heights fullback – who was playing both ways – caught the ball and was promptly hit by Sidney Cohen in the hardest flying tackle any of us had ever seen.

After that tackle, Sidney, who had always impressed us as something of a Momma's boy, was Papa's Boy forever.

The Kelvin fullback fell to the earth as if he were the Tower of Babel crumbling beneath the wrath of God. The ball bounced into the air and Torchy . . . Torchy was where he always is during a fumble. He would have scored touchdowns if he had had to go down the field on crutches. The same, I'm afraid, could not be said of the 200-pound fullback. Bruno Hogg lay unconscious on the field, dreaming strange, alien dreams of knishes and gefilte fish, blissfully unaware that, for once, he'd met his match and been vanquished utterly. Now we were only six points behind.

During the fourth quarter, the Kelvin line started tackling Torchy on every play. You'd see him out there, limping away from the action of the hand-off, holding up both arms to show everyone he didn't have the ball, and still they'd tackle him. So then Torchy started throwing passes – that way the whole stadium could see he didn't have the ball. But neither the Kelvin tackles nor the officials seemed to care. And that was when Torchy sent word into the bench that it was time for Luther Johnson to come out.

Luther was our secret weapon. His family had moved up from a black ghetto in Chicago last summer, where Luther had played end for the city high-school champions. He was a lanky six foot five, could lope along for miles faster than most people could sprint, and caught passes thrown anywhere within shouting distance.

Before vanishing in a mêlée of purple Kelvin sweaters, Torchy managed to get away a twenty-yard completion. On the next play, Luther caught a thirty-five yarder. Suddenly those River Heights players didn't seem to be strutting about so much. From the way they kept pointing, first to one player on our team, then to another, you could see that they were puzzling who to go after. Torchy might just choose to go limping across the goal line for the tying touchdown himself.

Our team wasn't sure, either, what to do next. You could hear them arguing about it in the huddle. Once Norm Mittlehaus's deep baritone voice could be heard demanding that they call a trick play and throw the ball to him for a change. Finally . . . finally . . . they came out of the conference, but before they could line up, one of the officials blew his whistle to signal they'd lost the down. Too much time in the huddle. So back they went to argue some more.

They were still arguing when they came out for the second down. Torchy looked pretty small out there as he limped into position behind the centre. Even without the limp, though, we would have recognized him by that hard whiplash voice of his, his black hair constantly falling down into his eyes and the fluid way he managed to move once the ball was snapped – hurt leg and all. He was like a particularly graceful predatory bird that's injured a wing.

Again the ball was sent arcing through the air, and again Luther was running along in that lope of his – this time across the Kelvin goal line. Everyone on the Kelvin team seemed out to intercept the pass, and all the possible receivers were immediately encircled by River Heights players. The ball, which was soaring a good two feet above everyone's hands, kept rising still, and looked as if it would fall uncaught in the end zone.

Luther didn't need to leap or spring to reach the ball. Suddenly he was just there – his black face a good three feet higher than the distraught white ones looking up at him in disbelief. At that moment, with all the players all frozen together in a portrait of triumph and defeat, Luther must have looked – to the Kelvin team – like the Black Angel of Death himself. They hung there for a moment, Luther's eyes ablaze with laughter, and his white teeth flashing savagely. Then they all broke apart and tumbled to the ground, and the roaring from the stands broke over them.

As both teams lined up again for the kick-off, Torchy moved toward the sidelines, his limp worse than ever. Though only five minutes remained, now that the score was tied, not a spectator there doubted for a moment that we would go on to win the game. Standing at the bench and looking at his teammates lining up, Torchy seemed a magician who had just worked a miraculous transformation. The fumbling rabble of players who had dragged out on to the field two hours before now looked like a company of young gods come to try their prowess on the fields of Olympus.

That was when the Kelvin team began their incredible march down the field. It all started after the kick-off, with the referee claiming the receiver hadn't been given five yards. When Mittlehaus objected, he was promptly kicked out of the game for unsportsmanlike behaviour, and the team given an additional penalty of another ten yards. On the next play, Kelvin's pass was incomplete, but we got called for being off-side. A few minutes later, and they kicked a single point from our thirty-yard line.

After a moment of doubt and disbelief, a few cheers broke, halting and uncertain, from the River Heights stands. Yet almost immediately a feverish silence gripped the stadium, preventing even the outraged protests of the North End supporters from gathering momentum. Furiously, the St. John's team gathered about the ball. There were only two minutes left in the game, barely enough time to set matters right. Torchy began calling signals, the players snapped into formation, the ball was hiked, and now they were all in motion. Every line in their bodies, the practised way in which they moved, spoke of an assurance and competence toward which they'd been building throughout the game. The fullback slashed into the line. Three yards, maybe four. Again the players gathered about the ball and signals were barked. Ends criss-crossed over the goal line, players blocked, changed directions, faked. And then the fullback – on a delayed plunge – slashed into the line again. But the Kelvin players held as fast as the walls of Jericho before they finally came tumbling down. Five yards.

For the third down, Kelvin didn't even bother sending back receivers. The play began as another plunge, with the two lines clashing and then becoming still for a moment. Suddenly Torchy began fading back, arm raised to throw – as deadly as a cobra – while Luther burst forward into open left field. Torchy waited till the last possible moment as the purple sweaters converged upon him; and then the ball was soaring free out of that jumble of players – as straight and true a pass as any receiver could hope for. Luther loped effortlessly toward where the ball would arc downward into his waiting hands, and we cheered with enough energy to split the stadium apart and bring the walls of that Philistine temple down upon our enemies' heads. And about us, the city shone as if made of molten glass – aflame in the radiance of the setting sun – gates garnished with pearl and gold and all manner of precious stones.

In the dazzled eyes of the frenzied North End fans, Luther, in his dented helmet, torn sweater, and baggy pants, was already a figure of glory. But suddenly a look of alarm and disbelief crossed Luther's face as he was brought up short in his tracks, then pitched down, face forward, into the turf – his outstretched arms empty – the ball arcing downward to bounce just beyond his fingertips.

His own disbelief was mirrored in the faces of the fans. He had been up-ended, not by a Kelvin tackle, but by a pair of snapped suspenders which had catapulted his pants violently downward so that they now hung about his ankles. While the ball bounced mockingly across the Kelvin goal line and the stands erupted in laughter, boos, and cheers, we glimpsed what looked like a white flag signalling defeat. And then the whistle blew to end the game.

It was right, I suppose, that we should have lost. Anything else would have been a lie. Afterward, as we pushed and elbowed our way out the gates, we were only too aware of the outraged glances being directed at us by our teachers from across the field. While behind us, in a mighty crescendo of triumph, rose the voices from the River Heights stands:

Send him victorious,
Happy and glorious,
Long to reign over us,
God save the King!

Those voices followed us right out of the stadium, and once out of high school, we fled in every possible direction. Harvey Zimmerman raced back to the General Hospital and eventually married one of those pretty nurses; Sam Markewicz was promoted to a junior partner in his father-in-law's clothing firm; Joel Greenberg went on to become a doctor before, finally, taking his own life; Marty Klein became a delivery man for a local dairy; and Luther Johnson got taken on by the CPR as a sleeping car attendant. As for Mr. Rockwood, the short, heavy-set English teacher who was the terror of Room 41, he was at last allowed to return to Kelvin – after his years of penance in the North End – but almost immediately he was forced into early retirement when he swatted a grade ten student he caught sneaking out to a drugstore on Spruce St. Most of the others – players, teachers, friends – I'm afraid I've lost sight of over the years. But often, when I'm least expecting it, a familiar face that really hasn't changed all that much will stare out at me from the eleven o'clock TV news, or from the society pages of the *Free Press*, or even, occasionally now as the years pass, from the obituary columns. When that happens, I fill in a little write-up of my own beneath a photograph I keep filed away in my memory.

But not only have familiar faces disappeared, familiar landmarks have vanished also, and during the last twenty-five years it has become more and more difficult to keep track of the city I once knew. The Royal Alexandra Hotel, where we held our graduation dance, is gone. Child's Restaurant at Portage and Main, where we'd all meet after a play or movie – no more. Even Osborne Stadium, where we played our football games, has vanished, replaced by a huge, expensive insurance company. Do the shouts of former high school battles ever echo within those heavy stone walls, I wonder, or have they been filed away, along with such names as Norm Mittlehaus, Joel Greenberg, Harvey Zimmerman, and the rest, as insurance statistics in grey steel filing cabinets?

With the passage of time, the North End, too, has changed. So final has its defeat become that it has even had thrust upon it a suburb with such street names as Bluebell, Marigold, Primrose, and Cherryhill. Over the years, that 200-pound fullback has managed to race clear across the city to score a touchdown right here in our home territory. Now we also have our false Eden.

In an attempt to exact some small measure of revenge, I bought a house in River Heights a few years ago and let the lawn go to seed, allowed the back gate to fall off the hinges, let the torn screens on the veranda go unrepaired, and filled the garage and backyard with old furniture and junk from my grandfather's house. But even I know that this attempt to plant a bit of the North End in the heart of River Heights doesn't begin to restore the balance.

The only time we ever came close to holding our own – and, better still, maybe even winning – was that night years before when a lone figure with a hard whiplash voice and black hair falling into his eyes came limping on to the field for part of a football game. He was one of those figures who, at the time, are filed away in a prominent place in your memory and are then, unaccountably, forgotten – unless, by chance, they spring to life again.

Quite recently, when I was passing a downtown parking lot in the evening, I heard the uniformed attendant barking out directions to a group of motorists who'd managed to snarl up traffic and block both exits at once. The dark figure moved with a fluid grace that I was sure I had seen before. There was something familiar about that limp and the way he jerked his head to glance over the lot – like an athlete assessing a new and difficult situation. Back and forth he darted among the honking cars as he signalled some forward, others backward. Until, with a flair that – under the circumstances – was really quite surprising, he had managed to untangle them all.

In the darkness, as he started back toward the booth at the entrance to the parking lot, he seemed to merge with the figure that had limped along the sidelines of the stadium so many years ago and shouted encouragement to a grumbling rabble of players. That night, for almost thirty minutes, under the stadium lights, he had discovered to us all a grace and a strength that flashed electrically from one player to another. And then they were no longer a grumbling rabble of players. They had become timeless, ancient, a group of immortals caught up in the trials of strength that would never end, Greek athletes who had just come to life out of stone. That night, as we had all watched in wonder, the city had flashed about us with sapphires and emeralds, jasper and amethysts – and how we had longed to believe that the city could stay like that forever.

Questions for Writing and Discussion

Discovering Meaning

1. Torchy Brownstone is presented as a hero in the story. He is a prominent figure in each section: in the opening, during the game, and in the closing image of a parking-lot attendant. Examine each portrait of him to determine what characteristics make him a hero. Sum up the author's conception of what makes a person a hero. Do you agree with the author's definition of a hero? Why or why not?
2. What observations is the author making about the characteristics of youth and middle age in the narrator's two portraits: one of himself and his friends as high school students, and the other, his description of them as adults?
3. Identify the themes that the author develops in the final section of the story.
4. What is the significance of the title of the story?

Exploring Method

1. The story is told by a first-person narrator as spectator, first of his city, then of the high school game, and finally of the effects of time on his friends and on the city. What is his tone – the narrator's attitude to his subject – in each of the sections? What added dimension does the author provide by using an adult narrator who is remembering his high school years?
2. In describing the players, the author refers to biblical figures and stories and to myth and legend. Identify the references and discuss their purpose in each context.
3. How does the author individualize the players so that the reader and the narrator, as a spectator at the game, can identify them?
4. The game is framed by opening and closing sections. What is the purpose of each? In the long middle section describing the game, how does the author sustain the suspense?

Suggestions for Writing

1. The narrator describes his schoolmates and then gives an account of their careers years later. Select a group of your friends and acquaintances in school and write a short sketch of each. Then add to each portrait a description as you imagine him or her twenty years later.
2. Examine the section in the story describing the game. Note the concrete verbs and verbals, the vivid metaphors and similes, the images of gold and jewels. Using the most effective passage in the story as a model, imagine yourself a spectator in a stadium and describe the most exciting part of a game.
3. Select a newspaper account of a sports event. Write an analysis comparing the quality of the writing in the article with the description of the game in the story. Consider the characteristics that make one journalism and the other effective fiction.
4. After the game, the narrator comments: "It was right, I suppose, that we should have lost. Anything else would have been a lie." Would a victory of the North Enders have made the story unrealistic? Why or why not? Rewrite the ending of the game to give the North Enders a victory. Which ending do you prefer? Why?

Examining Social Issues

1. The emphasis in sport is on competition. Is competitiveness a danger or an asset to society?
2. Torchy Brownstone enters the game despite his knee injury; Marty Klein is carried off the field by the Ambulance Corps. Discuss your views on violence in sports.
3. The narrator notes that years later, the 200-pound fullback from Kelvin had managed to "race clear across the city to score a touchdown right here in our home territory. Now we also have our false Eden." Explain what the author means by "false Eden." How does the game in the story serve as a "false Eden" for its spectators? Discuss other reasons for the special appeal of sports.

2

SUMMER

Early Adulthood
and Adulthood

Early Adulthood

I remember my youth and the feeling that
will never come back any more – the feeling
that I could last forever, outlast the sea, the
earth, and all men; the deceitful feeling that
lures us on to joys, to perils, to love, to vain
effort – to death; the triumphant conviction
of strength, the heat of life in a handful of
dust, the glow in the heart that with every
year grows dim, grows cold, grows small,
and expires – and expires, too soon, too
soon – before life itself.

Joseph Conrad
Youth

Many young people find that, despite their
adult stature and competency, they have no
standing in the adult world. They are in a
no-man's land where they have lost the
privileges and security of childhood but
have not yet gained acceptance as adults.
This is a difficult period. . . . Achieving
identity is a long and arduous process. The
course of self-understanding and self-
realization is not smooth. . . . Growth in self-
understanding implies a search, a struggle,
a continual endeavour. It is a process,
rather than an end result. The search for
self requires courage, humility, a
willingness to feel, a desire to grow.

Arthur T. Jersild
In Search of Self

A & P

John Updike

John Updike's stories are often concerned with pressures, reflections, and minor revelations in the lives of sensitive teenagers and young adults. Like Mark Twain, he often focuses on a contrast between childhood and adulthood. In his fiction, Updike sets individual human needs against society's demands. Within his characters he portrays tensions derived from the pressures of society, causing his characters to vacillate between their individual instinctive desires and the social codes, and finally to discover that freedom involves accommodation to some social restrictions. In fact, Updike is concerned in his fiction with what William Faulkner, in his Nobel Prize acceptance speech, identified as the theme of all great literature, "the human heart in conflict with itself."

Updike's fiction is memorable for the carefully refined style with which he records his characters' revelations and for the photographic accuracy with which he captures setting and small details to give his readers a sense of life as it is actually lived. He expresses his code as a writer in this way: "Fiction is a tissue of lies that refreshes and informs our sense of actuality. Reality is – chemically, atomically, biologically – a fabric of microscopic accuracies." His story "A & P" (1962) focuses on these "microscopic accuracies," details of characterization and setting brilliantly delineated.

In walks these three girls in nothing but bathing suits. I'm in the third checkout slot, with my back to the door, so I don't see them until they're over by the bread. The one that caught my eye first was the one in the plaid green two-piece. She was a chunky kid, with a good tan and a sweet broad soft-looking can with those two crescents of white just under it, where the sun never seems to hit, at the top of the backs of her legs. I stood there with my hand on a box of HiHo crackers trying to remember if I rang it up or not. I ring it up again and the customer starts giving me hell. She's one of these cash-register-watchers, a witch about fifty with rouge on her cheekbones and no eyebrows, and I know it made her day to trip me up. She'd been watching cash registers for fifty years and probably never seen a mistake before.

By the time I got her feathers smoothed and her goodies into a bag – she gives me a little snort in passing, if she'd been born at the right time they would have burned her over in Salem – by the time I get her on her way the girls had circled around the bread and were coming back, without a pushcart, back my way along the counters, in the aisle between the checkouts and the Special bins. They didn't even have shoes on. There was this chunky one, with the two-piece – it was bright green and the seams on the bra were still sharp and her belly was still pretty pale so I guessed she just got it (the suit) – there was this one, with one of those chubby berryfaces, the lips all bunched together under her nose, this one, and a tall one, with black hair that hadn't quite frizzed right, and one of these sunburns right across under the eyes and a chin that was too long – you know, the kind of girl other girls think is very "striking" and "attractive" but never quite makes it, as they very well know, which is why they like her so much – and then the third one, that wasn't quite so tall. She was the queen. She kind of led them, the other two peeking around and making their shoulders round. She didn't look around, not this queen, she just walked straight on slowly, on these long white prima-donna legs. She came down a little hard on her heels, as if she didn't walk in her bare feet that much, putting down her heels and then letting the weight move along to her toes as if she was testing the floor with every step, putting a little deliberate extra action into it. You never know for sure how girls' minds work (do you really think it's a mind in there or just a little buzz like a bee in a glass jar?) but you got the idea she had talked the other two into coming in here with her, and now she was showing them how to do it, walk slow and hold yourself straight.

She had on a kind of dirty-pink – beige maybe, I don't know – bathing suit with a little nubble all over it, and what got me, the straps were down. They were off her shoulders looped loose around the cool tops of her arms, and I guess as a result the suit had slipped a little on her, so all around the top of the cloth there was this shining rim. If it hadn't been there you wouldn't have known there could have been anything whiter than those shoulders. With the straps pushed off, there was nothing between the top of the suit and the top of her head except just *her*, this clean bare plane of the top of her chest down from the shoulder bones like a dented sheet of metal tilted in the light. I mean, it was more than pretty.

She had sort of oaky hair that the sun and salt had bleached, done up in a bun that was unravelling, and a kind of prim face. Walking into the A & P with your straps down, I suppose it's the only kind of face you *can* have. She held her head so high her neck, coming up out of those white shoulders, looked kind of stretched, but I didn't mind. The longer her neck was, the more of her there was.

She must have felt in the corner of her eye me and over my shoulder Stokesie in the second slot watching, but she didn't tip. Not this queen. She kept her eyes moving across the racks, and stopped, and turned so slow it made my stomach rub the inside of my apron, and buzzed to the other two, who kind of huddled against her for relief, and then they all three of them went up the cat-and-dog-food-breakfast-cereal-macaroni-rice-raisins-seasonings-spreads-spaghetti-soft-drinks-crackers-and-cookies aisle. From the third slot I look straight up this aisle to the meat counter, and I watched them all the way. The fat one with the tan sort of fumbled with the cookies, but on second thought she put the package back. The sheep pushing their carts down the aisle – the girls were walking against the usual traffic (not that we have one-way signs or anything) – were pretty hilarious. You could see them, when Queenie's white shoulders dawned on them, kind of jerk, or hop, or hiccup, but their eyes snapped back to their own baskets and on they pushed. I bet you could set off dynamite in an A & P and the people would by and large keep reaching and checking oatmeal off their lists and muttering "Let me see, there was a third thing, began with A, asparagus, no, ah, yes, applesauce!" or whatever it is they do mutter. But there was no doubt, this jiggled them. A few houseslaves in pin curlers even looked around after pushing their carts past to make sure what they had seen was correct.

You know, it's one thing to have a girl in a bathing suit down on the beach, where what with the glare nobody can look at each other much anyway, and another thing in the cool of the A & P, under the fluorescent lights, against all those stacked packages, with her feet paddling along naked over our checkerboard green-and-cream rubber-tile floor.

"Oh Daddy," Stokesie said beside me. "I feel so faint."

"Darling," I said. "Hold me tight." Stokesie's married, with two babies chalked up on his fuselage already, but as far as I can tell that's the only difference. He's twenty-two, and I was nineteen this April.

"Is it done?" he asks, the responsible married man finding his voice. I forgot to say he thinks he's going to be manager some sunny day, maybe in 1990 when it's called the Great Alexandrov and Petrooshki Tea Company or something.

What he meant was, our town is five miles from a beach, with a big summer colony out on the Point, but we're right in the middle of town, and the women generally put on a shirt or shorts or something before they get out of the car into the street. And anyway these are usually women with six children and varicose veins mapping their legs and nobody, including them, could care less. As I say, we're right in the middle of town, and if you stand at our front doors you can see two banks and the Congregational church and the newspaper store and three real-estate offices and about twenty-seven old freeloaders tearing up Central Street because the sewer broke again. It's not as if we're on the Cape; we're north of Boston and there's people in this town haven't seen the ocean for twenty years.

The girls had reached the meat counter and were asking McMahon something. He pointed, they pointed, and they shuffled out of sight behind a pyramid of Diet Delight peaches. All that was left for us to see was old McMahon patting his mouth and looking after them sizing up their joints. Poor kids, I began to feel sorry for them, they couldn't help it.

Now here comes the sad part of the story, at least my family says it's sad, but I don't think it's so sad myself. The store's pretty empty, it being Thursday afternoon, so there was nothing much to do except lean on the register and wait for the girls to show up again. The whole store was like a pinball machine and I didn't know which tunnel they'd come out of. After a while they come around out of the far aisle, around the light bulbs, records at discount of the Caribbean Six or Tony Martin Sings or some such gunk you wonder they waste wax on, sixpacks of candy bars, and plastic toys done up in cellophane that fall apart when a kid looks at them anyway. Around they come, Queenie still leading the way, and holding a little gray jar in her hand. Slots Three through Seven are unmanned and I could see her wondering between Stokes and me, but Stokesie with his usual luck draws an old party in baggy gray pants who stumbles up with four giant cans of pineapple juice (what do these bums *do* with all that pineapple juice? I've often asked myself) so the girls come to me. Queenie puts down the jar and I take it into my fingers icy cold. Kingfish Fancy Herring Snacks in Pure Sour Cream: 49¢. Now her hands are empty, not a ring or a bracelet, bare as God made them, and I wonder where the money's coming from. Still with that prim look she lifts a folded dollar bill out of the hollow at the center of her nubbled pink top. The jar went heavy in my hand. Really, I thought that was so cute.

Then everybody's luck begins to run out. Lengel comes in from haggling with a truck full of cabbages on the lot and is about to scuttle into that door marked MANAGER behind which he hides all day when the girls touch his eye. Legel's pretty dreary, teaches Sunday school and the rest, but he doesn't miss that much. He comes over and says, "Girls, this isn't the beach."

Queenie blushes, though maybe it's just a brush of sunburn I was noticing for the first time, now that she was so close. "My mother asked me to pick up a jar of herring snacks." Her voice kind of startled me, the way voices do when you see the people first, coming out so flat and dumb yet kind of tony, too, the way it ticked over "pick up" and "snacks." All of a sudden I slid right down her voice into her living room. Her father and the other men were standing around in ice-cream coats and bow ties and the women were in sandals picking up herring snacks on toothpicks off a big glass plate and they were all holding drinks the color of water with olives and sprigs of mint in them. When my parents have somebody over they get lemonade and if it's a real racy affair Schlitz in tall glasses with "They'll Do It Every Time" cartoons stencilled on.

"That's all right," Lengel said. "But this isn't the beach." His repeating this struck me as funny, as if it had just occurred to him, and he had been thinking all these years the A & P was a great big sand dune and he was the head lifeguard. He didn't like my smiling – as I say he doesn't miss much – but he concentrates on giving the girls that sad Sunday-school-superintendent stare.

Queenie's blush is no sunburn now, and the plump one in plaid, that I like better from the back – a really sweet can – pipes up, "We weren't doing any shopping. We just came in for the one thing."

"That makes no difference," Lengel tells her, and I could see from the way his eyes went that he hadn't noticed she was wearing a two-piece before. "We want you decently dressed when you come in here."

"We *are* decent," Queenie says suddenly, her lower lip pushing, getting sore now that she remembers her place, a place from which the crowd that runs the A & P must look pretty crummy. Fancy Herring Snacks flashed in her very blue eyes.

"Girls, I don't want to argue with you. After this come in here with your shoulders covered. It's our policy." He turns his back. That's policy for you. Policy is what the kingpins want. What the others want is juvenile delinquency.

All this while, the customers had been showing up with their carts but, you know, sheep, seeing a scene, they had all bunched up on Stokesie, who shook open a paper bag as gently as peeling a peach, not wanting to miss a word. I could feel in the silence everybody getting nervous, most of all Lengel, who asks me, "Sammy, have you rung up their purchase?"

I thought and said "No" but it wasn't about that I was thinking. I go through the punches, 4, 9, GROC, TOT – it's more complicated than you think, and after you do it often enough, it begins to make a little song, that you hear words to, in my case "Hello (*bing*) there, you (*gung*) happy *pee-pul* (*splat*)!" – the *splat* being the drawer flying out. I uncrease the bill, tenderly as you may imagine, it just having come from between the two smoothest scoops of vanilla I had ever known were there, and pass a half and a penny into her narrow pink palm, and nestle the herrings in a bag and twist its neck and hand it over, all the time thinking.

The girls, and who'd blame them, are in a hurry to get out, so I say "I quit" to Lengel quick enough for them to hear, hoping they'll stop and watch me, their unsuspected hero. They keep right on going, into the electric eye; the door flies open and they flicker across the lot to their car, Queenie and Plaid and Big Tall Goony-Goony (not that as raw material she was so bad), leaving me with Lengel and a kink in his eyebrow.

"Did you say something, Sammy?"

"I said I quit."

"I thought you did."

"You didn't have to embarrass them."

"It was they who were embarrassing us."

I started to say something that came out "Fiddle-de-doo." It's a saying of my grandmother's, and I know she would have been pleased.

"I don't think you know what you're saying," Lengel said.

"I know you don't," I said. "But I do." I pull the bow at the back of my apron and start shrugging it off my shoulders. A couple customers that had been heading for my slot begin to knock against each other, like scared pigs in a chute.

Lengel sighs and begins to look very patient and old and gray. He's been a friend of my parents for years. "Sammy, you don't want to do this to your Mom and Dad," he tells me. It's true, I don't. But it seems to me that once you begin a gesture it's fatal not to go through with it. I fold the apron, "Sammy" stitched in red on the pocket, and put it on the counter, and drop the bow tie on top of it. The bow tie is theirs, if you've ever wondered. "You'll feel this for the rest of your life," Lengel says, and I know that's true, too, but remembering how he made that pretty girl blush makes me so scrunchy inside I punch the No Sale tab and the machine whirs "pee-pul" and the drawer splats out. One advantage to this scene taking place in summer, I can follow this up with a clean exit, there's no fumbling around getting your coat and galoshes, I just saunter into the electric eye in my white shirt that my mother ironed the night before, and the door heaves itself open, and outside the sunshine is skating around on the asphalt.

I look around for my girls, but they're gone, of course. There wasn't anybody but some young married screaming with her children about some candy they didn't get by the door of a powder-blue Falcon station wagon. Looking back in the big windows, over the bags of peat moss and aluminum lawn furniture stacked on the pavement, I could see Lengel in my place in the slot, checking the sheep through. His face was dark gray and his back stiff, as if he'd just had an injection of iron, and my stomach kind of fell as I felt how hard the world was going to be to me hereafter.

Questions for Writing and Discussion

Discovering Meaning

1. What is your impression of the narrator? Describe his character.
2. What aspects of the consumer society does Updike satirize in his story?
3. Updike sets the values of teenagers against those of adults. What are the values of each? Do you agree with the author that a sharp division exists between the generations? Why or why not?
4. Discuss the theme of the story. How is it related to the last sentence?

Exploring Method

1. Updike uses a first-person narrator who tells his own story in the present tense. How does this use of point of view affect your response to the story? To the narrator?
2. The author delays the dramatic conflict until more than halfway through the story. What does the author achieve by presenting Lengel's confrontation with the girls so late?
3. Where in the story is the turning point, the incident in which

Sammy first indicates that he is being forced into a crisis of choice? Where is the climax, the incident in which his conflict is resolved? How does the author heighten the emotional impact in the climactic episode?
4. How are the following three images at the end of the story related to Sammy's decision to quit his job?
   a) The young married woman with her three children screaming about "some candy they didn't get."
   b) Sammy's glimpse of Lengel, "his back stiff, as if he'd just had an injection of iron."
   c) Outside the store, "the sunshine . . . skating around on the asphalt."

Suggestions for Writing

1. Reread the descriptions of the store and the customers. Using these passages as a model, describe a store you know from two viewpoints: as a customer, and as a cashier.
2. The girls leave before Sammy quits. Rewrite the ending using dialogue to dramatize Sammy's meeting with them outside the A & P. Write another dialogue between Sammy and his mother when he returns home.
3. The story describes Lengel as Sammy sees him. Rewrite the scene in which Sammy quits, once from Lengel's perspective, and again from the perspective of the cash-register "witch" whom Sammy describes in the opening paragraph.
4. Sammy says of the girls, "You never know for sure how girls' minds work (do you really think it's a mind in there or just a little buzz like a bee in a glass jar?)." Write a script for a documentary film using examples of women who have disproved this stereotype.

Examining Social Issues

1. At issue in this story is the question of propriety and decency. Is the manager right? Is Sammy's decision to quit justified? Is Sammy's attitude towards the customers and towards Lengel an oversimplification? If you were in Sammy's position, what would you do? Why?
2. In an essay, "A New Perspective of the Adolescent," the psychologists Sarah and Herbert Otto regard teen-age rebellion as constructive. They explain:

   The adolescent brings to the social scene an idealism, integrity and commitment. . . . He contributes a fresh viewpoint and often shows a keen ability for organizational analysis. If an institution shows lack of soundness in its functioning, the teenager will not accept this as the status quo but will ask "why?" and call for change and reform.

Some psychologists even claim that the young benefit from the challenge of pitting themselves against an established order, that the generation gap is a constructive force for society and for the young, if each generation is going to be an improvement over the older one and not merely a reflection of it. Do you agree with this view of teen-age rebellion? Why or why not?

3. The following is a supermarket box boy's description of his job, from Studs Terkel's book *Working:*

> You have to be very respectful to everyone – the customers, to the manager, to the checkers. There's a sign on the cash register that says: smile at the customer. Say hello to the customer. It's assumed if you're a box boy, you're really there 'cause you want to be a manager some day. So you learn all the little things you have absolutely no interest in learning. . . . I saw so much crap there I just couldn't take.

How does the box boy's view of his job apply to Sammy? How does Sammy's feeling about his job affect the way he sees the girls who enter the store?

4. Social philosopher and psychiatrist Erich Fromm, in his book *The Sane Society*, writes about the feeling of alienation and discontent of workers in modern industry. He observes:

> The alienated and profoundly unsatisfactory character of work results in two reactions: the ideal of complete laziness; the other a deep-seated, though often unconscious hostility toward work and everything and everybody connected with it.

Does this observation apply to Sammy? Why or why not? In your own work experience and in your encounters with other workers, have you found this response to work? Describe your experience. Suggest remedies for this condition.

The Man from Mars

Margaret Atwood

Critically acclaimed Canadian novelist, poet, and short-story writer Margaret Atwood, in a literary study, Survival: A Thematic Guide to Canadian Literature *(1972), explores the prevalent themes in Canadian fiction – victimization and survival. These themes can be seen in her own works, in their portrayal of the struggle for survival of the hidden inner self beneath the artificial surface of social behaviour, which often represses real feelings and natural instincts.*

Atwood's poems contain images drawn from the Canadian land-scape and explore such themes as love, pioneer life, and the depths of the subconscious and its relation to myths of ancient cultures. As a literary form, the short story is close to poetry in its intensity, brevity, and singleness of effect. Atwood's short stories, a bridge between her novels and her poems, achieve these poetic qualities and expand on the themes of her other writings.

Her ability to insert a telling phrase and the clarity and precision with which she records her characters' interaction with their set-ting and with one another give her writing liveliness and polish. "The Man from Mars," taken from her collection Dancing Girls *(1977), illustrates Atwood's skill as a writer of short fiction. The story derives its powerful impact from the blend of the comic and the tragic. The obsessive pursuit-flight pattern that controls the movement of the story is comic. The pursuer's terrifying loneliness and desperate search for a friend contain elements of the tragic.*

A long time ago Christine was walking through the park. She was still wearing her tennis dress; she hadn't had time to shower and change, and her hair was held back with an elastic band. Her chunky reddish face, exposed with no softening fringe, looked like a Russian peasant's, but without the elastic band the hair got in her eyes. The afternoon was too hot for April; the indoor courts had been steaming, her skin felt poached.

The sun had brought the old men out from wherever they spent the winter: she had read a story recently about one who lived for three years in a manhole. They sat weedishly on the benches or lay on the grass with their heads on squares of used newspaper. As she passed, their wrinkled toadstool faces drifted towards her, drawn by the movement of her body, then floated away again, uninterested.

The squirrels were out, too, foraging: two or three of them moved towards her in darts and pauses, eyes fixed on her expectantly, mouths with the ratlike receding chins open to show the yellowed front teeth. Christine walked faster, she had nothing to give them. People shouldn't feed them, she thought; it makes them anxious and they get mangy.

Halfway across the park she stopped to take off her cardigan. As she bent over to pick up her tennis racquet again someone touched her on her freshly bared arm. Christine seldom screamed; she straightened up suddenly, gripping the handle of her racquet. It was not one of the old men, however; it was a dark-haired boy of twelve or so.

"Excuse me," he said, "I search for Economics Building. Is it there?" He motioned towards the west.

Christine looked at him more closely. She had been mistaken: he was not young, just short. He came a little above her shoulder, but then, she was above the average height; "statuesque," her mother called it when she was straining. He was also what was referred to in their family as "a person from another culture": oriental without a doubt, though perhaps not Chinese. Christine judged he must be a foreign student and gave him her official welcoming smile. In high school she had been president of the United Nations Club; that year her school had been picked to represent the Egyptian delegation at the Mock Assembly. It had been an unpopular assignment – nobody wanted to be the Arabs – but she had seen it through. She had made rather a good speech about the Palestinian refugees.

"Yes," she said, "that's it over there. The one with the flat roof. See it?"

The man had been smiling nervously at her the whole time. He was wearing glasses with transparent plastic rims, through which his eyes bulged up at her as though through a goldfish bowl. He had not followed where she was pointing. Instead he thrust towards her a small pad of green paper and a ball-point pen.

"You make map," he said.

Christine set down her tennis racquet and drew a careful map. "We are here," she said, pronouncing distinctly. "You go this way.

The building is here." She indicated the route with a dotted line and an X. The man leaned close to her, watching the progress of the map attentively; he smelled of cooked cauliflower and an unfamiliar brand of hair grease. When she had finished Christine handed the paper and pen back to him with a terminal smile.

"Wait," the man said. He tore the piece of paper with the map off the pad, folded it carefully and put it in his jacket pocket; the jacket sleeves came down over his wrists and had threads at the edges. He began to write something; she noticed with a slight feeling of revulsion that his nails and the ends of his fingers were so badly bitten they seemed almost deformed. Several of his fingers were blue from the leaky ball-point.

"Here is my name," he said, holding the pad out to her.

Christine read an odd assemblage of Gs, Ys and Ns, neatly printed in block letters. "Thank you," she said.

"You now write *your* name," he said, extending the pen.

Christine hesitated. If this had been a person from her own culture she would have thought he was trying to pick her up. But then, people from her own culture never tried to pick her up; she was too big. The only one who had made the attempt was the Moroccan waiter at the beer parlour where they sometimes went after meetings, and he had been direct. He had just intercepted her on the way to the Ladies' Room and asked and she said no; that had been that. This man was not a waiter though, but a student; she didn't want to offend him. In his culture, whatever it was, this exchange of names on pieces of paper was probably a formal politeness, like saying thank you. She took the pen from him.

"That is a very pleasant name," he said. He folded the paper and placed it in his jacket pocket with the map.

Christine felt she had done her duty. "Well, goodbye," she said. "It was nice to have met you." She bent for her tennis racquet but he had already stooped and retrieved it and was holding it with both hands in front of him, like a captured banner.

"I carry this for you."

"Oh no, please. Don't bother, I am in a hurry," she said, articulating clearly. Deprived of her tennis racquet she felt weaponless. He started to saunter along the path; he was not nervous at all now, he seemed completely at ease.

"*Vous parlez français?*" he asked conversationally.

"*Oui, un petit peu,*" she said. "Not very well." How am I going to get my racquet away from him without being rude? she was wondering.

"*Mais vous avez un bel accent.*" His eyes goggled at her through the glasses: was he being flirtatious? She was well aware that her accent was wretched.

"Look," she said, for the first time letting her impatience show, "I really have to go. Give me my racquet, please."

He quickened his pace but gave no sign of returning the racquet. "Where are you going?"

"Home," she said. "My house."

"I go with you now," he said hopefully.

"*No,*" she said: she would have to be firm with him. She made a lunge and got a grip on her racquet; after a brief tug of war it came free.

"Goodbye," she said, turning away from his puzzled face and setting off at what she hoped was a discouraging jog-trot. It was like walking away from a growling dog; you shouldn't let on you were frightened. Why should she be frightened anyway? He was only half her size and she had the tennis racquet, there was nothing he could do to her.

Although she did not look back she could tell he was still following. Let there be a streetcar, she thought, and there was one, but it was far down the line, stuck behind a red light. He appeared at her side, breathing audibly, a moment after she reached the stop. She gazed ahead, rigid.

"You are my friend," he said tentatively.

Christine relented: he hadn't been trying to pick her up after all, he was a stranger, he just wanted to meet some of the local people; in his place she would have wanted the same thing.

"Yes," she said, doling him out a smile.

"That is good," he said. "My country is very far."

Christine couldn't think of an apt reply. "That's interesting," she said. "*Très intéressant.*" The streetcar was coming at last; she opened her purse and got out a ticket.

"I go with you now," he said. His hand clamped on her arm above the elbow.

"You . . . stay . . . *here,*" Christine said, resisting the impulse to shout but pausing between each word as though for a deaf person. She detached his hand – his hold was quite feeble and could not compete with her tennis biceps – and leapt off the curb and up the streetcar steps, hearing with relief the doors grind shut behind her. Inside the car and a block away she permitted herself a glance out a side window. He was standing where she had left him; he seemed to be writing something on his little pad of paper.

When she reached home she had only time for a snack, and even then she was almost late for the Debating Society. The topic was, "Resolved: That War Is Obsolete." Her team took the affirmative and won.

Christine came out of her last examination feeling depressed. It was not the exam that depressed her but the fact that it was the last one: it meant the end of the school year. She dropped into the coffee shop as usual, then went home early because there didn't seem to be anything else to do.

"Is that you, dear?" her mother called from the living room. She must have heard the front door close. Christine went in and flopped on the sofa, disturbing the neat pattern of cushions.

"How was your exam, dear?" her mother asked.

"Fine," said Christine flatly. It had been fine; she had passed. She was not a brilliant student, she knew that, but she was conscientious. Her professors always wrote things like "A serious attempt" and "Well thought out but perhaps lacking in élan" on her term papers, they gave her Bs, the occasional B+. She was taking Political Science and Economics, and hoped for a job with the Government after she graduated; with her father's connections she had a good chance.

"That's nice."

Christine felt, resentfully, that her mother had only a hazy idea of what an exam was. She was arranging gladioli in a vase; she had rubber gloves on to protect her hands as she always did when engaged in what she called "housework." As far as Christine could tell her housework consisted of arranging flowers in vases: daffodils and tulips and hyacinths through gladioli, irises and roses, all the way to asters and mums. Sometimes she cooked, elegantly and with chafing-dishes, but she thought of it as a hobby. The girl did everything else. Christine thought it faintly sinful to have a girl. The only ones available now were either foreign or pregnant; their expressions usually suggested they were being taken advantage of somehow. But her mother asked what they would do otherwise; they'd either have to go into a Home or stay in their own countries, and Christine had to agree this was probably true. It was hard, anyway, to argue with her mother. She was so delicate, so preserved-looking, a harsh breath would scratch the finish.

"An interesting young man phoned today," her mother said. She had finished the gladioli and was taking off her rubber gloves. "He asked to speak with you and when I said you weren't in we had quite a little chat. You didn't tell me about him, dear." She put on the glasses which she wore on a decorative chain around her neck, a signal that she was in her modern, intelligent mood rather than her old-fashioned whimsical one.

"Did he leave his name?" Christine asked. She knew a lot of young men but they didn't often call her; they conducted their business with her in the coffee shop or after meetings.

"He's a person from another culture. He said he would call back later."

Christine had to think a moment. She was vaguely acquainted with several people from other cultures, Britain mostly; they belonged to the Debating Society.

"He's studying Philosophy in Montreal," her mother prompted. "He sounded French."

Christine began to remember the man in the park. "I don't think he's French, exactly," she said.

Her mother had taken off her glasses again and was poking absentmindedly at a bent gladiolus. "Well, he sounded French." She meditated, flowery sceptre in hand. "I think it would be nice if you had him to tea."

Christine's mother did her best. She had two other daughters, both of whom took after her. They were beautiful; one was well married already and the other would clearly have no trouble. Her friends consoled her about Christine by saying, "She's not fat, she's just big-bones, it's the father's side," and "Christine is so healthy." Her other daughters had never gotten involved in activities when they were at school, but since Christine could not possibly ever be beautiful even if she took off weight, it was just as well she was so athletic and political, it was a good thing she had interests. Christine's mother tried to encourage her interests whenever possible. Christine could tell when she was making an extra effort, there was a reproachful edge to her voice.

She knew her mother expected enthusiasm but she could not supply it. "I don't know, I'll have to see," she said dubiously.

"You look tired, darling," said her mother. "Perhaps you'd like a glass of milk."

Christine was in the bathtub when the phone rang. She was not prone to fantasy but when she was in the bathtub she often pretended she was a dolphin, a game left over from one of the girls who used to bathe her when she was small. Her mother was being bell-voiced and gracious in the hall; then there was a tap at the door.

"It's that nice young French student, Christine," her mother said.

"Tell him I'm in the bathtub," Christine said, louder than necessary. "He isn't French."

She could hear her mother frowning. "That wouldn't be very polite, Christine, I don't think he'd understand."

"Oh, all right," Christine said. She heaved herself out of the bathtub, swathed her pink bulk in a towel and splattered to the phone.

"Hello," she said gruffly. At a distance he was not pathetic, he was a nuisance. She could not imagine how he had tracked her down: most likely he went through the phone book, calling all the numbers with her last name until he hit on the right one.

"It is your friend."

"I know," she said. "How are you?"

"I am very fine." There was a long pause, during which Christine had a vicious urge to say, "Well goodbye then," and hang up; but she was aware of her mother poised figurine-like in her bedroom doorway. Then he said, "I hope you also are very fine."

"Yes," said Christine. She wasn't going to participate.

"I come to tea," he said.

This took Christine by surprise. "You do?"

"Your pleasant mother ask me. I come Thursday, four o'clock."

"Oh," Christine said, ungraciously.

"See you then," he said, with the conscious pride of one who has mastered a difficult idiom.

Christine set down the phone and went along the hall. Her mother was in her study, sitting innocently at her writing desk.

"Did you ask him to tea on Thursday?"

"Not exactly, dear," her mother said. "I did mention he might come round to tea *some*time, though."

"Well, he's coming Thursday. Four o'clock."

"What's wrong with that?" her mother said serenely. "I think it's a very nice gesture for us to make. I do think you might try to be a little more co-operative." She was pleased with herself.

"Since you invited him," said Christine, "you can bloody well stick around and help me entertain him. I don't want to be left making nice gestures all by myself."

"Christine, *dear*," her mother said, above being shocked. "You ought to put on your dressing gown, you'll catch a chill."

After sulking for an hour Christine tried to think of the tea as a cross between an examination and an executive meeting: not enjoyable, certainly, but to be got through as tactfully as possible. And it *was* a nice gesture. When the cakes her mother had ordered arrived from The Patisserie on Thursday morning she began to feel slightly festive; she even resolved to put on a dress, a good one, instead of a skirt and blouse. After all, she had nothing against him, except the memory of the way he had grabbed her tennis racquet and then her arm. She suppressed a quick impossible vision of herself pursued around the living room, fending him off with thrown sofa cushions and vases of gladioli; nevertheless she told the girl they would have tea in the garden. It would be a treat for him, and there was more space outdoors.

She had suspected her mother would dodge the tea, would contrive to be going out just as he was arriving: that way she could size him up and then leave them alone together. She had done things like that to Christine before; the excuse this time was the Symphony Committee. Sure enough, her mother carefully mislaid her gloves and located them with a faked murmur of joy when the doorbell rang. Christine relished for weeks afterwards the image of her mother's dropped jaw and flawless recovery when he was introduced: he wasn't quite the foreign potentate her optimistic, veil-fragile mind had concocted.

He was prepared for celebration. He had slicked on so much hair cream that his head seemed to be covered with a tight black patent-leather cap, and he had cut the threads off his jacket sleeves. His orange tie was overpoweringly splendid. Christine noticed, however, as he shook her mother's suddenly braced white glove that the ball-point ink on his fingers was indelible. His face had broken out, possibly in anticipation of the delights in store for him; he had a tiny camera slung over his shoulder and was smoking an exotic-smelling cigarette.

Christine led him through the cool flowery softly padded living room and out by the French doors into the garden. "You sit here," she said. "I will have the girl bring tea."

This girl was from the West Indies: Christine's parents had been enraptured with her when they were down at Christmas and had brought her back with them. Since that time she had become pregnant, but Christine's mother had not dismissed her. She said she was slightly disappointed but what could you expect, and she didn't see any real difference between a girl who was pregnant before you hired her and one who got that way afterwards. She prided herself on her tolerance; also there was a scarcity of girls. Strangely enough, the girl became progressively less easy to get along with. Either she did not share Christine's mother's view of her own generosity, or she felt she had gotten away with something and was therefore free to indulge in contempt. At first Christine had tried to treat her as an equal. "Don't call me 'Miss Christine,' " she had said with an imitation of light, comradely laughter. "What you want me to call you then?" the girl had said, scowling. They had begun to have brief, surly arguments in the

kitchen, which Christine decided were like the arguments between one servant and another: her mother's attitude towards
each of them was similar, they were not altogether satisfactory
but they would have to do.

The cakes, glossy with icing, were set out on a plate and the teapot was standing ready; on the counter the electric kettle boiled.
Christine headed for it, but the girl, till then sitting with her
elbows on the kitchen table and watching her expressionlessly,
made a dash and intercepted her. Christine waited until she had
poured the water into the pot. Then, "I'll carry it out, Elvira," she
said. She had just decided she didn't want the girl to see her
visitor's orange tie; already, she knew, her position in the girl's
eyes had suffered because no one had yet attempted to get *her*
pregnant.

"What you think they pay me for, Miss Christine?" the girl said
insolently. She swung towards the garden with the tray; Christine
trailed her, feeling lumpish and awkward. The girl was at least as
big as she was but in a different way.

"Thank you, Elvira," Christine said when the tray was in place.
The girl departed without a word, casting a disdainful backward
glance at the frayed jacket sleeves, the stained fingers. Christine
was now determined to be especially kind to him.

"You are very rich," he said.

"No," Christine protested, shaking her head, "we're not." She
had never thought of her family as rich; it was one of her father's
sayings that nobody made any money with the Government.

"Yes," he repeated, "you are very rich." He sat back in his lawn
chair, gazing about him as though dazed.

Christine set his cup of tea in front of him. She wasn't in the
habit of paying much attention to the house or the garden; they
were nothing special, far from being the largest on the street;
other people took care of them. But now she looked where he was
looking, seeing it all as though from a different height: the long
expanses, the border flowers blazing in the early-summer sunlight, the flagged patio and walks, the high walls and the silence.

He came back to her face, sighing a little. "My English is not
good," he said, "but I improve."

"You do," Christine said, nodding encouragement.

He took sips of tea, quickly and tenderly, as though afraid of in-
juring the cup. "I like to stay here."

Christine passed him the cakes. He took only one, making a
slight face as he ate it; but he had several more cups of tea while
she finished the cakes. She managed to find out from him that he
had come over on a church fellowship – she could not decode the

denomination – and was studying Philosophy or Theology, or possibly both. She was feeling well-disposed towards him: he had behaved himself, he had caused her no inconvenience.

The teapot was at last empty. He sat up straight in his chair, as though alerted by a soundless gong. "You look this way, please," he said. Christine saw that he had placed his miniature camera on the stone sundial her mother had shipped back from England two years before. He wanted to take her picture. She was flattered, and settled herself to pose, smiling evenly.

He took off his glasses and laid them beside his plate. For a moment she saw his myopic, unprotected eyes turned towards her, with something tremulous and confiding in them she wanted to close herself off from knowing about. Then he went over and did something to the camera, his back to her. The next instant he was crouched beside her, his arm around her waist as far as it could reach, his other hand covering her own hands which she had folded in her lap, his cheek jammed up against hers. She was too startled to move. The camera clicked.

He stood up at once and replaced his glasses, which glittered now with a sad triumph. "Thank you, miss," he said to her. "I go now." He slung the camera back over his shoulder, keeping his hand on it as though to hold the lid on and prevent escape. "I send to my family; they will like."

He was out the gate and gone before Christine had recovered; then she laughed. She had been afraid he would attack her, she could admit it now, and he had; but not in the usual way. He had raped, *rapeo, rapere, rapui, to seize and carry off*, not herself but her celluloid image, and incidentally that of the silver tea service, which glinted mockingly at her as the girl bore it away, carrying it regally, the insignia, the official jewels.

Christine spent the summer as she had for the past three years: she was the sailing instructress at an expensive all-girls camp near Algonquin Park. She had been a camper there, everything was familiar to her; she sailed almost better than she played tennis.

The second week she got a letter from him, postmarked Montreal and forwarded from her home address. It was printed in block letters on a piece of the green paper, two or three sentences. It began, "I hope you are well," then described the weather in monosyllables and ended, "I am fine." It was signed, "Your friend." Each week she got another of these letters, more or less identical. In one of them a colour print was enclosed: himself, slightly cross-eyed and grinning hilariously, even more spindly than she remembered him against her billowing draperies, flowers exploding around them like firecrackers, one of his hands an equivocal blur in her lap, the other out of sight; on her own face, astonishment and outrage, as though he was sticking her in the behind with his hidden thumb.

She answered the first letter, but after that the seniors were in training for the races. At the end of the summer, packing to go home, she threw all the letters away.

When she had been back for several weeks she received another of the green letters. This time there was a return address printed at the top which Christine noted with foreboding was in her own city. Every day she waited for the phone to ring; she was so certain his first attempt at contact would be a disembodied voice that when he came upon her abruptly in mid-campus she was unprepared.

"How are you?"

His smile was the same, but everything else about him had deteriorated. He was, if possible, thinner, jacket sleeves had sprouted a lush new crop of threads, as though to conceal hands now so badly bitten they appeared to have been gnawed by rodents. His hair fell over his eyes, uncut, ungreased; his eyes in the hollowed face, a delicate triangle of skin stretched on bone, jumped behind his glasses like hooded fish. He had the end of a cigarette in the corner of his mouth, and as they walked he lit a new one from it.

"I'm fine," Christine said. She was thinking, I'm not going to get involved again, enough is enough, I've done my bit for internationalism. "How are you?"

"I live here now," he said. "Maybe I study Economics."

"That's nice." He didn't sound as though he was enrolled anywhere.

"I come to see you."

Christine didn't know whether he meant he had left Montreal in order to be near her or just wanted to visit her at her house as he had done in the spring; either way she refused to be implicated. They were outside the Political Science Building. "I have a class here," she said. "Goodbye." She was being callous, she realized that, but a quick chop was more merciful in the long run, that was what her beautiful sisters used to say.

Afterwards she decided it had been stupid of her to let him find out where her class was. Though a timetable was posted in each of the colleges: all he had to do was look her up and record her every probable movement in block letters on his green notepad. After that day he never left her alone.

Initially he waited outside the lecture rooms for her to come out. She said hello to him curtly at first and kept on going, but this didn't work; he followed her at a distance, smiling his changeless smile. Then she stopped speaking altogether and pretended to ignore him, but it made no difference, he followed her anyway. The fact that she was in some way afraid of him – or was it just embarrassment? – seemed only to encourage him. Her friends started to notice, asking her who he was and why he was tagging along behind her; she could hardly answer because she hardly knew.

As the weekdays passed and he showed no signs of letting up, she began to jog-trot between classes, finally to run. He was tireless, and had an amazing wind for one who smoked so heavily: he would speed along behind her, keeping the distance between them the same, as though he were a pull-toy attached to her by a string. She was aware of the ridiculous spectacle they must make, galloping across campus, something out of a cartoon short, a lumbering elephant stampeded by a smiling, emaciated mouse, both of them locked in the classic pattern of comic pursuit and flight; but she found that to race made her less nervous than to walk sedately, the skin on the back of her neck crawling with the feel of his eyes on it. At least she could use her muscles. She worked out routines, escapes: she would dash in the front door of the Ladies' Room in the coffee shop and out the back door, and he would lose the trail, until he discovered the other entrance. She would try to shake him by detours through baffling archways and corridors, but he seemed as familiar with the architectural mazes as she was herself. As a last refuge she could head for the women's dormitory and watch from safety as he was skidded to a halt by the receptionist's austere voice: men were not allowed past the entrance.

Lunch became difficult. She would be sitting, usually with other members of the Debating Society, just digging nicely into a sandwich, when he would appear suddenly as though he'd come up through an unseen manhole. She then had the choice of barging out through the crowded cafeteria, sandwich half-eaten, or finishing her lunch with him standing behind her chair, everyone at the table acutely aware of him, the conversation stilting and dwindling. Her friends learned to spot him from a distance, they posted lookouts. "Here he comes," they would whisper, helping her collect her belongings for the sprint they knew would follow.

Several times she got tired of running and turned to confront him. "What do you want?" she would ask, glowering belligerently down at him, almost clenching her fists; she felt like shaking him, hitting him.

"I wish to talk with you."

"Well, here I am," she would say. "What do you want to talk about?"

But he would say nothing; he would stand in front of her, shifting his feet, smiling perhaps apologetically (though she could never pinpoint the exact tone of that smile, chewed lips stretched apart over the nicotine-yellowed teeth, rising at the corners, flesh held stiffly in place for an invisible photographer), his eyes jerking from one part of her face to another as though he saw her in fragments.

Annoying and tedious though it was, his pursuit of her had an odd result: mysterious in itself, it rendered her equally mysterious. No one had ever found Christine mysterious before. To her parents she was a beefy heavyweight, a plodder, lacking in flair, ordinary as bread. To her sisters she was the plain one, treated with an indulgence they did not give to each other: they did not fear her as a rival. To her male friends she was the one who could be relied on. She was helpful and a hard worker, always good for a game of tennis with the athletes among them. They invited her along to drink beer with them so they could get into the cleaner, more desirable Ladies and Escorts side of the beer parlour, taking it for granted she would buy her share of the rounds. In moments of stress they confided to her their problems with women. There was nothing devious about her and nothing interesting.

Christine had always agreed with these estimates of herself. In childhood she had identified with the false bride or the ugly sister; whenever a story had begun, "Once there was a maiden as beautiful as she was good," she had known it wasn't her. That was just how it was, but it wasn't so bad. Her parents never expected her to be a brilliant social success and weren't overly disappointed when she wasn't. She was spared the manoeuvring and anxiety she witnessed among others her age, and she even had a kind of special position among men: she was an exception, she fitted none of the categories they commonly used when talking about girls; she wasn't a cock-teaser, a cold fish, an easy lay or a snarky bitch; she was an honorary person. She had grown to share their contempt for most women.

Now, however, there was something about her that could not be explained. A man was chasing her, a peculiar sort of man, granted, but still a man, and he was without doubt attracted to her, he couldn't leave her alone. Other men examined her more closely than they ever had, appraising her, trying to find out what it was those twitching bespectacled eyes saw in her. They started to ask her out, though they returned from these excursions with their curiosity unsatisfied, the secret of her charm still intact. Her opaque dumpling face, her solid bearshaped body became for them parts of a riddle no one could solve. Christine sensed this. In the bathtub she no longer imagined she was a dolphin; instead she imagined she was an elusive water-nixie, or sometimes, in moments of audacity, Marilyn Monroe. The daily chase was becoming a habit; she even looked forward to it. In addition to its other benefits she was losing weight.

All these weeks he had never phoned her or turned up at the house. He must have decided however that his tactics were not having the desired result, or perhaps he sensed she was becoming bored. The phone began to ring in the early morning or late at night when he could be sure she would be there. Sometimes he would simply breathe (she could recognize, or thought she could, the quality of his breathing), in which case she would hang up. Occasionally he would say again that he wanted to talk to her, but even when she gave him lots of time nothing else would follow. Then he extended his range: she would see him on her streetcar, smiling at her silently from a seat never closer than three away; she could feel him tracking her down her own street, though when she would break her resolve to pay no attention and would glance back he would be invisible or in the act of hiding behind a tree or hedge.

Among crowds of people and in daylight she had not really been afraid of him; she was stronger than he was and he had made no recent attempt to touch her. But the days were growing shorter and colder, it was almost November. Often she was arriving home in twilight or a darkness broken only by the feeble orange street-lamps. She brooded over the possibility of razors, knives, guns; by acquiring a weapon he could quickly turn the odds against her. She avoided wearing scarves, remembering the newspaper stories about girls who had been strangled by them. Putting on her nylons in the morning gave her a funny feeling. Her body seemed to have diminished, to have become smaller than his.

Was he deranged, was he a sex maniac? He seemed so harmless, yet it was that kind who often went berserk in the end. She pictured those ragged fingers at her throat, tearing at her clothes, though she could not think of herself as screaming. Parked cars, the shrubberies near her house, the driveways on either side of it, changed as she passed them from unnoticed background to sinister shadowed foreground, every detail distinct and harsh: they were places a man might crouch, leap out from. Yet every time she saw him in the clear light of morning or afternoon (for he still continued his old methods of pursuit), his aging jacket and jittery eyes convinced her that it was she herself who was the tormentor, the persecutor. She was in some sense responsible; from the folds and crevices of the body she had treated for so long as a reliable machine was emanating, against her will, some potent invisible odour, like a dog's in heat or a female moth's, that made him unable to stop following her.

Her mother, who had been too preoccupied with the unavoidable fall entertaining to pay much attention to the number of phone calls Christine was getting or to the hired girl's complaints of a man who hung up without speaking, announced that she was flying down to New York for the weekend; her father decided to go too. Christine panicked: she saw herself in the bathtub with her throat slit, the blood drooling out of her neck and running in a little spiral down the drain (for by this time she believed he could walk through walls, could be everywhere at once). The girl would do nothing to help; she might even stand in the bathroom door with her arms folded, watching. Christine arranged to spend the weekend at her married sister's.

When she arrived back Sunday evening she found the girl close to hysterics. She said that on Saturday she had gone to pull the curtains across the French doors at dusk and had found a strangely contorted face, a man's face, pressed against the glass, staring in at her from the garden. She claimed she had fainted and had almost had her baby a month too early right there on the living-room carpet. Then she had called the police. He was gone by the time they got there but she had recognized him from the afternoon of the tea; she had informed them he was a friend of Christine's.

They called Monday evening to investigate, two of them. They were very polite, they knew who Christine's father was. Her father greeted them heartily; her mother hovered in the background, fidgeting with her porcelain hands, letting them see how frail and worried she was. She didn't like having them in the living room but they were necessary.

Christine had to admit he'd been following her around. She was relieved he'd been discovered, relieved also that she hadn't been the one to tell, though if he'd been a citizen of the country she would have called the police a long time ago. She insisted he was not dangerous, he had never hurt her.

"That kind don't hurt you," one of the policemen said. "They just kill you. You're lucky you aren't dead."

"Nut cases," the other one said.

Her mother volunteered that the thing about people from another culture was that you could never tell whether they were insane or not because their ways were so different. The policemen agreed with her, deferential but also condescending, as though she was a royal halfwit who had to be humoured.

"You know where he lives?" the first policeman asked. Christine had long ago torn up the letter with his address on it; she shook her head.

"We'll have to pick him up tomorrow then," he said. "Think you can keep him talking outside your class if he's waiting for you?"

After questioning her they held a murmured conversation with her father in the front hall. The girl, clearing away the coffee cups, said if they didn't lock him up she was leaving, she wasn't going to be scared half out of her skin like that again.

Next day when Christine came out of her Modern History lecture he was there, right on schedule. He seemed puzzled when she did not begin to run. She approached him, her heart thumping with treachery and the prospect of freedom. Her body was back to its usual size; she felt herself a giantess, self-controlled, invulnerable.

"How are you?" she asked, smiling brightly.

He looked at her with distrust.

"How have you been?" she ventured again. His own perennial smile faded; he took a step back from her.

"This the one?" said the policeman, popping out from behind a notice board like a Keystone Cop and laying a competent hand on the worn jacket shoulder. The other policeman lounged in the background; force would not be required.

"Don't *do* anything to him," she pleaded as they took him away. They nodded and grinned, respectful, scornful. He seemed to know perfectly well who they were and what they wanted.

The first policeman phoned that evening to make his report. Her father talked with him, jovial and managing. She herself was now out of the picture; she had been protected, her function was over.

"What did they *do* to him?" she asked anxiously as he came back into the living room. She was not sure what went on in police stations.

"They didn't do anything to him," he said, amused by her concern. "They could have booked him for Watching and Besetting,

155

they wanted to know if I'd like to press charges. But it's not worth a court case: he's got a visa that says he's only allowed in the country as long as he studies in Montreal, so I told them to just ship him down there. If he turns up here again they'll deport him. They went around to his rooming house, his rent's two weeks overdue; the landlady said she was on the point of kicking him out. He seems happy enough to be getting his back rent paid and a free train ticket to Montreal." He paused. "They couldn't get anything out of him though."

"*Out* of him?" Christine asked.

"They tried to find out why he was doing it; following you, I mean." Her father's eyes swept her as though it was a riddle to him also. "They said when they asked him about that he just clammed up. Pretended he didn't understand English. He understood well enough, but he wasn't answering."

Christine thought this would be the end, but somehow between his arrest and the departure of the train he managed to elude his escort long enough for one more phone call.

"I see you again," he said. He didn't wait for her to hang up.

Now that he was no longer an embarrassing present reality, he could be talked about, he could become an amusing story. In fact, he was the only amusing story Christine had to tell, and telling it preserved both for herself and for others the aura of her strange allure. Her friends and the men who continued to ask her out speculated about his motives. One suggested he had wanted to marry her so he could remain in the country; another said that oriental men were fond of well-built women: "It's your Rubens quality."

Christine thought about him a lot. She had not been attracted to him, rather the reverse, but as an idea only he was a romantic figure, the one man who had found her irresistible; though she often wondered, inspecting her unchanged pink face and hefty body in her full-length mirror, just what it was about her that had done it. She avoided whenever it was proposed the theory of his insanity: it was only that there was more than one way of being sane.

But a new acquaintance, hearing the story for the first time, had a different explanation. "So he got you, too," he said, laughing. "That has to be the same guy who was hanging around our day camp a year ago this summer. He followed all the girls like that, a short guy, Japanese or something, glasses, smiling all the time."

"Maybe it was another one," Christine said.

"There couldn't be two of them, everything fits. This was a pretty weird guy."

"What . . . *kind* of girls did he follow?" Christine asked.

"Oh, just anyone who happened to be around. But if they paid any attention to him at first, if they were nice to him or anything, he was unshakeable. He was a bit of a pest, but harmless."

Christine ceased to tell her amusing story. She had been one among many, then. She went back to playing tennis, she had been neglecting her game.

A few months later the policeman who had been in charge of the case telephoned her again.

"Like you to know, miss, that fellow you were having the trouble with was sent back to his own country. Deported."

"What for?" Christine asked. "Did he try to come back here?" Maybe she had been special after all, maybe he had dared everything for her.

"Nothing like it," the policeman said. "He was up to the same tricks in Montreal but he really picked the wrong woman this time – a Mother Superior of a convent. They don't stand for things like that in Quebec – had him out of here before he knew what happened. I guess he'll be better off in his own place."

"How old was she?" Christine asked, after a silence.

"Oh, around sixty, I guess."

"Thank you very much for letting me know," Christine said in her best official manner. "It's such a relief." She wondered if the policeman had called to make fun of her.

She was almost crying when she put down the phone. What *had* he wanted from her then? A Mother Superior. Did she really look sixty, did she look like a mother? What did convents mean? Comfort, charity? Refuge? Was it that something had happened to him, some intolerable strain just from being in this country; her tennis dress and exposed legs too much for him, flesh and money seemingly available everywhere but withheld from him wherever he turned, the nun the symbol of some final distortion, the robe and veil reminiscent to his near-sighted eyes of the women of his homeland, the ones he was able to understand? But he was back in his own country, remote from her as another planet; she would never know.

He hadn't forgotten her though. In the spring she got a postcard with a foreign stamp and the familiar block-letter writing. On the front was a picture of a temple. He was fine, he hoped she was fine also, he was her friend. A month later another print of the picture he had taken in the garden arrived, in a sealed manila envelope otherwise empty.

Christine's aura of mystery soon faded; anyway, she herself no longer believed in it. Life became again what she had always expected. She graduated with mediocre grades and went into the Department of Health and Welfare; she did a good job, and was seldom discriminated against for being a woman because nobody thought of her as one. She could afford a pleasant-sized apartment, though she did not put much energy into decorating it. She played less and less tennis; what had been muscle with a light coating of fat turned gradually into fat with a thin substratum of muscle. She began to get headaches.

As the years were used up and the war began to fill the newspapers and magazines, she realized which Eastern country he had actually been from. She had known the name but it hadn't registered at the time, it was such a minor place; she could never keep them separate in her mind.

But though she tried, she couldn't remember the name of the city, and the postcard was long gone – had he been from the North or the South, was he near the battle zone or safely far from it? Obsessively she bought magazines and pored over the available photographs, dead villagers, soldiers on the march, colour blow-ups of frightened or angry faces, spies being executed; she studied maps, she watched the late-night newscasts, the distant country and terrain becoming almost more familiar to her than her own. Once or twice she thought she could recognize him but it was no use, they all looked like him.

Finally she had to stop looking at the pictures. It bothered her too much, it was bad for her; she was beginning to have nightmares in which he was coming through the French doors of her mother's house in his shabby jacket, carrying a packsack and a rifle and a huge bouquet of richly coloured flowers. He was smiling in the same way but with blood streaked over his face, partly blotting out the features. She gave her television set away and took to reading nineteenth-century novels instead; Trollope and Galsworthy were her favourites. When, despite herself, she would think about him, she would tell herself that he had been crafty and agile-minded enough to survive, more or less, in her country, so surely he would be able to do it in his own, where he knew the language. She could not see him in the army, on either side; he wasn't the type, and to her knowledge he had not believed in any particular ideology. He would be something nondescript, something in the background, like herself; perhaps he had become an interpreter.

Questions for Writing and Discussion

Discovering Meaning

1. Compare the two portraits of Christine, one as a student, the other as a young professional. How has she remained the same? How has she changed? Account for the change.
2. Select instances of Christine's behaviour that suggest rebellion against her family, and others that indicate she has absorbed her family's social attitudes.
3. How does Christine's position as the unattractive daughter with two beautiful sisters affect her self-image, her life at college, her life at home, and her fantasies and dreams?

Exploring Method

1. Atwood tells her story through a third-person narrator, with the focus on the responses of Christine, her central character. Select the details that suggest Christine's attitude to the foreign student. What is your impression of him? What details influenced your impression? Is your view like Christine's or different? Why?
2. How do the opening three paragraphs, tracing Christine's walk through the park, prepare the reader for her relationship with the foreign student?
3. What is the role of Elvira, the maid? Compare Christine's relationships with the maid and with the foreign student. Account for the differences.

Suggestions for Writing

1. This story can be read on several levels: as a dramatization of Christine's flight from a repressed layer of her own personality, with the student functioning as an image of her own alienation, or as a dramatization of Christine's initiation. Write an analysis of the story in which you support or reject one of these interpretations or develop an interpretation of your own.

2. In "On Friendship," Margaret Mead, the noted anthropologist, observes:

> The difficulty when strangers from two cultures meet . . . [is] the different expectations about what constitutes friendship and how it came into being. . . . For a Frenchman, a German, or an Englishman friendship is usually more particularized and carries a heavier burden of commitment. . . . There are real differences between these relations for Americans – a friendship may be superficial, casual, situational or deep and enduring. But to a European who sees only our surface behaviour, the differences are not clear.

Although Margaret Mead refers to Europeans and Americans and this story's focus is on a Canadian and an Asian, can you relate the conflict in this story to the contrasting views of friendship? Why or why not? Describe your encounter with a person of another culture. As you develop your story, illustrate what you have learned about yourself and about your friend.
3. Christine's father is puzzled by the foreign student's pursuit of his unattractive daughter. How might a girl's relationship with her father affect her social and emotional development? Write a personal account of your relationship with one of your parents in which you analyze its influence on your development.

Examining Social Issues

1. Christine's mother says that "the thing about people from another culture was that you could never tell whether they were insane or not because their ways were so different." To some people, "normal" means only the behaviour accepted by their own society; the behaviour of people from other societies seems to them insane. Do Christine and her mother share this view? How can such biases be overcome?
2. Identify the details in the story that suggest Christine's relationship with her family, particularly the underlying tensions between herself and her mother. Discuss the conflicts that occur between mothers and daughters.
3. After graduation, Christine starts a career and acquires an apartment of her own. We are given no hint in the story of whether she maintains relations with her family. Confronted with family pressures, young people often leave home even before they are ready to assume independence. Discuss ways of

preventing such an extreme breakdown in child-parent communication.

4. Christine's mother is anxious about her daughter's marriage prospects. What effects do such pressures have on daughters? Do such pressures on single women still exist? What is your view of women's demands for more options? Do you think that a single woman with a career can achieve contentment? Why or why not?

Eveline

James Joyce

James Joyce's early years are well known because of his first auto-biographical novel, Portrait of the Artist as a Young Man *(1916). He was born in a suburb of Dublin in 1882, a time of dramatic political change in Ireland. After obtaining a BA from University College in Dublin, he broke his ties with home, religion, and country, rejecting the provincialism of Irish intellectuals and nationalists to seek a broader vision and greater freedom on the Continent, and to practise art, in the words of his first novel, "in silence, exile, and cunning."*

Dubliners, *a collection of fifteen stories from which "Eveline" is taken, was intended as "a chapter in the moral history of Ireland." Beginning with sketches of a Dublin childhood, told in the first person, and moving to more objective studies of servants, politicians, and members of the middle class, all the stories in* Dubliners *are held together by a single theme, which Joyce describes as "paralysis"; that is, he portrays people who are emotionally, intellectually, and spiritually dead although they are physically alive.*

Joyce wrote a letter in which he explained that his book was intended to portray his native Dublin as the soul of that paralysis. He claimed that, as an agent of civilization, his book would be the first step towards the spiritual liberation of the city; Dubliners *would give his countrymen one good look at themselves in a nicely polished looking-glass. Ireland's response was a rejection of the book on moral grounds. After a tortuous ten-year struggle, Joyce got the book published in Ireland in 1914.*

Living in Trieste, Zurich, and Paris, Joyce wrote the novels that established him as one of the most influential writers in modern times. By the time of his death in 1941, Joyce had become a legend for his great contribution to literature. He remains today the modern master of literary art against whom all contemporary writers are measured. Richard Ellman, his biographer, has declared, "We are all still learning to be Joyce's contemporaries, to understand our interpreter."

Joyce's technique in Dubliners *is based on a blend of sympathy and objective observation. In his stories he is concerned not only with presenting specific details of description but also with the sound and rhythm of his words and sentences. He uses skilfully repeated key words to convey visual images and to suggest mood and atmosphere. Although the portraits in these stories appear realistic, they are symbolic: each character and each image emerges as a symbol of Dublin and its residents.*

Joyce himself was able to leave his native city in search of a fuller life, but the characters in his stories are unable to bring themselves to throw off their national "nets." His characters behave like most Dubliners: they catch an occasional glimpse of life beyond their own provincial existence but never penetrate through the dream stage, living and dying within their oppressive, decaying city.

She sat at the window watching the evening invade the avenue. Her head was leaned against the window curtains and in her nostrils was the odor of dusty cretonne. She was tired.

Few people passed. The man out of the last house passed on his way home; she heard his footsteps clacking along the concrete pavement and afterwards crunching on the cinder path before the new red houses. One time there used to be a field there in which they used to play every evening with other people's children. Then a man from Belfast bought the field and built houses in it – not like their little brown houses but bright brick houses with shining roofs. The children of the avenue used to play together in that field – the Devines, the Waters, the Dunns, little Keogh the cripple, she and her brothers and sisters. Ernest, however, never played: he was too grown up. Her father used often to hunt them in out of the field with his blackthorn stick; but usually little Keogh used to keep *nix* and call out when he saw her father coming. Still they seemed to have been rather happy then; and besides, her mother was alive. That was a long time ago; she and her brothers and sisters were all grown up; her mother was dead. Tizzie Dunn was dead, too, and the Waters had gone back to England. Everything changes. Now she was going to go away like the others, to leave her home.

Home! She looked round the room, reviewing all its familiar objects which she had dusted once a week for so many years, wondering where on earth the dust came from. Perhaps she would never see again those familiar objects from which she had never dreamed of being divided. And yet during all those years she had never found out the name of the priest whose yellowing photograph hung on the wall above the broken harmonium beside the colored print of the promises made to Blessed Margaret Mary

Alacoque.* He had been a school friend of her father. Whenever he showed the photograph to a visitor her father used to pass it with a casual word:

"He is in Melbourne now."

She had consented to go away, to leave her home. Was that wise? She tried to weigh each side of the question. In her home anyway she had shelter and food; she had those whom she had known all her life about her. Of course she had to work hard, both in the house and at business. What would they say of her in the Stores when they found out that she had run away with a fellow? Say she was a fool, perhaps; and her place would be filled up by advertisement. Miss Gavan would be glad. She had always had an edge on her, especially whenever there were people listening.

"Miss Hill, don't you see these ladies are waiting?"

"Look lively, Miss Hill, please."

She would not cry many tears at leaving the Stores.

But in her new home, in a distant unknown country, it would not be like that. Then she would be married – she, Eveline. People would treat her with respect then. She would not be treated as her mother had been. Even now, though she was over nineteen, she sometimes felt herself in danger of her father's violence. She knew it was that that had given her the palpitations. When they were growing up he had never gone for her, like he used to go for Harry and Ernest, because she was a girl; but latterly he had begun to threaten her and say what he would do to her only for her dead mother's sake. And now she had nobody to protect her. Ernest was dead, and Harry, who was in the church decorating business, was nearly always down somewhere in the country. Besides, the invariable squabble for money on Saturday nights had begun to weary her unspeakably. She always gave her entire wages – seven shillings – and Harry always sent up what he could but the trouble was to get any money from her father. He said she used to squander the money, that she had no head, that he wasn't going to give her his hard-earned money to throw about the streets, and much more, for he was usually fairly bad on Saturday night. In the end he would give her the money and ask her had she any intention of buying Sunday's dinner. Then she had to rush out as quickly as she could and do her marketing, holding her black leather purse tightly in her hand as she elbowed her way through the crowds and returning home late under her load of provisions. She had hard work to keep the house together and to see that the two young children who had been left to her charge

* Founder of the congregation of the Sacred Heart and the guardian of the values of home and family.

went to school regularly and got their meals regularly. It was hard work – a hard life – but now that she was about to leave it she did not find it a wholly undesirable life.

She was about to explore another life with Frank. Frank was very kind, manly, open-hearted. She was to go away with him by the night boat to be his wife and to live with him in Buenos Aires where he had a home waiting for her. How well she remembered the first time she had seen him; he was lodging in a house on the main road where she used to visit. It seemed a few weeks ago. He was standing at the gate, his peaked cap pushed back on his head and his hair tumbled forward over a face of bronze. Then they had come to know each other. He used to meet her outside the Stores every evening and see her home. He took her to see *The Bohemian Girl* and she felt elated as she sat in an unaccustomed part of the theatre with him.* He was awfully fond of music and sang a little. People knew that they were courting and, when he sang about the lass that loves a sailor, she always felt pleasantly confused. He used to call her Poppens out of fun. First of all it had been an excitement for her to have a fellow and then she had begun to like him. He had tales of distant countries. He had started as a deck boy at a pound a month on a ship of the Allan Line going out to Canada. He told her the names of the ships he had been on and the names of the different services. He had sailed through the Straits of Magellan and he told her stories of the terrible Patagonians. He had fallen on his feet in Buenos Aires, he said, and had come over to the old country just for a holiday. Of course, her father had found out the affair and had forbidden her to have anything to say to him.

"I know these sailor chaps," he said.

One day he had quarrelled with Frank and after that she had to meet her lover secretly.

The evening deepened in the avenue. The white of two letters in her lap grew indistinct. One was to Harry; the other was to her father. Ernest had been her favorite but she liked Harry too. Her father was becoming old lately, she noticed; he would miss her. Sometimes he could be very nice. Not long before, when she had been laid up for a day, he had read her out a ghost story and made toast for her at the fire. Another day, when their mother was alive, they had all gone for a picnic to the Hill of Howth. She remembered her father putting on her mother's bonnet to make the children laugh.

Her time was running out but she continued to sit by the win-

* A romantic operetta in which the heroine promises to escape from her home with the hero.

dow, leaning her head against the window curtain, inhaling the odor of dusty cretonne. Down far in the avenue she could hear a street organ playing. She knew the air. Strange that it should come that very night to remind her of the promise to her mother, her promise to keep the home together as long as she could. She remembered the last night of her mother's illness; she was again in the close dark room at the other side of the hall and outside she heard a melancholy air of Italy. The organ player had been ordered to go away and given sixpence. She remembered her father strutting back into the sickroom saying:

"Damned Italians! Coming over here!"

As she mused the pitiful vision of her mother's life laid its spell on the very quick of her being – that life of commonplace sacrifices closing in final craziness. She trembled as she heard again her mother's voice saying constantly with foolish insistence:

"Derevaun Seraun! Derevaun Seraun!"*

She stood up in a sudden impulse of terror. Escape! She must escape! Frank would save her. He would give her life, perhaps love, too. But she wanted to live. Why should she be unhappy? She had a right to happiness. Frank would take her in his arms, fold her in his arms. He would save her.

She stood among the swaying crowd in the station at the North Wall. He held her hand and she knew that he was speaking to her, saying something about the passage, over and over again. The station was full of soldiers with brown baggage. Through the wide doors of the sheds she caught a glimpse of the black mass of the boat, lying in beside the quay wall, with illumined portholes. She answered nothing. She felt her cheek pale and cold and, out of a maze of distress, she prayed to God to direct her, to show her what was her duty. The boat blew a long mournful whistle into the mist. If she went, tomorrow she would be on the sea with Frank, steaming towards Buenos Aires. Their passage had been booked. Could she still draw back after all he had done for her? Her distress awoke a nausea in her body and she kept moving her lips in silent fervent prayer.

A bell clanged upon her heart. She felt him seize her hand:
"Come!"

All the seas of the world tumbled about her heart. He was drawing her into them: he would drown her. She gripped with both hands at the iron railing.

"Come!"

* In a corruption of Gaelic, it means: "The end of pleasure is pain."

166

No! No! No! It was impossible. Her hands clutched the iron in frenzy. Amid the seas she sent a cry of anguish!

"Eveline! Evvy!"

He rushed beyond the barrier and called to her to follow. He was shouted at to go on but he still called to her. She set her white face to him, passive, like a helpless animal. Her eyes gave him no sign of love or farewell or recognition.

Questions for Writing and Discussion

Discovering Meaning

1. What is your impression of Eveline? Describe her character and background.
2. The influence of parents on children is a common theme in fiction. How have Eveline's parents shaped her character?
3. Why does Eveline reject the chance to escape?
4. What values are represented by (a) Eveline's father, (b) Frank, (c) Blessed Margaret Mary Alacoque, and (d) the yellowed photograph of the priest?

Exploring Method

1. Almost the entire story is told through Eveline's thoughts, in which the present is set against the past. Ordinarily such a pattern drains the story of a sense of immediacy, the feeling that the action is occurring before the reader's eyes. Does Joyce overcome this problem? Why or why not? How does he create suspense?
2. Describe the atmosphere or mood in the story. What details create the atmosphere? How does the atmosphere contribute to your understanding of Eveline's character?
3. The story can be divided into three sections. Identify the divisions and examine the parallels between the sections. How does the final section differ from the first two?
4. Throughout the story, Joyce dramatizes an opposition between the grip of paralysis on Eveline and her impulse to escape. How is the conflict reflected in the setting and in the contrast between Eveline's childhood and the present?

Suggestions for Writing

1. For young people, leaving home can be a painful experience. All separations contain elements of threat and fear of the unknown. Like Eveline, most young people experience a conflict between the will to become independent and the fear of measuring up to the new challenge. Two of the most dramatic separations for young people are leaving home to enter university, and, at the same time or later, moving beyond reliance on the economic shelter of the family home. Write two portraits of your future self, one leaving home to enter university, the other, taking your first job as an independent adult.

2. Write a narrative in which you put a modern teenager in Eveline's position. Before you write your story, examine the language Joyce uses in Eveline's thoughts. Note particularly the key words he repeats and the level of complexity of the vocabulary and sentence structure. Use these techniques as a model to portray your character and to heighten her conflict.

3. In the endings of Joyce's stories, you will find what the author calls an "epiphany," a moment in which the central character and the reader find that events have come into focus and that the theme and the significance of the symbols have become clear. Reread the last paragraph in the story and describe the significance of the ending for you. Does Eveline also experience a moment of recognition? Why or why not? Rewrite the ending portraying Eveline making the opposite choice. Use Joyce's images, but present them in such a way that they persuade her to leave with Frank.

Examining Social Issues

1. For young people, separation from home is an essential step in growth and development. Discuss ways in which home and school can prepare young people for this crucial event. Give examples from the experiences of your older friends or siblings.

2. Joyce portrays a daughter who is unable to free herself from the restrictions of her family. Psychologists Sarah and Herbert Otto, in their essay "A New Perspective of the Adolescent," have observed that the adolescent can be a growth catalyst in the family:

> The teenager extends an invitation to adults to participate in growth. . . . They offer parents an opportunity to break established and restricted habit patterns, habitual modes of perception and habitual modes of relating.

Do you agree with this view of today's teenagers? Support your answer with examples. How does your relationship with your parents confirm or deny this view of the teenager as a growth catalyst in the family?

3. Eveline is painfully aware of her alienation from her father and from the adults that she encounters at work. Contemporary social scientists disagree about the existence of a generation gap between the younger and older generations. Psychologist Kenneth Keniston, in his essay "Social Change and Youth in America," claims that the generations are completely estranged from one another – more so now than at any other period in history because of the rapid pace of change today. As a result, the young sense that "their parents are poor models for the kinds of lives they themselves will lead in their future years." In his essay "Youth in the Context of American Society," social scientist Talcott Parsons expresses his view that the generation gap has narrowed:

> As to youth's relation to the family, it seems probable that the institutionalizing of increased permissiveness for and understanding of youth-culture activities is a major factor. The newer generation of parents is more firmly committed to a policy of training serious independence. It tolerates more freedom, and it expects higher levels of performance and responsibility.

Which view, Keniston's or Parsons's, do you think is a better description of the relations between the generations? Support your view with your own and your friends' experiences.

4. The story "Eveline" is set in the first decade of this century. What obstacles prevent Eveline from leaving home and assuming independence? Theology professor Allen J. Moore, in his book *The Young Adult Generation: A Perspective on the Future*, describes the obstacles that prevent young people in this age from moving into early adulthood and independence:

> Young people of the present generation are coming of age in a historical period that is experiencing the breakdown of traditional communities, the crumbling of traditions and stated values, the diversification of adult models, the changing function of the family, and the increasing mobility of population. All these have increased the difficulty of moving from a youth world of dependency to an adult world of independency.

Do you agree with the author? Why or why not? Use your own experience to support your view.

Some Grist to Mervyn's Mill

Mordecai Richler

The Canadian satirist and humorist Mordecai Richler writes mostly realistic novels and short stories set either in the Montreal of his childhood or in London, England, where he lived for several years. His Montreal is not so much a physical region as the memory of a way of life in the old Jewish ghetto of his childhood. Of this setting, Richler has said, "No matter how long I continue to live abroad, I do feel forever rooted in St. Urbain Street. This was my time, my place, and I have elected to get it right." He brings the colour and variety of his city to life through the vividness of his sensory details and through his quick sketches of eccentric characters, portrayed mostly through dialogue.

Richler presents his fictional world with vitality and variety illuminated with flashes of comedy. His laughter ranges from exuberant humour to bitter satire that cuts through the surface of urban society to expose hypocrisy, pretension, acquisitiveness, search for social status, and indifference to aesthetic values of an uncultured middle class conditioned by the packaged idols of success in popular culture. In this environment, where an expectancy hovers over childhood, where the young are driven by their own aspirations and by their parents' ambition, Richler's protagonists are involved in a struggle to free themselves from the mental and emotional bonds of their community and to seek self-realization beyond the invisible walls of their ghetto.

"Some Grist to Mervyn's Mill" comes from The Street, *a collection of Richler's stories and sketches. Richler in his essay "The Uncertain World," reminiscing about his own agony as a beginning writer, describes his feeling about his first novel,* The Acrobat:

> *It was a totally private act, with the deep inner assurance that nobody would be such a damn fool as to publish it. That any editor would boot it back to me, a condescending note enclosed, enabling me to quit Paris for Montreal, an honourable failure, and get down to the serious business of looking for a job. A real job.*

Like young Richler in his essay, the protagonist in the story begins to suspect that composing a novel is self-indulgent. In a moment of doubt he says, "Maybe the novel I sent out is no good. Maybe it's just something I had to work out of my system." But with the buoyancy of youth, he turns from despair to confidence as he declares, "My talent is unquestioned," and he concludes at the end of the story, "For a writer . . . everything is grist to the mill."

Mervyn Kaplansky stepped out of the rain on a dreary Saturday afternoon in August to inquire about our back bedroom.

"It's twelve dollars a week," my father said, "payable in advance."

Mervyn set down forty-eight dollars on the table. Astonished, my father retreated a step. "What's the rush-rush? Look around first. Maybe you won't like it here."

"You believe in electricity?"

There were no lights on in the house. "We're not the kind to skimp," my father said. "But we're orthodox here. Today is *shabus.*"

"No, no, no. Between people."

"What are you? A wise-guy."

"I do. And as soon as I came in here I felt the right vibrations. Hi, kid." Mervyn grinned breezily at me, but the hand he mussed my hair with was shaking. "I'm going to love it here."

My father watched, disconcerted but too intimidated to protest as Mervyn sat down on the bed, bouncing a little to try the mattress. "Go get your mother right away," he said to me.

Fortunately, she had just entered the room. I didn't want to miss anything.

"Meet your new roomer," Mervyn said, jumping up.

"Hold your horses." My father hooked his thumbs in his suspenders. "What do you do for a living?" he asked.

"I'm a writer."

"With what firm?"

"No, no, no. For myself. I'm a creative artist."

My father could see at once that my mother was enraptured and so, reconciled to yet another defeat, he said. "Haven't you any . . . things?"

"When Oscar Wilde entered the United States and they asked him if he had anything to declare, he said, 'Only my genius.' "

My father made a sour face.

"My things are at the station," Mervyn said, swallowing hard. "May I bring them over?"

"Bring."

Mervyn returned an hour or so later with his trunk, several suitcases, and an assortment of oddities that included a piece of driftwood, a wine bottle that had been made into a lamp base, a collection of pebbles, a twelve-inch-high replica of Rodin's *The Thinker*, a bull-fight poster, a Karsh portrait of G.B.S., innumerable notebooks, a ball-point pen with a built-in flashlight, and a framed cheque for fourteen dollars and eighty-five cents from the *Family Herald & Weekly Star*.

"Feel free to borrow any of our books," my mother said.

"Well, thanks. But I try not to read too much now that I'm a wordsmith myself. I'm afraid of being influenced, you see."

Mervyn was a short, fat boy with curly black hair, warm wet eyes, and an engaging smile. I could see his underwear through the triangles of tension that ran from button to button down his shirt. The last button had probably burst off. It was gone. Mervyn, I figured, must have been at least twenty-three years old, but he looked much younger.

"Where did you say you were from?" my father asked.

"I didn't."

Thumbs hooked in his suspenders, rocking on his heels, my father waited.

"Toronto," Mervyn said bitterly. "Toronto the Good. My father's a bigtime insurance agent and my brothers are in ladies' wear. They're in the rat-race. All of them."

"You'll find that in this house," my mother said, "we are not materialists."

Mervyn slept in – or, as he put it, stocked the unconscious – until noon every day. He typed through the afternoon and then, depleted, slept some more, and usually typed again deep into the night. He was the first writer I had ever met and I worshipped him. So did my mother.

"Have you ever noticed his hands," she said, and I thought she was going to lecture me about his chewed-up fingernails, but what she said was, "They're artist's hands. Your grandfather had hands like that." If a neighbour dropped in for tea, my mother would whisper, "We'll have to speak quietly," and, indicating the tap-tap of the typewriter from the back bedroom, she'd add, "in there, Mervyn is creating." My mother prepared special dishes for Mervyn. Soup, she felt, was especially nourishing. Fish was the best brain food. She discouraged chocolates and nuts because of Mervyn's complexion, but she brought him coffee at all hours, and if a day passed with no sound coming from the back room my mother would be extremely upset. Eventually, she'd knock softly on Mervyn's door. "Anything I can get you?" she'd ask.

"It's no use. It just isn't coming today. I go through periods like that, you know."

Mervyn was writing a novel, his first, and it was about the struggles of our people in a hostile society. The novel's title was, to begin with, a secret between Mervyn and my mother. Occasionally, he read excerpts to her. She made only one correction. "I wouldn't say 'whore'," she said. "It isn't nice, is it? Say 'lady of easy virtue.'" The two of them began to go in for literary discussions. "Shakespeare," my mother would say, "Shakespeare knew everything." And Mervyn, nodding, would reply, "But he stole all his plots. He was a plagiarist." My mother told Mervyn about her father, the rabbi, and the books he had written in Yiddish. "At his funeral," she told him, "they had to have six motorcycle policemen to control the crowds." More than once my father came home from work to find the two of them still seated at the kitchen table, and his supper wasn't ready or he had to eat a cold plate. Flushing, stammering apologies, Mervyn would flee to his room. He was, I think, the only man who was ever afraid of my father, and this my father found very heady stuff. He spoke gruffly, even profanely in Mervyn's presence, and called him Moitle behind his back. But, when you come down to it, all my father had against Mervyn was the fact that my mother no longer baked potato kugel. (Starch was bad for Mervyn.) My father began to spend more of his time playing cards at Tansky's Cigar & Soda, and when Mervyn fell behind with the rent, he threatened to take action.

"But you can't trouble him now," my mother said, "when he's in the middle of his novel. He works so hard. He's a genius maybe."

"He's peanuts, or what's he doing here?"

I used to fetch Mervyn cigarettes and headache tablets from the drugstore round the corner. On some days when it wasn't coming, the two of us would play casino and Mervyn, at his breezy best, used to wisecrack a lot. "What would you say," he said, "if I told you I aim to out-Emile Zola?" Once he let me read one of his stories, *Was The Champ A Chump?*, that had been printed in magazines in Australia and South Africa. I told him that I wanted to be a writer too. "Kid," he said, "a word from the wise. Never become a wordsmith. Digging ditches would be easier."

From the day of his arrival Mervyn had always worked hard, but what with his money running low he was now so determined to get his novel done, that he seldom went out any more. Not even for a stroll. My mother felt this was bad for his digestion. So she arranged a date with Molly Rosen. Molly, who lived only three doors down the street, was the best looker on St. Urbain, and my mother noticed that for weeks now Mervyn always happened to be standing by the window when it was time for Molly to pass on the way home from work. "Now you go out," my mother said, "and enjoy. You're still a youngster. The novel can wait for a day."

"But what does Molly want with me?"

"She's crazy to meet you. For weeks now she's been asking questions."

Mervyn complained that he lacked a clean shirt, he pleaded a headache, but my mother said, "Don't be afraid she won't eat you." All at once Mervyn's tone changed. He tilted his head cockily. "Don't wait up for me," he said.

Mervyn came home early. "What happened?" I asked.

"I got bored."

"*With* Molly?"

"Molly's an insect. Sex is highly over-estimated, you know. It also saps an artist's creative energies."

But when my mother came home from her Talmud Torah meeting and discovered that Mervyn had come home so early she felt that she had been personally affronted. Mrs. Rosen was summoned to tea.

"It's a Saturday night," she said, "she puts on her best dress, and that cheapskate where does he take her? To sit on the mountain. Do you know that she turned down three other boys, including Ready-To-Wear's *only* son, because you made such a *gedille*?"

"With dumb-bells like Ready-to-Wear she can have dates any night of the week. Mervyn's a creative artist."

"On a Saturday night to take a beautiful young thing to sit on the mountain. From those benches you can get piles."

"Don't be disgusting."

"She's got on her dancing shoes and you know what's for him a date? To watch the people go by. He likes to make up stories about them he says. You mean it breaks his heart to part with a dollar."

"To bring up your daughter to be a gold-digger. For shame."

Mervyn soon fell behind with the rent again and my father began to complain.

"You can't trouble him now," my mother said. "He's in agony. It isn't coming today."

"Yeah, sure. The trouble is there's something coming to me."

"Yesterday he read me a chapter from his book. It's so beautiful you could die." My mother told him that F. J. Kugelman, the Montreal correspondent of *The Jewish Daily Forward*, had looked at the book. "He says Mervyn is a very deep writer."

"Kugelman's for the birds. If Mervyn's such a big writer, let

174

him make me out a cheque for the rent. That's my kind of reading, you know."

"Give him one week more. Something will come through for him, I'm sure."

My father waited another week, counting off the days. "E-Day minus three today," he'd say. "Anything come through for the genius?" Nothing, not one lousy dime, came through for Mervyn. In fact he had secretly borrowed from my mother for the postage to send his novel to a publisher in New York. "E-Day minus one today," my father said. And then, irritated because he had yet to be asked what the E stood for, he added, "E for *Eviction*."

On Friday my mother prepared an enormous potato kugel. But when my father came home, elated, the first thing he said was, "Where's Mervyn?"

"Can't you wait until after supper, even?"

Mervyn stepped softly into the kitchen. "You want me?" he asked.

My father slapped a magazine down on the table. *Liberty*. He opened it at a short story titled *A Doll For The Deacon*. "Mel Kane, Jr.," he said, "isn't that your literary handle?"

"His *nom-de-plume*," my mother said.

"Then the story is yours." My father clapped Mervyn on the back. "Why didn't you tell me you were a writer? I thought you were a . . . well, a fruitcup. You know what I mean. A long-hair."

"Let me see that," my mother said.

Absently, my father handed her the magazine. "You mean to say," he said, "you made all that up out of your own head?"

Mervyn nodded. He grinned. But he could see that my mother was displeased.

"It's a top-notch story," my father said. Smiling, he turned to my mother. "All the time I thought he was a sponger. A poet. He's a writer. Can you beat that?" He laughed, delighted. "Excuse me," he said, and he went to wash his hands.

"Here's your story, Mervyn," my mother said. "I'd rather not read it."

Mervyn lowered his head.

"But you don't understand, Maw. Mervyn has to do that sort of stuff. For the money. He's got to eat too, you know."

"Yeah. Yeah, sure." My father invited Mervyn to Tansky's to meet the boys. "In one night there," he said, "you can pick up enough material for a book."

"I don't think Mervyn is interested."

Mervyn, I could see, looked dejected. But he didn't dare antagonize my mother. Remembering something he had once told me, I said, "To a creative writer every experience is welcome."

"Yes, that's true," my mother said. "I hadn't thought of it like that."

So my father, Mervyn and I set off together. My father showed *Liberty* to all of Tansky's regulars. While Mervyn lit one cigarette off another, coughed, smiled foolishly and coughed again, my father introduced him as the up-and-coming writer.

"If he's such a big writer what's he doing on St. Urbain Street?"

My father explained that Mervyn had just finished his first novel. "When that comes out," he said, "this boy will be batting in the major leagues."

The regulars looked Mervyn up and down. His suit was shiny.

"You must understand," Mervyn said, "that, at the best of times, it's difficult for an artist to earn a living. Society is naturally hostile to us."

My father went into Mervyn's room. He smiled a little. Mervyn waited, puzzled. My father rubbed his forehead. He pulled his ear. "Well, I'm not a fool. You should know that. Life does things to you, but . . ."

"It certainly does, Mr. Hersh."

"You won't end up a zero like me. So I'm glad for you. Well, good night."

But my father did not go to bed immediately. Instead, he got out his collection of pipes, neglected all these years, and sat down at the kitchen table to clean and restore them. And, starting the next morning, he began to search out and clip items in the newspapers, human interest stories with a twist, that might be exploited by Mervyn. When he came home from work – early, he had not stopped off at Tansky's – my father did not demand his supper right off but, instead, went directly to Mervyn's room. I could hear the two men talking in low voices. Finally, my mother had to disturb them. Molly was on the phone.

Molly came by at seven-thirty on Friday night.

"Is there something I can do for you?" my mother asked.

"I'm here to see Mr. Kaplansky. I believe he rents a room here."

"Better to rent out a room than give fourteen ounces to the pound."

"If you are referring to my father's establishment then I'm sorry he can't give credit to everybody."

"We pay cash everywhere. Knock wood."

"I'm sure. Now may I see Mr. Kaplansky, *if you don't mind?*"

"He's still dining. But I'll inquire."

Molly didn't wait. She pushed past my mother into the kitchen.

Her eyes were a little puffy. It looked to me like she had been crying. "Hi," she said. Molly wore her soft black hair in an upsweep. Her mouth was painted very red.

"Siddown," my father said. "Make yourself homely." Nobody laughed. "It's a joke," he said.

"Are you ready, Mervyn?"

Mervyn fiddled with his fork. "I've got work to do tonight," he said.

"I'll put up a pot of coffee for you right away."

Smiling thinly, Molly pulled back her coat, took a deep breath, and sat down. She had to perch on the edge of the chair either because of her skirt or that it hurt her to sit. "About the novel," she said, smiling at Mervyn, "congrats."

"But it hasn't even been accepted by a publisher yet."

"It's good, isn't it?"

"Of course it's good," my mother said.

"Then what's there to worry? Come on," Molly said, rising. "Let's skidaddle."

We all went to the window to watch them go down the street together.

"Look at her how she's grabbing his arm," my mother said. "Isn't it disgusting?"

"You lost by a T.K.O.," my father said.

"*Thanks*," my mother said, and she left the room.

My father blew on his fingers. "Whew," he said. We continued to watch by the window. "I'll bet you she sharpens them on a grindstone every morning to get them so pointy, and he's such a shortie he wouldn't even have to bend over to . . ." My father sat down, lit his pipe, and opened *Liberty* at Mervyn's story. "You know, Mervyn's not *that* special a guy. Maybe it's not as hard as it seems to write a story."

"Digging ditches would be easier," I said.

My father took me to Tansky's for a coke. Drumming his fingers on the counter, he answered questions about Mervyn. "Well, it has to do with this thing . . . The Muse. On some days, with the Muse, he works better. But on other days . . ." My father addressed the regulars with a daring touch of condescension; I had never seen him so assured before. "Well, that depends. But he says Hollywood is very corrupt."

Mervyn came home shortly after midnight.

"I want to give you a word of advice," my mother said. "That girl comes from very common people. You can do better, you know."

My father cracked his knuckles. He didn't look at Mervyn.

"You've got your future career to think of. You must choose a mate who won't be an embarrassment in the better circles."

"Or still better stay a bachelor," my father said.

"Nothing more dreadful can happen to a person," my mother said, "than to marry somebody who doesn't share his interests."

"Play the field a little," my father said, drawing on his pipe.

My mother looked into my father's face and laughed. My father's voice fell to a whisper. "You get married too young," he said, "and you live to regret it."

My mother laughed again. Her eyes were wet.

"I'm not the kind to stand by idly," Mervyn said, "while you insult Miss Rosen's good name."

My father, my mother, looked at Mervyn as if surprised by his presence. Mervyn retreated, startled. "*I mean that,*" he said.

"Just who do you think you're talking to?" my mother said. She looked sharply at my father.

"Hey, there," my father said.

"I hope," my mother said, "success isn't giving you a swelled head."

"Success won't change me. I'm steadfast. But you are intruding into my personal affairs. Good night."

My father seemed both dismayed and a little pleased that someone had spoken up to my mother.

"And just what's ailing you?" my mother asked.

"Me? Nothing."

"If you could only see yourself. At your age. A pipe."

"According to the *Digest* it's safer than cigarettes."

"You know absolutely nothing about people. Mervyn would never be rude to me. It's only his artistic temperament coming out."

My father waited until my mother had gone to bed and then he slipped into Mervyn's room. "Hi." He sat down on the edge of Mervyn's bed. "Tell me to mind my own business if you want me to, but . . . well, have you had bad news from New York? The publisher?"

"I'm still waiting to hear from New York."

"Sure," my father said, jumping up. "Sorry. Good night." But he paused briefly at the door. "I've gone out on a limb for you. Please don't let me down."

My father showed Mervyn some clippings he had saved for him. One news story told of two brothers who had discovered each other by accident after twenty-five years, another was all about a funny day at court. He also gave Mervyn an announcement for the annual Y.H.M.A. *Beacon* short story contest. "I've got an idea for

178

you," he said. "Listen, Mervyn, in the movies . . . well, when Humphrey Bogart, for instance, lights up a Chesterfield or asks for a coke you think he doesn't get a nice little envelope from the companies concerned? Sure he does. Well, your problem seems to be money. So why couldn't you do the same thing in books? Like if your hero has to fly somewhere, for instance, why use an unnamed airline? Couldn't he go TWA because it's the safest, the best, and maybe he picks up a cutie-pie on board? Or if your central character is . . . well, a lush, couldn't he always insist on Seagram's because it's the greatest? Get the idea? I could write, say, TWA, Pepsi, Seagram's and Adam's Hats and find out just how much a book plug is worth to them, and you . . . well, what do you think?"

"I could never do that in a book of mine, that's what I think. It would reflect on my integrity. People would begin to talk, see."

Molly's father phoned the next morning. "You had a good time Mervyn?"

"Yeah. Yeah, sure."

"Atta boy. That girl she's crazy about you. Like they say she's walking on air."

Molly, they said, had told the other girls in the office at Susy's Smart-Wear that she would probably soon be leaving for, as she put it, tropical climes. Gitel Shalinsky saw her shopping for beach wear on Park Avenue – in November, this – and the rumour was that Mervyn had already accepted a Hollywood offer for his book, a guaranteed best-seller. A couple of days later a package came for Mervyn. It was his novel. There was a printed form enclosed with it. The publishers felt the book was not for them.

"Tough luck," my father said.

"It's nothing," Mervyn said breezily. "Some of the best wordsmiths going have had their novels turned down six-seven times before a publisher takes it. Besides, this outfit wasn't for me in the first place. It's a homosexual company. They only print the pretty-pretty prose boys." Mervyn laughed, he slapped his knees. "I'll send the book off to another publisher today."

My mother made Mervyn his favorite dishes for dinner. "You have real talent," she said to him, "and everything will come to you." Afterwards, Molly came by. Mervyn came home very late this time, but my mother waited up for him all the same.

His novel was turned down again.

"It doesn't matter," Mervyn said. "There are better publishers."

"But wouldn't they be experts there," my father asked. "I mean maybe . . ."

"Look at this, will you? This time they sent me a personal letter! You know who this is from? It's from one of the greatest editors in all of America."

"Maybe so," my father said uneasily, "but he doesn't want your book."

"He admires my energy and enthusiasm, doesn't he?"

Once more Mervyn mailed off his novel, but this time he did not resume his watch by the window. Mervyn was no longer the same. I don't mean that his face had broken out worse than ever – it had, it's true, only that was probably because he was eating too many starchy foods again – but suddenly he seemed indifferent to his novel's fate. I gave birth, he said, sent my baby out into the world, and now he's on his own. Another factor was that Mervyn had become, as he put it, pregnant once more (he looks it too, one of Tansky's regulars told me): that is to say, he was at work on a new book. My mother interpreted this as a very good sign and she did her utmost to encourage Mervyn. Though she continued to change his sheets just about every other night, she never complained about it. Why, she even pretended this was normal procedure in our house. But Mervyn seemed perpetually irritated and he avoided the type of literary discussion that had formerly given my mother such deep pleasure. Every night now he went out with Molly and there were times when he did not return until four or five in the morning.

And now, curiously enough, it was my father who waited up for Mervyn, or stole out of bed to join him in the kitchen. He would make coffee and take down his prized bottle of apricot brandy. More than once I was wakened by his laughter. My father told Mervyn stories of his father's house, his boyhood, and the hard times that came after. He told Mervyn how his mother-in-law had been bedridden in our house for seven years, and with pride implicit in his every word – a pride that would have amazed and maybe even flattered my mother – he told Mervyn how my mother had tended to the old lady better than any nurse with umpteen diplomas. "To see her now," I heard my father say, "is like night and day. Before the time of the old lady's stroke she was no sourpuss. Well, that's life." He told Mervyn about the first time he had seen my mother, and how she had written him letters with poems by Shelley, Keats and Byron in them, when all the time he had lived only two streets away. But another time I heard my father say, "When I was a young man, you know, there were days on end when I never went to bed. I was so excited. I used to go out and walk the streets better than snooze. I thought if I slept maybe I'd miss something. Now isn't that crazy?" Mervyn muttered a reply. Usually, he seemed weary and self-absorbed. But my father was irrepressible. Listening to him, his tender tone with Mervyn and the surprise of his laughter, I felt that I had reason to be envious. My father had never talked like that to me or my sister. But I was so astonished to discover this side of my father, it was all so unexpected, that I soon forgot my jealousy.

One night I heard Mervyn tell my father, "Maybe the novel I sent out is no good. Maybe it's just something I had to work out of my system."

"Are you crazy it's no good? I told everyone you were a big writer."

"It's the apricot brandy talking," Mervyn said breezily. "I was only kidding you."

But Mervyn had his problems. I heard from Molly's kid brother that Mr. Rosen had told him he was ready to retire. "Not that I want to be a burden to anybody," he had said. Molly had begun to take all the movie magazines available at Tansky's. "So that when I meet the stars face to face," she had told Gitel, "I shouldn't put my foot in it, and embarrass Merv."

Mervyn began to pick at his food, and it was not uncommon for him to leap up from the table and rush to the bathroom, holding his hand to his mouth.

"You know," my mother said, "he owes us seven weeks' rent now."

"The first day Mervyn came here," my father said, his eyes half-shut as he held a match to his pipe, "he said there was a kind of electricity between us. Well, I'm not going to let him down over a few bucks."

But something was bothering Mervyn. For that night and the next he did not go out with Molly. He went to the window to watch her pass again and then retreated to his room to do the crossword puzzles.

"Feel like a casino?" I asked.

"I love that girl," Mervyn said. "I adore her."

"I thought everything was O.K., but. I thought you were making time."

"No, no, no. I want to marry her. I told Molly that I'd settle down and get a job if she'd have me."

"Are you crazy? A job? With your talent?"

"That's what she said."

"Aw, let's play casino. It'll take your mind off things."

"She doesn't understand. Nobody does. For me to take a job is not like some ordinary guy taking a job. I'm always studying my own reactions. I want to know how a shipper feels from the inside."

"You mean you'd take a job *as a shipper*?"

"But it's not like I'd really be a shipper. It would look like that from the outside, but I'd really be studying my co-workers all the time. I'm an artist, you know."

"Stop worrying, Mervyn. Tomorrow there'll be a letter begging you for your book."

But the next day nothing came. A week passed. Ten days.

"That's a very good sign," Mervyn said. "It means they are considering my book very carefully."

It got so we all waited around for the postman. Mervyn was aware that my father did not go to Tansky's any more and that my mother's friends had begun to tease her. Except for his endless phone calls to Molly he hardly ever came out of his room. The phone calls were futile. Molly wouldn't speak to him.

One evening my father returned from work, his face flushed. "Son-of-a-bitch," he said, "that Rosen he's a cockroach. You know what he's saying? He wouldn't have in his family a faker or a swindler. He said you were not a writer, Mervyn, but garbage." My father started to laugh. "But I trapped him for a liar. You know what he said? That you were going to take a job as a shipper. Boy, did I ever tell him."

"What did you say?" my mother asked.

"I told him good. Don't you worry. When I lose my temper, you know. . . ."

"Maybe it wouldn't be such a bad idea for Mervyn to take a job. Better than go into debt he could – "

"You shouldn't have bragged about me to your friends so much," Mervyn said to my mother. "I didn't ask it."

"*I'm* a braggard? You take that back. You owe me an apology, I think. After all, *you're* the one who said you were such a big writer."

"My talent is unquestioned. I have stacks of letters from important people and – "

"I'm waiting for an apology, Sam?"

"I have to be fair. I've seen some of the letters, so that's true. But that's not to say Emily Post would approve of Mervyn calling you a – "

"My husband was right the first time. When he said you were a sponger, Mervyn."

"Don't worry," Mervyn said, turning to my father. "You'll get your rent back no matter what. Good night."

I can't swear to it. I may have imagined it. But when I got up to go to the toilet late that night it seemed to me that I heard Mervyn sobbing in his room. Anyway, the next morning the postman rang the bell and Mervyn came back with a package and a letter.

"Not again," my father said.

"No. This happens to be a letter from the most important publisher in the United States. They are going to pay me two thousand five hundred dollars for my book in advance against royalties."

"Hey. Lemme see that."

"Don't you trust me?"

"Of course we do." My mother hugged Mervyn. "All the time I knew you had it in you."

"This calls for a celebration," my father said, going to get the apricot brandy.

My mother went to phone Mrs. Fisher. "Oh, Ida, I just called to say I'll be able to bake for the bazaar after all. No, nothing new here. Oh, I almost forgot. Remember Mervyn you were saying he was nothing but a little twerp? Well, he just got a fantastic offer for his book from a publisher in New York. No, I'm only allowed to say it runs into four figures. Excited? That one. I'm not even sure he'll accept."

My father grabbed the phone to call Tansky's.

"One minute. Hold it. Couldn't we keep quiet about this, and have a private sort of celebration?"

My father got through to the store. "Hello, Sugarman? Everybody come over here. Drinks on the house. Why, of Korsakov. No, wise-guy. She certainly isn't. At her age? It's Mervyn. He's considering a five thousand dollar offer just to sign a contract for his book."

The phone rang an instant after my father had hung up.

"Well, hello Mrs. Rosen," my mother said. "Well, thank you. I'll give him the message. No, no, why should I have anything against you we've been neighbours for years. No. Certainly not. It wasn't *me* you called a piker. Your Molly didn't laugh in my face."

Unnoticed, Mervyn sat down on the sofa. He held his head in his hands.

"There's the doorbell," my father said.

"I think I'll lie down for a minute. Excuse me."

By the time Mervyn came out of his room again many of Tansky's regulars had arrived. "If it had been up to me," my father said, "none of you would be here. But Mervyn's not the type to hold grudges."

Molly's father elbowed his way through the group surrounding Mervyn. "I want you to know," he said, "that I'm proud of you today. There's nobody I'd rather have for a son-in-law."

"You're sort of hurrying things. Aren't you?"

"What? Didn't you propose to her a hundred times she wouldn't have you? And now I'm standing here to tell you alright and

183

you're beginning with the shaking in the pants. This I don't like."

Everybody turned to stare. There was some good natured laughter.

"You wrote her such letters they still bring a blush to my face – "

"But they came back unopened."

Molly's father shrugged and Mervyn's face turned grey as a pencil eraser.

I woke at three in the morning when I heard a chair crash in the living room; somebody fell, and this was followed by the sound of sobbing. It was Mervyn. Dizzy, wretched and bewildered. He sat on the floor with a glass in his hand. When he saw me coming he raised his glass. "The wordsmith's bottled enemy," he said, grinning.

"When you getting married?"

He laughed. I laughed too.

"I'm not getting married."

"Wha'?"

"Sh."

"But I thought you were crazy about Molly?"

"I was. I am no longer." Mervyn rose, he tottered over to the window.

"Have you ever looked up at the stars," he said, "and felt how small and unimportant we are?"

It hadn't occurred to me before.

"Nothing really matters. In terms of eternity our lives are shorter than a cigarette puff. Hey," he said. "Hey!" He took out his pen with the built-in flashlight and wrote something in his notebook. "For a writer," he said, "everything is grist to the mill. Nothing is humiliating."

"But what about Molly?"

"She's an insect. I told you the first time. All she wanted was my kudos. My fame . . . If you're really going to become a wordsmith remember one thing. The world is full of ridicule while you struggle. But once you've made it the glamour girls will come crawling."

He had begun to cry again. "Want me to sit with you for a while," I said.

"No. Go to bed. Leave me alone."

The next morning at breakfast my parents weren't talking. My mother's eyes were red and swollen and my father was in a forbidding mood. A telegram came for Mervyn.

"It's from New York," he said. "They want me right away.

There's an offer for my book from Hollywood and they need me."

"You don't say?"

Mervyn thrust the telegram at my father. "Here," he said. "You read it."

"Take it easy. All I said was . . ." But my father read the telegram all the same. "Son-of-a-bitch," he said. "Hollywood."

We helped Mervyn pack.

"Shall I get Molly?" my father asked.

"No. I'll only be gone a few days. I want to surprise her."

We all went to the window to wave. Just before he got into the taxi Mervyn looked up at us, he looked for a long while, but he didn't wave, and of course we never saw him again. A few days later a bill came for the telegram. It had been sent from our house. "I'm not surprised," my mother said.

My mother blamed the Rosens for Mervyn's flight, while they held us responsible for what they called their daughter's disgrace. My father put his pipes aside again and naturally he took a terrible ribbing at Tansky's. About a month later, five dollar bills began to arrive from Toronto. They came sporadically until Mervyn had paid up all his back rent. But he never answered any of my father's letters.

Questions for Writing and Discussion

Discovering Meaning

1. Compare the narrator's father and mother in their relations with Mervyn. What in their background accounts for their attraction to him? How does the parents' attitude to him differ from the Rosens'? What need does Mervyn fulfil for each member of the Hersh family?

2. In the first half of the story Mrs. Hersh supports and encourages Mervyn, and Mr. Hersh is suspicious of him. In the second half, the narrator observes, "And now, curiously enough, it was my father who waited up for Mervyn, or stole out of bed to join him in the kitchen." Explain the reason for the reversal.

3. Mervyn says, "My talent is unquestioned." What concrete evidence does the story offer to confirm his claim that he is a "creative artist"?

4. At the end, Mervyn says to the narrator, "Everything is grist to

185

the mill. Nothing is humiliating." What does he mean? What does Mervyn learn from his experience in Montreal?

5. Identify the targets of Richler's satire in the story.

Exploring Method

1. What is the effect of presenting Mervyn from the outside, in action and dialogue that is filtered through the perspective of the first-person narrator, the naive young son in the Hersh family? Why did Richler select the son rather than the mother or father or Mervyn as the narrator?
2. Describe the various pressures that Mervyn experiences. Since we do not enter Mervyn's mind, how does Richler convey these pressures and their effects on his protagonist?
3. Richler is particularly skilful in creating realistic characters through authentic dialogue and through brief, telling comparative details. Select the speech patterns and descriptive passages that individualize each of the following characters: Mervyn, Mrs. Hersh, Mr. Hersh, Molly Rosen.
4. Despite Mervyn's lie about a publisher's accepting his novel, how does the author retain the reader's sympathy for him?

Suggestions for Writing

1. Mr. Hersh tells Mervyn, "Well, I'm not a fool. You should know that. Life does things to you, but . . . You won't end up a zero like me. So I'm glad for you." Add a new opening to the story in which you give an account of what "life has done" to Mr. Hersh to make him feel like a "zero."
2. Mervyn is rebelling against his family's obsessive pursuit of material success. Mrs. Hersh tells him, "You'll find that in this house we are not materialists." From Richler's portrayal of the Hershes, do you agree with Mrs. Hersh? Why or why not? We see little of Mervyn's family in Toronto. Using a flashback in an appropriate place in the story, write a scene between Mervyn and his parents to suggest why Mervyn left home.
3. Do the Hershes victimize Mervyn or does he victimize them? Write an analysis of the story in which you explore the theme of victimization. Use references from the story to support your interpretation.
4. Both this story and Mavis Gallant's "Wing's Chips" dramatize the position of the creative artist in society. Compare the stories in these aspects:
   a) the nature of the community;

b) the community's attitude to the artist;

c) the narrator's attitude to the artist.

Examining Social Issues

1. Mrs. Hersh is portrayed as domineering, protective, and intensely ambitious for Mervyn, whom she has come to regard as a son. She is the stereotypical "Jewish mother," who has become a target for satire among novelists and comedians. Julius Segal, a psychologist, commends "Jewish" mothers in his book *A Child's Journey*. He notes that they are "committed, protecting, hovering, skin-close, truly loving parents." Sociologists John Rothchild and Susan Berns Wolf studied Sixties dropouts and concluded in their book, *The Children of the Counterculture*, that their children are suffering from the opposite phenomenon: "self-oriented, neglecting, and rejecting mothers."

   Researchers have discovered that not only disadvantaged parents but also educated, middle-class parents neglect their children. Discuss the effects on children of the "Jewish" type of mother and the self-involved type of mother. Illustrate your answer with your experience and your observations of your friends' mothers.

2. The story dramatizes the problem of a creative person in a materialistic world. Mr. Hersh suggests that Mervyn attract sponsors by referring to commercial products. Mervyn replies, "I could never do that in a book of mine. . . . It would reflect on my integrity." Whose view do you accept? Compare a "light reading" best-seller with a critically acclaimed "serious" novel you have read. What characteristics make the former a commercial novel and the latter a work of art?

3. Mervyn condemns his family's materialism. Carolyne Bird, a career counsellor, in her essay "The Job Market," a study of youth's attitude towards jobs, concludes:

   > Students don't want to work for a big company. . . . They don't want to sell. They don't want money or prestige as much as their elders do. And they don't want a job that forecloses their options . . . which is to say that a lot of them aren't thrilled by the prospect of a good, steady job with a future.

   Other, more recent studies have concluded that today's youth is more career-oriented. What is your opinion? Conduct a survey in your school to determine students' career goals. What conditions in society have influenced their views?

4. What are Molly Rosen's expectations from marriage to Mervyn? From your conversations and observations of friends and relatives, what do you think women expect from marriage? What are men's expectations? What is the role of romantic love in modern marriage? Compare your conclusions with a selection of movies and lyrics of popular songs with love themes. Do they reflect the views that you have discovered? Why or why not?

5. Psychologists identify several sources of pressure in the lives of late adolescents and early adults:

   • With the greater demand for specialization, the young are working harder at education, extending their schooling into early adulthood and prolonging their financial dependence on their parents.

   • With the wide range of career choices open to youth, evaluation becomes difficult and guidance is often lacking.

   • In an age of rapid technological change, parents, on whom youth must depend, seem out of tune with what young people sense to be the most significant developments of the time.

   • The unreality of the idealistic values presented to children clashes with the realities they encounter in the adult world.

   Which of these pressures are dramatized in the portrayal of the protagonists in "A & P," "Grids and Doglegs," and "Some Grist to Mervyn's Mill"? How does each protagonist cope with these pressures? On the basis of a survey you conduct in your school, expand the list of pressures. Explore ways of coping with them.

Adulthood

It is not until the early thirties that people
truly begin to settle down in the full sense
... life becomes less provisional. They
make deeper commitments, take on more
adult responsibilities, invest more of
themselves in family and personal interests,
and within this framework, pursue long-
range plans and goals. ... Alongside the nest
building and upward mobility of this period
is the inherent instinct to be free, not tied to
any structure no matter how great its
current satisfaction, or how alluring its
future promise.

Daniel Levinson
The Seasons of a Man's Life

To Earn My Living . . .

Gabrielle Roy

One of the most important French-Canadian writers, Gabrielle Roy, set her novels and stories either in Quebec, where she lived as an adult, or in Manitoba, her childhood home. "To Earn My Living..." is the last story in a collection of eighteen episodes in Street of Riches *(1957), stories unified by the childhood memories of the protagonist.*

The adult narrator charts the development of her awareness as she grows from childhood to young adulthood. The stories parallel the author's own life. The fictional Rue Deschambault, the setting of most of the episodes in the collection of stories, is modelled after St. Boniface, a suburb of Winnipeg where Gabrielle Roy was born and grew up. After graduating from school, like Christine, her protagonist in the story, she taught in a small prairie village.

"To Earn My Living ...," the final story in Street of Riches, *distils the values that emerge from the entire collection: a recognition of the dignity of each person in a universe where fortitude, endurance, and concern for others lessen the hardships in the present. The story is an affirmation of the challenge of earning a living, viewed through the gentle vision of the teacher, a young woman entrusted with other people's children. Her portrait of the tedious, confined life in the village is softened by her compassion as she expresses the faith that "every village in our parts ... always contains something more than hatred!" Particularly memorable is the brief portrait of the narrator's strong, protective mother – her self-sacrifice, her intuitive wisdom, her profound love for her daughter – qualities reflected in the narrator's tender commitment to others. The job and the weather in Gabrielle Roy's harsh landscape create a testing ground where her protagonist gains greater vigour and greater understanding of her capabilities.*

One evening in my tiny attic room, which I had whitewashed and which was austere in color, but crazy, too – stuffed with incongruous baggage – and just the way I wanted it, in this my refuge, Maman appeared, out of breath from her rapid ascent of two flights of stairs. She glanced about, seeking a place to sit, for I insisted that chairs were dull and would have only cushions scattered over the floor. I played the artist, still unaware that a writer is the most self-sufficient of beings – or the most lonely! – and that he could just as readily write in a desert, if in a desert he should still feel the need to communicate with his fellows. Be this as it may, I sought to create an "atmosphere" for myself, and Maman was abashed every time she penetrated into what she called my "mumbo jumbo." Yet was this surprising? In those days I was forever abashed at myself. Maman, very uncomfortable upon a narrow bench, at once broached the subject that had brought her. "Christine," she asked me, "have you considered what you're going to do with your life? Here you are in your last year of school. Have you given it any thought?"

"But I've told you, Maman. I should like to write. . . ."

"I'm talking seriously, Christine. You're going to have to choose an occupation." Her lips trembled slightly. "Earn your living . . ."

Of course I had already often heard this phrase, but it had never seemed that it might some day fully apply to me. It was upon this evening that its words dedicated me to solitude. To earn one's living! How mean, it seemed to me, how selfish, how grasping! Must life be earned? Was it not better to make a gift of it once for all, in some beautiful impulse? . . . Or even to lose it? Or – again – to stake it, to gamble it . . . Oh, anything! But to earn it, pettily, day by day! . . . That evening it was exactly as though someone had told me, "For the mere fact that you live, you must pay."

I think I never made a more disconsolate discovery: all life subject to money, every dream appraised in terms of its yield.

"Oh, maybe I'll earn my living by writing . . . a little later . . . before too long. . . ."

"You poor girl!" said my mother; and after a silence, after a sigh, she continued, "Wait first until you have lived! You've plenty of time. But in the meantime, in order to live, what do you expect to do? . . ."

Then she confessed to me, "Almost all the former earnings left by your father are gone, now. I was very careful with them; but we'll soon be at their end."

Then I saw clearly the endless piecing together, the hard role that had been Maman's; a thousand memories seized me by the throat: Maman mending clothes of an evening under an inadequate light, absorbed in trying to save money, sending us to bed early so that the fire need not be kept up. "Under the covers, you don't feel the cold. . . ." And I recalled a hundred occasions when I might have helped her, whereas she packed me off to study a sonata. And how she would tell me: "You give me a great deal more pleasure, you know, by being the first in your class than by helping with the dishes." And once, when I insisted upon taking her place at the hand-operated washing machine, she had said to me, "If you really want to lighten my work, go play the 'Moment Musical' while I go about my business. It's strange how that piece affects me; so gay, so airy, it drives all my weariness out the window!"

Yes, so it had been. But this evening I jumped from one extreme to the other. Now I ardently wanted to earn money. For Maman's sake, I think I even decided that I'd make a lot of it.

"Right off tomorrow," I declared to her, "I'll go look for work. No matter what! In a store, an office . . ."

"You in a store!" she exclaimed. "Besides, it requires some experience to sell things. No, there's no question of your earning a living at once, starting tomorrow, nor yet at haphazard. I can still keep you at your studies for another year."

And she told me what she wanted for me with all her heart: "If only you were willing, Christine, to become a teacher! . . . There is no finer profession, none more worthy, it seems to me, for a woman. . . ."

Maman had wanted to make all her daughters school-teachers – perhaps because she carried within herself, among so many shattered dreams, this lost vocation.

"It doesn't pay very well!"

"Oh! Don't talk like that. Should we value our lives by what we earn?"

"Since we must earn our livings, it's just as well to bargain for the highest price. . . ."

"Earn it, but not sell it," said Maman; "two very different things. Think it over, Christine. Nothing would please me more than to see you a teacher. And you would do wonderfully at it! Do think it over."

When as yet you scarcely know yourself, why should you not strive to realize the dream that those who love you have dreamed on your behalf? I finished my year at normal school, and then I went off to take my first school in one of our little prairie villages. It was a tiny little village, flat on its back, by which I mean really set flat upon the flatness, and almost entirely red in color, of that dark, dull redness you see on western railway stations. Probably the C.N.R. had sent paint to cover the station and its small dependent buildings – the tool shed, the water tower, the handful of retired railway cars which served as lodging for the section foreman and his men. Some must have been left over, which the villagers had bought at a cut rate, or even got for nothing, and they had put it on all their walls – or at least that was what I pictured to myself upon my first arrival. Even the grain elevator was red, even the house where I was to live, sheathed in sheets of tin several of which flapped in the breeze. Only the school had any individuality; it was all white. And that red village was called, still is called, Cardinal!

When she saw me, the lady with whom I was to board exclaimed, "Come, come! You're not the schoolteacher! Oh no; it's impossible!"

She adjusted her glasses to get a better look at me. "Why, they'll gobble you up in one mouthful!"

All through that first night I spent in Cardinal, the wind kept shaking the sheet metal that had come loose from this house, set off by itself on the outskirts of the village ... but – it's true – escorted by two sad small trees, themselves, like it, shaken by the wind. They were almost the village's only trees; they became very precious to me, and later on I was most saddened when one of them was killed by the frost.

That first night, though, the wind spoke cruelly to me. Why was the village so atrociously red? Was it the color of its dreadful boredom? Certain people had warned me, "It's a village full of hatred; everyone hates some person or some object. . . ." Yes, but every village in our parts, even if it is red, even if it stands alone on the nakedness of the plain, always contains something more than hatred! . . .

The next day I crossed the whole village; truth to tell, there was but one long street, and it, in fact, was the public highway, a broad dirt road; and the village was so tiny a thing, so silent, that the highway passed through it at the same pace as it did the open country. I think that at every window someone stood to spy at me. Behind their curtains, could they have known what it is to set forth one morning along a wooden sidewalk that echos your every step, in order, at the very opposite end of the suspicious village, to earn your living?

But since I had accepted the bargain, I wanted to live up to my end of it. "You give me so much in salary, I give you so many hours of work. . . ." No, it was not in that spirit that I wanted to do business with the village. I should give it all I could. And what would it give me in return? I did not know, but I gave it all my trust.

II

There were not many children that first day of school, and almost all of them very young. Everything went well. I began with geography; here was the subject I myself had liked best during my years as a student. It seems to me that geography is something that requires no effort, that you can't go wrong in teaching it, since it so captures your interest – perhaps because of the lovely big maps, each country indicated by a different color. And then it's not like history. In geography you don't have to judge peoples; no wars are involved, no sides need be taken. I spoke of the various crops raised in the different portions of the globe, in which regions grew sorghum, tapioca, bananas, oranges, sugar, molasses. . . . The children seemed delighted to learn whence came the things they liked best of all to eat. And I told them that they, too, in a sense labored for the happiness of others, since our Canadian wheat was known almost everywhere in the world and was very needful to sustain life.

When I returned, toward noon, to the house of red tin plate, Madame Toupin questioned me avidly. "Well? Did they eat you alive?"

Later on, Madame Toupin became my friend; since it was the one thing at which she best excelled, she was constantly reading my fortune in the cards. She foretold that I should travel a great deal, meet blond men, dark men. . . .

And indeed this is precisely what happened in very short order; on the Sunday following, a number of young men appeared at the sheet-metal house, in groups of four or five, who could not possibly all have come from nearby farms; some were from fairly distant villages. As the weather was fine, they sat themselves down upon a bench in front of the house. The spectacle of these boys in their Sunday best, sitting like bumps on a log, greatly astonished me, but, nothing daunted, I proceeded to take my walk, following the railroad right of way toward the little hills near Babcock. When I returned, rather late in the afternoon, the bench in front of the door was empty. Madame Toupin took me aside. "You're a strange girl," said she, "to leave your suitors flat like that. You are well liked for the moment, obviously enough; but if you continue to show your independence this way, it won't last; mark my words."

"What do you mean? Are those lads suitors of mine?" I asked Madame Toupin. "I never laid eyes on one of them before today, and why on earth did they all come in a group?"

"It gets around quickly in these parts," said Madame Toupin, "when a new schoolteacher comes to town, but I'm afraid that your distant manner has put your boy friends off for a long time. You'll certainly regret it this winter, for you'll have no one to take you to the parties. The boys have long memories around here."

"But what should I have done?"

"Sit down beside the boy who pleased you the most," replied Madame Toupin, "and thus make known your choice. Now I'm afraid it's too late to recover lost ground."

Other Sundays, being a little at loose ends, I began to cultivate the acquaintance, in one or another of the village houses, of its so shadowy people. The greater part of them became my friends, and practically everywhere the women got out their cards to tell my fortune. Ever since then I have clearly understood how much people stand in need of the novel, especially in a village like Cardinal, where new things almost never happen. Everything there was predictable: the preparations for sowing at certain set seasons, at others pure tedium. Then, too, the wind which sighed endlessly; even the monotonous pattern of dreams which the cards revealed.

Meanwhile, Madame Toupin had warned me, "Your trouble will begin when the older boys come to school. For the moment they are helping their parents with the threshing and fall plowing, but sometime in October you'll see the tough ones beginning to appear. I'm sorry for you, poor girl!"

Luckily they came one by one, which gave me the time to win them one by one . . . and in my heart I wonder whether these hard characters were not the more interesting. They forced me to be skillful, and to be just; they forced me to do many difficult things, true enough; they made me mount a tightrope, and once there, they never let me down. Everything had to be absorbing – arithmetic, catechism, grammar. A school without its rebels would be boresome indeed.

Thus the red village and myself were coming to know one another. Somehow I furnished it with a touch of that novelty which it loved above everything in the world, and it – I shall always remember – showed me the nobility of having to earn your living. And then winter fell upon us!

III

How well I recall its brutal coming, along our highway! November was about to begin. The deep frost, the snow, all the pain of winter came in a single night along that shallow road. The wind urged them on with cries and ugly gusts. The next day we were snowbound. I had a very hard time beating my way through the drifts, often sinking above my knees. But I thought it fun to see the immense tracks I left behind me.

Of course there weren't many scholars in attendance that

morning; in fact, by ten o'clock only the village children had put in an appearance. I imagine they had watched me going by their windows, and then that a number of them had thought of taking advantage of the trail I had opened. They had hastened to do so, for the wind quickly obliterated it.

But the farm children were nowhere to be seen. Used to thirty-five youngsters, I thought the dozen that now confronted me excessively well behaved, almost too docile. And when they had recited their lessons, when they had shown me their homework, what else was there left for me to do but tell them stories? For I knew I could have no illusions: often again would there be storms to keep the farm children from school. Were I to push the village pupils ahead, they would leave the others too far behind, and that could lead only to discouragement. In a way it was bitter to take advantage of the country children's absence and tell the others stories. But this, all the same, is what I did.

That day – so well do I remember it – we were as though cut off from the rest of the world in our warm little schoolhouse. In the cellar we had a big stove, and a register in the classroom floor. From time to time, one of my eldest students, lanky Eloi, would look at me, asking me a kind of silent question. I would nod at him. Then he would raise a trap door and climb down into the cellar to toss a few logs on the fire; shortly afterward the warmth would increase, while outdoors the driving snow seemed to fly even more violently. I toyed with the thought: "What fun to be shut up here with the children two or three days at a stretch, maybe even the whole winter! . . ."

I began, however, to miss those who were absent. I walked over to a window and tried to see in the distance, through the high whirling of the snow, the bit of path I had left behind in my passage; but at only a few feet from the building you could distinguish nothing.

Then, through the spirals of snow which seemed to climb in towers toward the sky, I suddenly descried something red – yes, two long scarves, their ends tossed in the wind, just as was the snow. It must be little Lucien and his sister Lucienne – by now I was well acquainted with the children's mufflers, and theirs were red. Their parents were from Brittany, having been at Cardinal for only five or six years, and they did not know how to read or write.

The two tots arrived almost frozen, their cheeks on fire. For prudence's sake, I rubbed their hands with fistfuls of snow; I helped them out of the coats that had stiffened over their bodies, and I kept them a little while standing on the register. Then they came to my desk with their readers and notebooks.

Later I learned that that morning they had made a great scene with their parents, who wanted to prevent their attempting the two miles on foot to school.

With me they were pliant. In their eyes, fixed upon mine, there was complete trust. I presume they would have believed me had I told them that the world was peopled with enemies, that they would have to cherish hatred for many men, even for whole peoples. . . .

But we – all of us together – were warm and happy. The two little ones recited their lessons. Right next to us the gale, like a misunderstood child, wept and stamped its feet outside the door. And I did not fully realize it yet – often our joys are slow in coming home to us – but I was living through one of the rarest happinesses of my life. Was not all the world a child? Were we not the day's morning? . . .

Questions for Writing and Discussion

Discovering Meaning

1. Describe the character of Christine's mother. What traits did Christine inherit from her?
2. Christine's mother tells her that she "would do wonderfully" as a teacher. How has her upbringing prepared her for this profession? What in her temperament promises that she will be a successful teacher?
3. Christine expresses the belief that "every village in our parts . . . always contains something more than hatred!" What does she find in the village that confirms this belief?
4. Before her encounter with the children, Christine reflects on the "bargain" she has made with the town: "I should give it all I could," she thinks, and then asks, "And what would it give me in return?" At the end of the story she concludes that she was living through "one of the rarest happinesses" of her life. Explain what she gives the town, what it gave her, and the source of her "rare happiness."
5. Explain the meaning of the last two questions: "Was not all the world a child? Were we not at the day's morning?"

Exploring Method

1. In the story, the first-person narrator recalls her past: her first experience of earning her living. Where in the story is the voice

of the older narrator evident? What does the author gain by her use of this point of view to tell her story?

2. Compare the adult narrator in this story with the adult narrator in Clark Blaise's story "Grids and Doglegs." Consider their attitudes towards their younger selves and the complexity of the language and the sentence structure.

3. Examine the three divisions in the story. What is the function of the ending in each section?

4. How are the atmosphere and the nature of the village conveyed by the author's use of colour, the description of the wind and snow, and the description of the villagers?

5. Examine the metaphors in the story. Explain how each clarifies thought, feeling, or sensation.

Suggestions for Writing

1. Christine's mother wanted to make all her daughters schoolteachers, "perhaps because she carried within herself, among so many shattered dreams, this lost vocation," Christine surmises. Write a portrait of your parents in which you illustrate the motives for their career expectations for you.

2. Christine says, "Since we must earn our livings, it's just as well to bargain for the highest price." Her mother replies, "Earn it, but not sell it." Explain the mother's remark. With whom do you agree? Support your view. Describe the dream occupation of your choice. Outline the steps in your education that will prepare you for your vocation. Which attitude to your job, Christine's or her mother's, will you assume? Why?

3. Christine believes that writers are self-sufficient, that they can write in a desert. They only need to feel a need to communicate. Her mother believes that writers need to experience life before they can write important works. She tells Christine, "Wait first until you have lived!" With whom do you agree? Why? Examine your purpose for writing: to use your imagination in poems and stories? To explain or give your opinion on a subject derived from your experience or thought? To argue for or against an issue? Do you ever write for impractical purposes: just to express yourself in a journal or a diary? Why or why not?

4. Christine says that she likes geography best because "you don't have to judge peoples; no wars are involved, no sides need be taken." Select the subject you like best and explain why it appeals to you.

5. What are the qualities of Christine as a teacher that make children walk two miles through bitter cold and snowdrifts to

attend her class? In your opinion, should a teacher be an instrument through whom facts are communicated, or should a teacher relate to students in a more personal way? Can the two roles be integrated? Illustrate your view by writing a portrait of a teacher you admire.

Examining Social Issues

1. Christine's mother urges her daughter to study and play the piano rather than to help with the housework. Do you approve of such an approach to rearing children? Why or why not? Illustrate your opinion by explaining your duties as a member of your family.
2. Christine accepts her mother's choice of a career for her. She asks, "When as yet you scarcely know yourself, why should you not strive to realize the dream that those who love you have dreamed on your behalf?" Analyze your motives for selecting your "dream career." Consider the influences on you of your parents' expectations, your aptitudes and interests, and other conditions.
3. Of the two attitudes towards work expressed in the story, "You give me so much in salary, I give you so many hours of work," and "I should give it all I could," which attitude does Christine assume in her job? According to social scientists, the former attitude to work is most common. Economist Peter Drucker, in *Concept of the Corporation*, observing workers in the automobile industry, notes:

> For the great majority of automobile workers, the only meaning of the job is in the paycheck, not in anything connected with the work or the product. Work appears as something unnatural, a disagreeable and stultifying condition of getting the paycheck, devoid of dignity as well as of importance. No wonder that the result is an unhappy and discontented worker – because a paycheck is not enough to base one's self respect on.

Write a list of questions about work attitudes and use it to conduct a survey of some workers in your community. Examine the results, draw conclusions, and determine the reasons for your findings.
4. In "The Man from Mars" and "To Earn My Living ..." daughter's are pressured to live out their mother's unfulfilled dreams. Compare the dream of each mother and the response of each daughter. Explain the reasons for the daughters' responses.

199

The Neilson Chocolate Factory

Irena Friedman

Born in the Soviet Union, Irena Friedman lived in Poland and Israel before moving to Canada. Herself an immigrant, her interest in other newcomers is no surprise. Her story "The Neilson Chocolate Factory," a reflection of this interest, is a sympathetic portrayal of the hardships of immigrant life in Canada.

The vivid details, the accurate recreation of her characters' dialects, the sharp images of diverse, vibrant colour in the urban setting impart vitality to each scene. To tell her story, Friedman uses a narrator recalling her past. The clarity with which she reconstructs an earlier experience is based on the psychological concept of "involuntary memory": a landscape, a strain of music, a snapshot glimpse of a face in a crowd can evoke an earlier experience with its network of images, sensations, and feelings. The most vivid writing derives from such an experience. Marcel Proust's series of novels Remembrance of Things Past, *Mark Twain's boyhood experience in* Tom Sawyer *and* Huckleberry Finn, *William Wordsworth's poetic landscapes – all owe their power to their ability to engage the reader's imagination by evoking the past vividly.*

In her story, Irena Friedman suggests this experience in her opening: the narrator, casually unwrapping a Neilson Crispy Crunch far away from Toronto, suddenly recalls the atmosphere of the neighbourhood where she once lived. She plunges into time to recollect an experience of the past with the vividness and immediacy of a present encounter.

This is a story which starts with the casual unwrapping of a Neilson Crispy Crunch, a name which suddenly – far away from Toronto – is as evocative as the warm fragrance of chocolate which forever lingered over the neighbourhood.

"What, a chocolate factory?" my friends would laugh. "In Toronto?"

It's true, the factory made the neighbourhood sound like the world-famous Berne or Haarlem, though in fact it was a rather undistinguished area which some called Little Italy and others

Little Portugal. Well, some of *us* called it that. The Italian and Portuguese immigrants who lived there were not likely to think of it as anything resembling their homelands. But though the winters were harsh and inflation kept rising, more and more of them seemed to move into the neighbourhood, planting tomatoes and vine in their backyards and sweeping the dry autumn leaves with a fervour equal only to their longing for the warm regions they had left behind. At four or five in the morning, one could see window after window light up in the houses around the factory as the men would get up to go to work, often labouring for twelve, fifteen hours a day while their wives scrubbed and laundered and waited on tables and the children played football on the icy streets. Only on Sundays, an air of contentment would settle over the neighbourhood and the smell of chocolate would give way to that of home-baked bread or roasting lamb. Only then did those rapidly maturing faces seem to relax as uncles and aunts would arrive and, taking little Giorgio or Rafael on their knee, ask:

"What are you gonna be when you grow up, hey?" while the child, barely able to restrain his pride, would answer: "Me, I'm gonna be a doctor," or – as inevitably – "Me, I'm gonna build chocolate factories!"

Some of the men on my street were employees of the Neilson factory, but the only person I knew was Manuel de Sousa, my landlord. The funny thing was, I could never find out just what he did there. An inscrutable Portuguese immigrant, his English seemed hopelessly inadequate whenever we had a disagreement. Which, I might have known from the start, the two of us – worlds apart – were bound to have our share of.

"Hello, I see you have a flat for rent," I said, that rainy September evening when I finally found him home. Manuel, I remember, glared at me as though I had come to expropriate him.

"How many?" he snapped after a prolonged scrutiny.

"One, only me," I said, smiling, trying not to look overly eager. But, almost at once, he started to close the door in my face.

"Too big, too expensive for you," he said and I wondered whether it would be in my favour to tell him I was a free-lance journalist and needed extra space for an office.

"Hundred and forty dollars, *too much!*"

Hundred and forty dollars, in Toronto, hardly seemed like too much. "How many rooms?" I asked.

"Three and one kitchen, no fridge, no stove."

"Oh I see." Even so, it seemed like a bargain – I could always pick these up second hand, I decided. "Can I see?" I asked. And at last, he stepped aside to let me pass.

"You no have husband?" he asked.

"No, I'm . . . not married." To say I was divorced would not, I suspected, help me get the flat. And I needed no more than one glance to know that I definitely wanted the place. An entire floor really, it was surprisingly beautiful – bright and immaculate, with a sun room and stained-glass windows. I was much too excited to notice, until the very end, the absence of one obvious room.

"No bathroom?" I asked, puzzled to have missed it and wondering why in the world he was acting so indifferent.

"Downstairs," he said, flicking off the lights.

And I, again: "Can I see?"

Well, it turned out the bathroom was in the basement and that I would have to share it with him. Though it was perfectly clean, I remember thinking it could be a problem, for – he told me then – he lived right there, across the hall from the bathroom. Now, it was my turn to feign nonchalance.

"You live alone?" I asked while he, with sudden defiance, snapped: "You want the flat, yes or no?"

I didn't understand any of it but I could take care of myself. I said yes, I would take it – quickly, before he could change his mind. Above all, I was puzzled that a man in his mid-thirties would own a three-storey house and live, alone, in the musty basement.

"You sure you can pay the rent?" he asked as I wrote out the first month's cheque.

"I'm sure," I said and, ignorant as I was, added: "Don't worry, I earn as much as a man."

Monday must have been the day they mixed the chocolate at the factory, for on those days the smell was so strong, one expected those red, home-grown tomatoes to have a cocoa taste. I moved into the flat the first Monday in October and I remember wondering whether I would eventually sicken of the sweet, persistent smell which Manuel, wearing his factory clothes, seemed to have brought with him right into my flat.

"So much furniture!" he said when I and two friends came back with my possessions from Montreal. "You buy it all?" he asked, looking, I remember, baffled and awed. He hovered around us, eyeing with inexplicable intensity the velvet couch, the Persian rugs. Now and then, he would give us a hand but mostly, he just stood there, pretending to busy himself with a light fixture or cupboard door, but looking the way a man might while handing over a family heirloom to a pawnbroker. He seemed curious too about my friends, Stuart and Jean-Paul.

"That man, the tall one, he your husband, no?" he said when the two of them had gone to return the trailer.

"I'm not married," I repeated. I couldn't understand why he should look so downcast about it. Did he, I wondered, feel uneasy about having a single woman in the house? Did he mind my bringing male friends over?

Stuart and Jean-Paul drove back that night and the next few days assured me Manuel was likely to keep a perfectly respectful distance. Both he and the Melos upstairs worked day and night, coming home, it seemed, only to eat and sleep. My desk was in the sun room, overlooking the garden, and each day, I would see him arrive in his chocolate-stained overalls and bend over the crisp, leafy plants, picking a ripe tomato, a green pepper. He pretended not to know I was there, though more than once, he must have heard the typewriter. His daily vegetable picking – slow and self-absorbed – was one of several rituals I was getting to know. Twice or three times a week, he would take out the garbage bins before going to work and, when he came home, carry them back under my windows where he would linger for suspiciously long moments, whistling and rattling the lids and, from time to time, glancing furtively into the lit-up living room. Once a week, on Saturdays, he would drive down to Kensington Market and return with heavy sacks of potatoes and newspaper-wrapped fish which he fried every Saturday before going out into the driveway to wash and polish his '71 Chevy. The car stood locked up in the garage all week, but he washed it faithfully all the same: once a week, after the trip to the market.

It was an unusually mild fall and I was beginning to discover the city – looking for curtain material in cluttered textile shops or for a paper lantern in Chinatown. Toronto seemed supremely organized for shopping purposes: Fabric and hardware stores on Spadina, second-hand furniture on Queen Street. Each day, the radius of familiar territory expanded and each day, the toy-like streetcars would bring me back to the more familiar streets I was beginning to think of as home. That was the fall I wore nothing but black until one day, I perceived the Italian and Portuguese widows smiling at me like unlikely but sympathetic sisters. I could see it so plainly in their eyes: Ah, so young, poor thing, and already in mourning! I didn't mind their silent solicitude. There was something comforting in that feeling of shared bereavement – shared anything, I suppose. But soon after that, my black outfit – skirt, sweater, leotards – began to seem like a parody of their loss and I went back to wearing green corduroy skirts and maroon sweaters – the clothes which, I had to admit, were more properly mine.

Manuel's place was directly under my living room and, judging from the area it occupied, must have consisted of no more than one small room where he slept and cooked his fish and his potatoes. I say *must have* because he seemed as secretive about his place as an adolescent hiding old *Playboys*.When, one evening, I knocked on his door to ask about the fuse box (which turned out to be in his room), he kept the door open a crack, so that all I could see was the pale green corner with its peeling paint. It was not until a day or two later, however, that I fully realized the extent of his shame, his pride.

That afternoon (it was Saturday and Manuel was, as usual, washing his car in the driveway), I found my telephone dead and opening the back door, asked whether I might use his. I would have preferred to ask Ava-Maria upstairs but I had seen her leave with her husband only a short while earlier, on their way to the market and laundry.

Manuel turned off the hose and said yes, he would bring it up in a minute. I noticed, while waiting, that the vine leaves had turned quite yellow and the tomatoes were beginning to rot. I thought, with some surprise, that he must have had a plug phone, but the surprise turned to pained astonishment when he came upstairs carrying an *unwired* telephone which he at once proceeded to connect to an old phone box out in the hall.

"Manuel, I am sorry . . . I didn't know you were going to – "

"No trouble, no trouble," he kept repeating, crouching on the floor with two screwdrivers.

"I'm sorry, really, I'm sorry."

"Is okay, you no have stove yet?"

"No, I'll probably get one this week."

"Everything costs too much money, no?" he smiled. He told me then about the job he used to have in the Sudbury mines and how, one winter, he slipped on the ice and broke his back.

"Nine months I no work," he said, "But Workmen's Compensation, they no pay me." He told me they paid only for work accidents. "And now," he said, "I wait another year for marry." He looked at my living room wistfully, then turned to face me again.

"I read your name in newspaper last week," he said, "Raoul and Ava-Maria, they want to know why you no have husband, I tell them you write for Toronto *Star*, right?"

"And you, what do you do?" I asked, just then more out of desire to change the subject than real curiosity.

"I work at Neilson Chocolate Factory."

"Yes, I know, but what do you do, exactly?"

"Chocolate, lots and lots of chocolate, mountains of chocolate," he said with a great gesture. "You like chocolate?"

"Yes, I like." I was gradually lapsing into his kind of speech.

"In Portugal, even in holidays, we no have much chocolate and now . . . I no like," he finished sadly. I was intrigued by his talk of marriage. He was always alone. He had no visitors, male or female. And he worked about fourteen hours every day.

"Do you have a fiancée?" I asked, dialing the telephone company.

"No," he said, "I no have enough money." He waited while I talked to the telephone people, watching the squirrels in the garden pluck the rose hips from his bushes and disappear quickly among the yellowing foliage of his vegetable garden. I too had no visitors that first month. I was new in Toronto and was just beginning to meet people.

Those first two weeks, while looking for a stove, I would often eat at Lydia's Roti Shop around the corner. Lydia was a big Jamaican with an enormous bust pressing against the white jersey she wore day in and day out. Her voluptuous, knowing body seemed strangely incongruous with the shy and self-effacing expression on her aging face. She looked like a woman whose adolescence had congealed below the lines and wrinkles of middle age. She was married to a man from Trinidad and her roti shop was a favorite hangout for other islanders. A mother to some and object of sexual fantasies to others, she kept the place open day and night, making excellent, the best, roti. I acquired a great taste for the spicy, cheap stuff and for the Caribbean music the customers played on the juke box. Bent over the oozing pancake, I would eavesdrop on their conversations.

"Listen to me, man, you let that woman have a finger and, I tell you, she'll soon want a hand!"

"Hey, man, you don't know what you talking about, Pearl and me, we – " The voices sharp and urgent and, whatever the subject, as inexplicably optimistic as that relentless music. They knew how to live it up, those islanders and, late at night, it was an especially good place to go to, the hot spice lingering in my mouth for a long time after. Barely five minutes away, Manuel's house – the street – was always a startling surprise after Lydia's shop. Everyone, it seemed, went to bed here by ten. Like Manuel and Raoul, they all had to get up at four or five in the morning and leave for work before it was quite light. I don't know whether Neilson's had a night shift or not, but the chocolate smell continued to hover over the neighbourhood long after the workers had gone to sleep.

Now that I think about it, my problems with Manuel seemed to start when I first hung up my curtains. At the time, I didn't give it a thought, but he seemed to take it as a personal affront that I should want to protect my privacy. Perhaps he thought it was a rebuke for his curiosity, perhaps he saw it as an assertion of immoral intentions (I say *intentions* because, living below me, he must have known my lifestyle was above reproach). In any case, he began greeting me with extreme coldness, looking at once guilty and accusing whenever we met on the stairs and muttering under his breath when I said "How are you?" It is possible, however, that his mood had nothing to do with me, for twice that week, some friend of his arrived at the house and, for a long time, banged on Manuel's door and called his name. It was sometime past nine and Manuel had just arrived from work, but he did not come to the door and I did not let the man in. If there was anything I understood, even then, it was that he would want no one to see his place.

It was the week before Hallowe'en and, every afternoon, some child would ring my bell and ask me to buy a Neilson chocolate bar.

"How much?" I would ask.

"One dollar."

"One dollar!" It seemed like a lot, even for a large bar, but – for some reason – they all pushed the same product and all, somewhat timidly, demanded one dollar. When I asked why it cost so much, they just stared at me with their dark, somber eyes; so that I was never sure whether they had understood me. Only one of them – a fat, red-cheeked boy with energetic gestures – did not lose his bearings. Perhaps someone had already prepared him for the question, for the words were hardly out of my mouth when, meeting my eyes, the boy said: "It's for the poor people, the Greek and Portuguese and Italian people." Something told me he was lying, but I bought the chocolate anyway and ate it all that same night. Only after it was finished did I start to curse the boy. The chocolate bar turned out to be full of almonds and probably worth close to a dollar, but all the same, I was by then quite certain that the boy had lied.

My search for an antique table took me to the outlying suburbs of Toronto where families renovating or selling a home would advertise in the paper, quickly disposing of their possessions for half the price an antique dealer might want. I had no car in those days and used public transit, speculating about a given area on the basis of passengers getting on and off the subway. At Rosedale, for example, there would be elderly, meticulously-dressed women, or bearded men who worked as editors or radio producers; at Davisville, secretaries and hairdressers would get off; at Finch, housewives with small children and businessmen returning home. Sometimes, I would wonder whether Manuel, or the Melos, ever made it to these parts of town, to the ravines and lake, and what they might have thought of the pink faces framed by coiffed hair or fur collars. Far from the city centre, the buses had the blank serenity of people on their way to church and the further away one got, the paler and more homogeneous the faces seemed.

Heading back, on the other hand, the buses and trains would become microcosms of cosmopolitan fervour: The Greek and Jamaican and Chinese returning home from factories and fish shops, chattering in a language they would have identified as English, though no English-speaking person could hope to understand more than the occasional word. Here, a Macedonian tailor might be heard discussing the sign for his shop with an Italian barber, or a black hosiery sorter her child's tonsilitis with a blonde Ukrainian mother. The further south one got, the more weary and uncouth the faces seemed. But the eyes – most often black, but sometimes blue or green – were strangely luminous and, glancing at my sixty-dollar boots or suede coat, bright with patience and hope.

Hallowe'en night brought the children to my door once again, this time in large groups of five or six, dressed as queens and gypsies and cowboys, and repeating their "Trick or treat" over and over, as though I might otherwise fail to understand their lisping command. They came well into the night, the sons and daughters of my weary neighbours who would greet me on the street, but cautiously, making it clear that some time would have to pass before they knew how to treat me. Judging from the quantity of Neilson chocolates in the children's bags, many of them indeed were employed at the factory, but the children – with their feather crowns and painted faces – had not yet lost their enthusiasm.

"Look at all the Burnt Almonds I got!" they'd say, or "Pepita's mother gave you more Rosebuds than me!"

Ah, how sweet must have been the sleep of those dark-eyed children who lived by the factory and who, night after night, drifted into dreams of luscious, aromatic plenty.

I had meanwhile settled down to a routine of work and relaxation – going out to the theatre, meeting new friends.

"Can you imagine?" my visitors would say, "tons and tons of chocolate processed every day, *yum!*"

I was beginning to have quite a few visitors and could not help but notice that each time a car would park in front of the house, one of my neighbours would be watching from the windows across. In a way, even then, I could appreciate their point of view: why, they must have asked, does she not go to work in the morning? Why does an attractive woman live all alone? And why, yes why, do all these men come to visit – in the morning, at night?

At first, I was amused and joked about it with my visitors, most of whom were in fact professional acquaintances. Soon, however, my life in the house became incomprehensibly difficult.

In the first place, Manuel was developing personal habits which made the bathroom unusually disagreeable. The bathroom, I should point out, had been unpleasant even before that. I couldn't possibly have known this that first day, but the plumbing was so cheap that flushing the toilet brought about a kind of gurgling in the drains of both sink and bath, sometimes so violent that it seemed as though any moment, both would overflow with toilet water. Now – it was the beginning of November – I began to find the yellow sink spattered with chocolate-like stains and strewn with black hair. A week later, Manuel stopped flushing the toilet, going on to make every conceivable effort to offend me. It was an unmistakable protest, but why? What was he trying to tell me? It wasn't long before I was allowed to find out.

All through October, I had lived with no heat whatsoever. Occasionally, at night, it would get rather cold but it had been for the most part a sunny, warm month and, knowing how hard Manuel worked for his money, I had not complained. Right after Hallowe'en, however, fall arrived, with surprisingly low temperatures and gusty winds which blew away the last leaves of vine Manuel had planted. The neighbourhood cats, which used to hide among the swiss chard, were now plainly visible in the balding garden and, every day, I would hear the hissing of their encounters intermingled with the howling of the wind. Still, the heat was not turned on and, reluctant to complain, I began to spend more and more time by the steamed-up windows of Lydia's shop. Going home, the sharp air made the chocolate seem to come from a great distance – as though heralding the approach of snow – and my warm breath would be visible in the chilly night. At last, I decided to speak to him.

"Manuel," I said, hearing him come home one night, "it's very cold now, could you please – "

He did not let me finish my sentence. "Yes," he said, "I wanting to speak to you. Today, when I come home for lunch, you have friend in your flat!"

"Yes?" I said, thrown off by his finger which pointed accusingly in my face. What did my friend have to do with the heat?

"All the time," he went on, "you have friends and friends, you make music, laughing – I can no sleep all night!"

"But Manuel," I said, "I've never had a friend later than eleven."

"You lying, you have friend after one last night!"

"Oh no, that was a long-distance call."

"No!"

"Yes!"

It went on like that for a while, Manuel claiming I had men overnight, I – truthfully – denying; Manuel repeating he couldn't get any sleep, asking when did I do any work anyway; and I, losing my patience, saying it was none of his business, I worked when I wanted to, I didn't have to keep his hours!

Well, that was just what he seemed to be waiting for.

"Yes, you must," he finally said. "From tomorrow, no friends and you go sleeping at ten, like everybody."

I could hardly believe my ears. "Look," I said, "you can't tell me what to do, the flat – "

"You no go to sleep and work, I want new tenant end of December!"

At last, I gave up. I couldn't understand his outrage, the obvious lies. I liked working at night so that, in fact, most of my friends came for lunch or tea and, as I had pointed out, no one had ever stayed past eleven, though I certainly did not want to be denied my rights.

What was I to do?

He couldn't evict me, I knew, but he could make life unbearable unless I complied with his wishes. That was clearly out of the question. I was not about to start retiring at ten. I could not possibly live without friends. And I couldn't – I had meanwhile forgotten all about it – go on without heat. It was all very well for Manuel and the Melos – they were out most of the time – but I – was he trying to freeze me out, I wondered; was there someone else he wanted to rent the place to?

I decided to talk to an acquaintance who worked for Legal Aid, making my way downtown through the first snowstorm of the season. Already, I was beginning to think I would probably have to go, but "It's out of the question," the lawyer said; my landlord could do nothing to evict me, unless – he said – unless he had relatives he wanted to rent the flat to. I don't know why, but it was only then that I remembered seeing Manuel go down the week before with two gallons of paint. I had thought nothing of it at the time but there, in the lawyer's office, I had an overwhelming intuition.

"Manuel," I confronted him that very night, "you are planning to move upstairs, aren't you?"

He looked confused as a child, then – all at once – belligerent. "How you know that?" he asked.

I just glared, looking – I hoped – confident and wilful.

"You speaking to Raoul?"

"No, no – Look," I finally said, "if you wanted the place to yourself, why didn't you tell me last month?"

He looked down at his feet. "I change my mind," he said, guiltily, but with a curious sense of pride.

"Are you getting married?"

"No – one, two years maybe."

"Then why do you suddenly want the flat, why?"

He shrugged his shoulders and would not tell me. One thing I did know: If he wanted the place for himself, there was nothing I could do. Like it or not, I would have to start looking for a new place. It was damn annoying and I wanted to insist that he owed me an explanation, at the very least. Yet, with some part of me I must have understood something because, despite it all, I could feel no hostility toward him.

"I'll be out end of the month," I said, turning to climb the stairs, but stopped by the offended look on his face.

"No!" he said, leaving his door unguarded for once, "you no have to go before end of December, I give you one month, two."

"Well, I don't want to stay any longer than I have to."

"But please," he begged, "you no understand, I . . . you Canadian, I Portuguese, you can no understand."

"Maybe not," I said and went up the stairs to my flat. I could hear him pacing downstairs for a long time after, well past eleven, anyway.

The colder it got, the more powerful the chocolate smell seemed to grow. By mid-November, the factory seemed to be stepping up its production toward Christmas and I hardly saw Manuel in the next two weeks. The day after our confrontation, the heat was turned on and, for the rest of that month, the bathroom was kept as immaculate as it had been at the start. The utter desolation of the garden, however, made it difficult to believe that I had lived in that house for less than two months. I had thought, when I learned I'd have to go, that I would look for a place downtown, away from the immigrants' disapproving eyes and their stifling lifestyle. But in the following days, as I'd pass Lydia's shop or watch the children play around the factory, the thought of leaving the street, of breathing plain winter air devoid of all sweetness, became as painfully sharp as first frost. There was only one apartment building on the street and, for days, I had ignored the red sign: APARTMENT FOR RENT. I wanted to be able to come and go, to pull up my blinds at ten or eleven without feeling like the scarlet lady in some small village.

Well, it was a two-bedroom apartment and though it had nothing special to recommend it, I took it on impulse one afternoon, on my way from the Italian grocery. I felt curiously fortunate once I paid the deposit – as though, after all, I had been permitted to stay close to home.

Manuel was a changed man after our encounter. He had painted his room downstairs and found a new immigrant to move in as soon as he moved up to the first floor. Once or twice, I heard visitors' voices downstairs and he seemed to have bought himself a radio. One day, he came back from the market with crated grapes and over the weekend made, he later told me, fifty bottles of wine, which left the basement area sticky with dark, purple stains and attracted innumerable fruit flies multiplying rapidly, though we sprayed and sprayed.

When Ava-Maria told him I had fallen and sprained my ankle, he came up to see me and, shy as a village boy, handed me a box of Neilson chocolates.

"One day you tell me you like chocolates, remember?"

"I remember," I said. "Thank you very much."

There was an awkward silence between us, then – looking up at the ceiling – he said: "I gonna help you move, OK?"

"Oh no," I protested, "really, it's not necessary."

But he looked as obstinate as he had that first day. "Yes," he said, "I gonna help you."

And that was that. He would not take no for an answer, saying he knew someone with a truck and that he and Raoul would help. I don't know why, but I could not bring myself to eat those chocolates, finally packing them with my kitchen stuff.

When the day came, they showed up as agreed, he and Raoul and Ava-Maria, the four of us carrying the bookshelves, the couch, the Tiffany lamp. We were all a little awkward, I think, but Manuel made every effort to help me forget that, all said and done, I was still getting evicted. At one point, Ava-Maria and I stood watching while Manuel and her husband manoeuvered the large secretarial desk which – Manuel insisted, laughing – could not have come through that door. Ava-Maria smiled and moved closer beside me.

"You still mad?" she asked, searching my eyes in the dark.

"I'm not . . . mad," I said, more embarrassed than ever.

"Manuel," she said, "he no like to live in basement after you come here."

"But why, has he told you why?"

She shrugged her shoulders, much as Manuel himself had done – as though, the gesture seemed to say, I could not possibly hope to understand.

"You are a woman and you Canadian," she said at last, "and you make lots of money – he no like that."

"But I'm not rich," I protested, "I have no money in the bank."

She only smiled – the slight, resigned smile an adult might bestow upon a slow child. "You no work in a factory," she said. "You born here."

The men meanwhile had managed to get the desk through the door, though the collapsible typewriter stand kept springing out.

"You gonna write lots of stories for Toronto *Star*, yes?" Manuel said, grinning, and I nodded, smiling back.

As soon as I get settled, I thought, I'm going to contact Neilson's and do a story for *Weekend* Magazine. I did phone their PR man several times that year and told his secretary what I wanted. She had a polished, executive-secretary's voice but her name was Miss Lopes. She said her boss, Mr. Amado, would call me back as soon as he was free. He never did.

Questions for Writing and Discussion

Discovering Meaning

1. Describe the character of Manuel de Sousa. What makes him decide to move upstairs to the narrator's flat? Why does he not give her formal notice of his intention rather than create unbearable conditions that force her to move?

2. Why does the narrator feel no hostility towards Manuel despite his intolerable treatment and his irrational demands?

3. After paying the deposit for the new apartment in the same neighbourhood, why does the narrator feel as though she has

been "permitted to stay close to home"? What traits in her character make her responsive to life in this neighbourhood?

4. Manuel says sadly, "In Portugal, even in holidays, we no have much chocolate and now . . . I no like." Why has he lost his taste for chocolates?

5. Manuel has difficulty accepting the freedom and independence of Canadian women. Does his attitude change at the end of the story? Why or why not?

Exploring Method

1. The first-person narrator recalls her life in the neighbourhood when she unwraps a Neilson Crispy Crunch. As a journalist, she is able to recreate the experience with the clarity and immediacy with which she encountered it in the past. What devices does the writer use to make the story as vividly alive for the reader as it is for the narrator recalling her experience?

2. The author indicates the narrator's lack of understanding of Manuel in the past and her present understanding of him as she recalls the past. Identify these moments of understanding. How do they function in the story?

3. What purpose does the author achieve in presenting an account of the narrator's tours downtown and through the suburbs of Toronto?

4. What techniques does the author use to convey the hardships of immigrant life in the area around the chocolate factory?

5. What is the function of these characters in the story: (a) the Portuguese women in black, (b) the local children, and (c) Ava-Maria Melos?

Suggestions for Writing

1. Compare the responses of these people to their new country:
   a) the Caribbean Islanders and the Portuguese;
   b) the children in the neighbourhood and their parents;
   c) the various cultural groups in the buses and trains and the immigrants living around the chocolate factory.
   Using a spokesperson for each group, write three dialogues in which your characters express their views of Canadian culture.

2. Referring to her disagreements with Manuel, the narrator observes, "I might have known from the start, the two of us – worlds apart – were bound to have our share." Describe a typical day in the life of each – the narrator and Manuel – illustrating the conditions that make their conflict inevitable.

3. Study the cultural mixture in your school. If you are a new Canadian, describe your experience in adjusting to other cul-

tural groups and to life in Canada in general. If not, interview some new Canadian students and describe their experience.

4. The author describes Lydia's Roti Shop. Study the three paragraphs beginning, "Those first two weeks, while looking for a stove, I would often eat at Lydia's Roti Shop around the corner." Using the paragraphs as a model, describe your favourite restaurant or the school cafeteria and its diners.

Examining Social Issues

1. Ava-Maria explains Manuel's behaviour to the narrator: "You are a woman and you Canadian, and you make lots of money – he no like that." Do such attitudes towards single, independent women still exist, or are they changing? Support your answer with examples.

2. The author describes the life of the immigrant men in this way: "Labouring for twelve, fifteen hours a day while their wives scrubbed and laundered and waited on tables and the children played football on the icy streets." In many families both parents have to work. What are the effects, good and bad, on children of having both parents working? What are the effects in single-parent families when the parent works? Use your own experience and your friends' experiences to support your answer.

3. In contrast to Manuel's and Ava-Maria Melos's "hopelessly in-adequate" English, the Portuguese secretary at Neilson's, Miss Lopes, has a "polished, executive-secretary's voice." A controversial issue in education is whether to teach children of cultural minorities in their own languages, at least for the first few years, or to require them to learn English right away. What is your opinion? Support your view with your own experience or with your observations of new Canadian friends at school.

4. Adults have answered the urgent questions that they posed in late adolescence: "Who am I to be?" and "Where am I going?" They can say "I am" and "I am here": they have developed satisfying identities with an adult self-image. They have made vocational choices that permit them to pursue a creative life with freedom and dignity; they are members of their communities, secure in their relations with others and prepared to participate in improving their society. Using these standards, rate the level of maturity of the main characters in "To Earn My Living . . . ," "Some Grist to Mervyn's Mill," and "The Neilson Chocolate Factory."

Mr. and Mrs. Fairbanks

Morley Callaghan

Morley Callaghan, one of Canada's foremost novelists and writers of short stories, has a distinctly individual style. His simple sentences, with few adjectives, and his colloquial dialogue capture the rhythm of North American speech. In his condensed descriptive passages, he often focuses on details that appear trivial but assume importance as the story unfolds.

Callaghan's early stories in A Native Argosy *(1929) are concerned with family relationships, with love, and with the need to maintain one's dignity when confronting a reality that has not measured up to the dream. The stories in his later collection* Now That April's Here *(1936), from which "Mr. and Mrs. Fairbanks" is taken, reflect the difficult social conditions of the Depression and are concerned with young lovers' problems, relations between parents and children, and a range of religious and moral issues. Callaghan's characters in* Now That April's Here *are unpretentious, ordinary people, but generally more sophisticated and intelligent than the bewildered rural characters in his earlier collection.*

The typical Callaghan story is a brief psychological drama that involves little action. The problem is posed and the story is told with ease and economy, as the author selects significant details, depicts mood, and moves his characters through a climax towards an ending; it may or may not resolve the original problem, but it leaves the issue lingering in the reader's mind. Sometimes, as in "Mr. and Mrs. Fairbanks," the conclusion returns to the same emotional atmosphere introduced at the beginning but the problem is perceived from a new perspective, in the light of a changed situation.

Callaghan's tone is consistently compassionate, yet objective. His stories leave the reader with a significant universal truth: that respect for individual dignity, patience, tolerance, and love can provide the best solution to human problems and the best basis for social relationships. "Mr. and Mrs. Fairbanks" leaves the reader with these truths. It captures the fragility of a young couple's relationship: the rapid shifts from happiness to despair and back to happiness that often occur in the difficult process of adjustment in marriage.

In the afternoon sunlight, young Mrs. Fairbanks and her husband were walking in the park. They had been married just a year. She was a small girl with fair bobbed hair, wearing a little tilted felt hat, who walked with a short light step. Her thin, boyish husband looked very tall beside her. They were walking close together as if sharing a secret that made them silent and a little afraid, but gradually an expression of uneasy discontent settled on Mrs. Fairbanks' plump smooth face. Sometimes she glanced up at her husband, not knowing whether to be upset or pleased by his eagerness. He looked as if he wanted to go striding forward into the sunlight with a wide grin on his face.

"I don't know why you seem so glad. Weren't you happy as we were before?" she asked suddenly.

"Sure we were happy, and everything is still working along splendidly," he said.

"In a way it would have been nice if everything could have remained as it was," she said. "I don't want to grow old."

"Why should you grow old," he said, bending down confidentially as if she were a little girl and didn't quite know what she wanted. "You just wait a while. You just wait till you get used to the idea, then you'll see what I mean."

"Tell me why you feel so good."

"I don't know why. It just makes me feel more expansive, more abundant, a kind of full and overflowing feeling," he said, grinning.

"That's very nice of you," she said, teasing him. "You don't have to put up with anything, though. You won't have to look like me."

"You just ought to see how you look, Helen," he said earnestly. "Your face is soft and plump and kind of all glowing, and your neck and shoulders are rounder and fuller than they ever were. You look lovely, Helen."

"But I'm scared, Bill."

"Why should you be scared? It's happening all the time, isn't it? It happens to nearly all women."

"I know. But I'm such a little coward, really I am. I can never stand anything. I'll be terribly scared," she said, hanging on to his arm tightly. And there was really a fear in her, a deep uneasiness mixed with wonder at what was taking place within her. She glanced up at the side of Bill's long face and smiled, for he couldn't conceal his ridiculous pride in himself. "I don't feel sure about anything," she thought to herself. "We hadn't counted on this at all. Everything will change now. The things we used to look forward to are already passing away." For a few moments she walked along holding her husband's arm with her eyes closed, and she knew his arm was squeezing her wrist as if he never wanted her to get away from him. Opening her eyes, she looked around the park in the strong sunlight and smiled up innocently at her husband. They smiled at each other, went walking along the dry path, and Mrs. Fairbanks wondered if any one passing would see her as Bill had seen her, glowing with contentment.

They were passing a bench by the walk where an old man with a short, red face, as if the blood had all gone to his head, was sitting. One half of the bench was shaded by his tired body. His hat was off and the sun was shining on straggly wisps of gray hair at his temples. One of his shoes was laced up with a piece of string. He was slouched back on the bench with his eyes closed, looking like a beggar who was too weary to beg even with his eyes. The moment Mrs. Fairbanks looked at him she forgot her own mild discontent. She stopped on the path, wanting to give something to the tired shabby man.

"I'm going to give him something," she said, looking up eagerly at her husband.

"Go ahead," he said. "Only you can't give to all the bums."

"He looks so tired with his eyes closed and the sun shining," she said. Smiling, she fumbled in her purse, feeling sure Bill wanted her to do anything that would make her happy. From her purse she took twenty-five cents and stepped over to the bench, saying to the man, "Please, here you are." She was smiling broadly, quite pleased with herself. Lifting his head quickly, the man opened his eyes and saw she was holding out her hand to him. He had pale blue watery eyes with red rims, and when he saw she was offering him money, he did not smile nor even open his mouth, he just turned his eyes up and looked at her steadily with simple dignity and then turned away.

"Oh, I'm so sorry," she said, drawing her hand back hastily.

But the old man merely nodded his head as she stepped back to her husband, took hold of his arm, and tried to walk him away rapidly.

"I feel terrible, something terrible," she said to Bill. A warm flush of colour came into her face, and her head began to feel hot from the embarrassment. "The poor fellow, he wasn't a beggar at all and I was insulting him like a clumsy stupid woman." Mrs. Fairbanks felt completely humiliated, but her pride, too, was hurt and soon she began to resent this humiliation which was becoming like a heavy weight of dejection inside her. She dared not look around. "It was a crazy thing to do," she said. "I feel terrible and I guess he feels terrible, too."

"It was an embarrassing situation all right," Bill said.

"He feels bad enough as it is and I probably made him feel worse," she said. "I felt like running away."

"There's no use feeling that way, dear. He's probably just an old fellow out of work, or maybe even he does work. You can't tell. It's all right. He ought to be grateful."

"If he was out of work it would make him feel more resentful."

"Forget about it, dear. There are plenty of men out of work these days and if you offer a bum a dime and he won't take it, well, lots will, so he's got no reason to be snooty."

"He wasn't a bum and it was a quarter, not a dime, that I offered him," she said shortly.

"Don't argue, just stop worrying."

"I'm not arguing. But I do wish you wouldn't seem so insensitive."

"I just don't want you worrying, pet. We've got to look after you now."

"Can't I sympathize with him? Can't I regret that he's sitting there looking so hopeless? Doesn't it make any impression on you at all?"

"Sure it does. But day after day you see a lot of guys like that and you get used to them."

"There's a ruthless streak in you, I guess, Bill. You haven't got much feeling. That's what I was saying to you a while ago when we first came into the park and you were strutting along beside me and not worrying about me at all. You were grinning and thinking of yourself," she said excitedly. "You thought it made a man feel so expansive. Thinking of yourself and not wondering at all what I'd have to put up with."

He tried to plead with her, coaxing her with soft words, but she pushed his arm away and walked on alone, a sullen frown remaining on her face. And for no reason, she began to think that the afternoon sunlight was hot and withering, drying up the little bit of freshness there was in the park. Now she had none of the contentment she had had half an hour ago, instead there was fear in her, not fear of physical pain, but a deeper fear that there would be only poverty and ugliness in their life in the city.

Around the park were the great upright surfaces of the skyscrapers with windows glistening in the afternoon sunlight. When they had got married they had both intended to go on working, she thought. Bill had been studying law, but he had decided they would have to wait too long to get married if he went on with it, so he had quit and got a job in an office. That night, not much more than a year ago, when they had decided to marry, he had said, "With the two of us working we'll get along in fine style," and they had both started to laugh, feeling strong and eager. Now she would have to stop working. She began to think of the cold expression that had come into the red-rimmed eyes of the old fellow when he looked up at her. He was old and near the end, all the suffering that had been in his life was there to see on the bench: she and Bill were young, she thought. But they were poor. They would be very poor. Suddenly she said, "I don't want to have a baby."

"Still being afraid, I suppose," he said irritably.

"Yes, I'm afraid. Why shouldn't I be? And why should you understand?"

"Please, pet, don't get excited. I'm very, very sorry if I irritated you. See how sorry I am? I just didn't want you to go on having unpleasant thoughts because they're not good for the baby."

"I tell you I won't have a baby. We'll do something. Besides we're too poor, and it would just mean a lot of misery and maybe more children afterward. We can't afford it. It would make me so old."

"But it's making you look lovelier than ever now."

"I never, never want to grow old. I'll not do anything to make me old."

"Well, I'm trying not to appear important," he said mildly, "but you're being very unreasonable, dear." Then he stopped and shrugged his shoulders. She saw that his eyes were full of angry resentment, as if she were rejecting him and he felt savage. She was glad to see him feeling like this and wanted to hurt him more. "If you want to talk so haughtily about what we ought to do in this world," she said, "why don't you see to it that we have more money? I've never worried you very much, though I've had to slave harder than ever since we got married."

"You knew all about that when you married me," he said. "Listen to you. You worked a long time before you married me and you didn't save a nickel, either."

"I want to go home," she snapped at him.

"That suits me," he said.

"We'll go back then."

They turned, walked back the way they had come, walking now a little more rapidly, as if anxious to get somewhere in a hurry. The sun was not shining so strongly on the path. Looking dogged and resentful, they kept a step away from each other, so their elbows would not touch. Mrs. Fairbanks was taking deep breaths. All the eagerness to quarrel had gone out of her, but she wanted to get home and throw herself on the bed and cry. With his great long legs Bill was covering the ground far too quickly for her and she was getting all out of breath, but she dared not beg him to go slower. His mouth was set firmly, a pouting, stubborn mouth that looked so much nicer when he smiled.

Soon they were passing again the bench where the old man was sitting, and Mrs. Fairbanks, hurrying and looking down at the ground, hoped they would not be noticed. And when they had passed, and she felt secure, she couldn't help looking back timidly like a little girl. The man on the bench, who had seemed so sad, was looking after them, and suddenly he smiled at her, smiling gently as if he had noticed in the first place that they had been happy and now were like two lovers who had quarreled. So she smiled at him timidly, and then quite warmly, feeling full of humility.

As she walked on, still thinking of the man on the bench, she felt more and more peaceful. She put out her hand and took hold of her husband's arm and he slowed down at once, thinking she was trying to get her breath. She was feeling glad and almost humble, as they walked along slowly, while gradually she accepted all the strange reverence for her that had been in her husband all day. They went walking along slowly and peacefully, and soon she was wondering if people could notice that she felt all soft and glowing.

Questions for Writing and Discussion

Discovering Meaning

1. The story contains several references to Helen Fairbanks as "a little girl" and as "innocent." Is she immature? Describe her conflict. What are her major concerns?
2. Contrast the husband's and wife's attitudes to the old man on the park bench. What do their contrasting views of him reveal about their characters?
3. Trace the references to "a smile" in the story. What is its effect in each of its appearances? Why is Helen Fairbanks reassured after the old man's smile at the end of the story? What theme emerges from the repeated references to "a smile"?
4. What problem does the story pose in the opening? What added insight into the problem does the ending provide?

Exploring Method

1. Why does Callaghan focus on the wife's thoughts and emotions rather than on the husband's? What do we learn about Bill

Fairbanks through his wife's reactions to him? Is her assessment of her husband reliable? Why or why not? Describe your impression of Bill Fairbanks. What details determined your view?

2. The structure of the story is circular: it begins and ends in the same way, with harmony between husband and wife. What other details contribute to the circularity of the story? How does this circular structure relate to Callaghan's observations about the couple's relationship?
3. What is the old man's function in the story?
4. In describing Callaghan's early stories, critics often refer to their "simplicity" and "transparency," meaning that the author uses short sentences and no big words, and that the simplicity of his style helps the reader see character, setting, and situation as they are. Examine the words and the sentences in the story to determine whether the author succeeds or fails to bring his reader close to his characters and the setting through the "simplicity and transparency" of his style.
5. One of Callaghan's themes is that the way we see reality is conditioned by how we feel at the moment. How does he use the image of sunlight in the story to illustrate this theme?

Suggestions for Writing

1. The story portrays a couple facing the prospect of parenthood, the wife with mixed feelings, the husband with pride. Write them a letter describing what characteristics you have observed in them that would make them ideal parents or showing why they lack the emotional maturity for parenthood.
2. In the exchanges between husband and wife during the quarrel, Callaghan portrays the pressures and frustrations that pregnancy can generate. Put yourself in the husband's or the wife's shoes and describe your feelings as a prospective parent.
3. The old man on the park bench silently observes the young couple. Write a monologue in which you record the old man's thoughts and feelings as the couple pass him. Reveal in your monologue the reasons for his response to Helen Fairbanks's offer and for his smile as they pass him a second time.

Examining Social Issues

1. This story is set in the 1930s, when women were often regarded as weak and childish. Helen Fairbanks is repeatedly referred to as a "little girl." Does this attitude towards her affect her feeling about the responsibility of parenthood? Why or why not?

From this story and from research, compare the condition of Canadian women in the 1930s with their present condition; how do you think the changes have affected women's attitudes towards pregnancy and motherhood?

2. Does the ending resolve Helen Fairbanks's fears, or will they return? Does a new baby strengthen a relationship between husband and wife, or do the changes create new tensions? Support your opinion with observations of your neighbours and relatives and what you can discover from your reading on the topic.

3. Psychologists have observed that for young couples the period of pregnancy and childbirth can be the most hazardous and upsetting stage of family life. The arrival of a child threatens to interfere with personal freedom, to disrupt earlier intimacy between husband and wife, and to undermine economic security: where previously there might have been two incomes, now there will be only one, at least for a while, and just when more money is needed to care for the infant. The new family is child-centred, and couples neglect their own and each other's needs. Which of these developments does Helen Fairbanks seem anxious about? How can a couple prepare for having children so that they may ease the tension of the transition period?

4. Marriages without children have become common. What is your view of childless marriages? What social pressures do these couples experience?

3

AUTUMN

Mid-Life

Mid-Life

Men at Crossroads
Upon reaching forty, whatever illusions he
might have had before, this is inevitably a
time of assessment. He knows fairly clearly
just where he has placed in life's battles –
and just about how much further he can go.
At this point, many beliefs and values – all of
those obvious "truths" that support a man
while he is "settling down" – may suddenly
come into question. For he's been engaged
in a huge effort, working toward the thing
that was supposed to make him happy in
some glorious, distant future. And now here
he is, and things suddenly don't seem clear.

Maggie Scarf
"Husbands in Crisis"

Women at Crossroads
Women sense this inner crossroad earlier
than men do. . . . Whatever options she has
already played out, she feels a "my last
chance" urgency to review those options she
has set aside and those that aging and
biology will close off in the now foreseeable
future. For all her qualms and confusion
about where to start looking for a new
future, she usually enjoys an exhilaration of
release. Assertiveness begins rising. There
are so many firsts ahead.

Gail Sheehy
Passages

Dwarf House

Ann Beattie

American novelist and short-story writer Ann Beattie explores the strange rituals of American suburban life, exposing the chaos beneath the bland surface. Beattie says of her writing, "Many of the simple flat statements that I bring together are usually non sequiturs *or bordering on being* non sequiturs – *which reinforces the chaos. I write in these flat simple sentences because that's the way I think."*

Ann Beattie's fiction records her own generation, who were of college age during the social turbulence of the Sixties. Convinced that the world has somehow gone wrong, her characters are listless and despondent, saddened by their passive lives and the vacuum that the end of the turmoil has created. In an article, "Stories from the American Front," on Ann Beattie, Margaret Atwood diagnoses the source of the emotional dislocation she portrays in her fiction:

> *There are no longer any ties that bind, not securely, not definitely: jobs, marriages, the commitments of love, even the status of parent or child – all are in a state of flux. Thus everything is provisional, to be reinvented tomorrow, and no one can depend on anyone else.*

In "Dwarf House," MacDonald is one of a succession of passive, despondent characters that Beattie develops more fully in her later fiction.

Beattie's style of writing and method of telling her story are different from the traditional approach. Writers of fiction customarily present a sequence of events as if remembered. They use the past tense to give the illusion not of experience being seen, but of experience remembered and recreated in the mind. Beattie uses the present tense, which gives her scenes and characters the revealing clarity and immediacy of a photograph just taken. She tells her story in dialogue that reflects the triviality, repetition, and contradictions common in ordinary speech. Her humour often derives from her use of non sequiturs – *statements that have no logical relation to one another. Beattie avoids long passages of description, occasionally using carefully recorded detail to set a scene or to reveal character. The deliberate flatness of the prose,*

the truthfulness of the dialogue, the simple assertive sentences,
and the present-tense verbs give her characters and scenes a three-
dimensional life-like quality.

"Are you happy?" MacDonald says. "Because if you're happy I'll leave you alone."

MacDonald is sitting in a small gray chair, patterned with grayer leaves, talking to his brother, who is standing in a blue chair. MacDonald's brother is four feet, six and three-quarter inches tall, and when he stands in a chair he can look down on MacDonald. MacDonald is twenty-eight years old. His brother, James, is thirty-eight. There was a brother between them, Clem, who died of a rare disease in Panama. There was a sister also, Amy, who flew to Panama to be with her dying brother. She died in the same hospital, one month later, of the same disease. None of the family went to the funeral. Today MacDonald, at his mother's request, is visiting James to find out if he is happy. Of course James is not, but standing on the chair helps, and the twenty-dollar bill that MacDonald slipped into his tiny hand helps too.

"What do you want to live in a dwarf house for?"

"There's a giant here."

"Well it must just depress the hell out of the giant."

"He's pretty happy."

"Are you?"

"I'm as happy as the giant."

"What do you do all day?"

"Use up the family's money."

"You know I'm not here to accuse you. I'm here to see what I can do."

"She sent you again, didn't she?"

"Yes."

"Is this your lunch hour?"

"Yes."

"Have you eaten? I've got some candy bars in my room."

"Thank you. I'm not hungry."

"Place make you lose your appetite?"

"I do feel nervous. Do you like living here?"

"I like it better than the giant does. He's lost twenty-five pounds. Nobody's supposed to know about that – the official word is fifteen – but I overheard the doctors talking. He's lost twenty-five pounds."

"Is the food bad?"

"Sure. Why else would he lose twenty-five pounds?"

"Do you mind . . . if we don't talk about the giant right now? I'd like to take back some reassurance to Mother."

"Tell her I'm as happy as she is."

"You know she's not happy."

"She knows I'm not, too. Why does she keep sending you?"

"She's concerned about you. She'd like you to live at home. She'd come herself . . ."

"I know. But she gets nervous around freaks."

"I was going to say that she hasn't been going out much. She sent me, though, to see if you wouldn't reconsider."

"I'm not coming home, MacDonald."

"Well, is there anything you'd like from home?"

"They let you have pets here. I'd like a parakeet."

"A bird? Seriously?"

"Yeah. A green parakeet."

"I've never seen a green one."

"Pet stores will dye them any color you ask for."

"Isn't that harmful to them?"

"You want to please the parakeet or me?"

"How did it go?" MacDonald's wife asks.

"That place is a zoo. Well, it's worse than a zoo – it's what it is: a dwarf house."

"Is he happy?"

"I don't know. I didn't really get an answer out of him. There's a giant there who's starving to death, and he says he's happier than the giant. Or maybe he said he was as happy. I can't remember. Have we run out of vermouth?"

"Yes. I forgot to go to the liquor store. I'm sorry."

"That's all right. I don't think a drink would have much effect anyway."

"It might. If I had remembered to go to the liquor store."

"I'm just going to call Mother and get it over with."

"What's that in your pocket?"

"Candy bars. James gave them to me. He felt sorry for me because I'd given up my lunch hour to visit him."

"Your brother is really a very nice person."

"Yeah. He's a dwarf."

"What?"

"I mean that I think of him primarily as a dwarf. I've had to take care of him all my life."

"Your mother took care of him until he moved out of the house."

"Yeah, well it looks like he found a replacement for her. But you might need a drink before I tell you about it."

"Oh, tell me."

"He's got a little sweetie. He's in love with a woman who lives in the dwarf house. He introduced me. She's three feet eleven. She stood there smiling at my knees."

"That's wonderful that he has a friend."

"Not a friend – a fiancée. He claims that as soon as he's got enough money saved up he's going to marry this other dwarf."

"He is?"

"Isn't there some liquor store that delivers? I've seen liquor trucks in this neighborhood, I think."

His mother lives in a high-ceilinged old house on Newfield Street, in a neighborhood that is gradually being taken over by Puerto Ricans. Her phone has been busy for almost two hours, and Mac-Donald fears that she, too, may have been taken over by Puerto Ricans. He drives to his mother's house and knocks on the door. It is opened by a Puerto Rican woman, Mrs. Esposito.

"Is my mother all right?" he asks.

"Yes. She's okay."

"May I come in?"

"Oh, I'm sorry."

She steps aside – not that it does much good, because she's so wide that there's still not much room for passage. Mrs. Esposito is wearing a dress that looks like a jungle: tall streaks of green grass going every which way, brown stumps near the hem, flashes of red around her breasts.

"Who were you talking to?" he asks his mother.

"Carlotta was on the phone with her brother, seeing if he'll take her in. Her husband put her out again."

Mrs. Esposito, hearing her husband spoken of, rubs her hands in anguish.

"It took two hours?" MacDonald says good-naturedly, feeling sorry for her. "What was the verdict?"

"He won't," Mrs. Esposito answers.

"I told her she could stay here, but when she told him she was going to do that he went wild and said he didn't want her living just two doors down."

"I don't think he meant it," MacDonald says. "He was probably just drinking again."

"He had joined Alcoholics Anonymous," Mrs. Esposito says. "He didn't drink for two weeks, and he went to every meeting, and one night he came home and said he wanted me out."

MacDonald sits down, nodding nervously. The chair he sits in has a child's chair facing it, which is used as a footstool. When James lived with his mother it was his chair. His mother still keeps his furniture around – tiny child's glider, a mirror in the hall that is knee-high.

"Did you see James?" his mother asks.

"Yes. He said that he's very happy."

"I know he didn't say that. If I can't rely on you I'll have to go myself, and you know how I cry for days after I see him."

"He said he was pretty happy. He said he didn't think you were."

"Of course I'm not happy. He never calls."

"He likes the place he lives in. He's got other people to talk to now."

"Dwarfs, not people," his mother says. "He's hiding from the real world."

"He didn't have anybody but you to talk to when he lived at home. He's got a new part-time job that he likes better, too, working in a billing department."

"Sending unhappiness to people in the mail," his mother says.

"How are you doing?" he asks.

"As James says, I'm not happy."

"What can I do?" MacDonald asks.

"Go to see him tomorrow and tell him to come home."

"He won't leave. He's in love with somebody there."

"Who? Who does he say he's in love with? Not another social worker?"

"Some woman. I met her. She seems very nice."

"What's her name?"

"I don't remember."

"How tall is she?"

"She's a little shorter than James."

"Shorter than James?"

"Yes. A little shorter."

"What does she want with him?"

"He said they were in love."

"I heard you. I'm asking what she wants with him."

"I don't know. I really don't know. Is that sherry in that bottle? Do you mind . . ."

"I'll get it for you," Mrs. Esposito says.

"Well, who knows what anybody wants from anybody," his mother says. "Real love comes to naught. I loved your father and we had a dwarf."

"You shouldn't blame yourself," MacDonald says. He takes the glass of sherry from Mrs. Esposito.

"I shouldn't? I have to raise a dwarf and take care of him for thirty-eight years and then in my old age he leaves me. Who should I blame for that?"

"James," MacDonald says. "But he didn't mean to offend you."

"I should blame your father," his mother says, as if he hasn't spoken. "But he's dead. Who should I blame for his early death? God?"

His mother does not believe in God. She has not believed in God for thirty-eight years.

"I had to have a dwarf. I wanted grandchildren, and I know you won't give me any because you're afraid you'll produce a dwarf. Clem is dead, and Amy is dead. Bring me some of that sherry, too, Carlotta."

At five o'clock MacDonald calls his wife. "Honey," he says, "I'm going to be tied up in this meeting until seven. I should have called you before."

"That's all right," she says. "Have you eaten?"

"No. I'm in a meeting."

"We can eat when you come home."

"I think I'll grab a sandwich, though. Okay?"

"Okay. I got the parakeet."

"Good. Thank you."

"It's awful. I'll be glad to have it out of here."

"What's so awful about a parakeet?"

"I don't know. The man at the pet store gave me a ferris wheel with it, and a bell on a chain of seeds."

"Oh yeah? Free?"

"Of course. You don't think I'd buy junk like that, do you?"

"I wonder why he gave it to you."

"Oh, who knows. I got gin and vermouth today."

"Good," he says. "Fine. Talk to you later."

MacDonald takes off his tie and puts it in his pocket. At least once a week he goes to a run-down bar across town, telling his wife that he's in a meeting, putting his tie in his pocket. And once a week his wife remarks that she doesn't understand how he can get his tie wrinkled. He takes off his shoes and puts on sneakers, and takes an old brown corduroy jacket off a coat hook behind his desk. His secretary is still in her office. Usually she leaves before five, but whenever he leaves looking like a slob she seems to be there to say good-night to him.

"You wonder what's going on, don't you?" MacDonald says to his secretary.

She smiles. Her name is Betty, and she must be in her early thirties. All he really knows about his secretary is that she smiles a lot and that her name is Betty.

"Want to come along for some excitement?" he says.

"Where are you going?"

"I knew you were curious," he says.

Betty smiles.

"Want to come?" he says. "Like to see a little low life?"

"Sure," she says.

They go out to his car, a red Toyota. He hangs his jacket in the back and puts his shoes on the back seat.

"We're going to see a Japanese woman who beats people with figurines," he says.

Betty smiles. "Where are we really going?" she asks.

"You must know that businessmen are basically depraved," MacDonald says. "Don't you assume that I commit bizarre acts after hours?"

"No," Betty says.

"How old are you?" he asks.

"Thirty," she says.

"You're thirty years old and you're not a cynic yet?"

"How old are you?" she asks.

"Twenty-eight," MacDonald says.

"When you're thirty you'll be an optimist all the time," Betty says.

"What makes you optimistic?" he asks.

"I was just kidding. Actually, if I didn't take two kinds of pills, I couldn't smile every morning and evening for you. Remember the day I fell asleep at my desk? The day before I had had an abortion."

MacDonald's stomach feels strange – he wouldn't mind having a couple kinds of pills himself, to get rid of the strange feeling. Betty lights a cigarette, and the smoke doesn't help his stomach. But he had the strange feeling all day, even before Betty spoke. Maybe he has stomach cancer. Maybe he doesn't want to face James again. In the glove compartment there is a jar that Mrs. Esposito gave his mother and that his mother gave him to take to James. One of Mrs. Esposito's relatives sent it to her, at her request. It was made by a doctor in Puerto Rico. Supposedly, it can increase your height if rubbed regularly on the soles of the feet.

He feels nervous, knowing that it's in the glove compartment. The way his wife must feel having the parakeet and the ferris wheel sitting around the house. The house. His wife. Betty.

They park in front of a bar with a blue neon sign in the window that says IDEAL CAFÉ. There is a larger neon sign above that that says SCHLITZ. He and Betty sit in a back booth. He orders a pitcher of beer and a double order of spiced shrimp. Tammy Wynette is singing "D-I-V-O-R-C-E" on the jukebox.

"Isn't this place awful?" he says. "But the spiced shrimp are great."

Betty smiles.

"If you don't feel like smiling, don't smile," he says.

"Then all the pills would be for nothing."

"Everything is for nothing," he says.

"If you weren't drinking you could take one of the pills," Betty says. "Then you wouldn't feel that way."

"Did you see *Esquire*?" James asks.

"No," MacDonald says. "Why?"

"Wait here," James says.

MacDonald waits. A dwarf comes into the room and looks under his chair. MacDonald raises his feet.

"Excuse me," the dwarf says. He turns cartwheels to leave the room.

"He used to be with the circus," James says, returning. "He leads us in exercises now."

MacDonald looks at *Esquire*. There has been a convention of dwarfs at the Oakland Hilton, and *Esquire* got pictures of it. Two male dwarfs are leading a delighted female dwarf down a runway. A baseball team of dwarfs. A group picture. Someone named Larry – MacDonald does not look back up at the picture to see which one he is – says, "I haven't had so much fun since I was born." MacDonald turns another page. An article on Daniel Ellsberg.

"Huh," MacDonald says.

"How come *Esquire* didn't know about our dwarf house?" James asks. "They could have come here."

"Listen," MacDonald says. "Mother asked me to bring this to you. I don't mean to insult you, but she made me promise I'd deliver it. You know she's very worried about you."

"What is it?" James asks.

MacDonald gives him the piece of paper that Mrs. Esposito wrote instructions on in English.

"Take it back," James says.

"No. Then I'll have to tell her you refused it."

"Tell her."

"No. She's miserable. I know it's crazy, but just keep it for her sake."

James turns and throws the jar. Bright yellow liquid runs down the wall.

"Tell her not to send you back here either," James says. Mac-Donald thinks that if James were his size he would have hit him instead of only speaking.

"Come back and hit me if you want," MacDonald hollers. "Stand on the arm of this chair and hit me in the face."

James does not come back. A dwarf in the hallway says to Mac-Donald, as he is leaving, "It was a good idea to be sarcastic to him."

MacDonald and his wife and mother and Mrs. Esposito stand amid a cluster of dwarfs and one giant waiting for the wedding to begin. James and his bride are being married on the lawn outside the church. They are still inside with the minister. His mother is already weeping. "I wish I had never married your father," she says, and borrows Mrs. Esposito's handkerchief to dry her eyes. Mrs. Esposito is wearing her jungle dress again. On the way over she told MacDonald's wife that her husband had locked her out of the house and that she only had one dress. "It's lucky it was such a pretty one," his wife said, and Mrs. Esposito shyly protested that it wasn't very fancy, though.

The minister and James and his bride come out of the church onto the lawn. The minister is a hippie, or something like a hippie: a tall, white-faced man with stringy blond hair and black motor-cycle boots. "Friends," the minister says, "before the happy mar-riage of these two people, we will release this bird from its cage, symbolic of the new freedom of marriage, and of the ascension of the spirit."

The minister is holding the cage with the parakeet in it.

"MacDonald," his wife whispers, "that's the parakeet. You can't release a pet into the wild."

His mother disapproves of all this. Perhaps her tears are partly disapproval, and not all hatred of his father.

The bird is released: it flies shakily into a tree and disappears into the new spring foliage.

The dwarfs clap and cheer. The minister wraps his arms around himself and spins. In a second the wedding ceremony begins, and just a few minutes later it is over. James kisses the bride, and the dwarfs swarm around them. MacDonald thinks of a piece of Hershey bar he dropped in the woods once on a camping trip, and how the ants were all over it before he finished lacing his boot. He and his wife step forward, followed by his mother and Mrs. Esposito. MacDonald sees that the bride is smiling beautifully – a smile no pills could produce – and that the sun is shining on her hair so that it sparkles. She looks small, and bright, and so lovely that MacDonald, on his knees to kiss her, doesn't want to get up.

Questions for Writing and Discussion

Discovering Meaning

1. Beattie opens her story with the word "happy" and repeats the word with comic variations throughout the story. Trace its use in different contexts in the story. What social comment does the author make on the pursuit of happiness in modern society?
2. Describe the character of the mother. She says of James, "He's hiding from the real world." What tendency in her own conduct makes this comment ironic?
3. James asks for a green parakeet, which is later released at the wedding. Explain the significance of the parakeet.

Exploring Method

1. The story is told in the third person and centred on MacDonald, through whom we perceive the other characters in the story. Why has the author used this point of view to tell her story rather than using James or his mother as the character through whom the action and characters are perceived?
2. The story has a six-part structure. Discuss the content of each division. How is each related to the theme of happiness?
3. Examine MacDonald's conflicting attitudes towards James. How does the author portray his conflict? In which episode is the conflict most evident?
4. Contrast Betty's smile with the bride's smile in the final paragraph. What observation is the author making about the theme of happiness through the contrast? Identify other contrasts Beattie uses to reinforce her view of happiness.
5. What is MacDonald's feeling at the end of the story? How is it

related to the author's satire of society's attitudes towards those who are different? How does Beattie prepare us for this ending?

Suggestions for Writing

1. In the bar, Betty and MacDonald discuss optimism and pessimism. In the eighteenth-century novel *Candide*, by Voltaire, the French philosopher and novelist, the pessimist Martin observes, "Man is bound to live either in convulsions of misery or in the lethargy of boredom"; in other words, human beings experience mood swings. Write three dialogues in which the speakers respond to this view of life: between MacDonald and Betty; between James and his bride; and between you and a friend.

2. John Ciardi, the American poet and critic, in the essay "What Is Happiness?" defines it in this way: "Happiness is in the pursuit itself, in the meaningful pursuit of what is life-engaging and life-revealing, which is to say, in the ideal of becoming." Compare Beattie's and Ciardi's definitions. Write your own definition of happiness, supporting it with specific examples and illustrations.

3. In the story, Beattie is critical of society's attitude towards the physically handicapped. Is Beattie's criticism valid? Why or why not? Write a letter to the editor of your local newspaper in which you suggest ways your community can help the physically handicapped to live a fulfilling life.

Examining Social Issues

1. How has the mother affected the life of each of her sons? How has she affected the relationship between the two brothers? Compare James's and MacDonald's relations with their mother. Are such relationships common in families? Use your own experience and the experiences of your friends to support your view.

2. Betty takes two kinds of pills to maintain the appearance of happiness. Through Betty, the author is satirizing the artificial smile with which secretaries, clerks, supermarket cashiers, and salespersons greet the public. How do you feel about this social custom? How do you react to it as a customer or as an employee?

3. James marries at the age of thirty-eight. In the life cycle, this

age is within the mid-life crisis, a time when men and women re-evaluate their lives and often make changes: some may change their jobs, seek a divorce, or move to another region. In what sense is James experiencing this mid-life transition? Why is he marrying so late in his life?

Xanadu

Audrey Thomas

Before settling in Canada, Audrey Thomas lived in the United States, England, and Ghana. Her fiction reflects this background. Thomas's characters are generally American, English, and Canadian women confronting an alien environment or culture, where their uncertainties appear more stark. As a stylist, Thomas is a daring experimentalist. In telling her story, she alternates between two views of the protagonist: a view of her inner thoughts and an external view of her social behaviour. This technique makes her stories subtle in implication and provides a probing psychological exploration of the female consciousness during intense moments of self-doubt. Thomas's stories appear fragmentary in detail, her protagonists confused, uncomprehending, anguished. They often do not understand the sources of their private fears.

The story "Xanadu," from Thomas's collection Ten Green Bottles *(1967), is such a psychological exploration of a woman.*

In the beginning it was hardly paradise. That first night, "the night of the dreadful overture," as she was to call it later, when they had arrived at last at the house, bones aching from the long drive up from the harbor (over a road so pock-marked with holes it looked, as her husband said, "as though an army had blown it up as they retreated"), heads reeling from that first sensuous shock which Africa invariably delivers to the European consciousness, only to discover that the house was in utter darkness and the steward who had been engaged for them by the university was dead drunk on the front veranda (had quite literally stumbled upon this last discovery and experienced a thrill of horror, thinking, for a moment, that the man was dead, not drunk); when they had solved the mysteries of hanging mosquito nets and sent the children off to bed with the remains of the picnic lunch inside them ("we couldn't find so much as a can opener"); when she had inhaled the general atmosphere of damp and decay (which even two Bufferin tablets and a large whiskey failed to dispel), had succumbed to self-pity and despair and anger, she did the only sensible thing a woman can do in such circumstances – put her head

237

in her hands and wept. "The whole thing seemed a vast conspiracy," she said to her friends later, "and I felt, somehow, that a large and highly organized 'un-welcoming committee' had been at work." Then she would add, with a small laugh at her own idiosyncrasies, "I attach great importance to beginnings, to signs and portents you might say. My Irish ancestry I suppose." What made it worse was the fact that her husband insisted upon treating the whole thing as a joke, an adventure. "Jason seemed to find it all so interesting, so novel. He kept sticking his head out the door and sniffing – like a great dog who wanted to be let out, or a child on his first night of vacation. I honestly think that if I had been the violent sort – " (a pause while she impishly regarded her listeners and smiled the delightful smile which had made her such a favorite with both men and women) " – if I had been the violent sort I would have killed him on the spot. There is nothing more irritating," she would continue in a half-humorous, half-philosophic tone, "than the sight of another person enjoying a situation which you yourself find absolutely intolerable. *He* couldn't wait for daylight because he wanted to explore. *I* couldn't wait for daylight because I wanted to find the way to the nearest travel office."

Yes, it made for an amusing tale, in retrospect, but it could hardly be called an auspicious beginning. The next morning, in spite of the terrible and tiring events of the day before, she awoke early; and being unable to return to sleep or to endure the sight of her husband's peaceful face on the pillow beside her, she dressed quickly and went down to the kitchen. She was surveying with distaste a platoon of small ants who were breakfasting off the dirty dishes of the night before when she heard a light tap, tap ("almost like a discreet cough") on the kitchen door. Thinking it might be someone from the university, someone who would apologize for their not having been met; for their having to arrive in the dark, the pouring rain, alone and helpless; for the drunken steward, the missing can opener, the musty sheets, for the whole initial fiasco, she flung open the door "as full of righteous indignation as a balloon about to pop." There on the stoop stood a large black man, the blackest man she had ever seen. He was clad only in a pair of khaki shorts and a tattered string vest. She was still in that state, not at all unusual for a European, when all Africans look alike; so, although she had seen the steward of the night before, had seen him clearly in the light of her husband's torch, she did not realize at first that the two men bore very little resemblance to one another and she immediately assumed that they were the same. Naturally she was furious, and she spoke to him very sharply. ("I nearly sent him away!")

"I thought my husband made it very clear to you last night that your services would no longer be required. And if you think you're getting any wages for yesterday's performance you're very much mistaken." He watched her, impassive yet without hostility, and waited politely until she had finished. "There was I, screaming at the poor man like some fishwife, and he never moved a muscle; never even, as I recall, batted an eye." (Of course she was elaborating a little here. In actual fact she had never raised her voice, was furiously calm, spoke slowly and methodically as though, with each word, she were giving him a sharp but precise blow from an unseen hammer. But it made a better story the other way, and she enjoyed the picture she created in her listeners' minds, enjoyed the implication that she, who seemed the mildest of women, had been, at the outset, the typical European bitch. "I was positively archetypal," she would cry, and wrinkle her delightful nose with laughter and pretended self-distaste.) Yet when she had finished her little speech, the man did not go away as she expected and she spoke to him again. "Well? What is it you want? You can hardly expect us to give you a reference, can you?"

"No, Madame. Please, Madame, I know nothin' about yesterday. I have only just arrived. Do you want a steward, Madame?" It was then that she looked at him closely, *really* looked at him, and realized her terrible mistake, her awful blunder.

"I'm terribly sorry," she said, and smiled her brilliant smile – the smile that had endeared her to countless cab-drivers, milkmen, and meter-readers (not to mention her wide circle of friends) back home. "I thought you were someone else. Our steward, I mean the steward engaged for us, was drunk when we arrived. We sent him away, and I thought you were he. I've been very rude to you. Forgive me." She found herself offering an apology where no apology had, in fact, been demanded. Perhaps precisely because none had been asked for, not even hinted at in the man's impassive but polite silence; or perhaps because the awareness of centuries of what one might call, euphemistically, European bad manners made her feel that an apology was due and overdue. He accepted the apology in the same way in which he had accepted the accusations – with a polite silence. Yet this very silence seemed to comfort her, seemed to indicate that he understood and approved first, the anger, and second, the apology. But all he did, verbally, was to repeat, "Please, Madame, do you need a steward?"

"Can you cook?" she asked. He could.

"Can you read and write?" He could do this as well. ("Although why I asked that question, then, when all I needed, all I was desperate for, was someone who could clean and scrub and make the wretched stove light, who could bring domestic order out of the chaos into which we had been plunged, I'll never know." She did not remember that she had overheard a woman on the boat say that it was a tremendous advantage if "they" could read and write.)

"Well, then," she said, "you're hired."

"Just like that?" her listeners would ask in wonder and admiration. "Just like that," she would reply with a laugh. "Call it instinct, call it what you will; I somehow felt that he was what we wanted, what we needed, and that it would be ridiculous to ask for letters of reference, or his job book, with all those ants crawling around and the children about to wake up and want their breakfast. It was as though I had rubbed a lamp and the genie had appeared. One doesn't," she added with a laugh, "ask a genie for his testimonials."

And indeed, it did seem like magic. In minutes the dishes were done, the kitchen swept ("the broom seemed to appear from nowhere") and a large pan of bacon and eggs was frying merrily on the stove. Full of excitement she ran up the stairs which she had descended with such foreboding just half an hour before. She found her husband in the children's room, searching through suitcases for clean underwear and socks, for dry sandals (the eldest had managed to step in a puddle the night before), and a missing Teddy bear. The room was in chaos, and for a moment she experienced a renewal of despair as she glanced at the disorder and the all-too-obvious grime of the room itself. But then she remembered her errand, her news. "Listen, Jason, we've got a steward." "We had a steward, you mean," he replied from the corner, where he was trying to persuade the eldest that one brown sandal and one red would look very gay.

"No," she shook her head slowly, triumphantly, "we've got one – a new one. I just hired him."

"Good," he said. And that was all. No questions were asked – nothing. It seemed to him the most natural thing in the world that a steward should appear out of nowhere, and that his wife should hire him on the spot. She was a little put out, a little irritated, that her announcement did not, somehow, seem worthy of blaring trumpets and waving flags. Something (it couldn't have been spite) made her ask, "What if he isn't any good?"

"He'll be good," said her husband. And he was. By the time they all trooped down to breakfast, the sitting room had been swept, the ashtrays emptied, and the table laid with an almost military precision. A pot of coffee stood ready (a hot pad placed carefully

240

under it, she noted with approval), a bowl of fruit was waiting at each place, and she settled herself at the head of the table with a shy, triumphant smile – like a soldier modestly returning home, his erect back and grave smile bearing mute witness to battles won and obstacles endured. Everything was delicious: crisp bacon, solid but not solidified eggs, a veritable regiment of toast lined up for their inspection. And all the time the steward moving to and fro, his sandals slapping efficiently on the terrazzo floor. Plates were whisked away and clean plates substituted; a second rack of toast appeared, more steaming coffee: all this done so quickly, so quietly that the large black man might have been another Ariel with hosts of spirits at his command. The children were delighted, intrigued.

"Did *he* get the breakfast, Mommy? What's his name?" It came as a shock to her, almost as a sensation of good manners breached, that she had, in fact, forgotten to ask him his name. So when he appeared again she turned her shy, brilliant smile on him once more, extended her smile to him, offered it, the way a friend will convey apology with the soft pressure of a hand.

"I'm terribly sorry. I forgot to ask you your name."

"Joseph, Madame." And then, a bit confused as to how to end the brief interview (for she had never dealt with servants before), she simply played her smile over his face once more and reached for the marmalade.

By noon, when they had all returned from an exploratory trip around the compound, had met the registrar and gracefully accepted his equally graceful apologies for thinking that their ship was due in on the tenth, not the ninth; had explained to him about the drunken steward and the lack of electricity; had been assured that the man, if he could be found, would be dealt with, and had been informed, again with a graceful apology, that the electricity was always off on Thursday evenings; when they had collected their mail and bought a few things at the little shop, they discovered that the chaos of the bedrooms had disappeared. Suitcases had been unpacked and set out on the upstairs veranda to air, the children's clothes had been carefully sorted and put away, beds had been stripped of their musty sheets, and mattresses laid outside to absorb the sun. They discovered Joseph in the bathroom, kneeling over the tub and methodically kneading dirt out of the mosquito nets. Even the missing Teddy bear had been found. And later, after a (by now) predictably delicious lunch, as she lay on her immaculate bed in a state of happy exhaustion and listened to the laughter of the children, who were taking turns on an ancient swing which her husband had discovered at the bottom of the garden, she decided that things had, after all, turned out for the best. She felt, somehow, that she almost owed that miserable creature of the night before a vote of thanks. For if they hadn't had to send him away, then she, in turn, would have sent Joseph away that morning. A bad beginning, she reflected philosophically, just before she dozed off, does not necessarily imply a bad ending.

Thus the days slipped by, each one like some perfect, exotic jewel set carefully and expertly into her golden chalice of contentment. What of mosquitoes? Joseph examined the nets each day, and sprayed the lounge each evening after dinner while they sipped a cup of coffee on the veranda. What of the rains? At the first tentative rumble Joseph ran swiftly through the house, shutting the louvres, bringing in the washing, checking that the candlesticks were ready if the electricity should go off and remain off after dark. What of the orange lady, the bean man, the itinerant traders – the steady stream of merchandise which arrived each day? Joseph took care of it all – made certain that only the biggest oranges at the smallest price, the choicest beans, the largest bunch of bananas, the most serious traders, ever passed her threshold. For the first time in more years than she cared to remember she felt "caught up" with the sheer mass of business necessary to maintaining a comfortable, well-run home. For the first time she could wake up in the morning without a moral hangover, a sense of things left undone or done too hastily, of buttons still missing or unmatched socks. Instead, at six o'clock came the gentle, cough-like knock announcing the arrival of morning tea. Then they dressed, and while her husband shaved and collected the books he would need that morning, she dressed the children for school. By six-thirty breakfast was on the table; by seven her husband had left; by seven-thirty the eldest child had been picked up by the little school bus which traveled the compound. She read and played games with the little one until it was eight-fifteen and his turn to be picked up for nursery school. How strange it seemed, at first, to take her coffee out on the veranda and contemplate the day before her, the day that would unroll like a red carpet under her feet, to choose what she wanted to do, to ignore unmade beds and dirty dishes, washing and ironing, what to serve for lunch. She felt almost as though she were a convalescent who was now recovering slowly but happily, aware perhaps for the first time of the small beauties of the world, the large beauty of being alive at all. Joseph took care of everything – everyone; moved swiftly and noiselessly in and out of their days, a dark brown shuttle weaving a gay-colored carpet for her delight.

Yet with all this idleness, this new and unaccustomed leisure, she wasn't bored – not for a minute. She embarked, first of all, on a plan of self-improvement, sent away for books which she had always meant to read, decided to brush up on her French, to begin German. "After all," she said to Jason one evening as they sat on the veranda observing the strange, almost embarrassed pink of the tropical sunset, "I may never have this chance again."

"Which chance is that?"

"The chance to spread my intellectual wings a bit, to grow – as a person, I mean."

"Begin," he said with a teasing smile, "by keeping still and watching that sky."

But his teasing never bothered her, and she was perceptive enough to realize that even the most sympathetic of husbands could not possibly understand what it was like to be suddenly released from all the never-ending pressures of housework, the domestic cares that had always, since the birth of their first child, hovered over her like a swarm of angry bees. "It was not that I had really minded, of course, at the time. I'm old-fashioned enough to believe that a woman's place *is* in the home, not in the office. It's just that one gets so run down, spiritually as well, without even noticing it – without having *time* to notice it I should say." Now, for the first time in many years, she could read a magazine through from cover to cover if she felt like it, at one sitting; she could have friends in for dinner without being conscious, as the evening wore on, of the great stack of unwashed dishes which would have to be dealt with when the final goodbyes had been said. Now, while the guests sipped their coffee on the veranda she could hear, as one hears a delightful, far-off tune, the sound of Joseph washing up in the kitchen. And every evening, before the children were bathed and put to bed (always clean pajamas, always a fresh and spotless towel), she sat down with them and read a story: one that they chose, however long, and not one that she had chosen because it was short and quickly gotten through. This hour with the children became very precious to her, and she would even linger over it, as one lingers over a delicious meal, asking the children questions about the characters, reading favorite bits again. The children responded gaily, affectionately, giggling with delight as she changed her voice and became the wicked old witch, the dwarfs, the three bears. She felt like a flower that had been tightly curled and suddenly, in the embrace of the sun, begins to expand.

Then too, there were the coffee mornings when she met the other faculty wives and discussed the advantages and disadvantages of life in the tropics; how difficult it was to get butter and tea, how easy to get fresh fruit. And, of course, they discussed the stewards. It took several weeks before she realized just how lucky they had been. Tales of broken crockery, sullenness, petty thievery; gradually it dawned on her that Joseph was something of a miracle, a paragon. Each week some new disaster was reported. One steward had been caught wearing his master's vests, another had burned a large hole in an heirloom tablecloth. Yet another had disappeared for five days and returned with no explanation at all (and was duly sacked). One woman, who had arrived only three months before, was on her eleventh boy, and *he* didn't seem at all satisfactory. She would come away from these coffee mornings feeling like a healthy woman who has just been regaled with stories of ghastly operations; she found it all hard to believe. But there was, of course, the initial experience, that first night, and almost as though she felt it necessary to defend herself, to justify her good fortune, she would recall her own lurid introduction and speculate with her friends on what would have happened if – ? For she could, in truth, find no fault with Joseph at all. "As a matter of fact," she confided shyly to her new friends, "he is far better at managing a household than I am." Then she would smile her delightful smile and throw up her hands in a pretty gesture of mock despair. It was as though they had all been panning for gold and she, the lucky one, had by chance discovered the richest hoard, the deepest vein, was carrying Joseph's virtues around in her pocket like a sack of golden pebbles. Every Tuesday, early, before the sun had begun to beat down in earnest, she and Joseph would set off in the station wagon for town. Wandering from shop to shop, a gay straw basket on her arm, she did the weekly marketing. (And always Joseph behind her like a cool black shadow.) She enjoyed these Tuesday mornings, enjoyed the colorful pageantry of the busy town, the gay clothes of the men and women – "black Romans in bright togas. How pale and insipid they make the Europeans look." She enjoyed bargaining with the boys who came rushing up with grapefruit, limes, oranges; enjoyed haggling with the "Mammys" over vegetables. Sometimes they would go to the large open-air market where it was her turn to wait quietly while Joseph quickly bargained for yams and sweet potatoes, bananas and pineapples. (He had explained to her, very politely, that the prices were raised for a white woman, and he could therefore obtain more value for her money if he bargained for her; said all this in a manner which indicated full recognition of this deplorable practice and yet somehow managed to convey the idea that such bargaining would be a pleasure for him because it would serve her and "the Master.") Although she could not understand what he said to the various traders, she accepted his prices as absolute and would never dream of interfering in these sometimes long and rather tedious harangues. And if she needed something at the end of the week, she did not hesitate to send him off alone, knowing that her money would be well spent and that he would not add on a six-pence here or a shilling there, as was the practice of many of her friends' boys. "There is something almost regal about him," she commented once to her husband. "It is as though everything that he does for me, for us, is done because he genuinely likes us, because he accepts us as people and not as employers. He serves without being servile – if you know what I mean."

They became familiar figures in the town, the small, fair woman in the straw hat and the huge black man. Even when she refused a purchase she would flash her smile and the sting was taken out of the refusal. And when the chattering, the crowding around became too much, she had only to turn to Joseph with a smiling, half-despairing look; a few sharp words in the vernacular and the vegetable boys, the fruit boys, the little crowd of beggars and loungers, would scatter like so many dark birds. It was wonderful to feel so protected, so well-looked-after. And of course, as though to keep her ever mindful of just exactly how wonderful it all was, there were always the Sundays – Joseph's day off. On Sunday morning there was no welcoming cup of tea, no immaculately laid breakfast table, no strong brown arms to deal with the tidying and washing up. On Sundays the magic world, her enchanted island as it were, disappeared. Joseph, like a huge black Prospero, retired to his cell, and she was left to work her own miracles. Strangely enough, in spite of the fact that she was rested and content, things always went wrong for her on Sundays. As though she were a bride of a few months, she found herself burning toast, over-cooking eggs, dropping a precious jar of marmalade on the floor. Jason and the children were really quite brutal about it, teased her unmercifully. "Who's Joseph's stand-in?" her husband would say to the eldest child. "I think she might do for a small-boy, don't you, but she'll never make a cook-steward." At first she entered into the game, dropping serviettes on purpose, laying the table backwards, making faces and muttering, "Yes, Master, yes, Master," under her breath, or "Sorry, Master." But after a while it began to hurt a bit, this patronizing attitude of theirs, and one Sunday, when the youngest had wept bitter tears because Joseph wasn't there to chop up the eggs in a special way, she left the table in anger and wept a few bitter tears of her own. After all, in the terrible heat, with a cantankerous stove, they could hardly expect her to be perfect. However, they all filed shyly up to apologize and she soon forgave them with her brilliant, if this time somewhat watery, smile. Nevertheless, although she may have forgotten and forgiven, something remained at the back of her consciousness, something unnamed, unobserved, as infinitesimal as a grain of sand in an oyster, as quiet as the hum of a solitary mosquito. Monday came, Joseph returned to work and everything seemed, on the surface, to be back to normal. If a bit of the old magic was gone, she would have been the last person to admit it, perhaps the last person to understand why. And except for the incident of the snake, things might have gone on, indefinitely, very much as before.

However, one morning, as she made her way across the courtyard with a small basket of wet clothes (for she refused to allow Joseph to wash out her underthings, felt, somehow, that this was too much to ask any man to do), a large python sluggishly uncurled itself from the clothes pole not three feet away from her. For the space of a heartbeat she stood rooted to the spot, hypnotized with terror. Then she ran, screaming, into the house. She was still locked in the farthest bedroom when her husband and the children came home for lunch. When she had been assured that the snake had been killed, she ventured forth and allowed herself to be led to the table. The children were very excited, for apparently Joseph had killed the snake and it was stretched out on a pole behind his quarters. Already a group of admiring neighbors had been to see it and marveled over its length and ugliness. It appeared that the eldest child knew all about snakes. "A python won't bite you, Mother. It crushes you to death. Or anyway, it crushes animals and things." He gazed at her with a condescending smile. But the terror of the morning was still so great in her mind that she scarcely heard the child, and his words bounced off her consciousness without wounding. She ate and drank mechanically and then, at her husband's insistence, went back upstairs to lie down. She had not yet spoken to Joseph, had not yet thanked him for killing the snake. To tell the truth, she was somewhat embarrassed about the whole thing. It was not that anyone would blame her for running away, for screaming, or even for hysterically locking herself in the bedroom. She knew that most people, men as well as women, have a violent reaction to snakes whatever their size. No, she was all right there, and her hasty retreat could hardly be called a social blunder. (As a matter of fact, the one woman on the compound who did show an interest in reptiles was thought by many of the others to be a bit "queer" and certainly slightly unfeminine.) Her embarrassment had to do with Joseph. Lying on the immaculate bed, shutters drawn against the glare, she faced up to the unpleasant fact that she did not want to thank her steward, that in fact she wished the snake had managed to get away. Now she was somehow in his debt, owed something to this dark man who could cope with anything. ("Something?" whispered a voice in her ear. "Everything.") She felt, for the first time, that she belonged to Joseph and not Joseph to her. And yet, the more she thought about it, the more she realized that the incident of the snake was just one example of the way in which Joseph had gradually made himself indispensable. Suddenly she heard the voices of her husband and the children, directly below the window. They must be coming back from viewing the snake, and the littlest child was obviously a bit frightened. "Will Joseph kill all the snakes, Daddy?" she heard him ask in an anxious voice. "Of course. That's what he keeps the big stick for." "But what will we do on Sundays?" said the child, and began to cry. "I'll tell you what," said his father, trying to jolly the child and aware, of course, that he was being overheard. "On Sundays, if we see any snakes we'll take some of Mummy's toast and hit them right between the eyes. I should think they wouldn't come around here a second time." The child began to giggle, and all three moved around the corner and out of earshot. This was the crowning blow. Not only had Joseph made himself a necessity in their household, but he was making her a family joke. Each time that he increased in importance, she diminished. It was unbearable. She felt stifled, afraid. All the little helps which Joseph had performed for her, all the larger duties which he had removed from her weary shoulders – each act now seemed like a golden thread binding her tighter and tighter to a conception of herself as a totally incompetent, albeit delightful, woman. She felt as though she had been tricked out of her rights, deceived. She lit a cigarette and lay, smoking, while she examined the problem, explored the wound the way a child will explore with his tongue the raw hole where a tooth should be. By tea time she had come to a decision.

The next morning, after her husband had left, after the children had been kissed and put on the bus, she gave Joseph a pound note and asked him to go into the market for some fruits and vegetables. She stood at the window for a long time, watching his erect figure grow smaller and smaller until he turned the bend in the road and disappeared. Almost regretfully she opened the silver chest and selected three coffee spoons, holding the heavy silver in her hands for a moment, hating to part with it for even a few hours. Then, with the spoons in her pocket, she made her way slowly, determinedly, across the courtyard toward the servants' quarters at the back of the house.

Questions for Writing and Discussion

Discovering Meaning

1. Analyze the protagonist's character. Consider the repeated references to her "brilliant" smile, her relationship with her husband and children, and her relations with the white community and with Joseph.
2. Compare the wife's and the husband's views of Africa and their attitudes to its people.
3. With her newly granted freedom, the protagonist plans to read books and to study foreign languages. Compare her plans with what she actually does with her leisure. Why does she fail to follow through her original plan? Would her relationship with her family and with Joseph have been affected if she had carried out her plan of self-development? Why or why not?
4. Why does she become irritated with her family's teasing as the story proceeds?
5. When the protagonist first meets Joseph, she apologizes to him for having mistaken him for the drunken steward. The narrator speculates about her motive: "Perhaps ... the awareness of centuries of what one might call, euphemistically, European bad manners made her feel that an apology was due and overdue." Explain the reference to "European bad manners." Cite examples of the protagonist's "bad manners" towards Joseph as the story unfolds. Why does she not thank Joseph for saving her from the python?

Exploring Method

1. In telling the story, the author shifts from a third-person narrator to the protagonist's direct speech in the first person. What is the effect of such a method of telling her story? Examine the frequent use of parenthetical passages. What is their purpose?
2. How does the author convey Joseph's efficiency? Examine the use of devices such as repetition, contrast, and the passive

voice (for example, "Suitcases had been unpacked . . . beds had been stripped" instead of "Joseph had unpacked the suitcases and stripped the beds").

3. The story is unusual for its style. Discuss the purpose and effect of these devices:
   a) parallel sentence structure;
   b) questions and answers;
   c) the use of literary allusions to *Arabian Nights* tales and to Shakespeare's *The Tempest*;
   d) similes and analogies.
4. Examine the opening and closing of each of the two parts of the story. What pattern emerges?
5. At the end of the story, the author does not disclose what the protagonist's decision is. We view the initial preparation only. What is her decision? What is the author's purpose in withholding the content of the protagonist's plan and ending the story before she completes it? How does the author prepare the reader for the protagonist's final act?

Suggestions for Writing

1. The title "Xanadu" is taken from Samuel Coleridge's lyrical fragment "Kubla Khan." The poem begins:

> In Xanadu did Kubla Khan
> A stately pleasure-dome decree
> Where Alph, the sacred river, ran
> Through caverns measureless to man
> Down to a sunless sea.

   Coleridge's poem creates an imaginative setting full of natural and artificial beauty with an underlying sense of the supernatural and mysterious. Read the entire poem and write an analysis of the story explaining why "Xanadu" is an appropriate title for the story.
2. The story provides a view of Africa from a range of perspectives. Write descriptions of Africa as seen from the varying perspectives of the protagonist, her husband, the faculty wives, and Joseph.
3. Through Joseph's efficiency, the protagonist is given a brief holiday from her domestic responsibilities. If you were granted an extended holiday from all responsibilities, including school work, describe how you would spend your time.
4. This story presents an ironic study of a woman. Irony occurs when authors present characters in such a way that while the

characters view themselves and their behaviour favourably, the author makes the reader aware of their faults. Identify the passages that provide an ironic view of the protagonist. For each, contrast your impression of her with her view of herself.

5. In the story, the protagonist and her family observe and comment on Joseph. We do not discover what Joseph thinks of the family. Add a scene, where you think it is appropriate in the story, in which Joseph describes his view of the family.

Examining Social Issues

1. As a wife and mother, the protagonist feels insecure, afraid of the responsibility of running a household in an alien country where conditions are unlike those in her own country. Initially she withdraws from her family, with the result that her husband spends much of his free time with the children. What is the effect on the children? What is your impression of the husband's behaviour towards his wife? Could he have made her adjustment less difficult? Why or why not?

2. The father in the story appears to have a warm, open relationship with his children. William Raspberry, a columnist in Washington, D.C., claims in "What Fathers Want to Tell Daughters" that fathers have difficulty expressing their feelings towards their children, particularly towards their teenage daughters. Addressing a father-daughter breakfast at his daughter's school, he said:

> We are not particularly competent as fathers. . . . Understand one last thing. We love you. It doesn't always seem that way. Many of us would break out into a cold sweat if we had to look our teen-age daughters in the eye and say "I love you.". . . We cannot talk to you about our love for you any more than we can talk to you about any number of things that we would like to discuss with you. If it weren't for your mothers, I don't know how you'd ever learn anything about dealing with your emotions, your feelings, your emerging womanhood.

Do you think this is generally true of fathers in North American society? Why or why not? Illustrate with examples of your own father and others you know.

3. The protagonist confesses, "I'm old-fashioned enough to believe that a woman's place *is* in the home, not in the office." Do her actions reflect this conviction? Why or why not? How do you react to her view of women? Illustrate your view with

examples from observing your mother and mothers of friends.

4. With her freedom from household duties, the protagonist observes that she is able to spend more time reading to her children at bedtime; she can read a story "they chose, however long, and not one that she had chosen because it was short and quickly gotten through." How do children benefit from parents reading to them before bedtime? Illustrate your answer with your own experience as a child; if you have read to the younger children in your family or to children you have taken care of, comment on your experience as a reader.

5. In the story, when the protagonist "inhaled the general atmosphere of damp and decay (which even two Bufferin tablets and a large whiskey failed to dispel)," she put her head in her hands and wept. In contrast, Joseph brings order out of chaos through patience and industry. What in the background of each accounts for the different responses? Do their different cultures make a difference? Why or why not?

"I Want a Sunday Kind of Love"

Herbert Gold

Herbert Gold is a prolific American novelist, short-story writer, and essayist. In his fiction, Gold condemns his generation's blind pursuit of the tokens of success and contrasts it with his father's generation, who experienced insecurity but took risks to gain a deeper, more meaningful life.

Gold's fiction is most impressive for its inventive use of language to capture the nervous energy of American urban life. With verve and colour, he rapidly develops vital, believable characters and establishes dramatic scenes against vivid realistic settings. The half-phrases, broken lines, and single exclamatory words in his dialogue reflect the turns and twists of ordinary speech and the individual mannerisms of the speakers. But just beneath the vitality and buoyancy is a darker vision of loneliness and dislocation. Gold's style creates the joy that the events he presents lack.

Dan Shaper had the court-given right to spend Christmas vacation with his children. He drove in this midwinter weather from New York to Cleveland through the wintry length of turnpike – slush and flats of New Jersey, sudden black mountains of Pennsylvania with their marred white tunnels, then slithering down through Ohio foothills – and not a stoplight after Manhattan until he approached Cleveland, his arm still embracing the wheel. He stopped for coffee at a Howard Johnson's, the coffee given by a pimply waitress, and then in the men's room studied the machine which, for an investment of eleven cents, cranked forth the Lord's Prayer engraved on a penny. A dime for labor, one cent for material.

He drove on until, again shaking with fatigue, he stopped at an identical Howard Johnson's, was offered coffee by a girl who had pimples in the same place, and retreated to possibilities for stamping the Lord's Prayer on the same or a similar penny. "Lest We Forget," the placard advised.

Like the famous drowning man, he thought of the ten years of his marriage, but with this difference: the marriage was the drowning, and afterward came the gasping and choking recovery. (Was that an unmarked patrol car behind him? Sometimes they used Edsels.)

Then he thought of Paula and Cynthia, love like lust eating at his belly, and his daughters saying, "Why do you have to stay away so long?" He bit hard into memory as if it were a plum. It was a black rock and his teeth hurt. And then he thought: "I need a wife of my own, wife and children with me every day. I need someone standing with me in the mirror." And thought: no other children could replace Paula and Cynthia, who were born of his first youth when he was a skinny boy, amazed that he could create plump living flesh.

And then thought: another coffee, another doughnut to keep him going. At least his stomach could take it. If the limits of love had been defined by pride and lust, left and right, his stomach could not still have taken doughnuts; but it still could. There was a new rock 'n' roll version of "Jingle Bells" on the radio. Fathers like him all over the world were flying, driving, training in to claim their visiting rights with their children – their stomachs jerking with excitement, hope and strain in their eyes, love and guilt and pride and an aching foot on the accelerator. Merry Christmas. God rest ye, merry gentlemen. "And now the Chipmunk Song, the newest Christmas classic . . ."

Shaper switched stations. He was near enough to Cleveland so that the pushbuttons now brought him the stations for which they had been set.

> For he shall reign for ever and ever
> He shall,
>   He shall,
> He shall reign for ever and ev-ev-ver.

All over America the fathers were returning to the scene of their defeat, their abdication, their flight. Some of them were thinking, like Dan Shaper: "Thank God I escaped! Thank God! I might have been caught forever!" Some of them were thinking, like Dan Shaper: "Regret, I should have tried once more, regret forever."

It was the late evening rush hour when he slid into the frayed edges of Cleveland. Neon and colored lights and sudden frosty forests of ripped-up evergreens beckoned to Christmas shoppers, while the men in vacant lots pounded their mitts together and promised "a nice tree, missus." Under a shelter marked in great letters $2.98! a woman sold teddy bears as large as teddy bears ever grow, and she had a portable coal stove to give her good cheer. The light changed; traffic urged him forward, down the outskirt slopes of the Alleghenies which lead into the flattened industrial town. Through the front vents of his car Shaper breathed the chilled exhaust from the tailpipe ahead of him.

If he could arrive at his friend's apartment before eight, he could call Paula and Cynthia. Or he could stop and call from a gas station. But he liked to talk with them, even by telephone, only when he was clean and shaved and combed, and the shaking fatigue of the five-hundred-mile drive eased by a drink. Then he could lounge at his ease through the first breathless words.

Cynthia, who was eight, would say, "I can say more things in Spanish now! *Buenos días*, Señor Daddy!"

"Señor Daddy too! Señor Daddy too!" would come Paula's protesting wail, twenty desperate squirming inches from the telephone.

"Shh. I'll let you talk. Wait till I'm finished, Paula. Daddy?"

"Yes, honeybear."

"We'll be ready tomorrow morning. You pick us up at nine. We'll be out on the front porch." She was very experienced at these arrangements, busy and bustling to get herself and her sister ready, experienced buffer state between her mother and her father.

"Now it's my turn!" came the distant wail.

"Now do you want to talk to Paula?"

"Yes," he would say.

"All right, Paula, now you talk."

And as Paula wrestled for the telephone, Cynthia's voice receded, becoming childish once again, all arrangements done, repeating merely: "Daddy. Daddy. Daddy?"

He sighed, emitting frost. He was not yet on the telephone with them. He was four blocks farther into the traffic; he had shifted gears four times; he had dreamed again, but it had only gotten him a few hundred yards deeper into Cleveland. There was another lot, festooned with lights, selling rootless and truncated, sap-frozen Christmas trees.

Driving through Cleveland on one of the many nights before Christmas, under fouled industrial skies seen through his greasy windshield, Shaper felt slush under his wheels, a flying soup of snow and dirt and salt, corroding the metal underbodies of automobiles; salt in the greasy air splashed up at nightfall into the traffic, wiping its film across the windshield, rhythmic swish of salt and glass; on the radio, once more God rested his merry gentlemen, followed by the Chipmunk Song. There were snowed-in, secretly salted sheep in the used-car lots. Hunched against the weather and the hurrying shoppers, the 1952 Studebakers and the older Fraziers ($100, nothing down) waited, and the sharp later models waited, too. GIRLS! ARE YOU HARD TO FIT? (A shoe store.) THRILL TO THE GLORY OF THE OPEN ROAD! (A driving school.) And THE ELBOW BAR, THE KNICK-KNACK-KNOOK, STEVE'S PLACE, STEAKS AND TEXAS-BURGERS!

DON'T ASK THE PRICE – YOU NAME IT! EVERYTHING GOES!

CHILI! STARLITE FOOD! DAY-OLD BAKED GOODS! (Slightly used apple pies? Shaper asked. Outgrown marshmallow cookies?) RED HOTS!

Where was that chicken store he remembered? CAPONS FOR SALE! "What's a capon, Daddy?" Cynthia had once asked him.

Answer: "A capon is a very tender chicken, given special treatment, nice and soft, honey."

At last he reached the apartment of his friend, Martie Grant. Warmth and greetings; this friend always saved his life. There was an amiable steam on the windows. His visits were special occasions; hot buttered rum and how are we doing? In answer to the question, Dan answered, "I dunno, chappie. Maybe I'm making out."

He had already called and the arrangements were fixed about seeing Cynthia and Paula on their front porch in the morning. He talked with his friend until they both grew drowsy, and then one more hot rum and a couple of salty crackers, and then to the sack. He made out: he fell asleep. That was all right, chappie, when what you need is sleep.

The children, thick in mufflers, were waiting on the porch when he drove up. They had been playing, waiting, talking; cocking their heads, they watched him turn into the driveway as if interested in his style as a driver.

"Hello, Daddy," said Cynthia very shyly.

"Hello, Daddy," said Paula.

He understood and said with shyness equal to theirs, "Hello, children. Let's get into the car."

Then out the driveway, down the street and around the corner; and then he had to pull over to the side of the curb, crunching frozen snow, when they flung their arms about him: "Oh Daddy, Daddy, Daddy!" It was as if they had feared that their mother could see through the walls. But they did not believe, as he sometimes did, that she could follow him around corners with an angry eye. There was now a swarming mass of daughters greeting father, and then, tousled, flushed, he patted them both and felt pleased by the happy tears all around.

"Okay. Now, what should we do?" he asked.

"Plans!"

"That's right, I have plans. Now listen – "

"What? What? What are we going to do?"

"A trip to the moon for lunch. Then Bermuda. Then a snack. Then quickly across two or three oceans for dinner, and then we'll – "

With relieved howls of laughter at so much eating, so much travel, they said, like happy little girls everywhere, "Oh, Daddy! I don't believe you."

"All right, then I'll have to show you."

And he would show them, would, *would*. If he had to take them to both the moon and Bermuda. Focused on his daughters, he believed that he could infuse them with his energy of feeling for them – right through the snow and ice and his yearning thrust across turnpikes.

"Why are you looking at me, Daddy?"

"I want to look at you, Paula."

"I outgrew the dress you gave me for my birthday already. Mommy says you never buy the right size."

"Tough shit."

"What's that?"

"That's the word for failure to calculate how fast a little girl can grow."

Slowly a smile appeared on her face. She had learned words on the playgrounds already. "Daddy, you're teasing. But when are we going to the television?"

He had promised them a tour at a local television station. It was part of the prolonged animal act of his "visitations" – legal poetry – where he challenged himself to amuse them without going to the movies. He had arranged to watch a local television show, a teen-age "dance party" with genuine rock 'n' roll celebrities and night-club performers doing a spot of afternoon propaganda with the Saturday kids. Two days later it was time and they were having a little meal, their version of oysters, soupe printanière, turbot, sauce Beaumarchais, poulard à l'estragon, macédoine de fruits – in other words, cheeseburgers with malted milk. "Oh, good, good!" said Cynthia, her dewy eyes shining.

"You like my cooking?"

"I like your *ordering*, Daddy," Paula said with great interest in precision. "*Gracias*, Pops!" and she flew up in an infestation of the giggles.

"Tell me about your Spanish class. Do you want some double bubble?"

"Bubble gum is for babies. We're too big," Cynthia said. "Now give us Chiclets."

"That's what we always have," Paula said. "Sometimes we have sugarless for our teeth."

"Sugarless and chlorophyll," said Cynthia.

Dan nodded solemnly. Paula's malted milk repeated warmly and she grinned. Cynthia was frowning with a sudden thought. "Mommy says you only buy us junk," she said.

"But," said Paula, "but I like your junk."

"Daddy, we like your junk." And Cynthia's smile for him, radiant up toward him. The word *junk* would always be a mystery for her, a beautiful and complicated word, like *serendipity* or *communion*. "Now tell us a story."

"Yes, Daddy. A once-upon-a-time story . . ."

The story concerned a prince who wanted more than anything else to be loved. Naturally, a magic potion came into the matter, and thus everyone loved him. But the once-upon-a-time prince remained unhappy because the potion had no effect on *him*, since for happiness to come of a love potion, it must above all make the once-upon-a-time prince love those who drink of his potion.

From that dreamy oblivion of the child which is so much like indifference and contains so much caring, Cynthia looked up at her father and said, "I know you do, Daddy."

"Know I do what?"

"What you said."

"What did I say?"

She laughed, thrilled because he had forgotten – he had not heard himself – the words had slipped out like his breath. But now he heard, he felt, he even saw himself repeating, "I love you, honeybear."

The waitress in the diner came up and said, "Mister, you must be a teacher to tell stories like that. My brat won't listen to any goddamn thing I tell her."

"My father's a lifesaver," Paula said. "He lives in New York. He knows how to save people's lives."

She had been much impressed by his efforts that summer to teach her to swim; she had overcome her fear of the water. Dan smiled because she remembered so well that he had been a junior lifesaver at the age of thirteen.

"Daddy," said Cynthia, "that magic potion made me hungry."

"*Thirsty*," her sister corrected her.

"Hungry *and* thirsty, Paula! Can we have, can we have . . . something?"

"Something! Something!" cried Paula.

They ate again, and this time Dan told a magic story that had no love and food in it. It was a poor magic story, of course, but the children did not object, scattering material ketchup and actual rootbeer on Formica. They liked his poor magic stories, too, and found food therein.

"You promised to take us to the TV station."

"Wait till he finishes the story, Paula."

Pout. Reproach.

"I know. I did. I will," he said.

Reversal of pout and reproach. They blinked at so many intentions. "Let's go," he said, and that was easy to understand.

Snowsuits, rubbers, hats, mittens, and a farewell to the nice and nosy waitress who thought it swell that a father took his daughters adventuring on a Saturday afternoon. Then salty slush, feet and wheels, and Shaper put his hand in his pockets to tip the boy who parked his car.

"You give everybody money," Cynthia observed.

"I sure do." But her face was bland. She was not kidding. She had noticed, was all.

"Can I have a penny?" said Paula. "For Chiclets? A nickel?"

The Saturday-afternoon dance party was a teen-age program which featured night-club stars visiting in town, and kids sucking from bottles of pop and dancing the Chicken or the Fish to records which were put on between the performances, interviews, and commercials. The disc jockey who ran this stew of "live entertainment" was called Fat Ed because he weighed nearly two hundred and fifty long and loose pounds and liked the sound of "Ed." He also wore heavy horn-rimmed glasses with a straight, wide flange of black plastic on each side pressing against his ears; pointed shoes, which made his fat little feet look like frog's flippers; and a smile like a frog's, separating his wide expanse of jowl from an equally generous slab of nose. He was an old acquaintance of Dan's, which in show biz means a lifelong friend or enemy. Since they were not in competition, it was friend and friendly-like. Thanks to this, Dan, Paula, and Cynthia could huddle together beneath the lights just out of camera range and watch the party doings. A shuffling band of stage personnel mystified the girls with their rushing of cameras up, their hustling of people to and fro, their muscular chaos of co-ordinated indecision. "This gets sent into the box at home," Dan elaborately whispered. "You mustn't talk. You can whisper back when I whisper to you. It's what you see in the box."

With florid elegance the deejay introduced Hennery Ford, middle-aged girl singer now appearing at that famous night-spot – "What's the name of that place, doll?"

She told him.

"Reet, Hennery doll. Say, you been in Miami Beach?" She nodded.

"That's great, Hennery, soaking up all those sun vitamins – Poor old Fat Ed, I have so many heartfelt responsibilities of live entertainment, I just don't have time – But now this here chick, she is – man, I mean the greatest. You know it, dontcha, kids?"

"We know it," screamed the studio visitors, heated by coke and awe.

The hot, stuck deejay wiped the acres of black plastic on his glasses, leaving the lenses fogged. He returned the folded hand-kerchief to his breast pocket. "Do you *know* it?"

"We *know* it!"

Busily Cynthia whispered to her father something which he did not hear. He answered, "Don't worry, they don't know anything." She smiled quickly, relieved.

"All right!" shouted the deejay. "So now she has chosen to sing for us one of her favorite hit tunes, a religious type love number with a rock 'n' roll beat – it'll live forever, and here's 'I Want a Sunday Kind of Love.' Hennery?"

Microphone, spots, SILENCE, hushed approval, and the sweaty operators rushing cameras in and out. Miss Ford, a wizened, peel-ing girl of about forty, stood smiling in the light, swaying slightly as her chapped and oiled lips opened over the words:

> I want a Sunday kind of love
> Like the kind I feel Above
> I want a Sunday kind of love
> From that One I'm thinking of –

Her mouth stretched over the sounds, her body swayed, the music shrilled forth; but she did not sing. The voice of Hennery Ford came from a record while the body of Hennery Ford mimed the gestures of singing.

"What did you say?" Dan whispered to Cynthia.

"*But she isn't singing!*" Cynthia whispered in shock and horror, discovering another instance of the world's corruption.

"She's very foolish," Paula said primly.

Later Dan would explain to them about idealism – how every-body wanted the song to be perfect, the way Hennery had recorded it originally; about pragmatism – how art is the politics of the possible; about mass media and the way of the world – that's how things are. In the meantime, this eight-year-old daughter had found public corruption condoned, and some of her disdain was directed against her father. "I want to go *right now!*" she said.

On the way out, Dan explained, "She has chapped lips like that from so much traveling. Maybe she has a cold, besides the change of climate." *Kachoo*, he said sympathetically.

"God bless you," said Paula, sure that her wish was His command. "I don't like that song. I like 'I'm itchy lak a man on a fuzzy tree, I'm all shook up.' "

"Paula, that's not right. It's 'Ah'm itchy *lak* a man on a *fuzzy* tree, Ah'm all – shook – *up*.' Daddy, let's go someplace else and you tell us a story about magic potions."

"Magic potions!" cried Paula.

"Again?"

"Tell it," said Cynthia, grinning, "just by moving your lips and we'll say the words, okay? Paula, what word am I saying?" And her lips squirmed over the enormous adult teeth that always surprised Dan, since it was still baby-teeth time when he stopped living with their mother. Her lips, glistening and pink, formed and re-formed over the teeth.

Paula watched, peered into her mouth, pulled back, solemnly imitated the gesture, and at last said loud and clear, "Fake! Fake! You were saying 'Fake'!"

"That's what my lips were saying," Cynthia said. "But that's what I think of 'I Want a Sunday Kind of Love' and Miss Hilary Ford."

"I guess you're right," said their father, obscurely troubled, as if somehow the children were judging him and putting him on the same side as poor Hennery-Hilary. Adults move their lips to music offstage; silently they pretend to sing; and what about Dan's willed gaiety with his girls? And did they not sense how terribly he sometimes flagged, their real father in town for a spree with them? Was he really so enthusiastic about milk shakes (magic potions) and the art museum (fairy tales)?

"It's the way of the world," he said.

"Singing like that?"

"Everything." But Cynthia patted his hand with one of her peculiarly adult, maternal gestures. It was like her salting his eggs. She wanted to be good to him for no purpose but that she was his daughter, and so she imitated the anxious gestures of her mother with that second husband whom she hoped to please and be pleased by. Logic, thought Shaper. (She had dumped a gagging amount of salt over the flattened yolk.) My daughter learns the gestures of love by monkeying around. She broods over my step-wife's gestures with the man who replaced me.

He ate egg. He wiped his mouth. He drank water and took toast. Another snack.

He would have liked a son, he suddenly thought – why? He asked himself why it came to him with such wrenching despair now, when Cynthia was so tender, Paula so sweet with their ideal, often absent, *real* father. All that rose to his mind was an image of the Square Deal Club football team, when at age twelve he had tackled a full-grown boy and, it turned out, broken his collarbone. Glory and shame and sudden hot tears making him sneeze. Well, why not have another child, more children? Why not have a wife again? He called for coffee; the girls called for milk, and dimes for the jukebox. Outside, the sky had turned black for these last days of the year. It could snow and snow and snow. He held Paula's hand and remembered his own grandfather shaking his hand, holding it, holding to life by an arthritic claw. The way ancient aunts kiss and uncles clutch, he thought, is how I hold my daughters.

It was time to take the children home after this last afternoon of his visit. The sky had clouded over again and there would be fresh snow as he aimed himself toward the highway. "What's the matter, Daddy?" Cynthia asked.

"I dunno, chappie. The weather. I'm sorry I won't be seeing you for another month."

"But you'll write to us," Paula said cheerfully.

"Yes. Yes."

A look of faint disdain and resentment crossed Paula's face, and her eye just passed to her thumb. No, she would not suck. She was too old for that. She would speak instead. "You don't come to see us often enough, Daddy. Mommy says we should call you 'Dan,' and we should call Mike 'Daddy.' "

"So," said Cynthia, statesmanlike, "we call you 'Daddy' when we're talking to you, because you're our *real* daddy – "

"And 'Dan,' " continued Paula like Mister Bones, "when we ask Mommy when you're coming to see us. She don't like us to ask."

"*Doesn't*," her sister corrected her. "You should say: 'Mike and Mommy *don't*,' but 'Mommy *doesn't*.' " She finished this moral and grammatical lesson by putting her finger in her mouth and ferociously pulling at the cuticle with her teeth.

He talked, sang, made rhymes, joked. Paula smiled, but Cynthia huddled against him as he drove. She stared with sleepy cunning at the panel showing gas, mileage, speed. Dan parked before their house and told them he had his suitcase all ready in the trunk. He was spending his last minutes with them, and then he would hurry again toward New York. Then there was silence. Somehow he had asked a question and Cynthia must answer.

She closed her eyes briefly, a gesture of restraint like a much older girl accused. She had a wide, unmarked forehead over the struggling lashes. She closed her eyes, planning. Her mother was training her excellently, but she still loved her father, she cared. Her *real* father, as she explained. And since she cared, really cared, this prematurely adult, scheming gesture of closing the eyes did not mean all that it seemed to mean. But still it meant something. She was angry because he was leaving so soon again; she was hurt, she wanted to touch and hurt him; she cared and was confused; she had something important to say and did not know how to say it. There was an item of information which would have to stand for all this. She opened and closed her eyes once more before she spoke; she squeezed something back into her brain behind the wide, hot, childish forehead. "Daddy," she said, "I didn't get your last letter."

"What do you mean? I'm afraid you don't get all my letters. How do you know about it at all?"

"I just know."

"What do you mean?"

"Rosalie" – the maid – "she said there was a letter. She said to go get it when I came home from school."

Cynthia shut her eyes again. "It must have got lost," she said.

Paula said, "I want to go inside." Dan said good-bye to his younger daughter, carried her across the snow to the door, kissed her. The wintry door opened for her; his invisible former wife took her back. Dan climbed back into the car with Cynthia. They sat awhile in thickening silence. "The letters I sent to you are supposed to be given to you," he said.

"I know, Daddy."

And they looked at each other like grownup lovers fleeing parents and family. Child, he thought; child of mine.

"I really love you awfully much, honey."

Impatient and a child again, she said, "I know. Why don't you ever wear black shoes, Daddy?"

"I like brown ones."

"Brown ones?"

Muffled in coats, they sat together in the front seat of the car as if there were more to say. It began to snow in little flakes colored yellow by industrial smoke, ragged-edged, yellow and faded. The fog of coal and steel and the fog of humid winter held the snow suspended in air, and then let it fall. He ran the motor to keep warm. The snow came down all over the city of Cleveland, and when the wiper of his car worked it left a smear, wiping the glass back and forth. He sat with his daughter before the house in which his former wife, her mother, lived, and explained to her why he wore brown shoes; why he did not wear rubbers; why some singers are fake and don't really sing; why the snow melted faster on the street than on the grass.

"Write to me anyway," she said.

"We'll figure something out, Cynthia."

"Will you?" she asked.

Fresh snow had shadowed his earlier footsteps by the time he took her to the door; evening had come. Half an hour later he was on the highway leading into the turnpike, which falls with hardly a pause through three states back to Manhattan. There in the new year he would like to find a wife and have children again.

Questions for Writing and Discussion

Discovering Meaning

1. What is your impression of Dan Shaper? Gold repeats Dan's thought that "he would like to find a wife and have children again" several times. At what points in the story's sequence does this thought appear? In these contexts, what does the recurring thought reveal about Dan's emotional state and about his character?

2. From the children's conversation and behaviour, what do you learn about their mother's attitude towards her former husband? How does this attitude affect the children? What are Dan's feelings about his former wife?

3. What effect does the visit to the television station have on the children? How does Dan see himself after this episode? Why do these effects occur?

4. What is the significance of the title?

Exploring Method

1. The story is told by a third-person narrator with events presented as the protagonist, Dan Shaper, perceives them. What is the effect on the reader of the author's use of this point of view? What would the author lose or gain by telling the story in the first person with Dan as narrator? Only twice in the story does the point of view shift from the father's to the children's

perspective before their parting with their father. Identify the passages that describe Paula's and Cynthia's thoughts. What is the purpose of these shifts in point of view?

2. Like most authors of short fiction, Gold summarizes less important events in his story and selectively highlights important events by describing them in greater detail or by using extended dialogue. Two prominent examples are the brief summary of the long drive from New York to Cleveland, in contrast to the expanded description of Dan's drive through Cleveland on his arrival, and Dan's recollection of one of his many telephone conversations with his daughters, presented in extended dialogue, with only a brief summary of his actual telephone conversation with them from his friend's apartment. What insight do these two examples of selective focusing provide into Dan's state of mind and his relationship with his daughters?

3. Through dialogue, Gold individualizes the children. What are the differences between them? How does the author make them life-like?

4. Dan's journey is circular – the drive through the garish world of American consumerism begins and ends on the highway. What is the effect of the circular structure?

Suggestions for Writing

1. This story portrays the effects of divorce on young children. Write a story in which you illustrate the effects of divorce on teenagers.

2. Dan's ex-wife does not appear in the story, yet she emerges as an individualized character. Describe her. Then write a scene in which she prepares her children for their visit with their father. Include dialogue between mother and daughters to illustrate your description of her character.

3. Dan spends the night at his friend's apartment before meeting his children in the morning. Gold summarizes the scene in one sentence: "He talked with his friend until they both grew drowsy, and then one more hot rum and a couple of salty crackers, and then to the sack." Expand the scene, including a conversation that provides insight into Dan's feelings and thoughts.

4. Write an analysis in which you identify the images and details that give this story a surface gaiety, and yet an underlying sadness.

Examining Social Issues

1. What aspects of the consumer society is Gold criticizing as he describes Dan's drives from New York to Cleveland, through Cleveland, and during his day with his children? Describe your own view of these familiar props of urban life.

2. Compare the images we see on television with the spectacle that the children and their father see in the television studio. What comment on television viewing does Gold make through his account? Do you agree with the author? Why or why not? What are the advantages and disadvantages of television viewing for young children? For teenagers?

3. Suzanne Gordon, a sociological writer, in her essay "The Geography of Loneliness," sees as one cause of divorce the fragmentation of the extended family and the loss of a sense of community:

> A disturbing effect of isolation from family, friends and community is the added difficulty it imposes in the average marriage. . . . A woman or man must be not only confidant and lover, but family, community, friend – all things to one other man or woman. In the past, relationships founded on larger family and close communities gave people some options if things weren't going well at home. Today when family bonds are weaker, more and more is being asked of the nuclear unit.

Do you agree with the author? What are other reasons for the high divorce rate?

4. Sociologists are debating whether the institution of the family can survive the rapid technological changes in society. Futurist Alvin Toffler, author of *The Third Wave*, explains that because technology, economics, and communication are undergoing dramatic changes and are emerging into a new stage that Toffler calls "The Third Wave" of development, the institution of the American family is fracturing:

> The frequently asked question, "What is the future of the family?" usually implies that as the Second Wave nuclear family loses its dominance some other form will replace it. A more likely outcome is that during Third Wave civilization no single form will dominate the family mix for any long period. Instead we will see a high variety of family structures. . . Again, this does not mean the total elimination or "death" of the nuclear family. It merely means that

from now on the nuclear family will be only one of the many socially accepted and approved forms. As the Third Wave sweeps in, the family system is becoming diversified right along with the production system and the information system in society.

Vance Packard contends in his essay "New Kinds of Families" that the family will survive because it fulfils a human need:

> While . . . the traditional economic functions of marriage have shrunk, there are two particularly compelling reasons looming why people will be marrying in the coming decade despite the relatively free availability of unmarried sexual partners:
> 1. The warm, all-embracing companionship that in marriage can endure through the confusion, mobility, and rapid social change of our times.
> 2. The opportunity to obtain immortality and personal growth for married individuals who perpetuate themselves through reproduction as they help mold personalities of their children and proudly induct them into the larger community.

Which opinion, Toffler's or Packard's, do you accept? Why? If you disagree with both of these social observers, explain your own view on the institution of the family in the technological society.

The Interview

Brian Moore

The novelist Brian Moore is an Irish expatriate who arrived in Canada in 1948 and made his home in Montreal for over a decade; there, like his protagonist Ginger Coffey, he worked for a newspaper – in Moore's case, the Montreal Gazette. *"The Interview" is taken from Moore's third novel,* The Luck of Ginger Coffey *(1960).*

In the novel, Moore dramatizes the plight of the English-speaking immigrant who encounters language, laws, culture, religious values, customs, manners that are similar to and modelled after those he left behind. Yet the Canadian adaptations tend to become distorted. Ginger Coffey, misled by surface similarities between the host country and his own, becomes confused when he encounters the realities of a corporate technological society that regards him as an anachronism. With humour and satire, Moore exploits the clash between old world impracticality and the North American myths of success and prestige.

Moore is a skilful stylist who responds sensitively and acutely to the sights and sounds of his environment. Particularly effective is his portrayal of his protagonist's thoughts, feelings, and dreams, which clash with the realities of his situation. What adds a touch of sunlight to the prevailing greyness of his protagonist's predicament is Moore's compassion. Ginger Coffey appears to be a failure, yet he is never completely defeated. He has inner resources that allow him to come to terms with his life and ultimately with his limitations.

Another characteristic that softens the depressing effect of Moore's fiction is his fine sense of comedy. Ginger Coffey is as much a comic character in his groundless hopefulness as he is pathetic. Ultimately, Moore suggests, humour is the magic element that makes life endurable.

. . . Coffey was hungry. He ate his sausages and helped himself to more gravy and potatoes. Fork halfway to his mouth, he noticed her standing in the door, her face pale, her eyes bright. Still in a rage. He put the forkful in his mouth and winked at her.

"How much *do* we have left?" she said.

He smiled, gesturing that his mouth was full.

"Answer me. The truth, mind."

Eighty and fourteen – well, make it an even – "About a hundred dollars," he said.

"Oh my God!" She went away.

He finished the spuds and wiped his plate with a bit of bread. What did Vera know about money anyway? An only child, brought up by a doting mother, pretty, with plenty of beaux, until she met and married him. And, even so, in all those years of marriage, the Army years, the years at Kylemore and in Cork, had she ever bloody starved? Had she? Give him credit for something. And remember, Vera, you married me for better or for worse. This is the worse. Ah, but supposing she won't put up with the worse?

Now that was nonsense. She loved him in her way and despite her temper. And she had Paulie. He could hear the two of them talking now in the living room. Paulie, home from her dance practice, had gone straight in to see Vera. And, as usual, not even hello for Daddy. They were like sisters, those two, always gossiping away about womany wee things he knew nothing about.

There was the phone. He got up to answer, because Vera hated the phone.

"Ginger?" It was Gerry Grosvenor. "Listen, how would you react to a hundred and ten a week?"

"Get away with you!"

"No, seriously, there's a job going as deskman on the *Tribune*. And the Managing Editor happens to be a friend of mine."

"Deskman?" Coffey said. "But Gerry lad, what's that? What does a deskman do? Make desks?"

"Copy editor," Grosvenor said. "Easy. This is on the international desk. All wire copy, very clean. It's just writing heads and putting in punctuation. Nothing to it."

"But I have no experience on a newspaper. I never wrote a headline in my life."

"Never mind that. Would you take the job?"

"Would a duck swim!"

"Okay. Wait. I'll call you back."

Coffey replaced the receiver and looked down the long railroad corridor hallway. Total silence from the living room, which meant she and Paulie had been listening. So he went in. "Hello, Apple," he said to Paulie. "Had a good day in school?"

"Was that Gerry?" Veronica asked in an angry voice.

"Yes, dear. He says he can get me a job. Hundred and ten dollars a week to start."

268

"What job?"

"On the *Tribune*. It's an editing job. I pointed out that I'd no experience, but he said not to worry."

"I'd worry," Veronica said, "if I were you. This isn't acting the glorified office boy, or playing poker and drinking pints in barracks."

He gave her a look intended to turn her into Lot's wife there on the sofa. Imagine saying that in front of Paulie!

"Go and have your supper, Apple," he told Paulie. He waited as, unwillingly, Paulie trailed out of the room. "Now, why did you say that in front of the child, Vera?"

"She might as well know."

"Know what?"

"What sort of a selfish brute she has for a father."

Suffering J! No sense talking, was there? He went out and, while he was in the bathroom, the phone rang again. He hurried up the corridor.

"Yes," she said to the phone. "Yes – wait, I want to explain something. I mean apropos of this afternoon. Ginger doesn't *have* our passage money home. He spent it. . . . Yes. . . . So that leaves me no choice, does it? . . . Yes . . . yes, here's Ginger. I'll let you tell him yourself."

"Ginger?" Gerry's voice said. "It's all set. I've given you a good build-up and old MacGregor wants to see you in his office at three tomorrow afternoon."

"Thanks a million, Gerry. But what did you tell him?"

"I told him you'd worked on a Dublin newspaper for two years and said, after that, you'd been a press officer in the Army, and then that you were a good public relations man for Irish whiskey out here. It sounded good, believe me."

"But, Holy God!" Coffey said. "It's not true. I never worked on a newspaper."

At the other end of the line there was a Remembrance Day hush. Then Grosvenor said: "Ginger, the point is, do you want this job or don't you?"

"Of course I do, but – "

"But nothing. Everybody bullshits out here. Every employer expects it. The point is to get in. After that, doing the job is up to you."

"But maybe I can't do it," Coffey said.

"Beggars can't be choosers," said Vera's voice. She reached out, took the receiver from him and said: "Thanks, Gerry, you're an angel. Thanks very much. . . . Yes. . . . Yes, I know. . . . Good night." She replaced the receiver, turned away, walked down the hall and went into their bedroom. He followed her but she shut the door. When he tried the door, it was locked.

"Vera? I want to talk to you?" . . .

On the fourth floor of the *Tribune*, the night's business was just beginning. Under fluorescent lights, lit all year round, a few reporters studied the afternoon papers. A police radio blared routine calls in a corner and in the nearby teletype room a jammed machine tintinnabulated incessantly, calling for attention. In the centre slot of a large horseshoe desk a fat man in a woollen cardigan sliced open the afternoon's crop of wire-service photographs. He looked up as Coffey approached. "Yes?"

"May I speak to Mr. MacGregor, please?"

"Boy! Take this man to Mr. Mac."

An indolent adolescent shoved a rubber cylinder down a communications tube, then hooked a beckoning finger. Across the City Room he led and down a corridor to a partitioned-off office on the opened door of which a small brass plaque announced MANAGING EDITOR. The boy pointed to the plaque, then went away, wordless. Inside, Coffey saw three young men in shirt sleeves looking over the shoulders of an old man who was seated at a large, scarred desk. He was a thin old man with a pale, bony face, a pumping blue vein in his forehead and eyebrows thick and crumbling as cigar ash. His voice, a Low Church Scottish rumble, could be heard clearly in the corridor. For once, Coffey was not comforted by the fact that he faced an older man.

"Dorrothy Dix? Where's Dorrothy Dix?"

"Here, Mr. Mac."

"O.K. Now, where's the funnies?"

"Here, Mr. Mac."

"Make sure that Blondie is up top and then Mutt and Jeff and *then* Moon Mullins. *Not* Rex Morrgan, M.D. Some bleddy rascal in the composing room changed the order in the Early last night."

"Right, Mr. Mac."

"O.K. Now, away with ye."

The three young men clutched up page proofs and galleys and rushed out, jostling Coffey in the doorway. For the love of J, how was he going to tell this sulphur-breathing Scottish Beelzebub that he was an experienced sub-editor? Grosvenor must be daft.

The old man spiked a scrap of paper, like Calvin downing sin. His eye picked out Coffey in the doorway.

"Come in. State your business."

"My – my name is Coffey. I believe Gerry Grosvenor spoke to you about me?"

"Grrosvenor? Och, aye, the cartoonist. Come in, come in, sit you down. Where's my notes? Aye, here we are. Deskman, aren't you?"

"Yes, sir."

"What paper did you work for in the Old Country?"

Confidence, Grosvenor had said. The time and tide that leads on to fortune. One good lie and – But as Coffey opened his mouth he was taken with a sort of aphasia. The old man waited, becoming suspicious. "I – ah – I worked on the *Irish Times*, sir."

"*Times*, eh? Good paper."

"Yes. Yes, isn't it?"

"Grrosvenor said you were in the Army?"

"Yes, sir."

"Officer, weren't you? Serve overseas?"

"I – I was in the Irish Army, sir. We were neutral during the war."

"Indeed?"

"I – I was press officer in the Irish Army," Coffey added, trying to correct the hostility in that "Indeed?"

"Press officer," the old man said. "Trying to keep the facts from the public, that is the services' job. However, I need a man who has some knowledge of wurrld events. Most Canadians have none. How about you?"

"I – ah – I try to keep up, sir."

"Grrosvenor tells me you were a publicity man for a whussky company."

"Yes, sir."

"Scotch whussky?"

"No, sir. Irish."

"No wonder you're out of a job, then. Did you wurrk on the foreign desk at the *Times*?"

"Yes, sir. Ah – part-time."

"What do you mean, part-time?"

"Well, ah – summer holidays and so on. Filling in."

The old man nodded and consulted his notes again. Coffey fingered his moustache. A good touch that summer holidays. He was pleased with himself for thinking of it.

"When was it you wurrked for the *Times*?"

"Oh – after I got out of the Army. About – ah – six years ago."

"How long did you wurrk there?"

"About" – what had Grosvenor said? – "about eighteen months."

"I see." The old man picked up one of the phones on his desk. "Give me Fanshaw," he said. "Ted? When you were in Dublin, did

you ever hear of a subbie on the *Times* by the name of Coffey? . . .
Aye, about five years ago . . . Hold on." He covered the mouthpiece and turned to Coffey. "What was the name of the foreign
editor?"

Coffey sat, his eyes on his little green hat.

"Well?"

He raised his eyes and read a title on the bookshelf behind
MacGregor. *Holy Bible.*

"Right, Ted," the old man told the telephone. "Disna' matter."
He put the phone down and glowered at Coffey under the crumbling ash of his eyebrows. "If you'd been a Scot," he said. "You'd
have come in here wi' references in your hand. But you carry
nothing besides your hat and a lot of cheek. Och, aye. You may
fool the likes of Gerry Grrosvenor, but there isn't an Irishman
born that I'd trust to pull the wuul o'er *my* eyes!"

Coffey, his face hot, stood up and put his hat on.

"Where are you going?" MacGregor said.

"I'm sorry I took up your ti – "

"Sit down! Are you hard up for a job? Tell me the truth."

"Yes, sir."

"O.K. Can you spell? Spell me parallel."

Coffey spelled.

"Correct. Are you married?"

"Yes, sir."

"Children?"

"One daughter, sir."

"*Hmm.* . . . Have you a vice?"

"Advice, sir?"

"Are you deaf? I mean, have you a weakness? Booze or horses
or wimmin? Own up now, for I'll find out, anyway."

"No, sir."

"O.K. You say ye've been a P.R. That may be. But what a P.R.
knows about the wurrkings of a newspaper could be written
twice over on the back of a tomtit's arse and still leave room for
the Lorrd's Prayer. So you'd best start at the bottom. Do you
agree?"

Coffey took a deep breath. He was too old to start at the bottom.

"Well? Don't stand there gawking."

"Well, sir, it depends. I'm not a boy of twenty."

"I'm proposing to start you off in the proofroom," the old man
said. "So that you can acquaint yourself with the rudiments of
our style. That's the best training there is."

"A – a p-p-proofreader, did you say, sir?"

"I did. My readers are not unionized, thank the Lord. And I happen to be shorthanded there at the moment. If you wurrk well, I might try you out on the floor as a reporter. You might even wind up as a deskman if you play your cards right. What do you say?"

"Well I – I'd have to think about that, sir. How much – how much would that pay?"

"Fifty dollars a week, which is more than you're wurrth. Start at six tonight. Go and think it over now, but let me know no later than half-past four, if you want the job."

"Thank you – "

"Clarence?" Mr. MacGregor shouted. "Where's Clarence?"

A fat man rushed in, notebook at the ready.

"What's the last two paras of Norrman Vincent Peale doing in the overset, Clarence?"

"Don't know, Mr. Mac."

"Bleddy well find out, then."

The fat man rushed out. Mr. MacGregor spiked another galley. "All right, Coffey. Good day to you."

Coffey went away. Fifty dollars a week, reading galleys. A galley slave ... He passed along a corridor lined with rolls of newsprint, wandered across the wide desert of the city room and out past the brass plaque to the elevator. The red light flashed above the elevator door. Going down. Down, down, all his high hopes failed; with Veronica waiting below, Veronica who wanted to know that the bad days were over, that they could move to a better place ...

"Ground floor," the elevator man said. "Ground floor. Out."

There she was under the big clock, the nervous beginnings of a smile on her face. Poor Kitten, it was not fair to her, not fair at all, she'd be in such a state –

Maybe, through Gerry Grosvenor, maybe he might just manage? Maybe. And so, he went towards her, his mind made up. Don't tell her now. Smile instead, be the jolly Ginger she used to love. He kissed her, squeezed her and said: "Steady as she goes."

"Did you get it, Ginger?"

"I did, indeed."

"Oh, thank God."

"Now, now," he said. "What's that? Sniffles? Come on, come on, it's laughing you should be. Listen – let's – let's go and have a cup of tea. How would you like to sail into the Ritz, just like the old days?"

"Oh, Ginger, I'm so glad for you."

"Glad for *me*? And aren't you glad for yourself, Kitten? Ah, it's going to be super. Just super. Come on now. We'll take a taxi."

"But we can't afford it, Ginger."

"Come on, come on," he said, out in the street now, signaling a cab. "Let me be the judge of that. In with you. Driver? The Ritz-Carlton Hotel, on the double!"

Questions for Writing and Discussion

Discovering Meaning

1. The story suggests that Coffey has been a failure for some time. What traits in his character have made him a failure? What admirable traits do you perceive in him?
2. How does Coffey deal with the strains of family relations?
3. Why does MacGregor offer Coffey a job, even though he knows that Coffey has had no previous experience?

Exploring Method

1. In telling the story, Moore shifts from the objective third-person narrator to focus on Coffey's thoughts and then into dialogue. How do these shifts in perspective help the reader to understand Coffey?
2. The interview is set within a frame: Coffey's opening quarrel with Veronica, and the ending with Coffey and Veronica on their way to the Ritz. What are the functions of the opening and closing?
3. Identify the religious imagery that Moore uses to present Coffey's impressions in the story. What does each image suggest about his attitudes towards Veronica and MacGregor? How are these religious allusions consistent with Coffey's background and character?
4. During the interview, what details help the reader to see and hear Coffey and MacGregor?
5. Examine the two settings: Coffey's apartment and the fourth floor of the *Tribune*. What is the atmosphere of each setting? What images create the atmosphere?
6. The interview begins with an ascent to the fourth floor of the *Tribune* and ends with a descent on the elevator, "Going down. Down, down . . . ." How does Moore relate this imagery of elevation and descent to Coffey's problems in the story?

Suggestions for Writing

1. What do you learn about the operation of a newspaper from the story? Look through your local newspaper, keeping in

mind Moore's satire of the Canadian press in the interview scene; then write an appropriate letter to the editor.

2. MacGregor tells Coffey, "I need a man who has some knowledge of wurrld events. Most Canadians have none." Do you agree with MacGregor? Prepare a questionnaire on world affairs and conduct a survey in your school. Do the results confirm or contradict your initial view? Most people get the news from the electronic media in capsule form. Write a comparison/contrast essay in which you examine how the newspaper differs from the television in presenting news; explain why reading the newspaper can be valuable for students.

3. Setting the scene and using dialogue to characterize the applicant and the interviewer, describe your first job interview or create a fictitious interview scene.

4. "The Interview" can be considered a tragicomedy. Write an analysis of the story identifying the elements of comedy and tragedy and explaining the effect of Moore's blending of the two elements.

Examining Social Issues

1. Unemployment imposes great strains on family relations. How is this evident in Coffey's home? What is the effect on Coffey of Veronica's attitude? How can family members help one another through such a crisis?

2. Coffey is an optimist who retreats from his problems into comforting dreams and illusions. Veronica is a realist who is painfully aware of their uncertain situation and feels insecure about the future. What are the prospects for a successful marriage between two such different people? Whose attitude, the optimist's or the realist's, contributes most to preventing a marriage breakdown in time of crisis?

3. After Veronica's harsh comment about Coffey's employment prospects, Coffey asks angrily, "Now, why did you say that in front of the child?" What are the effects of such conflicts on Paulie? What other effects do parents' quarrels have on children?

4. Using Gerry Grosvenor and MacGregor as examples, explain how the stresses of corporate life affect the personnel in managerial and executive positions. Interview people in your community with such jobs. Support your explanation with information you gather from your interviews.

5. When MacGregor offers Coffey a job "at the bottom" as a proof-reader, Coffey says, "I'm not a boy of twenty." Through Coffey, Moore dramatizes the problem of a man unemployed at

the age of thirty-nine. As technology advances and computers and robots proliferate, more workers will be unemployed. Especially affected will be the older worker whose experience is related to the old production methods. In such situations, what changes will occur in family life? What do you think are the government's and industry's responsibilities in planning to cope with mass unemployment?

6. According to psychologist Daniel Levinson, the following opposing tendencies emerge most insistently in mid-life.

   • People feel young, yet also have a sense of being old.

   • People become most aware of their own and others' mortality and of their destructive behaviour towards others, yet they wish to become more creative, to create products of value, and to advance human welfare.

   • People feel a need for attachment to others, yet an equally important need for separateness.

   This stage in the life cycle provides a unique opportunity to reconcile these conflicting feelings. Which of these oppositions are evident in the protagonists of " 'I Want a Sunday Kind of Love,' " "Xanadu," and "The Interview"? How well does each protagonist integrate these opposing tendencies?

4

WINTER

Old Age

Old Age

My eyes may be dulled, but the stray
thought that "this could be my last spring"
sharpens almost to pain my response to
swelling buds and the tender new green of
opening leaves. My ears are considerably
duller than they once were but the staccato
chant of some neighbour children swinging
a jump-rope in "hot pepper" rhythm is now
pure joy, whereas earlier it might have been
just noise. . . . I thrill to the knowledge that
I am still a part of the scene. . . . Anything
and everything now come to me with a
richness and poignancy they could not have
when time stretched out apparently
limitless.

Avis D. Carlson [eighty-five years old]
In the Fulness of Time

From the fine nursing home
unnoticed one afternoon
with saved-up money
from his children far away

He bolted across the lawn,
caught a streetcar downtown,
had two cheeseburgers, a malt,
and watched a double feature

His money all gone, he spent
the summer night on a park bench,
was found there the next morning
by his helpers young and hurt.

Donald Jones
"An Old Man's Lark"

Summer in the Mountains

Roger Angell

"Summer in the Mountains" is taken from Roger Angell's Stone Arbor *(1946), a collection of stories that originally appeared in* The New Yorker. *Angell's short fiction is concerned with well-to-do middle-class people nostalgic for the happier circumstances in their past. In a prose style that is concise and accurate in detail and dialogue, "Summer in the Mountains" dramatizes a common problem, that of the dispossessed woman who outlives her husband. She belongs to no family; she has no life of her own. She is like the few remaining possessions in her hotel apartment: transported from their original familiar home into an alien environment, they have "somehow lost their identity" and are "out of place and without companions."*

As fine writers always do, Angell dramatizes a problem movingly, without providing a solution.

Meg Porter had a look of determination on her face as she listened to her mother. Her eyes were fixed on her mother, and occasionally she raised her eyebrows or nodded slightly at a pause in the conversation, but her lips were clamped firmly together, as if to hold back any words she might later regret, as if no one could wring from her the mildest complaint or even a sigh of boredom or resignation. It was, nevertheless, a look of remarkable hostility, particularly from a woman of thirty whose face was normally pretty and animated. Both her husband and her mother had seen this look before; her mother, Mrs. Brockway, had, in fact, come to think it was her daughter's normal expression, and it worried her, but somehow she had never brought herself to speak of it. Larry Porter had once mentioned it to his wife. She ought to try, he had said, to appear happier and more interested when her mother was with them. She had no idea how bad it looked, he said, and Mrs. Brockway would think that that was the way her only daughter *felt* about her, which, of course, wasn't true. And besides, it made her look old. But Meg Porter somehow couldn't shake the habit. Now Larry, sitting across the room, tried to get her attention, to remind her again, but Meg wouldn't take her rigid stare away from her mother.

"And since Dr. Stout couldn't see me at any other time," Mrs. Brockway was saying, "naturally I had to call Mrs. Lincoln and tell her I wouldn't be able to come to the symphony after all. It was really a shame, because I do get out so little, you know. But the doctor had said to come back for a little checkup when I noticed that shortness of breath again, and Tuesday morning I just felt as if I couldn't take any air into my lungs. Of course, it wouldn't worry me if there were someone living with me in the hotel, but even with the elevator boys right outside that you told me I could call any time, it just isn't the same. I sometimes wonder what would happen if anything *did* happen to me and nobody there with me." Meg Porter opened her mouth suddenly and took a breath, but her mother held her hand up and smiled. "No," she said. "I know what both Dr. Stout and that other one said. I'm fine, perfectly fine, and there's really nothing to worry about. For my age. I'm not trying to scare you, Meg. I know you call up, and you know I love that. Nearly every day. And there's always the phone, in case anything . . . I really don't worry at all." She smiled bravely and shook her head. "It's just being alone, that's all. I'm afraid I'll never really be used to it. Of course, I don't have to tell you how much I appreciate – No, you told me not to use that word, didn't you?" She looked slyly at her daughter. "Well, how much I *love* that apartment and how glad I am knowing that it's mine, or almost mine. I always want you and Larry to know that I don't forget that or take it for granted. Ever. Well!" She smoothed her skirt carefully and then looked at Larry. "Where are you two going tonight?"

Larry Porter took his eyes off his wife. "It's just to cocktails with the Bradleys. You know – you met them here Christmas Eve. And then we thought we'd go to dinner at Luchow's. But we won't be late. Shouldn't be later than ten or so. Of course, we can always come back before then if you want to get home earlier. We could just pick up a hamburger."

"Don't be silly, Larry," Mrs. Brockway said. "I wouldn't dream of it. Jane and I always have a wonderful time together. You know I love looking after her. It's so much like the old days, with Meg. After her father died and before she went away to college. I'll bet she doesn't even remember how close we used to be."

"Of course I remember, Mother," Meg Porter said. She leaned forward and took a cigarette out of a box on the table beside her chair. "We used to play games. And we went to the theater. And – "

"And every summer to Chocorua," Mrs. Brockway said. "Larry,

you have no idea how she used to adore it there. Sometimes I wonder how you all ever started going to the beach."

"Jane is crazy about the beach, Mother," Meg said. "She wouldn't go any place else. And neither would I."

"Of course, dear," Mrs. Brockway said gently. "It isn't the place that counts. It's just being with people that counts. People you love. I just hope, Meg, that you're *with* Jane enough. She's such a responsive little girl, and you have no idea how suddenly it all ends. Before you know it, she'll be grown up and off married to somebody, with a busy life of her own and lots of friends and parties. And then you'll start thinking back about your life and you'll remember every hour you had together."

"Mother, for heaven's sake! You don't honestly think that I neglect – "

"Oh, no, Meg," Mrs. Brockway said, smiling again. "I just mean that Jane responds so. I hope you appreciate it. Why, I always look forward to these evenings we have together. Jane and I have such fine times it makes me feel like a real member of the family, just for a few hours, while you and Larry have a good time by yourselves. What I mean is, really, that at my age you know enough to appreciate a little child. They just *give* themselves, the way grownups can't. Nobody really understands that until they're as old as I am and their own children have gone."

"Oh, *Moth*-er," Meg said, helplessly dropping her hands.

Larry Porter stood up quickly, looking at his watch. "We'd better go, darling. It's past five-thirty. I'll tell Jane we're leaving. I think she's in her room watching that damned kid show again."

In the cab, a few minutes later, Meg was almost crying. "Oh, God, darling," she said to her husband, "why is she so awful, and why am I so awful to her? I've just got so that I think that every word is a hint or a slam or something, and I just can't stand it any more. There ought to be a compatibility test for parents and grown-up children to take together, and if they fail, there would be a law that said they couldn't see each other or couldn't live in the same city together. No, I don't mean that, either. I don't *really* feel that way – it's too hateful. It's just that Mother gets me all mixed up."

"I know," Larry Porter said. He lit a cigarette and handed it to her. "You had that look again. You never look that way except when she's there."

"I know I did. I can feel it coming over me and I can't stop it. Every time before she comes, I say to myself, This time will be different, this time we'll really get along, and she won't talk about herself and how lonely she is and how dreadful I am. But then the minute I see her I know it's going to be just the same."

"It's not your fault, Meg," Larry said gently. "It's just that she's old. That and the money."

"I know it. But we can't help the money. She needs it, and we want to give it to her. But why does she have to be so damned *grateful*? I've told her not to do that. It just ruins everything, and somehow it makes me feel as if we weren't doing enough for her, either. We all know she couldn't live with us, even if we had room. She doesn't really want that – she'd loathe it. And I'd go absolutely crazy and so would you."

"I wouldn't allow it." Larry said. "I'll never get us trapped with that."

"But what *does* she want?" Meg almost shouted. "I call her up. I have lunch with her. I go to the movies with her. We have her for dinner. We have her in to sit with Jane, because I honestly think she likes it. We get the best doctors for her and try to persuade her that she really is as well as she can expect. Why does she keep talking at me, then? Why does she make me feel so damned ungrateful and mean?"

Larry stared out at the passing lights for a moment before he answered. "I think," he said finally, "it's just that she's old and afraid, and she wants somebody to share that with her. And nobody can do it. You can't share being old with anybody."

Meg turned in the seat and quickly took hold of her husband's arm. "Don't let me get that way, Larry," she said urgently. She squeezed his arm hard. "Promise me you'll do that, Larry. Don't ever let me get like that. Don't let me do that to Jane, ever."

In the apartment, after she and the little girl had eaten the supper she had cooked, Mrs. Brockway went to the living-room windows to draw the curtains. She felt tired, and there was a vague pain in her side. Before dinner, she and her granddaughter had played a game on the floor, throwing dice that sent little racing cars around a numbered course. She hadn't understood the game well and the floor had made her knees ache, but Jane had seemed excited and happy, and they had played it twice. Now she stood for a moment by the window and looked out at the darkness that meant that soon the little girl would have to go to bed. After that, after an hour or two, the Porters would be back. She would hear them laughing and talking as they came out of the elevator, and they would come in looking excited and happy, and Larry would offer her a drink, which she would refuse, and then it would be time for her to leave and go back to the barren hotel apartment, with the uncomfortable bed, and the furniture that was not hers, and the steam heat that killed every plant she bought, and the silent telephone, and the strange voices in the hall late at night – all the ugly and frightening familiarities that had somehow become the place where she lived. There were a few of her possessions left there – the set of Thackeray of her husband's, and the Spode teacups, which she had to keep on the mantelpiece – but they no longer seemed like her own. Sitting there by herself in the evenings after she had turned off the loud, confusing television, she often studied these treasures of hers and tried to remember how they had looked back in her own apartment, the one she had shared with Meg – where in the bookcase the set of Thackeray had stood and how the cups had looked among the other familiar china on the shelves in the dining room. But she could no longer remember. When her furniture had gone (Meg had pointed out that it would be foolish and expensive to keep up her old place or to store all her books and pictures and furniture), her remaining treasures had somehow lost their identity. Out of place and without companions, they had become exactly the same as everything else in her bare rooms – somebody else's belongings, which she was now expected to live with for a time.

It was this she tried to explain to her daughter when she came to Meg's house and saw it full of the warmth of lived-with and familiar objects: an album of records that Jane had left open on the floor, the dachshund's worn cushion beside the fireplace, the clamshell ashtrays, which the three of them had collected on the beach the summer before – all the evidence of plans made long ago and happily accomplished. Seeing this after the cold emptiness of her own long afternoons, after the terrors of a sudden pain in the night with no one to call out to, Mrs. Brockway always wanted to tell her daughter what she had here in her home, to cry desperately to her, "You don't know! You're so lucky here and you don't know it. You can't know what it's like to be without it, when it's all forgotten, when your own belongings are gone, and your house empty, and there are no more plans." But somehow it never came out that way. When she tried (without complaining) to explain all this to Meg, it ended in a recital of her days, of what she had eaten and what the doctor had said. Meg always became impatient and angry, and Mrs. Brockway went away feeling ashamed, because she had said it all wrong.

"Grandma, look!"

The little girl had made a small tower out of the piled-up dice from the game, and now she sent one of the tiny racing cars crashing into it, knocking the dice onto the rug. "Bang!" she cried. "He hit the pylon on that turn and now he's out of the race. Dang! Dang! Dang! Here comes the ambulance!"

Mrs. Brockway sighed and closed the curtains. She would have to hurry. The little girl would have to be put to bed soon. There was less than an hour for the two of them to be together.

"Let's read now, Jane, shall we?" Mrs. Brockway said. "I'll sit on the couch and you can lie beside me, and we'll read anything you want. We'll have a nice, quiet time together, won't we, darling?"

"O.K.," Jane said. She dropped the racing car and ran over to the bookcase. "Here," she said, pulling out a book. "This one. Read me *The Tinder Box*, Grandma."

Smiling, Mrs. Brockway sat down on the sofa. Sometimes Jane was exactly the way her mother had been as a little girl. Like Meg, she was suggestible; at one moment she could appear frighteningly violent, but she could change her mood and her interest in a second. The similarity made the grandmother feel warm and happy. Now she took the book from the eight-year-old. "All right," she said comfortably, turning the pages. "*The Tinder Box* it is. I know that story. It has those wonderful dogs with the big eyes. Now you sit down beside me, and I'll start." The little girl quickly curled her legs on the sofa, and Mrs. Brockway put her arm around her, pulled her close, and began to read: "A soldier came marching along the highroad. One, two! One, two!"

As she read the familiar story, Mrs. Brockway kept glancing at the little girl's face, intent on the page. Looking at her, the grandmother felt calm. At these moments, she knew that the fears and pains of her hotel bedroom were not really part of her at all. She was the same as she had always been, capable of anything as long as there was someone near her whom she loved and could make happy. Meg could no longer accept that from her, but this little girl, her granddaughter, did. She knew Jane depended on her. All that was needed was for them to be together more often, not just for a few hours on an occasional evening.

When Mrs. Brockway finished the story, Jane didn't move but kept staring at the page with an intent and abstracted expression. Suddenly, before the child sat up, before it was time for her to go to bed, Mrs. Brockway wanted to do something to preserve the moment, plan something that she could take back with her to her room, like a possession of her own – a guarantee of love and happiness to come.

She tightened her arm about her granddaughter. "Jane," she said softly, "how would you like to come and live with me for a little while? Just we two together. Wouldn't that be fun? We do have such nice, happy times together it would be fun to do it for a longer time. I know a lovely place we could go, perhaps in the summer, when your school is over and Mum and your father might like to take a little trip by themselves. Would you like that, Jane?"

"Where would Mum and Dad go?" Jane asked quietly.

"Oh, I don't know. Perhaps to Europe for a few weeks or on a motor trip somewhere in the summer. I haven't asked them, but perhaps, if you would like it, I could suggest it and they might think it was a good idea. They haven't been off by themselves for so long that they might say yes. And then you and I could go to the mountains together, to a place I know. I used to go there every single summer with your mother. We could get a lovely cottage, and there are mountains all around, all with long Indian names. And there's a lake, where you could learn to swim, right where your mother did. And you can climb mountains, and we could take little trips. Would you like that, Jane?"

"Could I have a bulldog?" Jane asked. "Jennifer French, at the beach, has a bulldog, and Dad said maybe I could have one some- time – a dog of my very own. Could I have one in the mountains?"

"Well, maybe, Jane. It all depends." Mrs. Brockway gave her another little hug. "We'd have to see, but we certainly could try. Wouldn't it be fun?"

"Yes, Grandma," Jane said. She sat up and looked at Mrs. Brockway. "And we can take the bulldog to climb the mountains and take him to the lake, and he'll learn to swim with me, won't he?"

Mrs. Brockway laughed aloud; actually, the plan didn't seem impossible at all. They might do it this very summer. It wasn't too late. She would be very practical and write and ask about cot- tages first and then speak to Meg after she had heard, so that there could be no difficulties or arguments. It was the simplest thing in the world. A whole summer with Jane, every moment of the long months with someone she loved. She pulled the child close. "We'll make a little secret of this, Jane, won't we? You won't tell Mum tomorrow, and then we'll talk to her about it together some day soon and surprise her, and she'll be so glad you can go to the mountains just the way she did."

"Not tell Mum?" Jane said doubtfully.

"Not right away, darling. It'll be a surprise, see? And then when we do tell her, you can explain how very much you want to go and spend the whole summer with Grandma. And after that, who knows? Perhaps we can do it again and we can stay even longer together. And we could go for a little trip next Christmas, just the two of us, on the train. Oh, you'll see! We'll have fine times together, and we'll have a lot of them!"

Mrs. Brockway had been hugging the child close to her for a long time, and now Jane began to struggle under her arm. She pulled herself away and stood up, and Mrs. Brockway was astonished to see that there were tears in her eyes.

"Go away for *Christmas*?" Jane said in a frightened voice. "Where will Mum and Dad be? Won't they be here for Christmas?"

Mrs. Brockway was frightened now, too. "Of course, darling," she said quickly, putting her hands out toward the child. "Of course they will. You don't have to go away for Christmas if you don't want to." She hadn't meant to go so far with her talk and plans. All that could come later. She caught Jane's hand and pulled her back to the couch. "You don't have to go anywhere, Jane," she said, trying to make her voice warm and soothing again. "Just to the mountains. Just this summer in the mountains, darling. You and I together."

But Jane roughly jerked her arm free and took three quick and defiant backward steps away from her. Mrs. Brockway again reached her hands out toward her granddaughter, and as she searched hopelessly for the words to recapture what she had lost, she suddenly thought she saw on the red, tear-streaked face of the little girl a flicker of expression she had noticed before in the eyes of the young and the strong – a bright, animal look of rejection and fear.

Questions for Writing and Discussion

Discovering Meaning

1. Why is Meg hostile to her mother in the first scene? Does she fully explain the source of her hostility in the second scene, when she is in the cab with her husband? Examine her attitude and add other motives that she is perhaps unaware of or unable to express. She says she feels guilty. What is the source of her guilt?

2. In the last scene, Meg's mother thinks that she would like to tell her daughter how she feels now that her "house [is] empty" and "there are no more plans," but when they are together, she engages in trivial conversation. Who is responsible for this barrier that prevents mother and daughter from having meaningful communication?

3. Larry's judgement of Mrs. Brockway is that she is old and

afraid, that she needs someone to share that feeling with her, and that "you can't share being old with anybody." From your impression of Mrs. Brockway in the final scene, do you agree? Why or why not?
4. Precisely what is Mrs. Brockway's problem? Why are plans important to her? Why does she choose the plan to spend the summer in the mountains with her granddaughter?
5. Why does the child reject her grandmother's proposal?
6. Compare your impressions of Mrs. Brockway in the opening scene and in the final scene when she is alone with her granddaughter. In which scene are you most sympathetic with her? Why?

Exploring Method

1. In the opening scene, why does Angell present Mrs. Brockway as her daughter sees her? What would be lost or gained if the author had presented Mrs. Brockway in conversation without including her daughter's thoughts about her?
2. What is the purpose and effect of the author's setting alternating scenes against each other, one in which the daughter is expressing her feelings about her mother to her husband, the other revealing the mother's thoughts about herself and her relation with her daughter?
3. How are we prepared for Mrs. Brockway's proposal to her granddaughter to spend summer in the mountains together?

Suggestions for Writing

1. Describe Mrs. Brockway's problem. Include reasons for her loneliness and feeling of dislocation. Offer some solutions.
2. Write a letter to the Porters, as if you were a family friend, discussing their relationship with Mrs. Brockway. They seem to see her as a threat to their family; do you agree? Use your own experience with your grandparents and those of your friends to support your opinion.
3. Write two portraits of your grandparent or an old relative or friend: one from your perspective, the other from the old person's perspective.
4. Anthropologist Margaret Mead comments on the problems of the aged in an essay called "The Generation Gap": "Old people are immigrants in time, immigrants from an earlier world, living in an age essentially different from anything we knew before." Put yourself in Mrs. Brockway's position and describe

the changes that you find bewildering. Compare the present world with your past. To help you describe the past, interview old people in your family and in your neighbourhood.

Examining Social Issues

1. During the scene in the cab, Meg asks her husband to promise her that he will never let her become like her mother and cause Jane to feel the same resentment towards her as she feels towards her mother. Meg believes that people can prevent the kind of old age that her mother is experiencing. Her husband believes that fear and loneliness inevitably accompany old age and that these feelings are intensified because the aged cannot share their fear with anyone. What is your view?

2. Why do nuclear families like the Porters tend to exclude members of their extended families such as grandparents and other relatives? Psychologist Sonya Rhodes, in her book *Surviving Family Life: The Seven Crises of Living Together*, explains the contribution of grandparents living in the home of married children:

> Grandparents and great-grandparents are models and helpers in the family; they foster a sense of family history and pride. How the family copes with the aging and inevitable death of its oldest generation is a model of commitment and responsibility. The death of a grandparent or a great-grandparent often is a young person's experience with human mortality. These painful experiences help shape the lives of the youngest generation and prepare them for losses they will confront in their lifetime.

How do you respond to this view?

3. Philip Slater, in his book *The Pursuit of Loneliness*, is critical of the North American pursuit of privacy. He writes:

> Technological change, mobility, and the belief in individualism combine to rupture the bonds that tie individuals to a family, community, geographical location – bonds that give them a comfortable sense of themselves. . . . Obsessed with a desire for privacy, even within the family, North Americans are unique in their feeling that each member should have a separate room, and even a separate telephone, television, and car, when economically possible. We seek more and more privacy, and feel more and more alienated and lonely when we get it.

Does this criticism apply to the Porters in the story? Why or why not? Is our insistence on privacy making us "more and more lonely"? What are the benefits of privacy in family life? How does your family balance the need for privacy with the need for involvement?

4. The final sentence in the story makes a social comment on youth's attitude towards the elderly: Mrs. Brockway "saw on the red, tear-streaked face of the little girl a flicker of expression she had noticed before in the eyes of the young and the strong – a bright, animal look of rejection and fear." In a memo from the American National Institute of Senior Centers, Jack Weinberg, a psychiatrist, comments on this attitude among the young:

> In our value system, we believe the elderly are nonproductive, unattractive, useless, garrulous, old fashioned. . . . When we are young, we absorb these notions on a subconscious level and when we reach that age period we have a built-in system of self-deprecation, causing the elderly themselves to shun the notion of being old. Furthermore, the young in a society that's fashion conscious feel that the elderly are old-fashioned, and everything in our society that's old is to be discarded.

What is your view of this analysis? Describe your attitude to the elderly. Support your view with examples.

A Conversation with My Father

Grace Paley

Grace Paley is an acute observer of the chaos of urban life. With compassion and humour, her fiction records the disintegration of moral values and reveals how people ward off pain, fear, and loneliness through cheerful comments or through wry humorous remarks. The story that the narrator in "A Conversation with My Father" writes for her father illustrates Paley's predominant concern with the theme of motherhood. Her protagonists are lower-middle-class single mothers, often on welfare, struggling to hold their families together.

"A Conversation with My Father" was written in the tradition of the contemporary experimental literary movement called Postmodernism, represented by such writers as Richard Brautigan, Donald Barthelme, Kurt Vonnegut, John Barth, and John Hawkes. It is this Postmodernist approach to fiction that the father in the story rejects. Writers in this literary movement believe that the idea of a well-rounded, fully developed character in fiction belongs to an earlier age when the development of individualism was possible. In the modern mass society, this concept of character is outdated. Postmodernists, therefore, use types. Since characters are not individualized, biographical information is often blurred or ambiguous.

Unlike the fully developed plot in conventional fiction, which progresses chronologically, experimental fiction is composed of random, unconnected episodes dramatizing situations or incidents that emphasize a cyclical view of life – that is, the view that certain human experiences are universal and recur in every age, such as the generation conflict, a young person's initiation into adulthood, and our encounter with death.

In traditional stories, writers use a consistent point of view and often conceal their own identities by telling their stories through their protagonist's perspective and speech patterns. Experimental writers break the illusion of reality by using shifting points of view, moving from third person to first person with extended monologues revealing thought and feelings as they enter the consciousness of their characters. The traditional story is well constructed; the experimental story takes its order from the disturbed, fragmented consciousness of its characters. Settings in experimental stories are unimportant. The actual setting in these stories is the stage of the mind, where issues are raised and battles are fought.

Paley, through the "conversation" between father and daughter in this story, explores the validity of the Postmodernist writers' claim that the old themes can no longer be treated truthfully through conventional techniques.

M y father is eighty-six years old and in bed. His heart, that bloody motor, is equally old and will not do certain jobs any more. It still floods his head with brainy light. But it won't let his legs carry the weight of his body around the house. Despite my metaphors, this muscle failure is not due to his old heart, he says, but to a potassium shortage. Sitting on one pillow, leaning on three, he offers last-minute advice and makes a request.

"I would like you to write a simple story just once more," he says, "the kind de Maupassant wrote, or Chekhov, the kind you used to write.* Just recognizable people and then write down what happened to them next."

I say, "Yes, why not? That's possible." I want to please him, though I don't remember writing that way. I *would* like to try to tell such a story, if he means the kind that begins: "There was a woman . . ." followed by plot, the absolute line between two points which I've always despised. Not for literary reasons, but because it takes all hope away. Everyone, real or invented, deserves the open destiny of life.

Finally I thought of a story that had been happening for a couple of years right across the street. I wrote it down, then read it aloud. "Pa," I said, "how about this? Do you mean something like this?"

> Once in my time there was a woman and she had a son. They lived nicely, in a small apartment in Manhattan. This boy at about fifteen became a junkie, which is not unusual in our neighborhood. In order to maintain her close friendship with him, she became a junkie too. She said it was part of the youth culture, with which she felt very much at home. After a while, for a number of reasons, the boy gave it all up and left

---

* Guy de Maupassant (1850–93) wrote heavily plotted, ironic stories. Chekhov wrote realistic stories that often had no resolution and sometimes little plot.

291

the city and his mother in disgust. Hopeless and alone, she grieved. We all visit her.

"O.K., Pa, that's it," I said, "an unadorned and miserable tale."

"But that's not what I mean," my father said. "You misunderstood me on purpose. You know there's a lot more to it. You know that. You left everything out. Turgenev wouldn't do that.* Chekhov wouldn't do that. There are in fact Russian writers you never heard of, you don't have an inkling of, as good as anyone, who can write a plain ordinary story, who would not leave out what you have left out. I object not to facts but to people sitting in trees talking senselessly, voices from who knows where . . ."

"Forget that one, Pa, what have I left out now? In this one?"

"Her looks, for instance."

"Oh. Quite handsome, I think. Yes."

"Her hair?"

"Dark, with heavy braids, as though she were a girl or a foreigner."

"What were her parents like, her stock? That she became such a person. It's interesting, you know."

"From out of town. Professional people. The first to be divorced in their county. How's that? Enough?" I asked.

"With you, it's all a joke," he said. "What about the boy's father? Why didn't you mention him? Who was he? Or was the boy born out of wedlock?"

"Yes," I said. "He was born out of wedlock."

"For Godsakes, doesn't anyone in your stories get married? Doesn't anyone have the time to run down to City Hall before they jump into bed?"

"No," I said. "In real life, yes. But in my stories, no."

"Why do you answer me like that?"

"Oh, Pa, this is a simple story about a smart woman who came to N.Y.C. full of interest love trust excitement very up to date, and about her son, what a hard time she had in this world. Married or not, it's of small consequence."

"It is of great consequence," he said.

"O.K.," I said.

"O.K. O.K. yourself," he said, "but listen. I believe you that she's good-looking, but I don't think she was so smart."

---

* Ivan Turgenev (1818–83) wrote stories and novels deeply rooted in the culture of his time; his best-known novel, *Fathers and Sons*, deals with the conflict between generations.

"That's true," I said. "Actually that's the trouble with stories. People start out fantastic. You think they're extraordinary, but it turns out as the work goes along, they're just average with a good education. Sometimes the other way around, the person's a kind of dumb innocent, but he outwits you and you can't even think of an ending good enough."

"What do you do then?" he asked. He had been a doctor for a couple of decades and then an artist for a couple of decades and he's still interested in details, craft, technique.

"Well, you just have to let the story lie around till some agreement can be reached between you and the stubborn hero."

"Aren't you talking silly, now?" he asked. "Start again," he said. "It so happens I'm not going out this evening. Tell the story again. See what you can do this time."

"O.K.," I said. "But it's not a five-minute job." Second attempt:

Once, across the street from us, there was a fine handsome woman, our neighbor. She had a son whom she loved because she'd known him since birth (in helpless chubby infancy, and in the wrestling, hugging ages, seven to ten, as well as earlier and later). This boy, when he fell into the fist of adolescence, became a junkie. He was not a hopeless one. He was in fact hopeful, an ideologue and successful converter. With his busy brilliance, he wrote persuasive articles for his high-school newspaper. Seeking a wider audience, using important connections, he drummed into Lower Manhattan newsstand distribution a periodical called *Oh! Golden Horse!*

In order to keep him from feeling guilty (because guilt is the stony heart of nine tenths of all clinically diagnosed cancers in America today, she said), and because she had always believed in giving bad habits room at home where one could keep an eye on them, she too became a junkie. Her kitchen was famous for a while – a center for intellectual addicts who knew what they were doing. A few felt artistic like Coleridge and others were scientific and revolutionary like Leary.* Although she was often high herself, certain good mothering reflexes remained, and she saw to it that there was lots of orange juice around and honey and milk and vitamin pills. However, she never cooked anything but chili, and that

---

* Samuel Taylor Coleridge (1772–1834), an English Romantic poet, said he wrote his allegedly unfinished poem *Kubla Khan* in a hallucinatory state. Timothy Leary (1920–) is an American psychologist who promoted the use of psychedelic drugs in the 1960s.

no more than once a week. She explained, when we talked to her, seriously, with neighborly concern, that it was her part in the youth culture and she would rather be with the young, it was an honor, than with her own generation.

One week, while nodding through an Antonioni film, this boy was severely jabbed by the elbow of a stern and proselytizing girl, sitting beside him.* She offered immediate apricots and nuts for his sugar level, spoke to him sharply, and took him home.

She had heard of him and his work and she herself published, edited, and wrote a competitive journal called *Man Does Live By Bread Alone*. In the organic heat of her continuous presence he could not help but become interested once more in his muscles, his arteries, and nerve connections. In fact he began to love them, treasure them, praise them with funny little songs in *Man Does Live* . . .

> the fingers of my flesh transcend
> my transcendental soul
> the tightness in my shoulders end
> my teeth have made me whole

To the mouth of his head (that glory of will and determination) he brought hard apples, nuts, wheat germ, and soybean oil. He said to his old friends, From now on, I guess I'll keep my wits about me. I'm going on the natch. He said he was about to begin a spiritual deep-breathing journey. How about you too, Mom? he asked kindly.

His conversion was so radiant, splendid, that neighborhood kids his age began to say that he had never been a real addict at all, only a journalist along for the smell of the story. The mother tried several times to give up what had become without her son and his friends a lonely habit. This effort only brought it to supportable levels. The boy and his girl took their electronic mimeograph and moved to the bushy edge of another borough. They were very strict. They said they would not see her again until she had been off drugs for sixty days.

At home alone in the evening, weeping, the mother read and reread the seven issues of *Oh! Golden Horse!* They seemed to her as truthful as ever. We often crossed the street to visit and console. But if we mentioned any of our children who

---

* Michelangelo Antonioni (1912–) is an Italian film director (*Blow-up, Zabriskie Point*) whose neo-realist films investigate society.

were at college or in the hospital or drop-outs at home, she would cry out, My baby! My baby! and burst into terrible, face-scarring, time-consuming tears. The End.

First my father was silent, then he said, "Number One: You have a nice sense of humor. Number Two: I see you can't tell a plain story. So don't waste time." Then he said sadly, "Number Three: I suppose that means she was alone, she was left like that, his mother. Alone. Probably sick?"

I said, "Yes."

"Poor woman. Poor girl, to be born in a time of fools, to live among fools. The end. The end. You were right to put that down. The end."

I didn't want to argue, but I had to say, "Well, it is not necessarily the end, Pa."

"Yes," he said, "what a tragedy. The end of a person."

"No, Pa," I begged him. "It doesn't have to be. She's only about forty. She could be a hundred different things in this world as time goes on. A teacher or a social worker. An ex-junkie! Sometimes it's better than having a master's in education."

"Jokes," he said. "As a writer that's your main trouble. You don't want to recognize it. Tragedy! Plain tragedy! Historical tragedy! No hope. The end."

"Oh, Pa," I said. "She could change."

"In your own life, too, you have to look it in the face." He took a couple of nitroglycerin.* "Turn to five," he said, pointing to the dial on the oxygen tank. He inserted the tubes into his nostrils and breathed deep. He closed his eyes and said, "No."

I had promised the family to always let him have the last word when arguing, but in this case I had a different responsibility. That woman lives across the street. She's my knowledge and my invention. I'm sorry for her. I'm not going to leave her there in that house crying. (Actually neither would Life, which unlike me has no pity.)

Therefore: She did change. Of course her son never came home again. But right now, she's the receptionist in a storefront community clinic in the East Village. Most of the customers are young people, some old friends. The head doctor has said to her, "If we only had three people in this clinic with your experiences . . ."

"The doctor said that?" My father took the oxygen tubes out of his nostrils and said, "Jokes. Jokes again."

* Medicine for certain heart conditions.

"No, Pa, it could really happen that way, it's a funny world nowadays."

"No," he said. "Truth first. She will slide back. A person must have character. She does not."

"No, Pa," I said. "That's it. She's got a job. Forget it. She's in that storefront working."

"How long will it be?" he asked. "Tragedy! You too. When will you look it in the face?"

Questions for Writing and Discussion

Discovering Meaning

1. Compare the two parent-child relationships: father-daughter in the story and mother-son in the story the daughter writes for her father. Which relationship is more constructive? Why?
2. What does the father mean when he says of the mother in his daughter's story, "Poor woman. Poor girl, to be born in a time of fools, to live among fools"? Compare the father's and the daughter's attitudes to the woman in the story.
3. Compare the father's and the daughter's views on character and plot in fiction. Whose view do you support? Why?
4. After the daughter reads the second version of her story to her father, he says, "You have a nice sense of humor." What does he mean?
5. Explain the significance of the titles of the two periodicals in the daughter's story, *Oh! Golden Horse!* and *Man Does Live By Bread Alone.* How are these titles related to both stories: the story of the mother and son and the story of the father and daughter?
6. What does the father mean in his last remarks? Is he referring to his daughter's story or to his own predicament? Does the comment have a wider meaning beyond both the story and his own situation? Explain and support your answer.

Exploring Method

1. In your view, is the daughter's second version of the story an improvement over the first? Why or why not? Does "A Conversation with My Father" contain the weakness in presenting character and plot that the father objects to in his daughter's story of her neighbour? Why or why not?
2. In reply to her father's complaint about the decline of sexual morality, the daughter says that in "real life" people get mar-

ried, but not in her stories. She draws a distinction between life and art and then explains that she can never control her fictional characters. Does the second version of the story demonstrate her point about the growth of a character beyond the writer's control? Why or why not?

3. What are the differences in vocabulary and sentence structure between the two versions of the story that the daughter writes for her father, and the overall story about the conversation between the father and daughter? Which do you think is more effective? Why?

Suggestions for Writing

1. Using the daughter's plot, rewrite the story of the neighbour, adding your own improvements and creating your own ending.
2. In the conversation between father and daughter, Paley presents two views of fiction and life. Explain how their views of fiction are related to their views of life. Consider whether their differences illustrate the generational conflict. Write a dialogue between yourself and one of your parents that illustrates either the differences or the similarities in your views of life.
3. Select your favourite story or novel. Write a review of it, explaining the reasons for your choice. Whose view of fiction, the father's or the daughter's, does your story or novel illustrate?
4. Reread the explanation of Postmodernist fiction in the introduction to this story. Write an analysis of the two stories, the story of the father and daughter and that of the mother and son, identifying the components of experimental fiction in each.

Examining Social Issues

1. In the daughter's story, why does the mother become an addict? What is your opinion of the mother's motivation and behaviour?
2. In the daughter's story, how does the girl whom the son meets cure him of his addiction? Do you think this approach could be an effective way to cure addicts? Why or why not? How should parents deal with the problem of their children's drug abuse?
3. Compare the son's addiction with the mother's. Why is the son cured while his mother remains an addict? The daughter offers the father a more positive ending for the mother, in which she becomes a receptionist in a storefront clinic. The father insists that she will "slide back." Whose view do you accept? Why?
4. The daughter in the story is undergoing a painful experience:

helplessly watching her father die. The ending she gives her story in her conversation with him suggests that, like her fictional character's cure, a cure is possible for his illness. Should the dying be told the truth about their condition? Why or why not?

5. Although the father is dying, the conversation between father and daughter is not about death but about fiction. Sigmund Freud, in his essay "Our Attitude Toward Death," comments on this:

> We are prepared to maintain that death is the necessary outcome to life. . . . In reality, however, we are accustomed to behave as if it were otherwise. We display an unmistakable tendency to "shelve" death, to eliminate it from life. We try to hush it up. That is our own death, of course. No one believes in his own death. In the unconscious, everyone is convinced of his immortality.

How does Freud's observation apply to the father? To the daughter? Do you agree with Freud that this is the typical attitude to death? Why or why not? Give examples in our culture that support your view.

A Trip for Mrs. Taylor

Hugh Garner

The Canadian short-story writer Hugh Garner uses urban life of the lower middle class as the background for his fiction. Garner's fictional world is filled with little people oppressed by the shabbiness of their environment, facing dilemmas created by such problems as aging, unachieved goals, and loneliness. Garner examines not great, sensational conflicts, but the inner world of simple people, with compassion bordering on tenderness.

Garner's fiction is admirable for its sharp focus on accurate details of settings, its characters' histories, and its skill in capturing the natural rhythms of ordinary conversation.

"A Trip for Mrs. Taylor" is among the half-dozen stories that Garner himself listed as the best of the seventy-eight he wrote. The anecdote he told interviewer Allan Anderson provides an interesting insight into the author's life and into his method of writing:

> *I remember one time when I was completely broke. At eight o'clock that night I thought, "I'll write a piece and I'll use my mother. I'll think of my mother in this piece, and I'll write about an old lady who wants to take a trip but can't afford to take one." And I wrote a short story called "A Trip for Mrs. Taylor," and I wrote from eight o'clock that night until three in the morning. And the next morning I typed a fair copy and I took it up to* Chatelaine *magazine. Byrne Hope Sanders was editor then, and she took the story. At that time – and I suppose even today –* Chatelaine *doesn't want stories about old women – they want stories about young marrieds. But they read it, phoned me up and said: "We're buying the story." They've run it twice. I forget what I got, $300 or $400 for it, which allowed me to pay my rent.*

Mrs. Taylor got out of bed at five o'clock that morning; an hour ahead of her usual time for getting up. She moved around her attic room with the stealth of a burglar, making herself her morning cup of tea on the hotplate, and dressing quietly so as not to disturb her landlady, Mrs. Connell, on the floor below.

She dressed her tiny self carefully, donning a clean white camisole and her black Sunday frock. After she had drunk her tea and eaten a slice of thinly margarined toast she washed her cup and saucer in some water she had drawn from the bathroom the evening before, and put them away on her "kitchen" shelf in the clothes closet. Then she tiptoed down the steep stairs to the bathroom and washed her face and hands; "a lick and a spit" as she called it.

When she returned to her room her seventy-six-year-old face shone with wrinkled cleanliness and the excitement of the day. She combed her thinning grey hair and did it up with pins into an unsevere bun at the back of her head. Then, half-guiltily, she powdered her face and touched her cheeks with a rouge-tipped finger. Going over to her old trunk in the corner she extracted from its depths two pieces of jewellery wrapped in tissue paper. One of the pieces was a gold locket holding a faded photograph of her dead husband Bert, while the other was an old-fashioned gold chain bangle with a small lock shaped like a heart. She had lost the key to the bangle long ago, but it did not matter; her hands were now so thin that it slipped easily over her wrist.

When she had adjusted the jewellery she took her old black straw hat from its paper bag and put it on, primping a bit before the Woolworth mirror on the wall, smiling at herself and wishing that her false teeth were a little whiter.

All through her preparations she had been taking hurried glances at the alarm clock on the dresser, but now, when she was ready to go, she saw that she still had nearly two hours before train time. The train left at seven o'clock Standard Time, which was eight o'clock Daylight Saving, and here it was only a quarter to six. Still, it would take a half hour to get downtown to the station, and she couldn't afford to be late on this day of days.

She unclasped her small cardboard suitcase and carefully checked its contents once again. There was a clean change of underwear, a towel and soap, some handkerchiefs, two pairs of black lisle stockings, Bert's picture in its frame, and one of the two boys in uniform, her blouse and blue serge skirt, and the red velvet dress that Mrs. Eisen had given her the year before. The dress didn't fit her, but she liked its rich colour and the feeling of opulence it gave, just to possess it.

Picking up her heavy Bible from the top of the dresser she said to herself, "I really should take it along, I guess. It'll weigh me down, but I couldn't go anywhere without it." Quickly making up her mind she placed the Bible in the suitcase and fastened the lid. Then she sat down on the edge of the bed and let the wonderful coming events of the day take over her thoughts.

The idea for the trip had come to her about a week before, on the day she had received her July old-age pension cheque. She had been down to the main post-office, mailing a set of hand-crocheted runners to her daughter-in-law Ruth in Montreal when the idea struck her. Seeing all the holiday crowds hurrying into the maw of the station had prompted her to go in and inquire about train times.

The hurry and excitement of the place had brought back the nostalgic memories of those happier times when she and Bert and young Johnnie – yes, and young Bert too, who was killed in Italy – had gone away sometimes in the summer. Their trips hadn't been long ones, and their destination was usually the home of her dead cousin Flora in Jamesville, but they had been filled with all the hustle and bustle of getting ready, packing salmon and peanut-butter sandwiches for their lunches, and making sure Bert had the tickets. There had been the warm picnicky feeling going to the station on the streetcar, trying to keep young Bert from kneeling on the seat and brushing his feet on the man beside him (she wiped away a vagrant tear at the memory) and the awareness that she *belonged* to the crowds around her.

That was the thing she had missed most during the past few years, the feeling of being one with those about her. The knowledge that she was old and ignored by younger people sometimes caused her to wish she were dead, but then appalled by the irreverence of such thoughts she would take refuge in her Bible, which was now her only solace.

Her loneliness and the striving to live on her old-age pension made mere existence a hardship. Mrs. Connell, her landlady, was a kindly soul, not much younger than herself, but she had no conception of what it was like to be cooped up month after month in a dreary little room, without even a radio to keep you company, without even a cat or a dog or a canary – nothing, but the four walls, an electric plate, a bed and a dresser.

Of course, she told herself, she could have gone to live with Johnnie and Ruth in Montreal, but she'd seen too much of that sort of thing in the past. When Johnnie had married down there after the war she had felt a sinking in the stomach at the thought that he too was leaving her. "Come on down there with me, Ma," he had said, but she had sensed the reluctance behind his words. "I'm not going to be a built-in baby sitter for my grandchildren," she had answered, trying to cover her sense of loss and disappointment under her bantering words. She was independent, a woman who had run her own home for years, and brought up her two boys on the skimpy and unreliable wages of a labourer husband. But sometimes her independence melted under her silent tears, and she wished that once, just once, somebody would need her again.

But today was not the time for such gloomy thoughts. She glanced at the clock and saw that it was after seven. She stood up, straightened her hat once more, and picking up the heavy suitcase, made her way from the room, closing the door silently behind her. She had no wish to waken Mrs. Connell and have to answer the surprised questions of that lady; this trip was going to be a secret one, known only to herself.

She hurried down the street through the cloying warmth of the summer morning as fast as the heavy bag would allow her. When she reached the streetcar stop she put the suitcase down on the sidewalk and searched in the purse for a car ticket. There was very little money left from her pension cheque, but by doing without a few things to eat over the past week she had managed to save the expenses for the trip.

When the streetcar came along she climbed aboard and sat down near the front of the car. She was aware of the stares from the men and girls who were going to work, and she felt important for the first time in months. There was something friendly in the glances they gave her, and perhaps even a slight envy that she should be going away while they could only look forward to another stifling day in their offices and factories.

The downtown streets at this hour of the day were strange to her, but there was a tired camaraderie among the people getting on and off the car which brought back memories she had almost forgotten; once again she saw herself as a young woman going to work as they were, stepping down from the open-sided cars they had in those days, proud of her narrow waist and new high-buttoned boots. She felt almost young again and smiled apologetically as a thin girl in slacks nearly tripped over her suitcase.

As they neared the station several people carrying pieces of luggage boarded the car, and Mrs. Taylor smiled at them as if they were partners in a conspiracy. Most of them smiled back at her, and she felt that the anticipation and preparation for a journey was only exceeded by its actual beginning.

When she alighted from the streetcar a young man in army uniform took her suitcase from her, and holding her by the arm, led her across the street.

"This is a heavy bag for you to be carrying," he said in a conversational tone.

"It is a little heavy," she answered, "but I haven't far to go."

"Everybody seems to be going away today," he said. "I guess I won't get a seat on the northbound train."

"That's a shame," Mrs. Taylor answered, trying to keep up with the soldier's long strides. "Are you on leave?"

"Sort of. I was down here on a forty-eight-hour pass from camp. I should have been back last night."

"I hope you don't get into trouble," she said. She felt suddenly sorry for the young man – only a boy really. She wanted to tell him that both her sons had been overseas during the war, and that young Bert had been killed. But then she thought he might think she was bragging, or trying to make him feel bad because he'd been too young to go.

As they entered the cathedral-like station concourse she said to the young soldier, "I can manage now, thank you," and he stopped and placed the bag on the floor.

"If you're taking the northbound train I'll carry the suitcase to the gates for you," he offered.

"No. No, thank you. I'm taking the Montreal train," she answered.

"Well then, I'll have to leave you. Goodbye. Have a nice holiday," he said.

"Yes," she whispered, her voice cracking with emotion. As he walked away she shouted after him, "Good luck, son!" She watched him disappear into the crowd and felt a nameless dread for what might be before him. He was such a nice polite young boy, but what was more he was the first person outside Mrs. Connell and the man at the grocery store that she had spoken to all week.

The man at the ticket window seemed surprised as she bought her ticket, but he stamped it on the back and handed it to her without a word. When she asked him where to get the Montreal train he pointed across the station to a queue of people lined up before a pair of gates, and she picked up her suitcase and made her way towards it.

The crowd was a good-natured one, as she had known it would be, and she spent several minutes taking stock of the other travellers. It was unbelievable that so many people had woken up this morning as she had done, with the idea of catching the same train. All night as she had tossed and turned in anticipation of the morning these other people had probably been doing the same thing, unknown to her. The knowledge that they all shared the same sense of immediacy seemed to bring them closer together, and they were united in their impatience to be going.

But Mrs. Taylor was not impatient. She knew the value of time – she who had so little of it left – and this waiting with the others in the crowded station was as exciting to her as reaching the end of her trip – more so in fact.

She looked about her at the young people with their overnight bags and their tennis rackets; at the older men carrying haversacks and fishing rods, each looking a little sheepish like boys caught playing hookey; the three girls in the brand-new clothes whispering together ahead of her in the line; the young couple with the baby in the go-cart standing outside the queue, smiling at one another and talking together in French; the two priests in white panama hats who nodded solemnly and looked hot and cool at the same time in their black alpaca jackets.

This was what she had looked forward to all week! It was just as she had expected it to be, and she didn't care if the gates never opened; the best part of any journey was the waiting for the train.

There was the sound of a small scuffle behind her, and a young woman's tired voice said, "Garry, stop that right now!"

Mrs. Taylor turned and saw a slight dark girl wearing a shabby suit trying vainly to hold a young baby in her arms while she tugged at a little boy who was swinging on the end of a harness. The boy was trying desperately to break away.

"Here, young man, where do you think you're going!" Mrs. Taylor said sternly, bending down and catching him around the waist. The child stopped struggling and looked at her in surprise.

"He's been a little devil all morning," his mother said. "He knows I can't do much with him while I've got the baby in my arms."

"Now you just stand still!" Mrs. Taylor warned, letting him go and smiling at the young woman to show that she did not mean to override her authority.

"He'll stop for you," the girl said. "At home he'll do anything for his grandma, but when he knows I've got the baby to look after, he takes advantage of it."

Mrs. Taylor nodded. "I know; I had two boys myself," she said. "Is the baby a boy, too?"

"Yes. Four months."

Mrs. Taylor reached over and pulled the light blanket from the baby's face. "He's a big boy for four months, isn't he?" she asked.

She learned that the young woman's name was Rawlinson, and

that she was on her way to New Brunswick to join her husband who was in the Air Force. The girl's mother had wanted to come down to the station with her, but her arthritis had kept her at home. She also learned that the baby's name was Ian, and that his mother was twenty-two years old.

She in turn told the girl that she had lived alone since her oldest boy's marriage, and that Johnnie now lived with his wife and a young daughter in Montreal. In answer to the other's questions she also told the young woman that her husband and youngest son were dead, that she received the old-age pension, and that it wasn't enough in these days of high prices.

Mrs. Rawlinson said that a friend of her mother's went to the same church as Mrs. Taylor. Mrs. Taylor didn't recognize the woman's name, although she thought she knew who the girl meant: a stout woman with short-bobbed bluish hair who wore a Persian lamb coat in the winter.

She realized now that she had been starved for conversation, and she was so grateful for having met the young woman with the children.

"They should be opening the gates pretty soon," said the girl, looking at her wristwatch. "The train is due to leave in twenty minutes."

From the loudspeaker came the voice of the stationmaster announcing that the northbound train was due to leave. Mrs. Taylor thought about the nice young soldier who had overstayed his pass.

The little boy, Garry, indicated that he wanted to go to the toilet.

"Wait till we get on the train, dear," his mother pleaded desperately.

Mrs. Taylor said eagerly, "I'll hold the baby while you take him if you like."

"Will you! Gee, that's swell!" the young woman exclaimed. She handed the baby over, and Mrs. Taylor cradled him in her arm, while the young mother and the little boy hurried away.

She pulled back the blanket once again from the baby's face and saw that he was awake. She placed her finger on his chin and smiled at him, and he smiled back at her. The moment took her back more years than she cared to remember, back to a time when young Bert was the same age. She was filled with the remembered happiness of those days, and she thought, "I'd give up every minute more I have to live just to be young again and have my boys as babies for one more day." Then to hide the quick tears that were starting from her eyes she began talking to the baby in her arms, rocking back and forth on her heels in a gesture not practised for years.

When the woman and the little boy returned she gave up the baby reluctantly. She and the young woman stood talking together like old friends or like a mother and daughter-in-law. They discussed teething troubles, the housing shortage, and how hard it was to raise a family these days. They were so engrossed in their new-found friendship that they failed to notice when the man opened the gates.

The crowd began pushing them from behind, and Mrs. Taylor picked up her suitcase in one hand and grasped Garry's harness with the other. Then, followed by Mrs. Rawlinson and the baby they climbed the set of iron stairs to the platform.

Mrs. Taylor's feet were aching after the long wait at the gates, but her face shone with happiness as she steered the small boy alongside the train. The boy's mother drew up to her, and they walked together to the day-coach steps where a trainman waited to help them aboard.

"You've got your hands full there, Granny," he said, picking up the little boy and depositing him in the vestibule of the car.

She was pleased that he mistook her for the children's grandmother, and she beamed at him, not attempting to correct his mistake.

Inside the coach she led the way to a pair of seats that faced each other at the end of the car, and dropped into one with a tired sigh. Then she held the baby while its mother took the harness off Garry and placed her small case and shopping bags on the luggage rack.

"Am I ever glad to get aboard!" Mrs. Rawlinson exclaimed. "I'd been dreading the wait at the station. Now I've only got to change trains in Montreal and I'll be all set."

"It's quite a job travelling with children," Mrs. Taylor sympathized. "Don't worry, I know. I've done enough of it in my day," she said with slight exaggeration.

Mrs. Rawlinson laid the baby on the seat beside her, before sitting back and relaxing against the cushions. The coach soon filled up, and several people eyed their double seat enviously. Mrs. Taylor was glad she had been able to get well up in the queue at the gates.

When the train started she moved over close to the window and pointed out to the little boy the buildings and streets they passed, and the tiny inconsequential people they were leaving behind them. Young Garry shouted excitedly, "Choo-choo!" at every engine they passed in the yards.

The city looked hot and uncomfortable in the morning sun, and Mrs. Taylor was surprised that all the little ant-like people didn't simply jump on a train and get away from it. It was remarkable that the ones she could see walking the streets were strangers to her now, as if there was no connection between them and the people on the train. They were a race apart; an earthbound race separated from herself by movement and time, and the sense of adventure of her and her fellows.

She picked out landmarks as the train gathered speed; the streets she had lived on as a girl, now turned into industrial sites; the spinning mill where she had once worked; the soot-blackened park where she and Bert had walked so many years ago . . . .

"We won't be getting into Montreal until supper time," Mrs. Rawlinson said from the opposite seat, intruding upon her memories.

"No."

"I'll bet you'll be glad to get there and see your grand-daughter?"

Mrs. Taylor shook her head. "I'm not going to Montreal today," she said sadly. "I can't afford to go that far."

"But – but couldn't your son send you the fare?" asked the girl.

She had to protect Johnnie, who wasn't really mean, just forget-ful. "Oh, he could, but I've never really cared to go that far," she lied.

"Well – well, where are you going then?" the young woman asked, her curiosity getting the best of her.

"Not very far. Just up the line a piece," Mrs. Taylor answered, smiling. "It's just a short trip."

The train seemed to flow across the underpasses marking the streets. Soon the industrial areas were left behind, and they began rushing through the residential districts.

Mrs. Taylor was enthralled with the sight of the rows of houses as seen from the rear; yards waving with drying clothes, and every house having an individuality of its own. She only recog-nized some of the familiar streets after the train had passed them, they looked so different when seen from her hurtling point of vantage.

In a few minutes the train began to slow down for an outlying station, and the conductor came along the car collecting tickets. When Mrs. Taylor handed him her small bit of paste-board, he asked, "Are you getting off here, Madam?"

"Yes, I am," Mrs. Taylor replied, colouring with embarrass-ment.

"Have you any luggage?"

She pointed to the suitcase at her feet, ashamed to face the stares of those who were watching her.

"Fine. I'll carry it off for you," the conductor said calmly, as if old ladies took ten-cent train rides every day of the week.

She stood up then and said goodbye to the little boy, letting her hand rest for a long minute on his tousled head. She warned him to be a good boy and do what his mother told him.

"You must think I'm crazy just coming this far," she said to Mrs. Rawlinson. "You see, I've wanted to take a trip for so long, and this was sort of – pretending."

The young woman shook the surprised look from her face. "No, I don't, Mrs. Taylor," she said. "I wish you were coming all the way. I don't know what I'd have ever done without you to help me with Garry."

"It was nice being able to help. You'll never know how much I enjoyed it," Mrs. Taylor answered, her face breaking into a shy smile. "Goodbye, dear, and God bless you. Have a nice journey."

"Goodbye," the young woman said. "Thanks! Thanks a lot!"

Mrs. Taylor stood on the station platform and waved at the young woman and her son, who waved back at her as the train began to move again. Then she picked up her bag and walked along the platform to the street.

When she boarded a streetcar the motorman looked down at her and said, "You look happy; you must have had a swell vacation."

She smiled at him. "I had a wonderful trip," she answered.

And it *had* been wonderful! While all the others in the train would get bored and tired after a few hours of travel, she could go back to her room and lie down on the bed, remembering only the excitement and thrill of going away, and the new friends she had made. It was wonderful, just wonderful, she said to herself. Perhaps next month, if she could afford it, she would take a trip to the suburbs on the Winnipeg train!

Questions for Writing and Discussion

Discovering Meaning

1. Why does Mrs. Taylor take the trip? If she is going only a short distance, why does she pack such a heavy bag?
2. Garner portrays Mrs. Taylor with photographic detail. In such realistic stories, protagonists change as a result of their en-

counters with others. How has her encounter with Mrs. Rawlinson affected her?

3. How are the yearnings that Mrs. Taylor expresses earlier in the story fulfilled by her trip?

Exploring Method

1. The third-person narrator comments that "loneliness and the striving to live on her old-age pension made mere existence a hardship." What images suggest Mrs. Taylor's loneliness and poverty? What details make her a stock character – a generalized figure representative of the aged? What details individualize her?

2. Discuss the role of Mrs. Taylor's memory in characterizing her. How does Garner introduce her recollections naturally without stopping the action in the story?

3. Garner does not disclose Mrs. Taylor's actual destination until the end of the story. What is the effect of delaying the revelation? What clues does he include that foreshadow the outcome?

4. What is the function of the minor characters: Johnnie, young Bert, the soldier, and Mrs. Rawlinson?

5. Like Callaghan in "Mr. and Mrs. Fairbanks," Garner uses colourful images but a simple style devoid of literary pretentiousness. How is the style appropriate to the story?

Suggestions for Writing

1. The story suggests that the anticipation and the beginning of a trip can be more exciting than the journey itself. Describe a trip you have taken. Compare the anticipation with the actual trip and explain which was more exciting.

2. On the train, Mrs. Taylor identifies landmarks on the street where she had lived as a girl, a street that had been turned into industrial sites. Select an area in your home town and compare it as it appears to you now with the way it appeared to you when you were younger.

3. From what you learn about Mrs. Taylor's present life and from her recollections of herself as a girl and a young mother, write a portrait of her as you imagine she was at your age. Write a contrasting portrait of her as Mrs. Rawlinson sees her at the station.

4. Mrs. Taylor lives without a radio. How does she compensate

for the lack of this contact with the outside world? Describe how your life would be affected if radios, televisions, stereos, and tape players were no longer part of your life. What interests would you develop to fill the gap?

5. Compare Mrs. Taylor in this story with Mrs. Brockway in Roger Angell's "Summer in the Mountains" in these aspects:
   a) their characters and social class;
   b) their relations with their adult children;
   c) their attitudes towards aging.

6. Write a script for a documentary film on aging in North America. Use the characters in the stories you have read in this section as dramatic examples, and add interviews with the elderly and medical research on aging.

Examining Social Issues

1. Through his portrayal of Mrs. Taylor, Garner dramatizes a social condition – the plight of the aged. Discuss the hardships illustrated in this story. Which of Mrs. Taylor's problems can you see in old people around you? Have conditions improved at all for the aged since Garner wrote his story?

2. Sociologist Vivian Gornick claims that North America is one of the worst areas in the world in which to grow old; social scientist Merrill Clark believes that it is one of the best. Some people claim that the plight of the old is extremely pitiable; others argue that pity itself is part of the problem, that we are creating dependent old people by inducing self-pity through our attitude towards them. What is your view of these two controversies?

3. Simone de Beauvoir in her book about aging, *The Coming of Age*, writes:

   The purified image of themselves that society offers the aged is that of the white-haired and venerable sage, rich in experience, planing above the common state of mankind: if they vary from this, they fall below it. The counterpart of the first image is that of the old fool in his dotage, a laughing stock for children. In any case, either by their virtue or by their degradation, they stand outside humanity.

   How do the characters that Mrs. Taylor meets regard her? How does she regard herself? Do de Beauvoir's stereotypes apply to the view of the aged in our culture? Why or why not?

4. Modern research is critical of the stereotypes that de Beauvoir describes. On the basis of seven years of studies at the Univer-

sity of Chicago, Bernice Neugarten believes that real people do not match society's notions about them. She observes in *Growing Old*:

> Old persons do not become isolated and neglected by their families, although both generations prefer separate households. Old parents are not dumped into mental hospitals by cruel indifferent children. They are not necessarily lonely or desolate if they live alone. Few of them show signs of mental deterioration or senility, and only a small proportion ever become mentally ill.

Neugarten believes that even the terms "old" and "young" involve distorting stereotypes since chronological age is a poor basis for categorizing people. Instead of growing alike as they grow older, people become more distinct and individualized. Does Neugarten's conclusion apply to Mrs. Taylor? Why or why not? Using old people you have met as illustrations, give your opinion of this view of aging.

Heartache

Anton Chekhov

Anton Chekhov is universally regarded as one of the great masters of short fiction. More than any other writer, he was responsible for shaping the modern short story. He introduced the "slice of life" approach that writers have used for over a century. In such stories, the author records an ordinary but meaningful moment in a person's life that reveals the essence of a personality or provides a recognition of a universal truth.

"Heartache" (1886), one of the earliest of over 800 stories that Chekhov wrote, is regarded as a classic. As a representative Chekhov story, its subject is actual life: its plot preserves the shapelessness of life. Simplicity is its keynote. Its characteristics are brevity and compactness. In a letter to his brother on May 19, 1886, Chekhov wrote:

> *A writer should seize upon small details, arranging them so that the reader will see an image in his mind after he closes his eyes. For instance, you will capture the truth of a moonlit night if you will write that a gleam like starlight shone from the pieces of a broken bottle.*

With similar brevity and compactness, Chekhov evokes personality, often through a single detail. A repeated gesture provides a vivid portrait of Iona, the cabby, in the story "Heartache": "The driver clucks to the horse, cranes his neck like a swan, rises in his seat and, more from habit than necessity, flourishes his whip."

"TO WHOM SHALL I TELL MY SORROW?"*

Evening twilight. Large flakes of wet snow are circling lazily about the street lamps which have just been lighted, settling in a thin soft layer on roofs, horses' backs, peoples' shoulders, caps. Iona Potapov, the cabby, is all white like a ghost. As hunched as a living body can be, he sits on the box without stirring. If a whole snowdrift were to fall on him, even then, perhaps, he would not find it necessary to shake it off. His nag, too, is white and motion-

---

* From an old Russian song comparable to a Negro spiritual.

less. Her immobility, the angularity of her shape, and the stick-like straightness of her legs make her look like a penny ginger-bread horse. She is probably lost in thought. Anyone who has been torn away from the plow, from the familiar gray scenes, and cast into this whirlpool full of monstrous lights, of ceaseless uproar and hurrying people, cannot help thinking.

Iona and his nag have not budged for a long time. They had driven out of the yard before dinnertime and haven't had a single fare yet. But now evening dusk is descending upon the city. The pale light of the street lamps changes to a vivid color and the bustle of the street grows louder.

"Sleigh to the Vyborg District!" Iona hears. "Sleigh!"

Iona starts, and through his snow-plastered eyelashes sees an officer in a military overcoat with a hood.

"To the Vyborg District!" repeats the officer. "Are you asleep, eh? To the Vyborg District!"

As a sign of assent Iona gives a tug at the reins, which sends layers of snow flying from the horse's back and from his own shoulders. The officer gets into the sleigh. The driver clucks to the horse, cranes his neck like a swan, rises in his seat and, more from habit than necessity, flourishes his whip. The nag, too, stretches her neck, crooks her sticklike legs and irresolutely sets off.

"Where are you barging in, damn you?" Iona is promptly as-sailed by shouts from the massive dark wavering to and fro before him. "Where the devil are you going? Keep to the right!"

"Don't you know how to drive? Keep to the right," says the of-ficer with vexation.

A coachman driving a private carriage swears at him; a pedes-trian who was crossing the street and brushed against the nag's nose with his shoulder, looks at him angrily and shakes the snow off his sleeve. Iona fidgets on the box as if sitting on needles and pins, thrusts out his elbows and rolls his eyes like a madman, as though he did not know where he was or why he was there.

"What rascals they all are," the officer jokes. "They are doing their best to knock into you or be trampled by the horse. It's a conspiracy."

Iona looks at his fare and moves his lips. He wants to say something, but the only sound that comes out is a wheeze.

"What is it?" asks the officer.

Iona twists his mouth into a smile, strains his throat and croaks hoarsely: "My son, sir . . . er, my son died this week."

"H'm, what did he die of?"

Iona turns his whole body around to his fare and says, "Who

can tell? It must have been a fever. He lay in the hospital only three days and then he died. . . . It is God's will."

"Get over, you devil!" comes out of the dark. "Have you gone blind, you old dog? Keep your eyes peeled!"

"Go on, go on," says the officer. "We shan't get there until tomorrow at this rate. Give her the whip!"

The driver cranes his neck again, rises in his seat, and with heavy grace swings his whip. Then he looks around at the officer several times, but the latter keeps his eyes closed and is apparently indisposed to listen. Letting his fare off in the Vyborg District, Iona stops by a teahouse and again sits motionless and hunched on the box. Again the wet snow paints him and his nag white. One hour passes, another . . .

Three young men, two tall and lanky, one short and hunchbacked, come along swearing at each other and loudly pound the pavement with their galoshes.

"Cabby, to the Police Bridge!" the hunchback shouts in a cracked voice. "The three of us . . . twenty kopecks!"

Iona tugs at the reins and clucks to his horse. Twenty kopecks is not fair, but his mind is not on that. Whether it is a ruble or five kopecks, it is all one to him now, so long as he has a fare. . . . The three young men, jostling each other and using foul language, go up to the sleigh and all three try to sit down at once. They start arguing about which two are to sit and who shall be the one to stand. After a long ill-tempered and abusive altercation, they decide that the hunchback must stand up because he is the shortest.

"Well, get going," says the hunchback in his cracked voice, taking up his station and breathing down Iona's neck. "On your way! What a cap you've got, brother! You won't find a worse one in all Petersburg –"

"Hee, hee . . . hee, hee . . ." Iona giggles, "as you say –"

"Well, then, 'as you say,' drive on. Are you going to crawl like this all the way, eh? D'you want to get it in the neck?"

"My head is splitting," says one of the tall ones. "At the Dukmasovs' yesterday, Vaska and I killed four bottles of cognac between us."

"I don't get it, why lie?" says the other tall one angrily. "He is lying like a trouper."

"Strike me dead, it's the truth!"

"It is about as true as that a louse sneezes."

"Hee, hee," giggles Iona. "The gentlemen are feeling good!"

"Faugh, the devil take you!" cries the hunchback indignantly.

"Will you get a move on, you old pest, or won't you? Is that the way to drive? Give her a crack of the whip! Giddap, devil! Giddap! Let her feel it!"

Iona feels the hunchback's wriggling body and quivering voice behind his back. He hears abuse addressed to him, sees people, and the feeling of loneliness begins little by little to lift from his heart. The hunchback swears till he chokes on an elaborate three-decker oath and is overcome by cough. The tall youths begin discussing a certain Nadezhda Petrovna. Iona looks round at them. When at last there is a lull in the conversation for which he has been waiting, he turns around and says: "This week . . . er . . . my son died."

"We shall all die," says the hunchback, with a sigh wiping his lips after his coughing fit. "Come, drive on, drive on. Gentlemen, I simply cannot stand this pace! When will he get us there?"

"Well, you give him a little encouragement. Biff him in the neck!"

"Do you hear, you old pest? I'll give it to you in the neck. If one stands on ceremony with fellows like you, one may as well walk. Do you hear, you old serpent? Or don't you give a damn what we say?"

And Iona hears rather than feels the thud of a blow on his neck.

"Hee, hee," he laughs. "The gentlemen are feeling good. God give you health!"

"Cabby, are you married?" asks one of the tall ones.

"Me? Hee, hee! The gentlemen are feeling good. The only wife for me now is the damp earth . . . Hee, haw, haw! The grave, that is! . . . Here my son is dead and me alive . . . It is a queer thing, death comes in at the wrong door . . . It don't come for me, it comes for my son. . . ."

And Iona turns round to tell them how his son died, but at that point the hunchback gives a sigh of relief and announces that, thank God, they have arrived at last. Having received his twenty kopecks, for a long while Iona stares after the revelers, who disappear into a dark entrance. Again he is alone and once more silence envelops him. The grief which has been allayed for a brief space comes back again and wrenches his heart more cruelly than ever. There is a look of anxiety and torment in Iona's eyes as they wander restlessly over the crowds moving to and fro on both sides of the street. Isn't there someone among those thousands who will listen to him? But the crowds hurry past, heedless of him and his grief. His grief is immense, boundless. If his heart were to burst and his grief to pour out, it seems that it would flood the whole world, and yet no one sees it. It has found a place for itself in such an insignificant shell that no one can see it in broad daylight.

Iona notices a doorkeeper with a bag and makes up his mind to speak to him.

"What time will it be, friend?" he asks.

"Past nine. What have you stopped here for? On your way!"

Iona drives a few steps away, hunches up and surrenders himself to his grief. He feels it is useless to turn to people. But before five minutes are over, he draws himself up, shakes his head as though stabbed by a sharp pain and tugs at the reins . . . He can bear it no longer.

"Back to the yard!" he thinks. "To the yard!"

And his nag, as though she knew his thoughts, starts out at a trot. An hour and a half later, Iona is sitting beside a large dirty stove. On the stove, on the floor, on benches are men snoring. The air is stuffy and foul. Iona looks at the sleeping figures, scratches himself and regrets that he has come home so early.

"I haven't earned enough to pay for the oats," he reflects. "That's what's wrong with me. A man that knows his job . . . who has enough to eat and has enough for his horse don't need to fret."

In one of the corners a young driver gets up, hawks sleepily and reaches for the water bucket.

"Thirsty?" Iona asks him.

"Guess so."

"H'm, may it do you good, but my son is dead, brother . . . did you hear? This week in the hospital. . . . What a business!"

Iona looks to see the effect of his words, but he notices none. The young man has drawn his cover over his head and is already asleep. The old man sighs and scratches himself. Just as the young man was thirsty for water so he thirsts for talk. It will soon be a week since his son died and he hasn't talked to anybody about him properly. He ought to be able to talk about it, taking his time, sensibly. He ought to tell how his son was taken ill, how he suffered, what he said before he died, how he died. . . . He ought to describe the funeral, and how he went to the hospital to fetch his son's clothes. His daughter Anisya is still in the country. . . . And he would like to talk about her, too. Yes, he has plenty to talk about now. And his listener should gasp and moan and keen. . . . It would be even better to talk to women. Though they are foolish, two words will make them blubber.

"I must go out and have a look at the horse," Iona thinks. "There will be time enough for sleep. You will have enough sleep, no fear. . . ."

He gets dressed and goes into the stable where his horse is standing. He thinks about oats, hay, the weather. When he is alone, he dares not think of his son. It is possible to talk about him with someone, but to think of him when one is alone, to evoke his image is unbearably painful.

"You chewing?" Iona asks his mare seeing her shining eyes. "There, chew away, chew away. . . . If we haven't earned enough for oats, we'll eat hay. . . . Yes. . . . I've grown too old to drive. My son had ought to be driving, not me. . . . He was a real cabby. . . . He had ought to have lived. . . ."

Iona is silent for a space and then goes on: "That's how it is, old girl. . . . Kuzma Ionych is gone. . . . Departed this life. . . . He went and died to no purpose. . . . Now let's say you had a little colt, and you were that little colt's own mother. And suddenly, let's say, that same little colt departed this life. . . . You'd be sorry, wouldn't you?"

The nag chews, listens and breathes on her master's hands. Iona is carried away and tells her everything.

Questions for Writing and Discussion

Discovering Meaning

1. Describe Iona's relationship with his son. Where in the story do you begin to understand the depth of his grief?
2. What is Iona's conscious purpose of going out to the stable? Although he is unaware of it at the time, what is his real purpose?
3. Describe the effect of the final scene. Does the story generate a feeling of sadness for the "human condition" or anger at a social condition? What do you think Chekhov intended?

Exploring Method

1. What is the effect of Chekhov's use of the present tense to tell his story?
2. Chekhov's stories have been described as "a biography of a mood." Such stories can easily become offensively sentimental, inducing an emotional response more intense than is justified by the situation in the story. How does Chekhov maintain the reader's emotional distance from his protagonist? Consider his use of point of view, descriptive details, and dialogue.
3. Identify details describing the cabman and his actions that

prepare us for the narrator's explanation midway through the story, beginning, "The grief which has been allayed for a brief space comes back again and wrenches his heart more cruelly than ever."

4. What are the functions in the story of the two sets of passengers, the doorman, and the sleepy young cabman in the yard?
5. How does Chekhov prepare us for the last scene?
6. What effect does Chekhov gain by withholding information about the details of the son's death until just before Iona goes out to the stable?
7. In the last scene, Chekhov presents a simple man speaking about his grief to his horse. In what tone does the grief-stricken father speak? Such a scene can become either comic or sentimental. What devices does the author use to achieve a genuinely pathetic effect?

Suggestions for Writing

1. Most of us present a public image in our social and school and job-related encounters; we also have a private image, which is related to our inner thoughts and feelings and which we reveal only partially to those with whom we are intimate. One of the many fascinations of reading fiction is that the author provides us with an interior understanding of the characters that we rarely achieve with even our most intimate friends and relatives. Chekhov's story provides two views of Iona, as others see him and as the reader sees him. Describe Iona's public image as one of his passengers sees him. Then write another portrait of him as you – the reader, admitted to an intimate view – see him.
2. Describe your feelings as you read the story. Do you think the author has manipulated your emotional response? Why or why not?
3. This is a story of terrible loneliness. Compare the treatment of old age and loneliness in this story and in Garner's "A Trip for Mrs. Taylor." Explain any differences in the approaches to the theme.
4. "Heartache" suggests that people need to share their grief and that they have difficulty in finding anyone genuinely sympathetic to share it with. Some people, however, want to keep their grief to themselves. How would you classify yourself, as one who wants to share grief or one who wants to grieve alone? Illustrate your answer by writing about an incident from your

experience. The story also suggests that most people do not want to be burdened by other people's grief. What has been your experience? Describe a friend or relative who is willing to listen to your problems. Illustrate the characteristics that make him or her sympathetic.

5. Both in literature and in human experience, people suffer for a variety of reasons: trust betrayed, principles abandoned, ideals shattered, goals unrealized. Use your own experience or summarize a story or movie that dramatizes suffering from one of these causes; write a story using one of these themes.

Examining Social Issues

1. In his search for a listener, Iona thinks that a woman might be more sympathetic. From Iona's thoughts about women, what does Chekhov reveal about their position in Tsarist Russian society?

2. At the end of the story, Iona thinks, "I've grown too old to drive. My son had ought to be driving, not me. . . . He was a real cabby. . . . He had ought to have lived." This is an expression of a nineteenth-century Russian father's ambition for his son. In what ways have parents' ambitions for their children changed today? How are they the same? Support your view with examples.

3. All people experience suffering to some degree and in some way, not only physically but also emotionally and spiritually. Explore the following questions:

   • Is suffering a punishment for sins committed or laws broken, or is it the inescapable fate of everyone?

   • The poet John Donne, in his famous essay "The Sermon of the Bells," wrote, "Affliction is a treasure and scarce any man hath enough of it, for no man hath enough that is not ripened and matured by it." Is suffering a blessing in disguise? Can people grow through suffering? Does suffering bring its own reward in wisdom and moral sensitivity, or does suffering create only frustration and cruelty?

   • Many great writers, artists, and musicians have experienced great suffering. Does suffering generate great art, or is suffering an obstacle to artists' realization of their full potential?

"What I Have Lived For"

Three passions, simple and overwhelmingly strong, have governed my life: the longing for love, the search for knowledge, and unbearable pity for the suffering of mankind. These passions, like great winds, have blown me hither and thither, in a wayward course, over a deep ocean of anguish, reaching to the very verge of despair.

I have sought love, first, because it brings ecstasy – ecstasy so great that I could often have sacrificed all the rest of life for a few hours of this joy. I have sought it, next, because it relieves loneliness – that terrible loneliness in which one shivering consciousness looks over the rim of the world into the cold unfathomable lifeless abyss. I have sought it, finally, because in the union of love I have seen, in a mystic miniature, the prefiguring vision of the heaven that saints and poets have imagined. This is what I have sought, and though it might seem too good for human life, this is what – at last – I have found.

With equal passion I have sought knowledge. I have wished to understand the hearts of men. I have wished to know why the stars shine. And I have tried to apprehend the Pythagorian power by which number holds sway above flux. A little of this, but not much, I have achieved.

Love and knowledge, so far as they were possible, led upward toward heaven. But always pity brought me back to earth. Echoes of cries of pain reverberate in my heart. Children in famine, victims tortured by oppressors, helpless old people a hated burden to their sons, and the whole world of loneliness, poverty, and pain make a mockery of what human life should be. I long to alleviate the evil, but I cannot, and I too suffer.

This has been my life. I have found it worth living, and I would gladly live it again if the chance were offered me.

Bertrand Russell at ninety

Acknowledgements

This is an extension of the copyright page. Every reasonable effort has been taken to make this list of acknowledgements complete. The publishers would be grateful for information regarding any errors or omissions.

The editor gratefully acknowledges permission to reproduce material from the following sources.

Spring

"First Day in School," from *Who Has Seen the Wind*, by W. O. Mitchell. Reprinted by permission of Macmillan of Canada, a division of Gage Publishing Ltd.

"The Doll's House," by Katherine Mansfield. Copyright 1923 by Alfred A. Knopf, Inc. and renewed 1951 by John Middleton Murry. Reprinted from *The Short Stories of Katherine Mansfield*, by permission of Alfred A. Knopf, Inc.

"Wing's Chips," from *The Other Paris*, by Mavis Gallant. Reprinted by permission of George Borchhardt, Inc. and the author. Copyright © 1956 by Mavis Gallant.

"The Outlaw," from *The Lamp at Noon and Other Stories*, by Sinclair Ross. Reprinted by permission of the author's estate and McClelland and Stewart Limited, *The Canadian Publishers*.

"Growing Up in Victoria," by Joan Mason Hurley. Reprinted by permission of *Prism International*.

"Red Dress," by Alice Munro. From *Dance of the Happy Shades*, by Alice Munro. Reprinted by permission of McGraw-Hill Ryerson Limited.

"The Loons," by Margaret Laurence. Copyright © 1966 by Margaret Laurence. Reprinted from *A Bird in the House*, by Margaret Laurence, by permission of Alfred A. Knopf, Inc.

"Grids and Doglegs," from *Tribal Justice*. Copyright © 1974 by Clark Blaise. Reprinted by permission of Doubleday & Company, Inc.

"The Immortals," by Ed Kleiman. Reprinted from the *Journal of Canadian Fiction* 17, no. 18, with the permission of the author.

Summer

"A & P," by John Updike. Copyright © 1962 by John Updike. Reprinted from *Pigeon Feathers and Other Stories*, by John Updike, by permission of Alfred A. Knopf, Inc. Originally appeared in *The New Yorker*.

Sources

Anderson, Allan. "An Interview with Hugh Garner." *Tamarack Review*, December 1969.

Atwood, Margaret. "Stories from the American Front." *New York Times Book Review*, 26 September 1982.

de Beauvoir, Simone. *The Coming of Age*. New York: Putnam's, 1972.

Bird, Carolyne. "The Job Market." *New York*, 27 August 1973.

Carlson, Avis D. *In the Fullness of Time*. Chicago: Contemporary Books, 1977.

Ciardi, John. "What Is Happiness?" *Saturday Review*, 14 March 1964.

Conrad, Joseph. *Youth*. Garden City, N.Y.: Doubleday, 1968.

Drucker, Peter. *Concept of the Corporation*. New York: John Day, 1946.

Elkind, David. *A Sympathetic Understanding of the Child*. Boston: Allyn and Bacon, 1974.

Freud, Anna. *The Ego and the Mechanism of Defense*. New York: International Universities Press, 1948.

Freud, Sigmund. "Our Attitude Towards Death." In *Civilisation, War, and Death*, edited by John Rickman. Toronto: Clarke Brown, 1968.

Fromm, Erich. *The Sane Society*. New York: Holt, Rinehart and Winston: 1955.

Gordon, Suzanne. "The Geography of Loneliness." In *Lonely in America*. New York: Simon and Schuster, 1976.

Ionesco, Eugene. *Fragments of a Journal*. New York: Grove Press, 1968.

Jersild, Arthur T. *In Search of Self*. New York: Bureau of Publications, Teachers College, Columbia University: 1952.

Jones, Donald. *Medical Aid and Other Poems*. Lincoln, Nebr.: University of Nebraska Press, 1967.

Keniston, Kenneth. "Social Change and Youth in America." *Daedalus* 91, no. 1 (Winter 1962).

Kreisel, Henry. "The Prairie: A State of Mind." *Transactions of the Royal Society of Canada*, 4th ser. 6 (June 1968).

Levinson, Daniel. *The Seasons of a Man's Life*. New York: Ballantine Books, 1978.

Mayer, Nancy. *The Male Mid-Life Crisis: Fresh Starts after Forty*. Garden City, N.Y.: Doubleday, 1978.

Mead, Margaret. "The Generation Gap." *Science* 164, no. 3876 (1969).

Mead, Margaret. "On Friendship." In Margaret Mead and Rhoda Metraux, *A Way of Seeing*. New York: Dutton, 1970.

Moore, Allen J. *The Young Adult Generation: A Perspective on the Future*. Nashville, Tenn.: Abingdon Press, 1969.

Moustakas, Clark E. *The Young Child in School.* New York: Whiteside, 1956.

Neugarten, Bernice. "Grow Old Along with Me! The Best Is Yet to Be." In *Growing Old*, edited by Gordon and Walter Moss. New York: Simon and Schuster, 1975.

Otto, Herbert A., and Sarah Otto. "A New Perspective of the Adolescent." *Psychology in the School* 4, no. 1 (January 1967).

Packard, Vance. "New Kinds of Families." In *The Sexual Wilderness.* New York: David McKay, 1968.

Parsons, Talcott. "Youth in the Context of American Society." *Daedalus* 91, no. 1 (Winter 1962).

Raspberry, William. "What Fathers Want to Tell Daughters." *Los Angeles Times*, 22 March 1983.

Rhodes, Sonya, and Joseleen Wilson. *Surviving Family Life: The Seven Crises of Living Together.* New York: Putnam's, 1981.

Rothchild, John, and Susan Berns Wolf. *The Children of the Counterculture.* Garden City, N.Y.: Doubleday, 1976.

Russell, Bertrand. *The Autobiography of Bertrand Russell.* New York: Simon and Schuster, 1944-1969.

Scarf, Maggie. "Husbands in Crisis." *McCall's*, June 1972.

Segal, Julius, and Herbert Yahraes. *A Child's Journey: Forces That Shape the Lives of Our Young.* New York: McGraw Hill, 1978.

Sheehy, Gail. *Passages.* New York: E. P. Dutton, 1976.

Slater, Philip. *The Pursuit of Loneliness: American Culture at the Breaking Point.* Boston: Beacon Press, 1976.

Strang, Ruth. *The Adolescent Views Himself.* New York: McGraw Hill, 1957.

Terkel, Studs. *Working.* New York: Random House, Pantheon Books, 1974.

Toffler, Alvin. *The Third Wave.* New York: Wm. Morrow, 1980.

Weinberg, Jack. "Memo from The National Institute of Senior Centers," *Perspective on Aging*, June-July 1975.